George W. (George William) Cox

Tales of Thebes and Argos

George W. (George William) Cox

Tales of Thebes and Argos

ISBN/EAN: 9783741164163

Manufactured in Europe, USA, Canada, Australia, Japa

Cover: Foto ©Andreas Hilbeck / pixelio.de

Manufactured and distributed by brebook publishing software
(www.brebook.com)

George W. (George William) Cox

Tales of Thebes and Argos

THEBES AND ARGOS.

By the same Author.

TALES from GREEK MYTHOLOGY. Second Edition.
Square 16mo. price 3s. 6d. cloth, gilt edges.

The TALE of the GREAT PERSIAN WAR, from the
Histories of HERODOTUS. Fcp. 8vo. with 12 Woodcuts, price 7s. 6d.

TALES of the GODS and HEROES. Second Edition.
Fcp. 8vo. price 5s.

'AS the science of language has supplied a new basis for the science
of mythology, the science of mythology bids fair in its turn to open the
way to a new and scientific study of
the folk-lore of the Aryan nations.
Not only have the varied and formal
elements of language been proved to
be the same in India, Greece, Italy,
among the Celtic, Teutonic, and
Slavonic nations, but the names of
many of their gods, the forms of their
worship, and the mainsprings of
their religious sentiment also, have
been traced back of late years to one
common Aryan type. An excellent
account of these researches in comparative mythology has been given
by the Rev. G. W. Cox in the preface
to his *Tales of the Gods and Heroes*,—
a work which, together with his
Tales from Greek Mythology, ought
to be in the hands of every scholar
and of every schoolboy.'

SATURDAY REVIEW, Dec. 19, 1863

TALES

of

THEBES AND ARGOS.

BY THE

REV. GEORGE W. COX, M.A.

LATE SCHOLAR OF TRINITY COLLEGE, OXFORD.

LONDON:

LONGMAN, GREEN, LONGMAN, ROBERTS, & GREEN.

1864.

PRAYERS FROM JEREMY TAYLOR.

Lately published, price One Shilling.

A BOOK of FAMILY PRAYER, compiled chiefly from the Devotions of JEREMY TAYLOR and other Divines of the Seventeenth Century.

This Manual of Prayers, for the use of families, has been compiled chiefly from the Devotions of JEREMY TAYLOR, KEN, LAUD, SPINCKES, LAKE, HELE, and COSIN.

————

My dear Sir,

The permission to inscribe this volume with your name enables me to express my sincere thanks for the instruction and the genuine pleasure which I have received from your works in the sciences of Language and Comparative Mythology. The conclusions attained in the latter may be startling: but every step seems to be established with the closest as well as the most abundant evidence, while every inference, coming with all the weight of comparisons extended over more than the whole field of Aryan Mythology, throws a constantly increasing light on what had long been regarded as an incomprehensible and, in part, repulsive chapter in the history of the human mind.

I am, my dear Sir,

Very faithfully yours,

GEORGE W. COX.

PREFACE.

OF the tales related in this volume the greater number are legends belonging to the families of Œdipus and Perseus. I have endeavoured to give these dynastic stories of Thebes and Argos as nearly in their original form as seems to be possible when the conflicting versions of poets and mythologists are taken into account. An examination of these tales can scarcely fail to show their affinity, or rather their identity, with many of the legends already recounted in the preceding volume, 'The Gods and Heroes.' But this task has led (it would seem necessarily) to an analysis of the great legend of the Trojan war, as well as of some other myths which are narrated in the so-called Homeric hymns. If it can be shown that the Iliad is, in its framework and in all its more prominent features, the counterpart of the great epics of Northern Europe, and that the story of Achilleus is only a more magnificent version of the legends of Perseus, Theseus, Meleagros, or Bellerophon, some steps will be gained towards a determination of the process by which the Iliad was brought into its present shape. It may be some apology for the length to which I have found myself compelled to carry the Introduction to this volume, if it should in any measure serve to solve the difficulties which have gathered round this subject. Mr. Grote, in his History of Greece, has filled up or corrected much that was deficient or erroneous in the speculations which have issued from the school of Wolf and Lachmann; but, appreciating the characteristics of the Iliad far more keenly than Colonel Mure or Mr. Gladstone, he has not availed himself of the aid which he might have obtained from the researches of comparative mythologists. If the results attained by the latter are of any value, the method employed in attaining them must be capable of indefinite extension. With this conviction, I have ventured to examine the great epics of the Greek heroic age, and to express the conclusions which seem to be borne out by every portion of what, with Mr. Grote, I believe to be the original Achilléis, and (with scarcely less force) by the Odyssey.

Yet perhaps the attempt to bring out more

clearly the real nature of the Greek legends, and so to rebut all charges of conscious immorality from poets or mythographers, is one for which not much of apology will be demanded. The mythical stories of gods devouring their children, of unnatural marriages, and other horrors, were painful to the mind of many a Greek poet, and were indignantly thrust aside as unworthy of belief. Mr. Dasent has felt the weight of the same burden in treating of Norse mythology; and even comparative mythologists may look back to their school-days as to a time when the mythical tales presented little to attract and very much to repel them—when, in short, they merely strained the memory without exciting a single kindly feeling. If the science, which lays bare to us so much of the inner life of ages long preceding the dawn of contemporary history, has rent away the dark veil which shrouded the origin of these tales, it is a service for which all may well be grateful. If its method is right, then we may be assured that the Greek, the Norseman, the Hindu, and the Teuton did not sit down at the same time to frame immoral stories about divine or heroic beings, and succeed, each without the slightest knowledge of the rest, in producing and multiplying versions of one and the same story. The growth of

mythology followed inevitably on the separation
of tribes: the era of its birth was not a period of
gross, conscious, and determined depravity, breaking in on the steady march of ages. The history
of Aryan civilisation furnishes no evidence of any
such interruption.

I need scarcely say that, in relating the legends
of Perseus, I have had no wish that my tales
should be compared with the more elaborate narratives, founded on these myths, which form part
of the Rev. C. Kingsley's 'Heroes.' His occasional departure from what would seem to be the
spirit of the original myth is but a slight blemish
in a work of singular beauty.

NOTE.

The method of giving Greek names in English has not yet been completely determined, although it seems to be generally agreed that the English form should approach as closely as possible to the Greek. I venture therefore to hope that I may be acquitted of pedantry, in adhering to the rule which, in a note on the orthography of Greek names prefixed to the Tale of the Persian War, I proposed to myself as the most convenient in the present state of the question. That rule must, of course, be relaxed as the Greek forms become more familiar to English readers.

A list, containing the principal names occurring in this volume, with their quantities marked, will be found in the second edition of the Tales of the Gods and Heroes.

CONTENTS.

INTRODUCTION.

TALES.

TALES

OF

THEBES AND ARGOS.

———+———

INTRODUCTION.

THE historian Hecatæus expressed an honest pride when he asserted that his sixteenth ancestor was a god.[1] The value of his genealogy would have been enormously enhanced, if *Original value of Greek legends.* the intervening generations could have been reduced to six or even to a smaller number. The extension of the line not only removed him further from the immortal being whose blood flowed in his veins, but it weakened the memory of the family legend which related the incidents of its origin. Each house, which boasted of its descent from Zeus or Heracles or any other of the gods, preserved the memory of the mortal maiden who so became the mother of a noble line.[2] But

[1] Herodotus, ii. 143.

[2] The Hesiodic Catalogue of Women was specially designed to furnish a complete list of all such unions of heavenly beings with the daughters of men. In this supernatural origin lay the chief,

B

these family legends were intrusted for the most
part to the frail vehicle of oral tradition; and con-
stant variations so transmuted the old tales as not
unfrequently to blot out all their original features.
Lying out of the circle of national literature,
even after the latter had been reduced to writing,
they had none of the safeguards which the
metrical form [1] and the jealous rivalry of rhapsodists [2] provided for the great national epics.

But if the citizen lived at so late a day that the
attempt to trace back his own line to its divine
Tradi- founder became presumptuous and useless,
tions of
epony- he could still take refuge in the legends
mous
heroes. which traced the origin of his city, his tribe,
or his clan to some one of the glorious beings who
were free from the doom of old age or death.
Every country, every autonomous town, nay, even
many a hamlet, thus had its eponymous hero; [3]
and the strength and vigour of each community

if not the whole, value of Greek genealogies. See, further, Grote
History of Greece, Part I. ch. xix.

[1] Tale of the Great Persian War, p. 276.

[2] Gladstone, Homer and the Homeric Age, vol. i. p. 57.
Grote, History of Greece, vol. ii. p. 182.

[3] The practice might be carried to any extent by multiplying
the children of the more prominent mythical personages. Thus
the fifty sons of Lycáon supplied eponyms for as many Arcadian
townships. Many of these, as Phigalos, Trapezeus, Thnokos,
Akakos, Mantineus, Haliphthoros, are, like Pleuron, Kalydon,
and Orchomenos among the Æolidæ, mere names. Pausanias,
viii. 3.

determined the care with which the memory of
this affinity was preserved. Each smaller town
might boast its own immortal founder, or, for
lack of such, it might fall back on the common
origin of the larger society to which it belonged.

If, however, the Ionian and the Dorian, the
Argive, the Athenian, and the Spartan, thus
linked their own age with the ages of the
gods, the jealousy with which they guarded
the ancient legends which preserved these
pedigrees, was not more remarkable than
their persuasion that these legends had each
their plain and indelible characteristics.　That
they looked upon them as genuine narratives of
actual fact, it is almost superfluous to assert.
Political alliances were made, and national
quarrels excited or appeased, by appeals to the
exploits or the crimes of mythical heroes.　The
Persian king, before setting foot on European
soil, secured the neutrality of Argos by claiming
a national affinity with the son of Danaê.[1] On the
eve of the fight at Platææ, the Tegeatans did not
scruple to waste precious moments in support of
a claim founded on the exploits of the fabulous
Echemos, while the Athenians held that they
rebutted this claim by bringing up their ancient
kindness to the banished Heracleidæ.[2] The tale
of Othrysdes was regarded by Sparta and 'Argos

(margin note: These traditions were treated by the Greeks as historical.)

[1] Herodotus, vii. 150.　　[2] Ibid. ix. 26, 27.

as a sufficient ground for inserting a special article into a treaty made during the Peloponnesian war.[1]

But if they were thus convinced of their historical truth, they felt still more certain that the legends of one state or city were essentially distinct from those of another. The Athenian never doubted that the tales which he had heard about Erechtheus or Theseus had nothing in common with the legends of Argos, Thebes, or Pheræ, beyond those incidents of local intercourse which were acknowledged by the narrative. The Arcadian, when he told the tale of Zeus and Callisto, never supposed that it was repeated by the Thessalian in the story of Phœbus and Corônis. Perseus, Cadmus, Jason, Achilleus, moved each in their own circle, and had left behind them a history seemingly as distinct as that of Athens and Sparta from the days of Leonidas and Themistocles.

Each clan or tribe regarded its own traditions as distinct from any others.

This conviction was a dream. But it has its parallel in the scornful assurance with which the British soldier would even now repudiate all affinity with the Hindu whom he holds in subjection. They who can see a little further know that this kindred is a fact too stubborn to be denied, while they perceive

This belief was wholly without foundation.

---

[1] Tale of the Persian War, p. 380. Sir G. C. Lewis accepts the groundwork of the legend as historical (Credibility of Early Roman History, vol. ii. p. 515).

also that the national traditions of Hellenes, of Dorians and Ionians, with the political legends · of Athenians, Thebans, Thessalians, Spartans, Argives, move in the same charmed circle and revolve more or less closely round the same magic point. The great family legend of the Perseidæ is as magnificent a subject for an epic as that of the wrongs and woes of Helen. Its incidents are not less marvellous, its action is scarcely less complicated. Like the tale of Troy, it forms a coherent whole, and exhibits an equal freshness of local life and colouring. It serves, therefore, the more completely to prove the extent to which the Hellenic local legends sprang up from a common source, and to furnish the means of detecting the common element in isolated traditions with which they may seem to be not even remotely connected.

To the citizen of the town of Argos the mere name of Perseus sufficed as a conclusive mark, separating him from all who traced their origin to Theseus or to Cadmus. Yet his designation as a destroyer of noxious things linked the son of Danaê at once with other heroes of Greek mythology. If Perseus won or deserved his name because he slew the deadly Gorgon or the Libyan sea-monster, Phœbus Apollo had also killed the mighty serpent Python, and Bellerophon received his title as the slayer of the

fearful Belléros. It was the arbitrary sentence of
the cruel and cowardly Polydectes which sent Perseus on his weary errand to the caves of the Graiæ
and the Gorgons; but it was no less the relentless
hatred of the mean and false Eurystheus which
made the life of the high-souled Heracles a
long series of unrequited labours. Nay, Apollo
himself was driven forth to serve as a bondman
in the house of the kindly Admêtos, and, with
Heracles, to look in vain for a recompense from
the treacherous Laomedon. If, in doing the
bidding of the Seriphian king, Perseus encountered overwhelming dangers, Theseus surmounted
perils not less appalling, for the same reason and
from the same motives, while his victory over
the Minotauros only repeats the slaughter of the
Libyan dragon by Perseus. Thus, then, as un-
willing workers, as destroyers of unclean or hurtful things, Perseus, Theseus, Bellerophon, and
Heracles are expressions of the same idea. If,
again, his name as the child of the golden shower
points to the splendour of his birth, so also
Phœbus springs to light in Delos or in Lykia,
while the gloomy prison-house in which he is
born has its parallel in the sleep or death of
night, which is the parent of the Delphian god.
If it is the hope and the boast of Perseus that
before his life's labour is done he will bring back
Danaê to the home which she had left when he

was a babe,[1] so also Heracles meets at the close of
his toils the maiden Iolê whom he had wooed and
won while his life was in its morning. From
the island in the eastern sea Perseus journeys
through many lands to the dark home of the
Graiæ in the far west; but Heracles also wanders
from Argos to the distant gardens of the Hesperides, Bellerophon is driven from Lykia (the land
of light) and dies on the shore of the western sea,
while Kephalos seeks in the Leucadian gulf the
love which he had lost in Attica.[2] In his attack
on the Gorgon maiden, Perseus is armed with
the sword which slays everything on which it
falls; but Apollo is also the invincible Chrysaor,
and Artemis carries the unerring spear which is
fatal to the guileless Procris and the less innocent Corônis or Callisto. On the golden sandals
Perseus moves through the air quicker than a
dream; but the golden chariot also bears Helios
and Phaethon across the blue vault of the heaven,
and when Achilleus tries his armour, it bears him
aloft like a bird upon the wing.[3] After slaying

[1] The very name of Danaê, which is found with the first syllable
lengthened in the Shield of Heracles, 229, supplies the link between the Sanskrit Dahanâ and the Greek Daphnê. Danaos
also comes from Egypt, as Memnon the son of Eôs comes to Ilion
from Ethiopia.
[2] The Leucadian cape is naturally chosen by the local Athenian
legend. Max Müller, Comparative Mythology, p. 55.
[3] τῷ δ' ἄρα πτερὰ γίγνετ', ἄειρε δὲ ποιμένα λαῶν. Il. xix. 386.

the sea-dragon, Perseus wins Andromeda; after
killing the Minotauros, Theseus wins Ariadne.
In unselfishness of character and the determination to face rather than to shrink from danger,
there is no difference between Perseus and Theseus, until the latter returns from Crete, or,
again, between Perseus and Bellerophon, or even
Paris in the days when they called him Alexandros,
the helper of men. Perseus is the strongest and
the most active among the people in all manly
exercises. So, too, none can vie with Apollo in
the use of the bow, and the children of Niobê fall
not less surely than the Pythian dragon. If, again,
Perseus is the child of a mother of whom we know
little more than the name, gentle, patient, and
. long-enduring, the same neutral colouring is seen
in Hecabê,[1] the mother of the flaming Paris; in
Leto, who gives birth to Phœbus, the destroyer, in
Delos; and in Alcmênê, from whom is born the
mightiest of heroes, Heracles. The life of Perseus
closes in darkness. He has slain his grandfather,
and he has not the heart to remain in his ancient
home; but Kephalos also cannot abide at Athens
after he has unwittingly slain Procris, and both
depart to die elsewhere.

Without going further, we have here no very in-

---

[1] Gladstone, Homer &c. vol. ii. p. 155. See also the Gods and
Heroes p. 23.

sufficient evidence, if we sought to prove a close connection, or even a complete identity, between Identity of the legends of Perseus, Bellerophon, Theseus, and other mythical beings. Perseus, Bellerophon, Theseus, Kephalos, Paris, and Apollo.   If we cease to confine ourselves to a single legend, the coincidences might be indefinitely multiplied, while any other legend may be submitted to the same treatment which has just been applied to that of Perseus. If Kephalos, having won the love of Procris, is obliged to leave her for a time, Apollo in like manner is compelled to desert Corônis (x.) If Procris yields her affection to one whom she almost believes to be Kephalos, the guilt of Corônis is not many shades deeper, while both are alike smitten by the fatal spear of Artemis.   In the legends of Thebes, Athens, Argos, and other cities, we find the strange, yet common, dread of parents who look on their children as their future destroyers.   The Trojan Hecabê, faint and negative in character as Leto herself, dreams that she becomes the mother of a flaming fire, and Priam casts forth her child to die on the heights of Ida.[1] The same portion falls to the lot of Œdipus on the slopes of Kithairon, while Perseus is intrusted to the mercy of the deep sea. Nay, the legends interchange the method by which the parents seek the death of their children; for

[1] See ' Œnônê,' in the Gods and Heroes.

there were tales which narrated that Œdipus was
shut up in an ark which was washed ashore at
Sikyon.[1]   In every case the child grows up beautiful, brave, and strong. Like Apollo, Bellerophon,
and Heracles, they are all slayers of monsters. The
son of the gloomy Laïos[2] returns to destroy the
dreaded Sphinx, as Perseus slays the Gorgon and
the Minotauros falls by the sword of Theseus. They
have other features in common. The fears of their
parents are in all cases realised.   Acrisios and
Laïos are killed by Perseus and Œdipus, while
Paris lights the torch which burns Ilion to ashes.
All of them love fair maidens, and are somewhat
prone to forsake them. The desertion of Ariadne,
of Dêianeira, and Corônis, finds its parallel in the
abandonment of Œnônê by Paris. After doing
marvellous things, they return not unfrequently
to the maiden whom they loved at the beginning
of their career, or to the mother from whom they
had parted long ago. Heracles finds Iolê by his
funeral pile on Œta, while Œnônê cheers Paris
in his last hour on Ida.   Still more significantly,
Œdipus marries Iocastê[3] (the connection of the

---

[1] This version of the tale calls him a son of Eurycleia, a name
which belongs to the same clan with Euryganeia, Eurydikê,
Eurymedê, &c.

[2] In Laïos we have the same neutral colouring which is common to the characters of Hecabê and Leto.

[3] The violet or purple colour can be traced through many
Greek mythical names. Iolaos is the son of Iphicles, the twin

name with that of Iolê is manifest), and the unwitting sin thus committed becomes the starting-
point of a more highly complicated history.
Wonderful, again, as is the seeming variety of
action and incident in these legends, the recur-

brother of Heracles (Asp. Herad. 74). Through Epaphos and
Danaos, the line of Heracles is traced back to Io, in whom is
brought out the favourite image of the bull, as a figure of Indra
or the sun. (See Max Müller, Comparative Mythology, p. 57.)
The names of Iasion (loved by Demêtêr and slain by Zeus), of
Iaso (the daughter of Asclepios), and Jason, were referred to the
idea of healing (ἴασις); but Æschylus derived Lykios, as an
epithet of Apollo, from the destruction of wolves—

Λύκει' ἄναξ, Λύκειος γενοῦ
στρατῷ δαΐῳ—   Theb. 145.

and thus unconsciously explained the transformation of Lycáon
into a wolf. These names may therefore have had the same
origin with that of Iamos, which is directly referred to the violet
beds under which he was hidden by the serpents (of the night).
Again, we are told that 'Ιήϊος, as a name of Apollo, is to be referred not to ἰάομαι, but to the cry ἰή. To the same origin is
referred Ἴακχος, the name of Dionysos. Yet it is at the least possible, if not probable, that both these names originally expressed
colour, not sound; for we are not concerned to determine the
meaning assigned to such words by the Greeks, any more than
we are bound to accept Aristotle's derivation of δικαστής from
δίχα στῆς. Professor Max Müller has remarked that the idea of
the poisoned robes of Medeia and Deianeira may have come from
a fancied connection of the name Iolê with ἰός, poison (Comp.
Myth. p. 55). He has also noted that the ideas of sound and
colour are closely connected. 'Thus it is said (Rv. vi. 3,6), the
fire cries with light: the two Spartan Charites are called Κλητά
and Φαεννά, i.e. Clara, clear-sounding and clear-shining. Of
the rising sun, it is said in the Veda, "the child cries "' (Ib. p. 62).

rence of the same imagery, freshened by ingenious modifications, is not less remarkable.
If Heracles begins his career of marvels by
strangling the serpents who have twined round
his limbs, the youthful Apollo slays the huge
snake Pytho, and Perseus smites the snaky-haired
Medusa. The serpents in their turn win the victory when Eurydikê falls a victim on the banks
of the Hebros, or assume a more kindly form in
the legends of Iamos (VII.) and Melampus. The
former they shelter in the thickets, because, as
with Perseus, Œdipus, and Paris, his kinsfolk seek
his death, while to Melampus, by cleansing his
ears, they impart a new power, so that he may
understand the voices and the song of birds.[1] The
spotless white bull bears Europa across the waters
of the sea; the glistening ram [2] soars through the
air with the children of Nephelê, or the mist.
Phaethûsa and Lampetiê drive the cattle of Helios
to their pastures, and Hermes steals the herds of
Phœbus before he is scarce an hour old. The
cattle, in their turn, assume an unkindly aspect.
The Minotauros plagues the Cretans, the Mara-

[1] Melampus, like Heracles, is wakened by the serpents. The
night wakens the sun.

[2] The connection of the ram with the bull (Indra) is still
further shown in the unfading and incorruptible golden fleece.
Nor must it be forgotten that this fleece is recovered by Jason,
who is, again, married to Medeia, the possessor of the fatal robe
of Helios, which reappears in the legend of Dôianeira.

thonian bull ravages the fields of Attica. The former is killed by the child of the golden shower, the latter by the son of Æthra, the pure air.

The very names occurring in these tales have a significance which the Greek language itself interprets, whenever they tell us of the great heroes whose lives run so strangely in the same magic groove. Œdipus loves Iocastê, as Heracles loves Iolê : he is also the husband of Euryganeia, who spreads the light over the broad sky. The names of Phaethon, of Phaethûsa and Lampetiê, the children of Neaira, all tell their own tale. As in the names of Iolê and Iocastê, the violet colour recurs in that of the child Iamos, and Euryganeia reappears in Eurydikê, as well as in Eurymedê, the mother of Bellerophon, while slaughter or death is portended by the names of Leto and Apollo, of Perseus and Bellerophon. In the obscure mythology of Tegea, when the name of Heracles is introduced, the maiden whom he chooses is Augê, the brilliant.[1] She, too, like Danaê, is driven away by the terror of her father, and in the far eastern land becomes the mother of Têlephos, who, like Paris and Œdipus, is exposed on the rough hill-side, and whose office as the bringer of light is seen again

[margin note: Significance of the names employed in Greek mythology.]

[1] Paus. viii. 4, 6. Grote, History of Greece, vol. i. p. 243.

in the name of Telephassa, the mother of Europa.
So, again, when the genealogy of Phthia is to
be mingled with that of Elis, it is Protogeneia
(the earliest dawn) who becomes the mother of
Aëthlios (the toiling, struggling sun), who is the
father of Endymion, the tired sun at his setting,
in whose child Eurydikê we see again the morrow's
light restored to its former brightness.[1] So, in the
end, Paris is slain by the arrows which Apollo
gave to Philoctetes, and under the eye of Selênê
Endymion sleeps in Latmos.

 Thus, in the marvellous tales which recounted
the mighty deeds of Perseus and Heracles, the
The le-
gend of
Perseus
would, of
itself,
suffice for
a longer
epic than
the Iliad. people of Argos saw a coherent whole—
the chronicle of the great actions which
distinguished the founders of their state
from those of any other. Yet the tale of
Perseus, and still more that of Heracles, is re-
echoed in the legends of Theseus; and even more
significant is the fact of their utter unconscious-
ness that the life of Perseus is, in all its essential

[1] Pausanias, v. 1, 2. Aëthlios is the husband of Calykê, the
night. By some law of probability, better known to himself than
to others, Pausanias chooses to marry Endymion to Asterodia,
rather than to Selênê, as the mother of his fifty children. He
was making a distinction without a difference. Mr. Grote gives
the several versions of the myth (vol. i. p. 188, &c.); but he is
mistaken in supposing that the names Aëthlios and Endymion
are of late introduction, although their connection with the Olym-
pic games undoubtedly was.

features, repeated in that of his great descendant Heracles. Heracles, again, in some of his acts, is linked with Theseus, and thus the *epos* of Argos is twisted into a complicated chain with that of Attica. These legends taken together, or even a portion of them, might well be expanded into a far longer poem than the Iliad; and there is therefore the less reason for surprise if the Iliad itself, on examination, is found to relate part only of a more extended legend, or to exhibit under a different colouring modified versions of a single story. If in the mythology of a single city we have the ideal of Perseus recurring in the tale of Heracles, there is the less reason for wonder if the Hellenic Achilleus is but the counterpart of the Trojan Alexandros, otherwise called Paris,—nay, if the character of Achilleus recurs in that of other Hellenic heroes. The Iliad, or rather, as Mr. Grote would say, the Achilléis,[1] sings of the wrath of the Phthiotic chieftain, who is also the child of the sea-goddess Thetis, and this wrath is followed by a time of gloomy and sullen inaction. The glorious hero, the lightning of whose countenance struck terror into his enemies, hangs up his weapons and hides his face. The sun has passed behind the veil of the storm-cloud. The expression is literally forced

The story of the Iliad is only part of a more extensive legend.

---

[1] History of Greece, vol. ii. p. 236 et seq.

from us: we cannot withhold the metaphor. But
so was it with the men of Calydon while Meleagros lay sullen and angry in his secret chamber
with his beautiful wife Cleopatra. So complete
is the identity of the two charactors, so thoroughly
does it rebuke his moody anger, that the episode
of Meleagros is recited at length by Phoinix,
in the hope that it may appease the fury of
Achilleus.[1]   But the issue with both is the
same; and that issue is repeated in the history of
Paris. Meleagros comes forth at last to the aid
of his people, and Achilleus at last makes up his
quarrel with Agamemnon, to avenge the death of
Patroclos. All these are doomed, after their time
of obstinate inaction, to an early and violent
death, preceded by a brief outburst of their former
splendour. That such was to be the lot of his great
hero, the Homeric poet knew well; but, unconscious
as he may have been of the source of the materials
of which he made such splendid use, he chose,
with a poetical instinct never surpassed, to close
his tale when Achilleus grants the prayer of
Priam and yields to him the body of his dead
son Hector. The struggle has been long and
gloomy; but the hero who left his home in the
full flush of radiant manhood, must at the last
exhibit the nobleness of his nature, even if its

[1] Iliad, ix. 529–599.

splendour has been somewhat marred by the wayward stubbornness which rejected alike all comfort and all counsel. The storm-cloud has passed away, and the beaten vapours fly from the face of the triumphant sun.

Nor are resemblances of detail wanting to show that Eastern and Western legends have in the Iliad been blended together. Achilleus is wrathful because Agamemnon, the king, has taken from him the fair maiden Brisêis, whom he won with his bow and his spear. Paris rests sullenly on his luxurious couches because he will not, at the bidding of his father and his kinsfolk, give up Helen, whom he had brought away from Argos. And if Achilleus comes forth from his tent to slay Hector, while the name of Paris is made a by-word and a reproach, yet it is from Paris, aided by Apollo, that Achilleus receives his death-wound. *Mingling of Eastern and Western legends.*

Such a blending of the mythology of different cities or countries would necessarily issue in a highly complicated story. But it is obvious, at the same time, that no historical inferences can be drawn from the mere fact of such a complication. Rightly convinced that the tale of Troy, with its marvellously *No historical conclusions can be drawn from the complications so caused.* vivid details and astonishing incidents, must have some foundation, Dr. Thirlwall is disposed to refer it to some great expedition in which the

chieftains of Western Hellas were combined against
an Asiatic power ruling in Ilion.[1]   The evidence
of such a fact may be found in isolated statements
contained in the Iliad, but scarcely in the plot
of the story.   If it may be assumed from the
form of the prophecy of Poseidon that princes
claiming descent from Æneas ruled in the poet's
time ,in the Troad,[2] no light is thrown by it on
the existence of that chief or on the reality of
the Trojan war.   The ruins of Tiryns attest the

[1] History of Greece, ch. v.   Dr. Thirlwall is struck by the
contrast of the futile efforts of Agamemnon and his host
with the success of Heracles in his attack on Troy during
the reign of Laomedon. He makes some plausible historical
conjectures to account for this difference.   But the tale
explains itself. Heracles is a transformation of the invincible
sun-god; and his might therefore beats down every enemy.
Agamemnon and his host represent Gunnar and his followers in
the Northern epic; and these are of kin to the powers of darkness.   They can do nothing, therefore, in spite of their numbers,
until aided by Achilleus, the sunlike hero.   Such, at least, is the
burden of the Achilléis.   The interpolated Iliad was the result of
a patriotic feeling struggling against the laws of mythical speech.
Dr. Thirlwall sees clearly that the abduction of Helen may
have been 'a theme for poetry originally independent of the
Trojan war,' and he rightly insists that the tale of the war,
'even if unfounded, must still have had some adequate occasion
and motive.'   This is indisputable: but hypotheses connecting it
with Greek colonies in Asia explain nothing; the comparison of
Greek legends among themselves and with other systems of mythology explains all.
[2] Iliad, xx. 307-8.   It is, after all, the merest inference.   See
Grote, History of Greece, vol. i. p. 428.

truthfulness of Homeric description; the walls of Mykênæ bear out the statement that it was once the seat of a dynasty which ruled over many islands and all Argos; but archæological evidence tells us nothing of Perseids or of Pelopids.

But if we can trace this recurrence of the same ideal in different heroes, and of the same imagery in the recital of their adventures, in Hellenic mythology alone, the marvel is intensified a thousandfold when we compare this mythology with the ancient legends of Northern Europe or of the far-distant East. There is scarcely an incident in the lives of the great Greek heroes which cannot be traced out in the wide field of Teutonic or Scandinavian tradition; and the complicated action of the Iliad, or rather of the whole legend of which the Iliad forms a part, is reproduced in the Eddas and the lays of the Volsungs and the Nibelungs. If the Greek tales tell us of serpent-slayers and the destroyers of noxious monsters, the legends of the ice-bound North also sing of heroes who slay the dragons that lie coiled round sleeping maidens. If the former recite the labours of Heracles and speak of the bondage of Apollo, Sifrit and Sigurdr are not less doomed to a life of labour for others, not for themselves. If Heracles alone can rescue Hesionê from a like doom with Andromeda, or bring back Alkêstis from the land of Hades, it is

Substantial identity of Greek and Norse mythology.

c 2

Sigurdr only who can slay the serpent Fafnir, and
Ragnar Lodbrog alone who can deliver Thora from
the dragon's grasp.[1] If, at the end of his course,
Heracles once more sees his early love—if Œnônê
comes again to Paris in his death hour—so Brenhyldr lies down to die with Sigurdr who had forsaken her. If Achilleus and Baldr can only be
wounded on a single spot, Isfendiyar, in the Persian epic, can only be killed by the thorn thrown
into his eye by Rustem. If Paris forsakes Œnônê,
and Theseus leaves Ariadne mourning on the barren shore, so also Sigurdr deserts Brenhyldr, and
Gudrun to him supplies the place of Aiglê or
of Helen. If the tale of Perseus is repeated in
the career of Heracles, the legend of Ragnar
Lodbrog is also a mere echo of the nobler story
which told of the sunbright Sigurdr. It is scarcely
necessary to enter into more minute detail. How
completely the whole Northern mythology of
Europe is founded on the great tragedy of Nature
has been shown, in a way which leaves nothing to be
desired, by Professor Max Müller and Mr. Dasent.[2]
The harmony of this Northern mythology with
that of Homer and the Hellenic legends generally I have endeavoured to point out in the

---

[1] Gods and Heroes, Introduction, p. 64.

[2] Max Müller, Comparative Mythology, in Oxford Essays for
1856, p. 66, &c. Dasent, Popular Tales from the Norse, Introduction.

introduction to the 'Tales of the Gods and Heroes.'

But at this point we encounter a difficulty which, if not removed, must prove fatal to the method which the science of Comparative Mytho- Conclulogy applies to the legends of the East and drawn from a West. If that science has guided us to comparison of any measure of the truth, it has taught us Greek with Norse something not merely of the growth of legends. tales which recount the actions of deified heroes, but of the conceptions from which sprang the highest deities of Olympus—Artemis, Dêmêtêr, Apollo, and Zeus himself. It has identified Phœbus with Helios, Heracles, Perseus, Artemis. It has traced the several aspects of his character through the phases presented in the legends of Theseus, Kephalos, Daphnê, Endymion, Bellerophon, and Meleagros. It has taught us that he is the child of Zeus and Leto, while the maiden Persephonê is sprung from Zeus and Dêmêter. It tells us of Ouranos looking down on Gaia, and of Gaia returning the love of Ouranos by her unbounded fertility. It speaks of the toiling sun, visiting all the regions of the earth as he ascends or goes down the slope of heaven, and of earth as yielding to him her fruits, wherever his light may exercise its beneficent power. It speaks of Zeus as the son or the husband of Gaia, and of the tears which fell in raindrops

from the sky when he mourned for the death of
his son Sarpêdon. It seems to tell us, then, of a
mythological or religious system which, simple at
the first, became at the last excessively complicated,
and, further, that this system was the result not
of philosophical generalisations, but of the consciousness of an exuberant life which was extended
from man to every object which he beheld in the
visible creation. It seems to show that once upon
a time, while the ancestors of European nations
and tribes were still comparatively united, men
had uttered as the simple phrases of every-day
speech what became afterwards the groundwork
of elaborate religious systems—that once upon a
time they spoke of the dawn coming from the
chambers of the night, while the night herself
was struggling with the birth of the brilliant sun
—that the new-born sun saw, and loved, and pursued the dawn, which vanished at his touch.   It
seems to teach us that out of such phrases, which,
slightly varied, were expanded into the tales of
Kephalos and Procris, of Corônis and Apollo,
grew finally the more definite personalities of
Zeus and Phœbus, of Leto and Daphnê, of
Artemis and Heracles. Hence whatever in the
later Greek religious system there was of direct
anthropomorphism or of a fetiche nature-worship
would be the result of later thought and of
attempts to arrive at philosophical abstractions,

and not the maimed and distorted relics of a higher knowledge once possessed but now only not forgotten.

If the theory which makes the growth of Greek mythology from the first a philosophical process can be established, then the results of com- Mr.Glad-parative mythology must be abandoned as theory of of no value, and we must be content to logy as look on the points of resemblance between ruption of an Greek, Teutonic, Scandinavian, and Eastern dogmatic mythology, as a problem utterly beyond our tion. powers to solve or even to grapple with.   In either case it is a question of evidence.   In his studies on Homer and the Homeric age, Mr. Gladstone sought to bring together the evidence that the Greek theogony was a distortion of primitive dogmatic revelation—that Zeus, Hades, and Poseidon stood in place of the Christian Trinity, while Leto represented the mother of the Redeemer, whose attributes are divided between Apollo and Athênê.   The objections which seem to be conclusive against the hypothesis of an original dogmatic revelation, of such a kind at least as that of which Mr. Gladstone speaks, have been considered already ;[1] and it is perhaps unnecessary to reply at greater length to a theory which, however ingenious and however forcibly urged, has nothing but its own plausibility to

[1] Tales of the Gods and Heroes, Introduction, pp. 14–40.

appeal to for acceptance. Dr. Döllinger's position [1] lies open to no charges of fanciful
extravagance; it needs, therefore, to be the
more carefully examined, as professing to
be a legitimate deduction from the state of religion, or rather of religious *cultus*, among the
Greeks in historical times. This state was, in
the opinion of Dr. Döllinger, the result of an
attempt to reduce a variety of conflicting systems
and notions into one harmonious whole. In it
were mingled the mysticism of Egypt and the
orgiastic ritualism of the East, with the rude
nature-worship of the older and less civilised ages;
and his purpose is to trace the several ideas so
amalgamated to their original sources. With this
view he is obliged to assume that in his primæval
innocence man was enabled 'to conceive of the
Divinity as a pure, spiritual, supernatural, and
infinite being, distinct from the world and exalted
above it.' The loss of this conception and the
yearning for something in its place led to the
deification of material nature, which 'unfolded
herself to man's nature as a boundless demesne,
wherein was confined an unfathomable plenitude
of powers, incommensurable and incalculable, and
of energies not to be overcome.' With this was
developed a sympathy for naturalism, 'and thus

(margin note: Theory of Dr. Döllinger.)

man, deeper and deeper in the spells of his en-
chantress, and drawn downwards by their weight,
had his moral consciousness overcast in proportion, and gave the fuller rein to impulses which
were merely physical.'¹ This deification of natural
powers led, as Dr. Döllinger believes, first of all
to the worship of the elements—of ether as the
vault of heaven, of the earth as its opposite ; of
fire as the warming and nourishing, the consuming
and destroying power; of water as the element of
moisture separated from that of earth. To this
succeeded astrolatry in the East, and geolatry in
the West, where the idea of the earth as a suscep-
tible and productive agent led to the distinction
of male and female divinities. But the actual
Greek religion of the heroic and later ages was a
blending of the several notions derived from sup-
planted races, Leleges and Carians, Thracians and
Pelasgi, together with importations from Asia and
Egypt.² Thus Gaia and Helios, Zeus and Hêrê,
belong to the Pelasgic stock, while Poseidon was
introduced by Carian and Phœnician visitors of
the coasts of Hellas.³ Pallas Athênê was also
Pelasgian, as a goddess of nature and the elements.
Apollo, likewise Pelasgian, ' has so many features
in common with Athênê, that in many respects

¹ The Gentile and the Jew in the Courts of the Temple of
Christ, vol. i. p. 66.
² Ibid. p. 68.   ³ Ibid. p. 80.

one might call him an Athênê of the male species.'
Artemis was in continental Greece Pelasgian,
while at Ephesus she exhibits an Asiatic character and becomes 'a sort of pantheistic deity.' From
the Pelasgi also came Hestia, Hermes, and Aphroditê; but Ares was the god of the Thracian race,
'which, having penetrated into Bœotia and the
Peloponnese, took his worship along with them.'
Of the rest Dêmêtêr was Pelasgic, Hephaistos
came from the Thracians of Lemnos, and Dionysos from the more distant East; while Hades was
almost an afterthought, not much worshipped,
and not greatly cared for by the people.[1]

The picture drawn by Dr. Döllinger of the
great Olympian deities may in all its particulars
be strictly true. It is possible or probable
that ideas utterly foreign to the Greek
mind may have been imported from Phrygia,
Phœnicia, or Egypt, and that the worship
so developed may have embodied philosophical conceptions of nature and of the powers at
work in it. But the question which calls for an
answer cannot be determined by the most masterly portraiture of the great gods of Olympus;
and Dr. Döllinger's hypothesis does not enable us
to answer it. It starts on an assumption for
which we have no evidence; and all the evidence

This theory starts on an assumption for which there is no evidence.

---

[1] The Gentile and the Jew in the Courts of the Temple of
Christ, vol. i. p. 93.

that is furnished by the book of Genesis, and still
more all that is furnished by the study of language, militates against the idea that man started
originally with a conception of God 'as a pure,
spiritual, supernatural, and infinite being, distinct
from the world and exalted above it.' How soon
he might have risen to this conception, had his
lot been different from what it has been, it is
impossible to say; but if we are to argue simply
from statements before us, we may affirm that men
were, from the first, conscious of the existence of a
Being more powerful than themselves, whom they
were bound to obey, but we can scarcely maintain
more.   This sense of duty, and still more the
sense of shame following on a violation of it,
would show that the groundwork of that relation
was the goodness and justice of the Being with
whom they had to do.   But in this conviction
there was nothing to determine their ideas on the
objects and phenomena of the natural world.
Feeling a conscious life in himself, man would,
until corrected by experience, attribute the same
conscious life to everything that he saw or felt.
The sun and moon, the cloud and the wind, would
be living beings not less than himself; but he
could not embody them in anthropomorphic forms,
so long as the names by which he spoke of them
retained their original meanings.   Still less could
he start with a primary worship of the elements

until he had learnt to regard as abstractions the
objects or powers, which, it would seem, he looked
upon only as living beings. Three ways lay before
him. He might, like Abraham in the old Arabian
legend,[1] be led by the rising and setting of the
sun and stars to the conviction that they were
simply passive instruments in the hands of an
almighty and a righteous God; or he might, as
he forgot his old language, invest with an anthropomorphic life, the deities with which he peopled
the whole visible creation; or, lastly, he might
bow down crushed beneath the dead weight of
nature, and yield himself a living slave to a
loathsome and degrading fetichism. Of these
three courses the first was chosen only by the
Hebrew people, and even by them feebly and fit-
fully; the second was followed by the tribes of the
Hellenic stock; the third has been rejected by
every portion of the great Aryan family of nations.
These, as they journeyed from their ancient home,
carried with them the old language and the old
morality; but the measure in which they forgot
the meaning of proper names would determine
the extent to which new gods should be called
into existence. But this developement, as the
result, primarily, of a corruption of language,
would not be, in the strictest sense, a religion,
and the moral sense of the worshipper would not

[1] Milman, History of the Jews, book i.

be darkened in proportion to the number of the
gods whom he venerated. Dr. Döllinger's hypothesis, not less than the theory of Mr. Gladstone,
would require a continually increasing degrada-
tion; but a comparison of the Homeric and
Hesiodic poems is conclusive against it. There is
no evidence that the Greeks of the seventh or
sixth centuries before the Christian era had their
'moral consciousness more overcast' than the
Greeks of the tenth or twelfth; there is much to
lead us to the contrary conclusion.

But Dr. Döllinger's theory requires him to deal
with Carians, Leleges, and Pelasgi; and the chain
of his argument becomes weakest where it Histori-
should have the greatest strength. His spe- cal specu-
                                             lations of
culations may be masterly, and his conclu-   Dr. Dol-
                                             linger.
sions forcible, but we lack the means of determining
their truth. Mr. Grote, in his 'History of Greece,'
hesitates to speak of any events as historical facts
before the first recorded Olympiad, i. e. 776 B.C.
Sir Cornewall Lewis holds the researches of
scholars respecting the primitive history of the
Hellenic or Italian tribes as 'not less unreal than
the speculations concerning judicial astrology or
the discovery of the philosopher's stone and the
elixir of life.'[1] Dr. Döllinger must have evidence,
not accessible to either, to warrant the assertion
that the chief seats of the Pelasgians were Arcadia,

[1] Credibility of Early Roman History, vol. i. p. 297.

Argolis, and Perrhæbia, and that the immigration
of the Doric and Æolic races took place precisely
in the year 1104 B.C.[1]

His analysis thus leaves the Greek mythology,
as he found it, a strange and perplexing riddle.

It omits all notice of the marvellous likeness between Greek and Scandinavian
legends; it does not even attempt to explain why each Greek god should have
certain special attributes and not others.

They leave the real diffi-culties of Greek mytho-logy unex-plained.

It does not tell us why Heracles and Perseus
and Bellerophon and Apollo should all be made to
serve creatures meaner and weaker than themselves—why Heracles and Zeus should have a
thousand earthly loves, and Artemis and Athênê
none.   Still less does it explain why the character
of Heracles and Hermes should sometimes assume
a comic aspect, which is never allowed to weaken
the serious majesty of Athênê, or Dêmêtêr, or
Apollo.

But, without reference to the systems of other
nations, the mythology of the Greeks *seems* of
itself to point out the track which must be
followed if we seek to solve the problem of
its birth. It is impossible to read the legends
of Heracles and Demeter, of Theseus, Cadmus, Perseus, and other great mythical
personages, without feeling that a few simple

Greek mytho-logy, of itself, seems to point out the means of solving them.

---

[1] Jew and Gentile &c. vol. L pp. 08, 74.

phrases might well have supplied the germ for
the most complicated of these traditions.   Every
incident in the myth of the Eleusinian Démêtêr
may be accounted for, if only men once said
(with the conviction that the things of which they
spoke had a conscious life), 'The earth mourns
for the dead summer.   The summer lies shut up
in the prison of Hades, the unseen ; '—or, as in the
language of the Norseman, 'She sleeps in the
land of the Niflungs, the cold mists, guarded by
the serpent Fafnir.'   The tale of Endymion seems
to speak for itself : 'The moon comes to gaze on
her beloved, the sun, as he lies down to sleep in
the evening.'   In the story of Niobê we seem to
see the sun in his scorching power, consuming
those who dare to face his dazzling brightness ; in
that of Orpheus we seem to hear his lamentation
for the beautiful evening which has been stung by
the serpent of the night, and which he brings
back to life only to lose her at the gates of day.
In the myth of Europa we have the journey of
the sun from the far East to the Western land,
until Têlephassa, the far-shining, sinks down
wearied on the Thessalian plain.   Still more
transparent appear the tales of Kephalos and
Daphnê.   Procris, even in the mouth of the
Greek, is still the child of Hersê, the dew, Eôs
is still the morning, Kephalos still the head of
the bright sun.   In Daphnê we seem to behold

the dawn flying from her lover, and shrinking
before his splendour. In the Homeric hymn,
Leto, the night, dark and still as death, promises
that Phœbus shall long abide in Delos, the bright
land. Doubtless she made the same promise to
the Lykians; but the sun cannot tarry, and he
hastens westward to slay the serpent of darkness.
In Heracles we see the sun in other guise, toiling
and suffering, loving and beloved wherever he
goes, seeking to benefit the sons of men, yet
sometimes harming them in the exuberance of
his boisterous strength. In the tale of Althæa,
we read the sentence that the bright sun must
die when the torch of day is burnt out. In
Phaethon we seem to see the plague of drought
which made men say, 'Surely another, who cannot guide his horses, is driving the chariot of the
sun.' The beautiful herds, which the bright and
glistening daughters of early morning feed in the
pastures of Thrinakia, seem to tell us of the
violet-coloured clouds which the dawn spreads
over the fields of the blue sky. In Bellerophon,
as in Perseus, Theseus, and Heracles, we find
again the burden laid on the sun who must toil
for others, although the forms of that toil may
vary. Perseus goes to the dwelling of the Graiæ,
as men might have said, 'The sun has departed
to the land of the twilight.' When Perseus slays
Medusa, the sun has killed the night in its solemn

and deathlike beauty; while the wild pursuit of
the immortal Gorgons seems to be the chase of
Darkness after the bright sun, who, with his
golden sandals, just escapes their grasp as he
soars into the peaceful morning sky, the Hyper-
borean gardens, which sorrow, strife, and death can
never enter. In the death of Acrisios we have the
old tale which comes up in many another legend,
where Œdipus mourns that he has unwittingly
slain his father, and the maiden Iolê, like Œnônê,
dies on the funeral pile of Heracles.

If the Greek legends by themselves thus exhibit, or
seem to exhibit, their ancient framework, the Norse
tradition points not less unmistakably in the
same direction. If any now can be found
to assert that the one set of legends were
copied from the other, he not only maintains
a theory which, in Mr. Dasent's words, hangs on
a single thread,[1] but he displays a credulity
which need not shrink from the avowal that the
whole of the ' Arabian Nights' Entertainments ' is
a genuine and veracious history. The wildest

The Norse mythology points in precisely the same direction.

[1] Popular Tales from the Norse, Introduction, p. xliii. In the
chapter on Diffusion of Myths, Mr. Dasent has completely disposed of all charges of copying, in every form in which such
objections can be urged. Some of the most remarkable incidents
of Greek mythology are to be found in the folk-lore of English
counties. The story of the fatal brand of Meleagros survives in
the traditional tales of North Devon. See Mr. Tugwell's North
Devon Scenery Book.

D

prejudice can scarcely shelter itself behind these treacherous and crumbling barriers, although it may urge that, whether in Teutonic or Greek mythology, the dawn, the evening, and the night, the toiling and capricious sun, are already persons with human forms and a fixed local habitation. But even this position would be greatly strained. Mr. Grote himself allows that what he terms allegory is one of the constituent elements of Greek mythology.[1] But, even if we admit the objection in its full force, we lack but a single link to complete the chain of evidence and turn an overwhelming probability into fact. Have we any records of that old time in which men spoke as Greek and Norse myths seem to tell us that they did? Have we any actual relics of that speech in which men talked of Daphnê as chased by Phœbus, even while Daphnê was still the common name of the dawn, and Phœbus meant still simply the sun?

The Vedic hymns of the Mantra period stand forth to give us the answer, but they do so only to exhibit a fresh marvel. While they show to us the speech which was afterwards petrified into the forms of Greek mythology, they point to a still earlier time, of which no record has come down, and of which we can have no further evidence than that which is furnished by the laws which determine the

The missing link is supplied in the older Vedic poems.

---

[1] History of Greece, vol. i. p. 2.

growth of language. Even in the Mantra period, the earliest in all Sanskrit, and therefore (as exhibiting the earliest form of thought) the earliest in all human literature,[1] the whole grammar is definitely fixed, and religious belief has assumed the character of a creed. And if in them man has not lived long enough to trace analogies and arrive at some idea of an order of nature, he has grown into the strongest conviction that behind all the forms which come before his eyes there is a Being, unseen and all-powerful, whose bidding is done throughout the wide creation, and to whom men may draw nigh as children to a father.

When, therefore, in these hymns, Kephalos, Procris, Hermes, Daphnê stand forth as simple names for the sun, the dew, the wind, and the dawn, each recognised as such, yet each endowed with the most perfect consciousness, we feel that the great riddle of mythology is solved, and that we no longer lack the key which shall disclose its most hidden treasures. When we hear the people saying, 'Our friend the sun is dead. Will he rise? Will the dawn come back again?' we see the death of Heracles or Kephalos and the weary waiting while Leto struggles with the birth of Phœbus. When on the return of day we hear the cry—

The key to all Aryan mythology.

[1] Max Müller, History of Sanskrit Literature, pp. 528, 557.

D 2

'Rise! our life, our spirit is come back, the
darkness is gone, the light approaches,'
—we are carried at once to the Homeric hymn,
and we hear the joyous shout of all the gods when
Phœbus springs to life and light in Delos.[1] The
tale of Urvasî and Purûravas[2] (these are still
the morning and the sun) is the tale of Orpheus
and Eurydikê. Purûravas, in his dreary search,
hears the voice of Urvasî saying, 'I am gone like
the first of the dawns. I am hard to be caught
like the wind.' Yet she will come back to him
at the close of the night, and a son, bright and
beaming, shall be born to them. Varuṇa is still
the wide heaven, the god 'who can be seen by
all,' the lord of the whole earth; but in him we
recognise at once the Greek Ouranos, who looks
lovingly on Gaia from his throne in the sky. Yet
more we read the praises of Indra, and his great
exploit is that

'He has struck the daughter of Dyaus [Zeus],
a woman difficult to vanquish.

'Yes, even the daughter of Dyaus, the mag-

___

[1]   ἐκ δ' ἔθορε πρὸ φόωσδε· θεαὶ δ' ὀλόλυξαν ἅπασαι.

Hymn. Apoll. 119.

[2] In the Essay on Comparative Mythology, Professor Max
Müller has given not only the older forms of this myth, but a
minute analysis of the play of Kalidâsa on this subject. This
poem is very instructive, as showing that the character of the
Homeric Achilleus adheres as closely to the original idea as do
those of Urvasî and Purûravas in the later poetry of Kalidâsa.

nified, the Dawn, thou, O Indra, a great hero, hast ground to pieces.

'The Dawn rushed off from her crushed car, fearing that Indra, the bull, might strike her.

'This her car lay there well ground to pieces: she went far away.'

The treatment is rude, but we have here not merely the whole tale of Daphnê, but the germ of that of Europa borne by the same bull across the sea. More commonly, however, the dawn is spoken of as bright, fair, and loving, the joy of all who behold her.

'She shines upon us like a young wife, rousing every living being to go to his work.

'She rose up, spreading far and wide [Euryganeia, Eurydikê], and moving towards every one. She grew in brightness, wearing her brilliant garment. The mother of the cows [the morning clouds, the Homeric herds of the sun], the leader of the days, she shone gold-coloured, lovely to behold.

'She, the fortunate, who brings the eye of the god [Kephalos], who leads the white and lovely steed (of the sun), the Dawn was seen revealed by her rays; with brilliant treasures she follows every one.

'Shine for us with thy best rays, thou bright Dawn, thou who lengthenest our life, thou the love of all, who givest us food, who givest us wealth in cows, horses, and chariots.

'Thou, daughter of the sky [Dyaus, Zeus], thou high-born Dawn, give us riches high and wide.'[1]

We can but wonder at the marvellous exuberance of language, almost every expression of which may manifestly serve as the germ of a mythical tale. We say, 'The fire burns, the wood crackles and smokes.' They said,

Germ of mythical tales.

'Neighing like a horse that is greedy for food, it steps 8ut from the strong prison; then the wind blows after his blast; thy path, O Agni [Ignis], is dark at once.'

The Latin carried with him the name to little purpose. In the hands of the Greek, similar phrases on the searching breath of the wind grew up into the legend of Hermes. Nor can it be said that the instinct of the Greek was less true than that of the old Aryan poet to the sights of the natural world. If we recur with feelings of undiminished pleasure to the touching truthfulness of the language which tells of the Dawn as the bright being whom age cannot touch although she makes men old, who thinks of the dwellings of men and shines on the small and great, we feel also that the Homeric poet, even while he spoke of a god in human form born in Delos, was not less true to the original character of the being of whom he sang. He thought of the sun rising in

Truth-fulness of mythical descrip-tion.

---

[1] Max Müller, *History of Sanskrit Literature*, p. 551.

a cloudless heaven, and he told how the nymphs bathed him in pure water and wrapped him in a spotless robe.[1] But while they swathed him in golden bands, the great sword was not yet belted to his. side,[2] for thus far he showed to men only his beneficent brightness. Still, although the stress of the hymn lies wholly on the promise of Leto that her child shall have his chief home in Delos, the poet feels that Delos alone can never be his home, and so he sang how Apollo went from island to island, watching the ways and works of men—how he loved the tall sea-cliffs and every jutting headland and the rivers which hasten to the broad sea, even though he came back with ever-fresh delight to his native Delos.[3]

Thus the great mystery of Greek as of other

---

[1] ἔνθα σε, ἥϊε Φοῖβε, θεαὶ λόον ὕδατι καλῷ
     ἁγνῶς καὶ καθαρῶς· σπάρξαν δ' ἐν φάρεϊ λευκῷ
     λεπτῷ, νηγατέῳ.   Hymn. Apoll. 120.

[2]   πέρι δὲ χρύσεον στρόφον ἧκαν·
     οὐδ' ἄρ' Ἀπόλλωνα χρυσάορα θήσατο μήτηρ.   Ib. 122.

[3] Αὐτὸς δ', ἀργυρότοξε, ἄναξ, ἑκατηβόλ' Ἄπολλον,
     ἄλλοτε μέν τ' ἐπὶ Κύνθου ἐβήσαο παιπαλόεντος,
     ἄλλοτε δ' αὖ νήσους τε καὶ ἀνέρας ἠλάσκαζες.

        .   .   .   .   .   .

     πᾶσαι δὲ σκοπιαί τε φίλαι καὶ πρώονες ἄκροι
     ὑψηλῶν ὀρέων, ποταμοί δ' ἅλαδε προρέοντες·

        .   .   .   .   .   .

     ἀλλὰ σὺ Δήλῳ, Φοῖβε, μάλιστ' ἐπιτέρπεαι ἦτορ.
                                         Ib. 140.

mythology is dispelled like mist from the mountain side at the rising of the sun. All that
is beautiful in it is invested with a purer
radiance; while much, if not all, that is
gross and coarse in it, is refined, or else its gross-
ness is traced to an origin which reflects no disgrace on those who framed or handed down the
tale. Thus, with the key-note ringing in our ears,
we can catch at once every strain that belongs to
the ancient harmony, although it may be heard
amid the din of many discordant voices. The
groundwork of Greek mythology was the ordinary
speech which told of the interchange of day and
night, of summer and winter; but into the super-
structure there may have been introduced any
amount of local or personal detail, any number of
ideas and notions imported from foreign philosophical or religious systems. The extent of such
importations is probably far less than is generally
imagined; but, however this may be, the original
matter may still be traced, even where it exists
only in isolated fragments. The bull which bears
Europa away from Cadmos (Kedem, the East)[1] is
the same from which the dawn flies in the Vedic
hymn. It is seen again as the Minotauros, the

---

[1] Niebuhr (in his Lectures on Ancient History, vol. i. p. 239)
sees that the tale points to the East; but from the words Cadmus,
and Banna as occurring in the Boeotian dialect only, he is perfectly convinced of the 'Phœnician origin of Thebes.'

offspring of Pasiphaê (who gives light to all), and
reappears still further disguised in the Maratho-
nian bull. The robe with which Medeia poisons
the daughter of Creon was a gift from Helios, the
burning sun, and is seen again as the poisoned robe
which Dêianeira sends to the absent Heracles—
as the deadly arrow by which Philoctetes mortally
wounds the Trojan Paris—as the golden fleece
taken from the ram which bears away the children
of (Nephelê) the mist—as the sword which Ægeus
leaves under the stone for Theseus the son of
Æthra, the pure air—as the spear of Artemis which
never misses its mark—as the sword of Perseus
which slays all on whom it may fall—as the
unerring weapons of Meleagros—as the fatal lance
which Achilleus alone can wield. The serpents
of night or of winter occur in almost every tale,
under aspects friendly or unkind. The dragon
sleeps coiled round Brenhyldr or Aslauga, as the
snakes seek to strangle the infant Heracles or
sting the beautiful Eurydikê. But in Southern
climes night has its softer moods; and the serpents, in the dim twilight of morning, place Iamos
on the violet beds, or open the ears of Melampus
to the song of the early birds. If the power of the
sun's rays is set forth under such different forms,
their beauty is signified by the golden locks of
Phœbus over which no razor has ever passed,[1] by

[1] Φοῖβος ἀκερσεκόμης (Il. xx. 39), a significant epithet which,

the flowing hair which streams from the head of
Kephalos and falls over the shoulders of Perseus
and Bellerophon. They serve also sometimes as a
sort of Palladium, and the shearing of the single
golden lock which grew on the top of his head
leaves Nisos, the Megarian king, powerless as
the shorn Samson in the arms of the Philistines.
In many of the legends these images are mingled
together, or recur under modified forms. In
the tale of Althæa, there is not only the torch of
day which measures the life of Meleagros, but
the weapons of the chieftain, which no enemy
may withstand. In that of Bellerophon, there
are the same invincible weapons, while the horrible Chimæra answers to the boar of Calydon,
or to that of Erymanthos, which fell by the arm
of Heracles.

The name of Heracles brings us to the strange
border-ground in which the character of some of
Comic aspect of certain mythical charac- ters. the gods assumes a jovial or even a comic
aspect. The language of the Vedic hymns
at once shows why this should be the portion of some among the greater gods, and not of
others. Phœbus, Athênê, and Orpheus, as repre-
senting the pure effulgence of the sun, Hestia as
the unsullied fire upon the hearth, Dêmêtêr as

---

of itself, would suffice to give birth to such a legend as that of
Nisos and Skylla. The shearing of the locks of the sun must be
followed by darkness and ruin.

the nourishing mother of all living things, Poseidon as the lord of the mysterious sea, Hades and Persephonê as rulers of the unseen land, pass under no conditions which may detract from their purity or their majesty. It was far otherwise with Ouranos or Zeus, the heaven and the sky, whose relations to the earth, when described under anthropomorphic forms, exhibit a mere unbounded license and its results of envy, jealousy, and strife in the home of the gods. If Heracles was in the outset simply the toiling and wandering sun, he, like the sun, must have his children in every land, and the series of his adventures must, from time to time, exhibit an uncouth and grotesque character.[1] Wherever he

Burlesque in the character of Heracles.

---

[1] This aspect of the myth is well illustrated by the tale of Heracles and Echidna (Herod. iv. 9). This uncouth story has, however, not a single feature peculiar to itself. Heracles sleeps, and his herds are stolen. Like Apollo, in the hymn to Hermes, he must go in search of them. He comes into a gloomy land, like Perseus into the land of the Graiæ, and there in the dusk he sees a creature with something of the beauty and ghastliness of Medusa. For a time she will not let him depart. The sun must abide awhile in the dark cave of night after his setting. In the morning she restores the herds; or, in other words, she yields them to Phaethûsa and Lampetiê, the children of Neaira. The violet clouds (Iolê) again go before Heracles. But with Echidna he leaves, as Ægeus left with Æthra, weapons not to be yielded up except to one who can wield them like himself. The legends of Theseus and Perseus are mingled in the dynastic myth which Herodotus ascribes to the Scythian tribes.

goes, he has his loves and his toils; but his tasks
frequently need nothing but sheer brute strength
for their fulfilment, and mere force suggests the
idea of moral weakness or absence of mental
vigour.   Hence he is the careless slave of beings
weaker than himself, and like a burly slave he
seeks solace for his hard lot in wine and riotous
laughter] and song.[1]   The cry of mourning is

---

[1] In short, Heracles, so regarded, is a mere giant, exulting in
his strength like Briareos, and seeking to make of life one long
holiday. The idea of Samson was certainly not derived from
the Greeks; yet his character, as drawn by Dr. Stanley, agrees
in every feature with that of Heracles, as exhibited in the
Alkêstis of Euripides and in the stories of his many loves.
While claiming for Samson, somewhat mysteriously, a position
which 'most nearly resembles that of the founder of a monastic
order,' he speaks of him as 'the most frolicsome, irregular, un-
cultivated creature that the nation ever produced. Not only was
celibacy no part of his Nazarite obligations, but not even ordinary purity of life. He was full of the spirits and the pranks,
no less than of the strength, of a giant. His name, which Jose-
phus interprets in the sense of "strong," was still more characteristic. He was "the sunny,"—the bright and beaming, though
wayward, likeness of the great luminary whom the Hebrews
delighted to compare to a "giant rejoicing to run his course,"
"a bridegroom coming forth out of his chamber." Nothing can
disturb his radiant good-humour. His most valiant, his most
cruel actions, are done with a smile on his face and a jest in his
mouth' (Lectures on the Jewish Church, p. 368). This character
is the more remarkable, as the sense of the comic was wholly
wanting in the Jews as a people. They spoke of a laugh of
scorn and hatred: the laughter of mere mirth seems to have been
unknown to them, as it was little known to the Romans. Like

hushed at his coming into the house of Admêtos;
but, although he knows that the chieftain has lost
some one whom he dearly loved, he sees in the
fact no reason whatever why he should lose his
dinner. So he jokes on with the slave who stands
aghast at the strength of his appetite, and when
he learns the true cause for the sorrow of his host,
he assures him with a careless smile that his
brawny arm will be more than a match for Tha-
natos, the power of death; and, lastly, when he
brings back Alkêstis in disguise, he has a keen
relish for the unwillingness which Admêtos exhibits to be on with the new love before he is off
with the old, while admitting that the likeness
to his lost wife is very surprising.

The broad burlesque so introduced may be dismissed as the heightened colouring added by later
poets; but the Homeric hymn to Hermes
betrays an enjoyment of humour, if not so
coarse, yet fully as great as that which is
shown by Euripides. The reason is plain. In
the old speech of which the Vedic songs have
preserved to us the fragments, Hermes was the
hound of the gods, the wind, as Agni (Ignis) is
the fire.[1] In this form of a hound he stands by

Phœbus, Samson is ἀπερσεκόμης; and when his locks are shorn,
he incurs the ruin which falls to the lot of Nisos

[1] 'An unexpected light has been thrown on many an enigmatical form in the Hellenic mythology by recent researches regard-

the side of Artemis,[1] or goes forth to drive the
cattle of the sun to their pastures. But, like the
fire, which at its first kindling steps out with the
strength of a horse from its prison, the wind may
freshen to a gale before it be an hour old, and
sweep before it the mighty clouds big with the
rain that is to refresh the earth. Where it cannot
throw down, it can penetrate. It pries unseen
into holes and crannies, it sweeps round dark
corners, it plunges into glens and caves; and when
the folk come out to see the mischief that it has
done, they hear its mocking laughter as it hastens
on its way. These few phrases lay bare the whole
framework of the Homeric legend, and account
for the not ill-natured slyness and love of practical
jokes which enter into the character of Hermes.[2]

ing the earlier divinities of India. The hoary mysterious forms
of the Erinnyes are no Hellenic invention: they were immigrants
along with the oldest settlers from the East. The divine greyhound Saramâ, who guards for the lord of heaven the golden
herd of stars and sunbeams, and for him collects the nourishing
rain-clouds of heaven to the milking, and who, moreover, faithfully conducts the pious dead into the world of the blessed,
becomes, in the hands of the Greeks, the son of Saramâ, Saru-
meyâs, or Hermeias.' Dr. Mommsen, in this passage (History
of Rome, vol. i. p. 18), is at least arguing from evidence. His
ground is less sure when he suggests (p. 80) that the non-burgesses
resident in Rome appear to have paid the king a tax for pro-
tection, and then refers subsequently to such payment as a fact
(p. 94).

    [1] Gods and Heroes, p. 102.   [2] Horace, Odes, i. 10.

The babe leaves the cradle before he is an hour old.   The breath of the breeze is soft and Analysis of the hymn. harmonious at first, as the sounds which he summons from his tortoise lyre.[1]   But his strength grows rapidly;[2] with mighty strides he hastens from the heights of Kyllênê, until he drives from their pastures the cattle of Apollo, obliterating the foot-tracks after the fashion of the autumn winds, which cover the roads with leaves and mire.[3]   In his course he sees an old man working in his vineyard, and, like a catspaw on the surface of the sea, he whispers in his ear a warning of which but half the sound is caught before the

[1] Hymn to Hermes, 24.   He finds the tortoise and makes the lyre, and plays on it as soon as he has stepped out of the cave, and before he goes on his plundering expedition.

It is at this point that the legend of Hermes runs into that of Orpheus, who represents (Tales from Greek Mythology, p. 111) the Vedic Rhibus, or Arbhus.   In these Mr. Kelly sees an image of the wind.   'We see how the cruder idea of the Ribhus, sweeping trees and rocks in wild dance before them by the force of their stormy song, grew, under the beautifying touch of the Hellenic imagination, into the legend of that master of the lyre whose magic tones made torrents pause and listen, rocks and trees descend with delight from their mountain beds, and moved even Pluto's unrelenting heart to pity' (Indo-European Traditions and Folk-lore, p. 17).   Mr. Kelly seems to lay an undue stress on the theory which finds in Aryan mythology an expression chiefly of the effects of clouds and winds.

[2] Hymn to Hermes, 65.

[3] Ibid. 75

breeze has passed away. All the night long [1] the wind roared, or, as the poet says, Hermes toiled, till the branches of the trees, rubbing against each other, burst into a flame; and so men praise Hermes as the giver of the kindliest boon —fire. [2] The flames, fanned by the wind, consume the sacrifice; but Hermes (the wind), though hungry, tastes not of it; [3] and when the morning has come he returns to his mother's cave, and, in the words of the poet, passes through the keyhole like the sigh of a summer breeze, or mist on a hill-side. [4] The wind is tired of blowing, or, in other words, the feet of Hermes patter almost noiselessly over the floor, [5] till he lies down to sleep in his cradle, which he had left but a few hours before. The sun rises, and finds to his discomfiture that the

---

[1] Hymn to Hermes, 140.

[2] Ibid. 110 et seq.:

Ἑρμῆς τοι πρώτιστα πυρήια πῦρ τ' ἀνέδωκεν.

The assertion seems to be inconsistent with the legend of Prometheus. The idea of the two stories appears, however, to be not the same; and this, of itself, might suffice to account for the difference.

[3]
ὀδμὴ γάρ μιν ἔτειρε, καὶ ἀθάνατόν περ ἰόντα,
ἡδεῖ'· ἀλλ' οὐδ' ὧς οἱ ἐπείθετο θυμὸς ἀγήνωρ,
καί τε μάλ' ἱμείροντι, περᾶν ἱερῆς κατὰ δειρῆς.

Hymn to Hermes, 131.

[4]
διὰ κλήϊθρον ἴδυνεν,
αὔρῃ ὀπωρινῇ ἐναλίγκιος, ἠΰτ' ὀμίχλη. Ib. 147.

[5] Ib. 149: ἦκα ποσὶ προβιβῶν.

herds are gone. He too sees the hedger of Onchestos, who thinks, but is not sure,[1] that he had
seen a babe driving the cows before him. The
sun hastens on his way, sorely perplexed[2] at the
confused foot-tracks, covered with mud and strewn
with leaves, just as if the oaks had taken to walking on their heads.[3] But when he charges the
child with the theft, the defence is grounded on
his tender age. Can the breeze of a day old,[4]
breathing as softly as a babe new born, be guilty
of so much mischief? Its proper home is the summer land [5]—why should it stride wantonly over
bleak hills and bare heaths? But, with an instinct
singularly true, Hermes is represented as closing
his defence with a long whistle,[6] which sounds
very much like mockery and tends perhaps to
heighten the scepticism of Apollo. The latter
seizes the child, but a loud blast[7] makes him suddenly let go; and the child, once again quiet,
complains of unkind treatment, and appeals to his
father[8] (the sky). Zeus refuses to accept his
plea of infancy; but when Hermes brings back

[1] Hymn to Hermes, 208.
[2] Ibid. 349.
[3] Ibid. 219.
[4] Ibid. 273: χθὶς γενόμην.
[5] Ibid. 267-8.
[6] Ibid. 260: μάκρ' ὑποσυρίζων, ἅλιον τὸν μῦθον ἀκούων.
[7] Ibid. 296. The expression, anthropomorphised, is very
coarse. Its original meaning is perfectly plain and harmless.
[8] Ibid. 312.

E

the cows, the suspicions of Apollo are again roused,[1]
and, dreading his angry looks, the child strikes his
tortoise lyre, and wakes sounds so soft and tender[2]
that the hardest-hearted man cannot choose but
listen.   Never on the heights of Olympus, where
winds perhaps blow strong, as they commonly do
on mountain summits, had Phœbus heard a strain
so soothing.[3]   Like the pleasant murmur of a
breeze in the palm groves of the South, it filled
his heart with a strange yearning,[4] carrying him
back to the days when the world was young and
all the bright gods kept holiday, and he longed
for the glorious gift of music[5] which made the
life of Hermes a joy on the earth.   His prayer is
at once granted.   The wind grudges not his music
to the sun;[6] he seeks only to know the secrets
which his own eyes cannot penetrate,[7] for Phœbus
sits in the high heaven by the side of Zeus, knowing the inmost mind of his father, and his keen
glance can pierce the depths of the green sea.
This wisdom the sun may not impart.   Hermes
cannot rise to the height of heaven, but there are
other honours in store for him, many and great.
He shall be the guardian of the herds of heaven;
his song shall cheer the sons of men and lessen
the sum of their suffering; his breath shall waft

[1] Hymn to Hermes, 405 et seq.   [5] Ibid. 419.
[2] Ibid. 445, 450.   [6] Ibid. 422.
[3] Ibid. 457.   [4] Ibid. 465.   [7] Ibid. 472, 532.

the dead to the world unseen, and when he wills
he may get wisdom by holding converse with
the hoary Thriæ far down in the clefts of Parnassus.[1] The compact is ratified by the oath of
Hermes that he will do no hurt to the shrine of
Apollo,[2] who declares that he loves nothing so
well as the fresh breeze of heaven.[3] True to the
last to the spirit of the myth, the poet adds that
his friendship for man is not equal to his love for
the sun. Hermes has a way of doing men mischief, while they are asleep.[4]

Thus has the Greek bard expanded into a
coherent poem a myth of which the germ had
long lain beneath a few scattered phrases
which told of Saramâ, the hound of the
gods, who guards the cattle for the lord
of heaven. Whatever embellishment it
may have received from his genius, the
humour manifest throughout the tale is not his
own creation. It was involved in the very truthfulness of the conception, although this conception
was worked out with an unconscious fidelity which
is indeed astonishing; for the poet, probably, would
hardly have identified Hermes with the winds of
heaven as confidently as, when he told of Selênê
watching over Endymion, he must have felt that

The myth of Hermes peculiarly congenial to the Greek mind.

---

[1] Hymn to Hermes, 555.　　　[3] Ibid. 527.
[2] Ibid. 526.　　　　　　　　　[4] Ibid. 578.

he was speaking really of the moon and the sun.
But the comic vein thus developed was one peculiarly congenial to the liveliness of the Greek
mind.   Brought out more prominently in the
character of Heracles, this laughter-loving spirit
passed easily into a biting satire of the whole
Greek theology in the 'Battle of the Frogs and
Mice' (xx.), where Athênê herself becomes the
subject of a profane merriment which Homer
hesitates not to indulge in at the expense of
Arês, Hephaistos, and Aphroditê.   The relations
of Zeus and Hêrê, in the Iliad, have also their
ridiculous side, but this is the result of the same
causes which degraded the character of Heracles
to that of a drunken reveller.

   If the greater number of Greek legends have
been thus reduced to their primitive elements,
Dynastic   the touch of the same wand will lay open
legends.   many more which may seem to have grown
up on quite another model. Even the dynastic
legends of Thebes will not wholly resist the
method which has disclosed so many secrets.
For other tales the work is done.   There is
absolutely nothing left for further analysis in the
stories of Orpheus and Eurydikê, of Kephalos and
Procris, of Selênê and Endymion, Niobê and Leto,
Dêmêtêr and Persephonê, Cadmus and Europa,
Daphnê and Apollo.   Not an incident remains
unexplained in the legends of Heracles, of Althæa

and the Burning Brand, of Phaethon, Memnon, and Bellerophon. If there are bypaths in the stories of Ariadne, Medeia, Semelê, Prometheus, or of the cows of the sun in the Odyssey, they have been followed up to the point from which they all diverge. It will be seen that the tales contained in the present volume present no difficulties which have not been already encountered in other legends.

The great dynastic story of Argos is made up of a solar myth, recounted at length in the adventures of Perseus and repeated in those of Heracles. Perseus is the child of the golden shower, and of Danaê, Daphnê, Dahanâ, the dawn, and he is doomed, like other solar children, to be the slayer of the sire to whom he owes his life. His weapons are those of Apollo and Hermes. The sword of Chrysaor is in his hand, the golden sandals on his feet. His journey to the land of the Graiæ, the dim twilight, is only another form of the journey of Heracles to the garden of the Hesperides. When from the home of the Graiæ he went to the cave of the Gorgons, the story sprang from the mythical phrase, 'The sun is gone from the twilight land to fight with the powers of darkness.' But night has a twofold meaning. There is the darkness which must yield to the sun and die, and there is the absolute darkness which the sun can never penetrate. The former is the mortal Medusa, the latter her deathless sisters. The story ran that Medusa compared her own beauty with that of Athênê, but the solemn grandeur of the starlit night could be no rival for the radiant goddess on whom rested the full glory of Zeus and Phœbus. When from the Gorgon land he wandered to the shores of Libya, the story introduced an adventure which recurs in a hundred forms. Andromeda, Ariadne, Brenhyldr, Aslauga, Hesionê, Dêianeira, Philonoê, Medeia, Iocastê, were all won after the slaughter of monsters or serpents, while the triumphant return of Danaê with her son to Argos, after his toil is ended, is but the meeting of Heracles with Iolê, the return of the sun in the evening to the mother that bare him in the morning.

In the tale of Iamos the serpents of the night perform a kindly office, but it is Apollo who touches his ear that he may understand the speech of birds, while in another myth the serpents themselves convey this gift to Melampus. The story of Skylla is a tangled skein, in which several threads of solar legend have been mingled. Minos is himself a son of Zeus and the husband of Pasiphaê, whose name speaks of her at once as the child of Helios. The daughter of Nisos is smitten with the glorious beauty of his countenance, as is Echidna with that of Heracles;

Reproductions of solar myths.

but the golden lock of her father, while it remains unshorn, is an invincible safeguard to the city against the assaults of Minos. The love of Skylla is not thus to be disappointed. The lock is shorn; and the name of the maiden (as the rending monster) shows how well she has served the malignant powers of darkness. The tale of Asclepios is almost an echo of the story of Kephalos and Procris; but the child of Corônis, like Iamos, Melampus, and Medeia, inherits not so much the brightness of the sun as his power of seeing into hidden things, and so, by a more than earthly wisdom, drawing forth the healing powers of herbs and roots. The character of Theseus bears a closer resemblance to that of Heracles [1] than of Perseus. He is a slayer of monsters, and more especially of robbers and evil-doers, while, like Heracles, he forsakes those whom he loves, and has many loves in many lands. Armed with a sword welded of the same metal with the sword of Apollo and the spear of Achilleus, he, like Skythês in the tale of Echidna, wins the inheritance of his fathers, and becomes a companion of Meleagros, whose life is bound up with the burning brand. His descent to Hades is indeed

[1] Dr. Thirlwall lays stress on this resemblance (History of Greece, vol. i. ch. v.); but his efforts are directed towards a discovery of the historical facts underlying the legend—a poor prey for a mighty hunter.

disastrous; but the mishap is repaired by aid of
another solar legend. It is Heracles who de-
livers the wooer of Persephoné.[1]

Another solar tale is brought before us in the
transparent legend of Tantalos; but it tells us not
The legend of Tantalos. so much of his might and his exploits as of
his wealth and his wisdom and the fearful
doom inflicted for his sin. The palace of the
Phrygian king is but the golden house of Helios
from which Phaethon went forth on his ill-
starred journey. His wisdom is that keen insight
into the counsels of Zeus, which Phœbus cannot
impart even to Hermes, the messenger of the
gods.[2] His frequent converse with the king of
gods and men is an image of the daily visit of
Helios to the dizzy heights of heaven. The theft
of nectar and ambrosia[3] finds its parallel in the
stealing of the fire by Prometheus; and the gift
thus bestowed on his Phrygian people is but the

---

[1] In short, it becomes clear that attributes, now assigned to a
vast number of personages, were originally interchangeable; and
thus the Greek myths, by themselves, point to a state of things
which is realised in the earlier Vedic poetry, where 'there are
as yet no genealogies, no settled marriages between gods and
goddesses. The father is sometimes the son, the brother is the
husband, and she who in one hymn is the mother is in another
the wife' (Max Müller, Comp. Myth.). The subject is more
fully entered into in the History of Sanskrit Literature, p. 532
et seq.

[2] Hymn to Hermes, 534.   [3] Pindar, Ol. i. 100.

wealth which the sun brings from the sky and
bestows lavishly on the children of men. The
hound given to him in pledge by Pandareôs carries us to the hymn of Hermes. It is the mighty
Sarameyâs, who chases the clouds over seas and
mountains, always felt but never seen, a gift
which the sun may receive, but cannot yield up
again. The slaughter of Pelops, and the serving
up of his limbs to Zeus at the banquet, is as
horrible as the tale which relates the birth of
Erichthonios,[1] but its meaning is as clear and as
innocent. The genial warmth of the sun brings
to light and life the fruits of the earth which is
his bride; his raging heat kills the very offspring
in which he had delighted, and offers it up a
scorched and withered sacrifice in the eyes of Zeus,
the sky. The sentence passed upon him is in still
closer accordance with the old mythical language.
When Hermes first kindled a fire by rubbing together the dried branches of the forest, and slew
one of the oxen of Phœbus in solemn sacrifice, he
appeased not his hunger,[2] for the wind may kindle
the fire, but it cannot eat of that which the fire
devours. So, too, Tantalos may gaze on sparkling
waters and golden fruits; but if he stoops to drink
or puts forth his hand to the laden branches, the
water is dried up as by the scorching wind of the

[1] Apollod. iii. 14, 6.   [2] Hymn to Hermes, 130–135.

desert, and, in the words of the Homeric poet,[1]
only black mud and gaping clay remain in place
of flowing water, and the leaves wither away beneath the fierce glare of tropical noonday. In
the rock which threatens to crush him, we see
again only the misshapen Polyphêmos hurling
down huge crags on the ships of Odysseus—the
unsightly offspring of the stormy sea—the huge
cumulus cloud whose awful blackness oppresses
both eye and heart as an omen of impending
doom.

The myth of Ixion brings before us simply the
action of the sun under another phase. It belongs, perhaps, to the least attractive class
of Greek legends, but its origin is as simple
as that which gave birth to the repulsive story of
Erichthonios. Like the name of Orpheus, that of
Ixion cannot be explained by a reference to any
Greek words; but it is identified with the Sanskrit
akshivan, the being who turns on a wheel, and
M. Bréal well remarks[2] that no room is left for
doubt when, in many a passage of the Vedic hymn,
we read of the wheel of the sun, and the battle
waged by Dyaus, the heaven, to snatch it from the
grasp of night. So Ixion loves Hêrê, the queen
of the æther, the pure heaven, because Indra
loves the Dawn and Phœbus longs for Daphnê.

The
story of
Ixion.

---

[1] Odys. xi. 187.
[2] Le Mythe d'Œdipe, in Revue Archéologique for Sept. 1863.

But he is also wedded to the clouds, and becomes
the father of the Kentaurs, in whom again are
seen the Sanskrit Ghandharvas,[1] the bright clouds
in whose arms the sun reposes as he journeys
through the sky. And so the tale went, that in
the clouds he saw the image of the lady Hêrê, and
paid the penalty of his unlawful love. The idea
of toil, unwillingly borne, again came in, for Ixion
is *akshivan*, whose wheel can never rest, as the
sun cannot pause in his daily career. The legend
is almost transparent throughout. As the wealth
of Tantalos was the fruit which the genial sunshine calls up from the earth, the treasure-house
of Ixion is the blazing form of Helios, the abyss
of intolerable splendour which scorches the body
of Hesioneus.[2] The darkness and gloom which
follows the treacherous deed of Ixion, is a time of
plague and drought, during which the hidden sun
was thought to bow himself before the throne of
Zeus. But even yet the doom pursues him. He
has scarcely sought pardon for one offence before
he is ready to commit another. Hêrê, the queen,
whose placid majesty reflects the solemn stillness
of the blue heaven, fills with a new love the heart
which had once beaten only for Dia, as Heracles
lived at first only in the love of Iolê. Each day
his love grows warmer, as the summer sun gains a

---

[1] Le Mythe d'Œdipe.
[2] εἰς βόθρον πυρὸς μεστόν. Diod. iv. 69.

greater power. But the time of vengeance is at
hand. As he goes on his way, he sees a form, as
of Hêrê, reposing on the arms of the clouds; but
when he draws nigh to embrace her, she vanishes
like Daphnê from the gaze of Phœbus Apollo, or
Eurydikê from that of Orpheus.

The elements of a more modern ethical belief
are introduced into the dynastic legends of Thebes.
Intro- As in the tale of Crœsus, and still more as
doction
of ethical in the great trilogy of Æschylus, we have in
senti-
ment. them something like a philosophy of life.
The fortunes of Eteocles and Polyneikes show how
the sins of the fathers are visited upon the children.[1]
But, although it is easy to see how, when once the
results of old mythical phrases were submitted to
a moral criticism, the new turn so given to the
tale might give birth to an entirely new narrative,
the earlier part of the legend exhibits the framework of many another tale of Greek mythology.
Œdipus is the son of Iocastê, whose name suggests that of Iolê, Iamos, or Iobates. Laïos, like
Acrisios, Priam, and Aleos, dreads his own child,
and exposes him on a rough hillside,[2] while his

---

[1] It is a fearful tale, oppressive from the gloom which pervades
it. Mr. Dasent is impressed with the same feeling by much of
the Northern mythology; but he insists on assigning the features
with which he finds fault to a corruption of morals, not of speech.
See Gods and Heroes, p. 76.

[2] As the tale of Paris went, on Ida. But the Sanskrit Idâ is
the earth, the wife of Dyaus; and so we have before us the

gloomy and negative character is in complete accord with that of Hecabê or Leto. But the prophecy of Apollo must be fulfilled. Œdipus, like Paris, Telephos, and Perseus, grows up far away from his home, and, like them, remarkable for strength, beauty, and vigour. The suspicion that he is not the child of his supposed mother,· Meropê, sends him forth to Delphi, and the homicide of Laïos is the death of the parent of the sun, as the latter starts on his career. Then, like Perseus, Theseus, and Bellerophon, Œdipus, in his turn, must destroy the monster which vexes the land of Cadmus; but with the strength of Heracles he unites the wisdom of Medeia and Asclepios, and the Sphinx, baffled by the solution of her riddle, leaps from the rock and dies. This monster belongs, beyond doubt, to the class of which Python, Typhon, Fafnir, and Polyphêmos are examples. None of these, however, express precisely the same impressions. Fafnir is the dragon of winter, who guards the fruits of the earth within his pitiless folds. The Sphinx is the dark and lowering cloud, striking terror into the hearts of men, and heightening the agonies of a time of drought, until Œdipus, who knows her mysterious speech—as the sun was said, in a still earlier age, to understand the mutterings of the

mythical phrase, 'The rays of the sun at its birth rest level on the earth, or on the hillside.'

rumbling thunder—unfolds her dark sayings, and
drives her from her throne, just as the cloud,
smitten by the sun, breaks into rain, and then
vanishes away.[1]   His victory is won.   The bright
being has reached his goal, and the fair Iocastê
becomes his bride.   This point marks the close of
the original myth; but Iocastê, his .wife, is also
his mother, and the morality of men could not
recognise a form of speech in which the same
person might at once be the son and the husband
of another.   The relations of anthropomorphous
gods were no longer interchangeable, as they
appear in the earlier Vedic hymns.   From the
union of a mother with her son the moral sense
of the Greek would turn with horror, and, unconscious of the real nature of the incident so related,
he would look at once for an awful recompense
from the sleepless Erinnys of the murdered Laïos.
Iocastê dies in her marriage-chamber, as Œnônê
dies on the funeral pile of Paris, and, in something of the spirit of the old tale, Œdipus must
tear out his own eyes, as the light of the setting
sun is blotted out by the dark storm-cloud.

[1] M. Bréal, in his masterly analysis of the myth of Œdipus,
connects the name Sphinx with the verb σφίγγω, as the shutting
in of the rain within the cloud. The Bœotian name φίξ may
throw some doubt on the explanation, but it cannot affect the
general character of the legend.

For the meaning of the name Laïos, see M. Bréal, Le Mythe
d'Œdipe, p. 209.

Henceforth, the story is the expression of Greek ethics, until, in the last scene (in the company of Theseus, the solar hero of Attica), Œdipus goes forth to die, amid the blaze of the lightning, in the sacred grove of the Eumenides.

The blinded Œdipus dies unseen; but in his last hours his eye had rested on Antigonê, the fair and tender light, which sheds its soft hue over the eastern heaven, as the sun sinks in death beneath the western waters. But, whether in the slaughter of his father or his marriage with Iocastê, Œdipus was but fulfilling his doom. These things must be so. Heracles must see Iolê in the evening, as surely as the sun, once risen, must go across the sky and then sink down into his bed beneath the earth or sea. It was an iron fate from which there was no escaping; and this idea accounts for the awful 'Aνάγκη, the invincible necessity, which urges on the wretched Œdipus, and explains the origin of that theological belief which finds its mightiest expression in the dramas which tell us of the sin of Agamemnon and the vengeance of Clytæmnestra.

We approach at last the immortal epic of the Greek heroic age. Not much of the Hesiodic theogony is to be found in either the Iliad or the Odyssey. It was no part of the poet's pur- *Extent of Homeric mytho-logy.* pose to recount formally the birth or descent of gods or heroes. But we have no warrant for

asserting that he was ignorant of legends which he
has not mentioned ; and arguments drawn simply
from his silence are either inadmissible or must
be received with the keenest scrutiny.[1] Zeus is
with him the son of Cronos. He knew therefore
of dynasties among the gods; and the weight of
proof lies with those who maintain that he had
never heard the story of Prometheus. He knew
that Achilleus was to die young, although that
knowledge is but incidentally displayed, unless we
assume that the Iliad was written by a single poet,
and that that poet was also the author of the whole
Odyssey. He knew that Paris was called Alexandros; and it is impossible to show that he was
unaware of the reasons for which that name was
given. Nay, the change which has come over
the character of Paris is one of the most marked
features in the Homeric description of that hero.
He knew also that the whole expedition of the
Achaians against Troy was but an incident in the
life of Paris, for the very cause of the war is that
Paris came and stole Helen from the house of
Menelaos. He knew further, for he tells us
plainly, that the inaction of Achilleus had its
counterpart in the inaction of Paris. And if he
tells us how, after his long fit of sullen anger,
Achilleus came forth in all his old energy, he also
knew that Paris was not to be always idle, and

[1] See also the Gods and Heroes, p. 69.

that from him Achilleus himself was to receive his
death-wound.[1]   How marvellously the whole life
of Paris, in which the Trojan war is but one of
the later scenes, exhibits a true picture of the
sun's course from its rising to its setting, the
poet perhaps may have never known.   It is of the
very essence of mythology that the original signification of the names, which serve as the groundwork of its narratives, should be only in part
remembered.   The author of the hymn to Hermes
little knew probably that he was simply relating
the rivalry of the wind and the sun ; but he knew
enough of the attributes of Hermeias to write a
poem, almost every line of which points to the
mythical speech of which the tale is a petrifaction.
The author of the Iliad may not have known
or felt that Achilleus was but the Hellenic reflection of the seducer whom he sought to punish;
but his language throughout the poem harmonises
strangely with the mythical phrases which speak
of the lord of day when he hides away his face
behind the clouds.   He could not know that the
Norseman even then, wandering in regions which

---

[1]   ἤματι τῷ ὅτε κέν σε Πάρις καὶ Φοῖβος Ἀπόλλων

ἐσθλὸν ἐόντ' ὀλέσωσιν ἐνὶ Σκαιῇσι πύλησιν.   Il. xx. 360.

I may perhaps be pardoned for making frequent quotations
from the text of the Iliad; but in an analysis leading to conclusions which may be regarded with suspicion on the ground of
novelty, I felt that I ought at each step to give the authority
for my assertions.

F

for the Achaian had no existence, was framing the
tale which grew up into the epic of the Volsungs
and the Nibelungs; and that in that tale Agamemnon and his hosts warring against Paris were
represented by Gunnar and his followers planning
the death of Sigurdr. With the cause of the expedition to Troy he had no immediate concern. He
tells us, in passing, the cause of the war, but his
theme is the wrath of the great chieftain from
Phthia, and he has kept to that theme with
wonderful fidelity, if not to the Greek nature, yet
to the old mythical speech. For it seems impossible to withhold the admission, that those portions of the poem which relate exclusively to the
independent exploits of their chiefs were at a later
day embodied into a poem which was not an Iliad,
but an Achilléis. The arguments of Colonel
Mure [1] and Mr. Gladstone [2] in no way meet the
objections (seemingly unanswerable) of Mr. Grote [3]
against the original continuity of the poem in its
present form. Nor, if it be necessary to account

[1] Critical History of Greek Literature, book ii. ch. xvi.
[2] Homer and the Homeric Age. Aoidos.
[3] History of Greece, Part I. ch. xxi.; and see more particu-
larly the note on the embassy to Achilleus. This note seems
conclusively to dispose of every attempt to maintain the original
unity of the present Iliad on the ground of a supposed moral
consistency in the character of Achilleus, while it also shows
that the writer of the Achilléis knew nothing of the first effort
for reconciliation.

for the insertion of the Ilias, have we far to go
for a reason. The theme chosen by the author
of the Achillêis confined him to a period of comparative inaction. The valour of the Achaians
could only be asserted by an independent poem,
which showed that they were not helpless [1] even
without the aid of the great son of Peleus. It is
not surprising that the two poems should have
been gradually blended together.[2]

Thus was produced an epic as magnificent as it
is complicated; but through all its intricacy may
be traced the thread of the original myth; The tale of the Achillêis.
and the fact that it may be so traced is the
more remarkable as we realise the extent to which
the process of disintegration has been carried on.
If the poem does not exhibit the systematised
theogony of Hesiod, still Phœbus is already a

[1] Colonel Mure, strangely enough, sees in Il. ii.–vii. nothing
but a catalogue of disasters, bringing misery and disgrace on the
Argive hosts (Crit. Hist. Gr. Lit. vol. i. p. 256). Mr. Grote, far
more truly, says that the great chiefs are 'in full force at the
beginning of the eleventh book' (History of Greece, vol. ii.
p. 239).

[2] It would seem that the chief error of Wolf and his followers
was the attempt to fix the date of this combination, which they
attribute to Peisistratos. Mr. Grote has shown that of this fact
we have no evidence, while the regulations for the rhapsodists
given by Solon furnish strong evidence against any such notion.
Comparative mythologists might probably decline to give even
an approximate date; but the reduction of the Iliad even to its
present shape is probably the work of a far earlier time than is
generally supposed.

person distinct from Helios, Artemis, or Athênê;
Hecabê is no longer identified with Selênê;
Zeus is no longer one with Ouranos. Only a few
signs remain of the interchangeable character
which is so prominent in the gods of the earlier
Vedic poems. And, further, the Iliad necessarily
exhibits the later elements which must spring up
with the growth of a definite religion and the
developement of something like civil government.
Still, on the Trojan shore, facing the island of
Tenedos, the old tale is repeated, which assumes
a form still more gloomy in the mythology of the
North. The mighty Achilleus, over whose childhood had watched Phoinix (the purple cloud),[1] is
there to fight, but, like Bellerophon, as he insists
emphatically, in no quarrel of his own.[2] A hard
toil is before him, but, as with Heracles, the
honour which he wins is not to be his own.[3] Like
Heracles again, and Perseus and Theseus, his limbs
are strong, and his heart knows no fear. In place
of the sword of Apollo, the Chrysaór, he has the
unerring spear which no mortal can wield but
himself.[4] Still, like Heracles and Apollo and

---

[1] Another name, expressive of the class to which belong Iolê,
Iolaos, &c.

[2]   οὐ γὰρ ἐγὼ Τρώων ἕνεκ' ἤλυθον αἰχμητάων
      δεῦρο μαχησόμενος, ἐπεὶ οὔ τί μοι αἴτιοί εἰσιν. Il. i. 153.

[3]   τιμὴν ἀρνύμενα Μενελάῳ σοί τε, κυνῶπα.   Il. i. 159.

[4]   τὸ μὲν οὐ δύνατ' ἄλλος 'Αχαιῶν
      πάλλειν, ἀλλά μιν οἶος ἐπίστατο πῆλαι 'Αχιλλεύς.

                                           Il. xvi. 142.

Perseus and Bellerophon, he is practically the
servant of one on whom he looks down with a
deserved contempt.[1] On him falls all the labour
of war, but the spoil which he wins with his bow
and spear must pass into the hands of Agamemnon,[2]
as those of Heracles fall to the lot of Eurystheus.
Still he has his consolation. He is cheered by
the love of Hippodameia[3] (the tamer of the
horses of the sun), as the love of Iolê spurred
Heracles at the beginning of his toils. But even
Brisêis he must now give up, as Heracles was
compelled to part from Iolê. At the very thought
of losing her, his passion overleaps all barriers;
but his rage is subdued by the touch of Athênê,
the daughter of Zeus, the sky.[4] He must yield,
but with Brisêis vanishes the light of his life,
and he vows a solemn vow that henceforth in
the war the Achaians shall look in vain for his
aid.[5] He hangs up his sword and spear in his

[1] This contempt is fully expressed, L 225-231.
[2]   τὸ μὲν πλεῖον πολυάϊκος πολέμοιο
        χεῖρες 'μαὶ διέπουσ' · ἀτὰρ ἤν ποτε δασμὸς ἵκηται,
        σοὶ τὸ γέρας πολὺ μεῖζον.   Il. i. 167.
[3] Brisêis being a mere patronymic.
[4] Il. i. 195. It is at the least singular that, while Brisêis
comes from Lyrnessos, Diomêdê, who takes her place, belongs to
the south-western Lesbos (Il. ix. 658). So Œnônê lives on Ida, and
Helen in the far west. Iolê is the daughter of Eurytos (another
name of the class Euryganeia, &c.), in the eastern island Euboa;
Dêianeira lives in the western Calydon.
[5] Il. i. 240.

tent, takes off his glittering armour, and the
Argive warriors see the face of the bright hero
no more. Yet even the fierceness of his wrath
cannot avail to keep entirely in the background
another feature in which he resembles Paris,
Heracles, Theseus, Jason. Brisêis is gone, but
Diomêdê, the daughter of Phorbas, supplies her
place, as Œnônê gives way to Helen, Iolê to
Dêianeira, and the wise Medeia to the daughter
of the Argive Creon. But the mind of Achilleus
remains unchanged. His wrath is terrible as the
wrath of the angry sun, and he bids Thetis, his
mother, go to the throne of Zeus (the sky) and
pray him to send such a storm as may well make
the Achaians rate their king at his true value.[1]
The darkness thickens, but at first the Achaians
care not. Zeus alone knows and proclaims that
the fortunes of the Argives themselves must
remain under the cloud until Achilleus again goes
forth to the battle.[2] His words are soon accomplished. The knowledge that the great champion
of the Argives no longer takes part in the war in-
spires the Trojans with fresh strength. The storm-
clouds rise with greater volume when the light
of the sun is blotted out of the sky. Still the
great chiefs of the Argives stand forth in un-
abated confidence ;[3] but Agamemnon, Odysseus,

---

[1] Il. i. 407–412.   [2] Il. viii. 477.   [3] Il. i. 1–68.

and Diomêdês are soon wounded in the fight, and
the Achaians begin to realise their grievous loss.
Their misery excites the compassion of Patroclos,
in whom the character of Achilleus is reflected,
as is that of Helios in Phaethon.[1] Melted by the
tears of his friend, Achilleus gives him his own
armour, and bids him go forth to aid the Argives.
But with this charge he joins a caution. Phaethon
must not touch with his whip the horses of
Helios, and Patroclos must not drive the chariot
of Achilleus on any other path than that which
has been pointed out to him.[2] But although
Patroclos can wear the armour of Achilleus, he
cannot wield his spear.[3] The sword and lance of
Apollo and Perseus, of Artemis and Theseus,
may be touched by no other hands than their
own. Patroclos is ready for the fight, and yoked
to the car of Achilleus stand the immortal horses
Xanthos and Balios (golden and speckled as a
summer sky), which Podargê (the swift breeze)
bare to Zephyros (the strong west wind) near

[1] Mr. Grote has remarked this. 'Patroclus has no substantive
position : he is the attached friend and second of Achilleus, but
nothing else' (History of Greece, vol. ii. p. 236). Colonel Mure,
however, discerns in the contrast between the two strong evidence
of Homer's 'knowledge of human nature' (Crit. Hist. Gr. Lit.
vol. i. p. 285).
[2] μὴ σύ γ' ἄνευθεν ἐμεῖο λιλαίεσθαι πολεμίζειν. Il. xvi. 89.
[3] ἔγχος δ' οὐχ ἕλετ' οἶον ἀμύμονος Αἰακίδαο, κ. τ. λ.
Il. xvi. 140.

the shore of the ocean stream.[1] The sun is
breaking for a moment through the mist. Like
hungry wolves, the Myrmidons (the streaming
rays) stand forth to arm themselves at the bidding of their chieftain.[2] For a time the stréngth
of Achilleus nerves the arm of Patroclos, so
that he can smite Sarpêdon, the great chief of
the Lykians, in whose veins runs the blood of
Bellerophon, and for whom the bitter tears of
Zeus fall in big drops of rain from the sky
(Dyaus).[3] But the transient splendour is soon
dimmed. It was but the semblance of the sun
looking out from the dark cloud; and Patroclos,
therefore, meets his doom. But the poet recurs
unconsciously to the old myth, and it is Apollo
who disarms Patroclos,[4] although it is Hector

---

[1] Il. xvi. 151. These horses are the immortal Harits, the
Greek χάριτες. They also reappear under the name drvân, in
the feminine drushí, and are finally embodied in the Greek god of
love ῎Epos. Iris, the rainbow, is referred to another root; but
Iros, the name of the beggar in the Odyssey, is clearly the same
as Iris, and stands simply for a messenger. To assign it to another origin, even incorrectly, would only be to repeat the process which connected the violet clouds of morning with the idea
of poison. See Max Müller, Comp. Myth. pp. 81, 83.   .

[2] Il. xvi. 166.

[3]   αἱματοέσσας δὲ ψιάδας κατέχευεν ἔραζε.   Il. xvi. 459.

[4] Il. xvi. 790, κ. τ. λ. This was a strict mythical necessity;
yet Colonel Mure lays great stress on it, as showing the cowardice
and brutality of Hector (Crit. Hist. vol. i. p. 281). The result of
his false method is, that he finds himself compelled on every occasion to vilify the Trojans for the exaltation of their enemies.

who slays him. The immortal horses weep for
his death and the fall of their charioteer Automedon, while Zeus mourns that ever he bestowed
them as a gift on so mean and wretched a thing
as man.[1] In the fearful struggle which follows
for the body of Patroclos, the clouds are seen
fighting a fierce battle over the sun, whose splendour they have for a time extinguished. The
ragged and streaming vapours which rush across
the sky have their counterpart in the throng of
the Trojans who fling themselves like hounds on
the wounded boar.[2] But a fiercer storm is raging
behind the dark veil. Beneath the 'black cloud
of his sorrow,' the anguish of Achilleus is pre-
paring an awful vengeance.[3] The beauty of his
countenance is marred, but the nymphs rise from
the sea to comfort him,[4] as folk still say, 'the sun
drinks,' when the long rays stream slantwise from
the clouds to the waters beneath. One desire
alone fills his heart, the burning thirst for vengeance; but when Thetis warns him that the
death of Hector must soon be followed by his

In a less degree, Mr. Gladstone's criticism lies open to the
same remark.

[1] Il. xvii. 444.   [2] Il. xvii. 725.

[3]   ὣς φάτο· τὸν δ' ἄχεος νεφέλη ἐκάλυψε μέλαινα.

Il. xviii. 22.

[4] Il. xviii. 36. These nymphs are only half anthropomorphised. Their names still express their own meaning.

own,[1] his answer is that the destruction of his
great enemy will be ample recompense for his
own early doom. Even Heracles, the dearest of
the sons of Zeus, had submitted to the same hard
lot.[2] His mind is made up. He retains still the
unerring spear. It remains only that he should
wait for the glistening armour wrought on the
anvil of the fire-god Hephaistos. But, although
the hour of his vengeance is not yet come, his
countenance still has its terrors, and the very
sight of his form [3] fills the Trojans with dismay,
as they hear his well-known war-cry. His work
is in part done. The body of Patroclos is recovered as the sun goes down unwillingly into
the streams of ocean.[4] Then follows the awful
vow of Achilleus. There shall be a goodly
mourning for Patroclos. The life-blood of twelve

[1] Il. xviii. 96. The real nature of this myth becomes still
more transparent, when looked at through the bald statements of
Apollodorus (iii. 13, 8). Troy, he says, cannot be taken without
Achilleus: the sun alone can subdue the dark clouds. But Thetis
knows that, after Troy is taken, Achilleus must die. The sun
must set, after his victory over the mists. So she disguises
Achilleus in woman's garb, as the light clouds half veil the
early risen sun.

[2] Il. xviii. 117.

[3] Il. xviii. 205. Here the sun is not unclouded. So Achilleus
has about his head (χρύσεον νέφος) a golden cloud, and the glory
streams from him like smoke going up to heaven. The rays of
the sun are bursting from the cloud.

[4] Il. xviii. 240.

Trojans shall gush in twelve streams on the altar
of sacrifice,[1] like the torn and crimsoned clouds
which stream up into the purple heaven when
the angry sun has sunk beneath the sea. But the
old phrases, which spoke of Helios or Heracles as
dying in the arms of Iolê, still spoke of both as
coming forth conquerors of the power which had
seemed to subdue them; and, true to the ancient
speech, the poet makes Thetis assure her son that
no hurtful thing shall touch the body of Patroclos,
and that, though it should lie untended the whole
year round, his face should wear at its close a
more glorious and touching beauty.[2] The end
draws nigh. The very helmsmen leave the ships
as they hear the cry of Achilleus calling them
once again to battle.[3] His wrongs shall be re-
dressed. Agamemnon, the king, will yield to him
the maiden whom he had taken away, and with
her shall come other maidens not less fair, and
gifts of priceless beauty.[4] But, with a persistency

---

[1] Il. xviii. 336.

[2] ἦν περ γὰρ κῆταί γε τελεσφόρον εἰς ἐνιαυτόν,
αἰεὶ τῷδ' ἔσται χρὼς ἔμπεδος ἢ καὶ ἀρείων. Il. xix. 33.

[3] Il. xix. 44.

[4] Il. xix. 140. This is the first submission made by Agamemnon in the Achilléis. It may be noted that here he not
only acquits himself of guilt (86), but, in order to fix the blame
on Zeus, recites a tale which is essentially a separate poem, and
may have existed long before, or apart from, the Ilias or Achilléis,
as may have been the case with such lays as that of Meleagros.

which, except by a reference to the sources of the
myth, is at best a dark riddle, Agamemnon asserts
his own innocence. ' I am not guilty,' he said.
' The blame rests with Zeus and Moira (who fixes
the lot of man), and Erinnys, who wanders in the
air.' So the old wrong is atoned. The gifts are
placed before him. The fair maidens come forth
from the tent, but, with a singular fidelity to the
old legend, Brisêis comes last of all,[1] beautiful
and pure as in the hour when he parted from
her,[2] even as Œnônê, in her unsullied loveliness,
appears by the side of the dying Paris. Then
it is that Achilleus forgives the wrong done
to him, but repeats the riddle which lurked
in the words of Agamemnon. It was not anything in the son of Atreus which could really call
forth his wrath. ' He could never, in his utter
helplessness, have taken the maiden from me
against my will; but so Zeus would have it, that
the doom of many Achaians might be accomplished.'[3] So he bids them go and eat and make
ready for the fight; but when Agamemnon would
have Achilleus himself feast with them, the answer is that the time for the banquet is not yet
come. His friend lies unavenged, and of neither
meat nor drink will he taste until his last fight is
fought and won.[4] The same truthfulness to the

---

[1] ἴστ', ἀτὰρ ὀγδοάτην Βρισηΐδα καλλιπάρηον. Il. xix. 245.
[2] Il. xix. 261.   [3] Il. xix. 274.   [4] Il. xix. 210.

old idea runs through the magnificent passage
which tells of the arming of Achilleus. The
helmets of the humbler warriors are like the cold
white vapours which gather in the north.[1] But
when Achilleus dons his armour, a glorious light
flashes up to heaven, and the earth laughs at its
dazzling radiance.[2] His shield gleams like the
blood-red moon as it rises from the sea.[3] His
helmet glitters like a star, and each hair in the
plume glistens like burnished gold. When he
tries the armour to see whether it fits his limbs,
it bears him like a bird upon the wing.[4] Last of
all, he takes down his spear, which none but himself can handle, while Alkimos and Automedon
(the strong and mighty) harness his immortal
horses. As he mounts the chariot, he bids them
bear him safe through the battle and not leave
him to die as they had left Patroclos. Then the
horse Xanthos bows his head and warns him of
the coming doom. Their force is not abated.
They can still run swifter than the swiftest wind;
and their will is only to save the lord whom they
serve and love. But the will of Zeus is stronger
still, and Achilleus too must die.[5] It is a kindly

---

[1]   ὡς δ' ὅτε ταρφειαὶ νιφάδες Διὸς ἐκποτέονται
      ψυχραί, ὑπὸ ῥιπῆς αἰθρηγενέος Βορέαο.   Il. xix. 358.

[2]   αἴγλη δ' οὐρανὸν ἷκε, γέλασσε δὲ πᾶσα περὶ χθὼν
      χαλκοῦ ὑπὸ στεροπῆς.   Il. xix. 363.

[3] Il. xix. 374.   [4] Il. xix. 386.   [5] Il. xix. 387-417.

warning, and the hero takes it in good part. 'I know,' he says, 'that I shall see my father and my mother again no more; but the work of vengeance must be accomplished.' Then, before the great strife begins, Zeus bids all the gods (the powers of the heaven) take each his side. He alone will look down serenely on the struggle as it rages beneath him.[1] Many a Trojan warrior falls by the spear of Achilleus, and the battle waxes fiercer, until all the powers of heaven and earth seem mingled in one wild turmoil. The river Scamandros is indignant that the dead body of Lycaon, the (bright) son of Priam, should be cast into its waters, and complains to Achilleus that his course to the sea is clogged by the blood which is poured into it.[2] But Achilleus leaps fearlessly into the stream, and Scamandros calls for aid to Simoeis. The two rivers swell, and Achilleus is almost overborne.[3] It is a war of elements. The sun is almost conquered by the raging rain. But another power comes upon the scene, and the flood yields to Hephaistos, the might of fire.[4] Fiercer yet grows the strife. The gods themselves struggle wildly in the fray,

---

[1] Il. xx. 22. The sky itself, regarded as the pure æther, in which Zeus dwells (κελαινεφές, αἰθέρι ναίων), cannot be conceived as taking part in the contest, although the clouds and lightnings beneath it may.
[2] Il. xxi. 219.   [3] Il. xxi. 325.   [4] Il. xxi. 345.

while Zeus laughs at the sight.[1] Artemis falls
smitten by Hêrê, and her arrows (the sun's rays)
are gathered up by Leto (the dark power) and
carried to the throne of Zeus.[2] But, through all
the wild confusion of the strife, Achilleus hastens
surely to his victory. Before him stands his
enemy, but the spell which guarded the life of
Hector is broken, for Phœbus has forsaken him.[3]
In vain he hurls his spear at Achilleus, in vain
he draws his sword. Still Achilleus cannot reach
him through the armour of Patroclos,[4] and the
death-wound is given where an opening in the
plates left his neck bare. The prayer of Hector
for mercy is dismissed with contempt, and, in
his boundless rage, Achilleus tramples on the
body,[5] as the blazing sun seems to trample on the
darkness into which it is sinking.

[1]   ἐγέλασσε δέ οἱ φίλον ἦτορ
γηθοσύνῃ, ὅθ' ὁράτο θεοὺς ἔριδι ξυνιόντας.   Il. xxi. 390.
The æther looks down in grim serenity on the wild battle in the
air beneath.

[2] Il. xxi. 490–505.

[3] Il. xxii. 213: λίπεν δέ ἑ Φοῖβος 'Απόλλων.
Too much stress can scarcely be laid on these words. In the
first place, they make the slaying of Hector quite as much an act
of butchery as Colonel Mure represents the death of Patroclos to
be on the part of Hector. In the second place, they remove both
incidents out of the reach of all ethical criticism.

[4] Il. xxii. 322.

[5] Il. xxii. 395, κ. τ. λ. This is a trait of brutality scarcely to
be explained by a reference to the manners of the heroic age.

At this point, in the belief of Mr. Grote, the
original Achilléis ended. 'The death of Hector

The close
of the
Achil-
léis. satisfies the exigencies of a coherent scheme,
and we are not entitled to extend the oldest
poem beyond the limit which such necessity
prescribes.'[1] The force of the objection depends
on the idea by which the poet, either consciously
or unconsciously, was guided in his design.   The
sudden plunge of the sun into the darkness
which he has for a moment dispelled would be
well represented by an abrupt ending with the
death of Hector. The 'more merciful temper'
which Achilleus displays in the last book would
not only be necessary 'to create proper sympathy
with his triumph,' but it would be strictly in accordance with the idea of the sun setting in a broad
blaze of generous splendour after his victory over
the black mists, even although these are again to
close in fierce strife when he is dead.[2]   It is this
transient gleam of more serene splendour which
is signified by the games over which Achilleus
presides genially after the slaughter of the Trojan
captives, whose blood reddens the ground, just as
the torn streamers rush in crimsoned bands across
the sky after a storm. Yet it is not easy to suppose

The mystery is solved when we compare it with the mythical
language of the earlier Vedic hymns.
   [1] History of Greece, vol. ii. p. 266.
   [2] Odyssey, xxiv. 41, 42.

with Mr. Grote that the Achillêis ended with the
twenty-second book as it now stands, for that
book closes with the mourning of Andromachê
for Hector, which, even in the eyes of a Greek,
would hardly heighten the glory of the conqueror;
and the author of it certainly knew of the visit of
Priam, which is related in the last book, for he
makes the old man express his intention of going
to Achilleus when he first learns that his son is
dead.[1] But the feeling of the old solar myth is
once more brought out prominently in the case of
Hector. With the aid of Apollo, the god who
fights for the Trojans as the eastern people, he
had been the great champion of his country. The
desertion of Apollo left him at the mercy of his
enemy, as the departure of day is the triumph of
the night. But his body, like the body of Patroclos,
must still be preserved from all corruption. The
ravenous dogs and birds are chased away by
Aphroditê,[2] and Apollo wraps it in mist and
covers it with a golden shield.[3] From the Odyssey
we learn that the idea underlying the story of the
death of Achilleus was that of an expiring blaze of
splendour, followed by the darkness of the storm.
Over his body the Achaians and Trojans struggle
in mortal conflict, like the clouds fighting over
the dead sun; and only the might of Zeus puts an

[1] Il. xxii. 415.   [2] Il. xxiii. 185.   [3] Il. xxiv. 20.

G

end to the strife, for the winds alone can drive away the clouds. Then the sea nymphs rise, fair as the cloudless skies of night, and wrap the form of the dead hero in a spotless shroud.

Thus the whole Achilléis is a magnificent solar epic, telling us of a sun rising in radiant majesty, soon hidden by the clouds, yet abiding his time of vengeance, when from the dark veil he breaks forth at last in more than his early strength, scattering the mists and kindling the ragged clouds which form his funeral pyre, nor caring whether his brief splendour shall be succeeded by a darker battle as the vapours close again over his dying glory. The feeling of the old tale is scarcely weakened when the poet tells us of the great cairn which the mariner shall see from afar, on the shore of the broad Hellespontos.[1]

If this, then, be the common groundwork of the Achilléis and the epics of Northern Europe, the arguments of Mr. Grote against the original continuity of the Iliad in its present form are indefinitely strengthened. The Trojan war itself becomes simply a scene in a long drama,[2] of the other acts of which

The whole Achilléis is a solar epic. (marginal note)

The Trojan war is simply one scene of a long drama. (marginal note)

---

[1] Odyssey, xxiv. 82.

[2] Much blame, perhaps not undeserved, has been bestowed on the critics who formed the epic cycle and sought to find the sequence of the several legends on which the poems included in

the poet incidentally betrays his knowledge. The
life of Achilleus runs in the same groove with
that of Alexandros or Paris; the personality of
Patroclos is a dim reflection of that of Achilleus;
the tale of Meleagros is simply an echo of the
legend which, in its more expanded form and with
heightened colours, relates the exploits of the son
of Peleus.

With this groundwork, the original Achilléis
may have ended with the twenty-second book or
have been extended to the twenty-fourth. The
Apart from considerations of style, there is trasted
nothing in the story to militate against with the Achil-
either supposition. If it ended with the léis.
earlier book, the poet closed his narrative with
the triumphant outburst of the sun from the
clouds which had hidden his glory. The poet
who added the last two books was inspired by the
old phrases which spoke of a time of serene
though shortlived splendour after the sun's great
victory. But with this tale of the Achilléis,
whatever may be its close, the books which
relate the independent exploits of Agamemnon
and his attendant chiefs cannot possibly be made
to fit. They are the expression of an almost

that cycle were founded. So far as they sought an historical
sequence they were wrong. Yet their feeling that there was a sequence in these tales was not altogether without foundation. But
the sequence is one of phenomena, not of facts in human history.

unconscious feeling that the son of Peleus and
Thetis was a being not sufficiently akin to Achaians
to satisfy the instincts of national pride and
patriotism.[1]   It is of course possible—in the
opinion of Mr. Grote, it may be even probable—
that the same poet who first sang the wrath
of Achilleus afterwards inserted the exploits of
Odysseus, Ajax, and Diomedes.   The question is,
after all, not material.   If Mr. Grote is right in
thinking that the last two books are an addition,[2]
then the closing scene which exhibits Achilleus
in his more genial aspect existed as a distinct
poem, and the final complement of this lay is
found far apart in the closing book of the Odyssey.
The perfect harmony of that picture of the hero's
death with the spirit and language of the Achilléis
may be an argument for ascribing both Iliad and
Odyssey to the same author;[3] but it seems to

[1] Both Colonel Mure and Mr. Gladstone search vigorously for
every vestige of patriotism in the character of Achilleus.   It is
very hard to find any, and harder still to see any in the passages
which they adduce.   It does exist in Hector, and the reason
why it should exist in him is manifest.

[2] History of Greece, vol. ii, p. 266.

[3] This is not the place to enter into the question relating to
the unity of the Odyssey.   As Mr. Grote insists, it is impossible
to shut our eyes to the unity of plan which pervades the poem.
In the Iliad we look in vain for any such unity, and are forced
to strange shifts in order to establish a continuous unity of any
kind.   But it seems impossible to prove that no part even of the
Odyssey ever existed in the form of separate lays.   The tale of

furnish a much stronger warrant for asserting
that more than one poet derived his inspiration
from the mythical speech which, even in the Greek
heroic age, still retained more than half its life.
Nay, in the Ilias itself the legend of Meleagros,
recited, it may be noted, by the same Phoinix
who guarded Achilleus in his earlier years, exhibits
still more forcibly the method in which phrases
but partially understood, and incidents which had
each received a local colouring and name, were
wrought into the tales whether of the Calydonian
chieftain, or Paris, or Achilleus.   In times which
even then were old, such phrases formed the
common speech of the people; such incidents
expressed the phenomena of their daily life; and
this language was strictly the language of poetry,
literally revelling in its boundless powers of creation and development.   In almost every word lay
the germ of an epic; it is the less wonderful, therefore, if each incident was embodied in a separate
legend, or even reproduced in the independent
tales of separate tribes. A hundred Homers may
well have lit their torch from this living fire.

Nor can we well shut our eyes to the fact,
that in the main story of the Odyssey Ground-
the Homeric poet has set the same solar work of the Odyssey.

the death of Achilleus seems to point to a different conclusion;
and this may also be said of the longer lay of Demodocos and
of the episode of the solar herds in Thrinakia (Od. xii).

strain in another key. When Odysseus goes to
Troy, he is simply a chieftain in the great host of
Agamemnon, as Grimhildr aids Gunnar in his plots
against Sigurdr.   Regarded thus, he is himself of
kin to the dark powers, the clouds and the winds,
who veil the earth in gloom.   But once taken to
Troy, the army of the Achaians must be brought
away again; and if the poet was guided by the old
idea, he would represent all of them as coming
to an untimely end or dying by a violent death;
and this is the fate of most of them.   But round
the chieftain of each tribe would gather again all
the ideas suggested by the ancient myths; and the
light reflected from the glory of the great Phthiotic
hero might well rest on the head of Odysseus, as
he turns to go from Ilion. Thus would begin a
new career, not altogether unlike that of Heracles
or Perseus. Throughout the whole poem, the one
absorbing desire which fills the heart of Odysseus
is to reach his home once more and see the wife
whom he had been obliged to leave in the spring-
time of his career, as Heracles was torn from Iolê.
There are grievous toils and many hindrances on
his way; but nothing can turn him from his course.
He has to fight, like Heracles and Perseus, Theseus
and Bellerophon, with more than mortal beings and
more than earthly powers, but he has the strength
which they had to overcome or to evade them.   It
is true that he conquers chiefly by strength of will

and sagacity of mind; but this is again the phase
which the idea of Helios, the great eye of day, as
surveying and scanning everything, assumes in
Medeia, Prometheus, Asclepios, Iamos, and Melampus. The other phase, however, is not wanting.
He too has a bow which none but he can wield,[1]
and he wields it to terrible purpose when, like
Achilleus, after his time of disguise, he bursts on
the astonished suitors, as the sun breaks from the
storm-cloud before he sinks to rest. So, again, in
his westward wanderings (for this is the common
path of the children of Zeus or Helios), he must
encounter fearful dangers. It is no unclouded sky
which looks down on him as he journeys towards
rocky Ithaca. He has to fight with Cyclopes and
Læstrygonians, he has to shun the snares of the
Seirens and the jaws of Skylla and Charybdis, as
Perseus had to overcome the Gorgons and Theseus
to do battle with the Minotauros. Yet there are
times of rest for him, as for Heracles and Bellerophon. He yearns for the love of Penelope, but

---

[1] Odyssey, xxi. 405, κ. τ. λ. The phraseology of the poet here
assumes, perhaps without his being fully aware of it, the same
tone as that which tells of the arming of Achilleus. Others have
tried with all their might to bend the bow. Odysseus stretches
it without the least effort (ἄτερ σπουδῆς), and the sound of the
string is like tho whizzing of a swallow in its flight. In an
instant every heart is filled with dread, and every cheek turns
pale (πᾶσι χρὼς ἐτράπετο), and, to complete the imagery, they
hear at the same moment the crash of thunder in tho sky.

his grief can be soothed for a while by the affection
of Kirkê and Calypso, as Achilleus found solace
in that of Diomêdê, and Heracles awhile in that
of Dêianeira. Nay, wherever he goes, mortal
kings and chiefs and undying goddesses seek to
make him tarry by their side, as Menelaos sought
to retain Paris in his home by the side of the
Spartan Helen, and as Gunnar strove to win
Sigurdr to be the husband of his sister. So is it
with Alkinoös; but, in spite of the loveliness and
purity of Nausicaâ, Odysseus may not tarry in the
happy land of the Phæeakians, even as he might
not tarry in the palace of the wise Kirkê or the
sparkling cave of the gentle Calypso. At last he
approaches his home, but he returns to it unknown
and friendless. The sky is as dark as it was while
Achilleus lay nursing his great wrath behind the
veil of his sorrow. Still he too, like Achilleus, knows
how to take vengeance on his enemies; and in
stillness and silence he makes ready for the mortal
conflict. His foes are many and strong, and, like
Patroclos against Hector, Telemachos [1] can do but
little against the suitors, in whom are reflected the
Trojan enemies of the Achaians, the scowling
storm-clouds, ready to rush like hounds on the
wounded boar. But for him also, as for Achilleus,
there is aid from the gods. Athênê, the daughter
of the sky, cheers him on, and restores him to the

---

[1] Grote, History of Greece, vol. ii. p. 238.

glorious beauty of his youth, as Thetis clothed her
child in the armour of Hephaistos and Apollo
directed his spear against Hector. Still in his
ragged beggar's dress, like the sun behind the rent
and tattered clouds, he appears in his own hall on
the day of doom. The old bow is taken down
from the wall, and none but he can be found to
stretch it. His enemies begin to fear that the
chief has indeed returned to his home, and they
crouch in terror before the stranger, as the Trojans
quailed at the mere sight and war-cry of Achilleus.
But their cry for mercy falls as vain as that of
Lycaon or Hector, who must die to avenge the
dead Patroclos, as the doom of the suitors is come
for the wrongs which they have done to Penelope.
The fatal bow is stretched. The arrows fly deadly
and unerring as the spear of Artemis, and the
hall is bathed in blood. There is nothing to stay
his arm until all are dead. The sun-god is taking
vengeance on the clouds and trampling them down
in his fury. The work is done; and Penelope sees
in Odysseus the husband who had left her long
ago to face his toils like Heracles and Perseus.
But she will try him still. If indeed he be the
same, he will know his bridal chamber and the
beautiful robes which his own hands had wrought.
Iolê will try whether Heracles remembers the
beautiful network of violet clouds which he spread
as her couch in the morning. The sun is setting

in peace. Penelope, fair as Œnônê and as pure
(for no touch of defilement must pass on her, or
on Iolê, or Daphnê, or Brisêis), is once again by
his side. The darkness is utterly scattered; the
corpses of the suitors and of the handmaidens who
ministered to them cumber the hall no more. A
few flying vapours rush at random along the sky,
as the men of Ithaca raise a feeble clamour in
behalf of the slain chieftains. Soon these too are
gone. Penelope and Odysseus are within their
bridal chamber. Œnônê has gone to rest with
Paris by her side; but there is no gloom in the
house of Odysseus, and the hero lives still, strong
and beautiful as in the early days. The battle is
over. The one yearning of his heart has been
fulfilled. The sun has laid him down to rest

In one unclouded blaze of living light.

But unless the marvellous resemblance (may it
not be said, the identity?) of the Greek, the Trojan, and the Teutonic epics can be explained
away, it follows that in Achilleus and in
Paris, in Meleagros and Sigurdr, in Ragnar
Lodbrog and Theseus, in Perseus, Heracles,
Bellerophon, and Odysseus, we have pictures drawn from the same ideal as regarded
under its several aspects. It mattered not which
of these aspects the poet might choose for his
theme. In each case he had more than the frame-

How much of the Iliad or Odyssey belongs to the invention of the poet?

work of his story made ready to his hand. The
departure of Achilleus from his own land to fight
in a quarrel which was not his own—the transfer
of the spoils won by him to a chief of meaner
spirit than his own—his unerring spear and immortal horses—the robbery of Briseis or Hippodameia—the fierce wrath of Achilleus, which yet
could leave room for the love of another in her
place—the sullen inaction from which he refuses
to be roused—the dismay of the Achaians and the
exultation of the Trojans at his absence from the
fight—the partial glory spread over the scene by
the appearance of Patroclos, only to close in the
deeper gloom which followed his overthrow—the
fury of Achilleus behind the dark cloud of his
sorrow—the sudden outburst of the hero, armed
with his resistless spear and clad in armour more
dazzling than that which he had lost—the invincible might which deals death to Hector and his
comrades—the blood which streams from the
human victims on his altar of sacrifice—his for-
giveness of Agamemnon for that which Agamemnon of himself would have been powerless to do
—the warning of his own early death which he
receives from the horse Xanthos—the battle of
the gods, as they take part in the storm which rages
in the heavens and on the earth—the swelling of
the waters, their brief mastery over the hero,
their conquest by fire—the generous splendour

which follows the accomplishment of his vengeance
—the sudden close of his brilliant but brief career
—the fierce battle fought over his dead body, are
incidents which the poet might introduce or omit
at will, but the spirit of which he was not free to
alter. The character of Achilleus was no more
his own creation than the shifting scenes in the
great drama of his life. The idea of his picture no
more originated in himself than the idea of Sigurdr
in the mind of the more rugged poet of the North.
The materials were not of his own making; and
the words of Mr. Gladstone acquire a stronger
meaning, though not the meaning which he designed to convey, when, insisting that there must
be a foundation for the Homeric theogony and
for the chief incidents in the war of Troy, he
said that poets may embellish, but they cannot
invent.[1] Their course was marked out for them,

[1] Homer and the Homeric Age, vol. ii. p. 10.

The great epic of Virgil raises a distinct question, on which I
must not here enter. It is, however, manifest that epic poetry,
composed in a time of highly artificial civilisation, stands on a
wholly different ground from the true epic of a simple age, the
growth of generations from the myth-making talk of the people.
The tradition which brought Æneas to Italy was not of Virgil's
making; and in taking him for his hero, he bound himself to
give the sequel of a career which had been begun in the Iliad.
Nor is it without significance that Æneas, like Odysseus, moves
from east to west, fighting, with whatever success, against the
powers of the air and sea. His visit to the shades below may
have been directly suggested by the poems which Virgil had
before him as his model; but it must have been a genuine tra-

but the swiftness with which each ran his race de-
pended on his own power.   The genius of the
Homeric poets was shown, not in the creation of
their materials, but in the truthful and magnificent
colouring which they throw over a legend which,
in weaker hands, might exhibit but a tinsel glitter.

But if there is this affinity between the character of the Achaian and the Teutonic heroes,
it follows that that character is neither *The portraits*
strictly Achaian nor strictly Teutonic.   It *of the
greater
chief-*
cannot be regarded as expressing the real *tains and
heroes*
morality either of the one or of the other. *are not
strictly*
Any attempt to criticise them as genuine *true to
national*
pictures of national character[1] must be fol- *character.*

dition which led Virgil to tell how he left Creûsa, as Heracles left
Iolê, and as Ariadnê was deserted by Theseus. So, again, in the
war with Turnus for the possession of Lavinia is reflected the
war at Troy for Helen, and the contest in the Odyssey with the
enemies who strive to win the rightful bride of Odysseus. In
this war Æneas, like other solar heroes, is successful, and like
them, after his victory, which is followed by a time of tranquil
happiness, he plunges into the Numician stream, as Kephalos
and Bellerophon sink to sleep in the western waters of the
Leucadian gulf.

The same type reappears in Romulus; and the key is found
to his legendary history as well as to that of Cyrus, of Chandra-
gupta, and of the progenitor of the Turks. All these tales repeat
the exposure of the infant Œdipus, or Telephos, or Iamos, or
Alexandros. See further the Tale of the Persian War, p. 318,
note 2. The same myth is seen under another aspect in the
legend of Servius Tullius.

[1] The wish to base his criticism on this foundation has led

lowed by that feeling of repulsion which Mr.
Dasent openly avows for the Greek mythology,

Mr. Gladstone to assume, without evidence, that the cause of
Achilleus was substantially that of right and justice, and that
the apology made by Agamemnon in Il. xix. 67 is essentially
different from the apology made in ix. 120. But, in the first
place, it is difficult to see that 'justice is' more 'outraged in the
person of Achilleus' (Homer &c. vol. iii. p. 370) than it is in the
person of Agamemnon. If the former is compelled to part with
Briseis, the latter has also been obliged to give up the daughter
of Chryses, for whom, with a plainness of speech not used either
by Achilleus or even by Paris in deserting Œnônê, he avows
his preference over his wedded wife Clytæmnestra (Il. i. 110).
Moreover, the taking of Briseis is the sole act of Agamemnon, in
which his councillors and the people take no part. Yet Mr.
Gladstone holds it to be a 'deadly wrong,' justifying Achilleus in
visiting his wrath on an army which had nothing whatever to
do with it. The truth is, that, by an analysis of this kind, we
may prove that Achilleus was mad, but we can never show that
his character was either common or even known among the
Achaians. The mere sufferings of Agamemnon must be allowed
to be at least equal to those of Odysseus, unless we adopt a code
which would better befit the Confederate slave-owners than
Englishmen; but it is almost a slander on Agamemnon to say
that his apology 'comes first in his faltering speech' given in
Il. xix. 67. If there he says

ἃψ ἐθέλω ἀρέσαι, δόμεναί τ' ἀπερείσι' ἄποινα,

he had said precisely the same thing in Il. ix. 120, &c., and
there also confesses, that he had been infatuated. In fact, Mr.
Gladstone is furnishing conclusive evidence in proof of the assertion that the writer of the nineteenth book knew nothing of the
ninth. But it is hard to yield a self-chosen position; and Mr.
Gladstone therefore holds that the apology of the former book
is a valid atonement, although it is, word for word, the same
as that which is contained in the latter. The very fact that

and which he also feels in part for the Teutonic.
In either case, his moral indignation is thrown

Achilleus is so ready, and even eager, to visit on the whole
army the sin of the individual Agamemnon, shows how utterly
destitute his character is of real patriotism. If anything more
were needed to exhibit the falsity of such critical methods, it
would be furnished by Colonel Mure's remarks that the aim of
Homer is not to show, with Mr. Gladstone, the justice of the
cause of Achilleus, but to prove that both he and Agamemnon
were equally in the wrong (Crit. Hist. Gr. Lit. vol. i. p. 277).
Both sides are equally deserving of blame: the one must be
punished, the other convinced of his folly. This is the result of
taking Homer to be a moral philosopher or preacher who, to
adopt Mr. Gladstone's favourite Horatian motto, tells us all about
human life and duty much better than Chrysippus and Crantor.
Indeed, there seems to be no limit to violent interpretations of
the text of Homer, if any such hypothesis is to be entertained.
It is Mr. Gladstone's belief that the last book of the Iliad was
added to show that Achilleus 'must surrender the darling object
of his desire, the wreaking of his vengeance on an inanimate
corpse' (Homer &c. vol. iii. p. 395). His ambition might, perhaps, have been more dignified; but, such as it was, it had
surely been gratified already. If he was not contented with
tying the body to his chariot-wheels and dragging it about till
every feature was disfigured, what more did he want? The
whole of this moral criticism of epical characters is ludicrously
out of place; and such criticism can be applied least of all, as a
means of determining national character, to the hero who (in
order to beat Hector, in every respect, as Mr. Gladstone asserts,
his inferior) is made invulnerable, like Baldr and Rustem, in all
parts but the heel, and, clad in armour wrought by Hephaistos,
wields a spear (guaranteed never to miss its mark) against an
enemy, who, acknowledging his inferiority, yet faces him from
the high motive of patriotism and duty, and whom he is unable
to overcome except by the aid of Athênê and after he has been
deserted by Apollo.

away. There was, doubtless, quite enough evil
in the character of the Norseman and the Greek;
but it never assumed that aspect which is common
to the great heroes of their epic poetry. We
look in vain elsewhere for an instance of the
same unbounded wrath arising from a cause
which the Achaian would be rather disposed to
treat too lightly, of an inaction which cares not
though all around him die, of a bloody vengeance
on meaner enemies when his great foe has been
vanquished, of the awful sacrifice of human victims—a sacrifice, even in the heroic age, completely alien to the general character of the
Achaians. But every one of these characteristics
is at once exhaustively explained, when they are
compared with those of all the other great legendary heroes. The grave attempt to judge
them by a reference to the ordinary standard of
Greek, or rather of Christian and modern morality,
has imparted to the criticism of Colonel Mure an
air almost of burlesque. In his analysis of the
Iliad, the motives which sway Achilleus are taken
to pieces as seriously as if he were examining the
conduct of Themistocles or Archidamos. It might
be well to speak of the 'defective principles of
heroic morality;'[1] of the sarcasms of Achilleus
against Agamemnon, in the first book, as 'unwar-
ranted at this stage of the discussion;'[2] of the

[1] Crit. Hist. Gr. Lit. vol. i. p. 275.   [2] Ibid. p. 277.

'respectful deference to the sovereign will of
Agamemnon' as a duty 'inculcated by the poet,'
and 'scrupulously fulfilled by the other chiefs,'[1] if
the poet, in Mr. Grote's words, were telling us of
a Trojan war ' without gods, without heroes, without Helen, without Amazons, without Ethiopians
under the beautiful son of Eôs.'[2] Colonel Mure
lays great stress on the 'ethic unity' with which
the incidental references to the early death of
Achilleus invest the whole poem, and he finds a
deep 'knowledge of human nature' 'in the adap-
tation to each other of the characters of the hero
and his friend,' where Mr. Grote sees little more
than a reflection.[3] But his anxiety to exalt the
character of Achilleus has led him, in one instance
of no slight moment, to vilify unduly that of his
antagonist. 'The proudest exploit of Hector, his
slaughter and spoliation of Patroclos, is so described as to be conspicuous only for its ferocity.
The Greek hero, after being disabled by Apollo, is
mortally wounded by another Trojan, when Hector
steps in with the finishing blow, as his butcher
rather than conqueror.'[4] If it be to the dispa-
ragement of Hector that he should have the aid
of a god, the poet is not the less careful in saying
that Achilleus could not slay Hector until Phœbus

[1] Crit. Hist. Gr. Lit. vol. i. p. 278.
[2] History of Greece, vol. i. p. 434.   [3] Ibid. vol. ii, p. 238.
[4] Crit. Hist. Gr. Lit. vol. i. p. 28

H

Apollo had deserted him. But if Colonel Mure
anxiously seeks out apologies for the wrath,[1] the
inaction, and the furious revenge of the hero, his
criticism utterly fails to explain the very incidents
which seem most deeply to have impressed him.
It does not explain why he should choose inaction
as the mode of avenging himself against Agamemnon. It does not show *why*, during his
absence, 'the gods had, at his own request, de-
creed victory to Hector, rout and slaughter to the
Greeks'[2]—why in him 'no affection, amiable or
the reverse,' should 'exist but in overpowering
excess'[3]—why he should be 'soothed by the fulfilment of his duties as mourner,' why the games
should 'usher in an agreeable change,' or why
'we should part with Achilles at the moment best
calculated to exalt and purify our impression of
his character.'[4]   Still less does it explain why,
before the final struggle, the gods should be let
loose to take whichever side they might prefer.
Colonel Mure seems to imply that they were all
sent to take the part of the Trojans.[5] Mr. Grote,
with a far keener discernment of the character of
this part of the poem, insists that 'that which
chiefly distinguishes these books is the direct, inces-
sant, and manual intervention of the gods and
goddesses, formally permitted by Zeus, and the

[1] Crit. Hist. Gr. Lit. vol. i. p. 284.   [2] Ibid. p. 287.
[3] Ibid. p. 289.   [4] Ibid. p. 291.   [5] Ibid. p. 288.

repetition of vast and fantastic conceptions to
which each superhuman agency gives occasion,
not omitting the battle of Achilles against Ska-
mander and Simois, and the burning up of these
rivers by Hephæstus.' In his judgment this interference mars the poem and 'somewhat vulgarises'
the gods.' But, while he thinks that the poet has
failed in a task where success was impossible, he
has not explained why the poet should feel himself compelled to undertake it.

But if Mr. Gladstone strains every effort to save
the character of Achilleus, Colonel Mure is not
less zealous in behalf of the chieftain of
Ithaca. If Achilleus 'represents the grandeur of the heroic character as reflected in
the very excess of its noblest attributes,' Odysseus,
in his belief, 'represents its virtue, possessing as
he does, in greater number and higher degree
than any other chief, the qualities which in
that age constituted the accomplished king and
citizen.'¹ The matter is brought to a plain issue.
The Odyssey is 'a rich picture-gallery of human
life as it existed in that age and country,'³ and we
are to see in Odysseus a favourable specimen of
the manners and habits of his people. It is quite
possible, by Colonel Mure's method, so to represent him. But if we speak of him as one whose

The cha-
racter of
Odys-
seus.

---

¹ History of Greece, vol. ii. p. 264.
² Crit. Hist. Gr. Lit. vol. i. p. 301.   ⁴ Ibid. p. 380

B 2

'habitual prudence was modified, or even at times overcome, by his thirst for glory and by an eager pursuit of the marvellous'[1]—if we say that he never uttered an untruth or practised a manœuvre for a base object[2]—if we speak of him as inculcating in his adventures 'the duty incumbent on the most vigorous minds, not only to resist but to avoid temptation'[3]—are we really speaking of the Odysseus of Homer? If such a method may account for some features in his character, will it in the least explain his character as bound up with the whole structure of the poem? Will it not leave the groundwork of the tale and its issue a greater mystery than ever? Will it explain why Odysseus, like Heracles and Philoctetes, should use poisoned arrows[4] — why, without scruple, he should tell lies while he desires to remain unrecognised, why he should never depart from the truth when speaking in his own character—why he hesitates not to lurk in ambush for an unarmed man,[5] and stab him behind his back, and speak of the deed without shame—why

---

[1] Crit. Hist. Gr. Lit. vol. i. p. 393.

[2] Ibid. p. 395.   [3] Ibid. p. 403.

[4] Odyssey, i. 263. Dr. Thirlwall (History of Greece, vol. i. p. 182) refers to this passage as showing the 'manifest disapprobation' of the poet. It is, at the least, very faintly expressed. Zeus, possibly as being above law, gives the poison, and Athênê sees no harm in his so doing.

[5] Odyssey, xiii. 260.

he should wish to pry into everything in heaven
or on earth, or in the dark land beneath the
earth [1]—why nothing less than the slaughter of
all his enemies will satiate a wrath not much more
reasonable than that of Achilleus? Still more:
will it explain why Penelope weaves and unweaves
her web—why, when Odysseus returns, she is
restored by Athênê, the daughter of the sky, to
all her early loveliness,[2] while on him rests once
more all the splendour of his ancient majesty —
why the nurse who recognises him should be Eurycleia,[3] and the maiden who reviles him should be
Melantho [4]—why his dog Argos, although forsaken
and untended, retains something of his former
beauty and at once recognises his old master[5]—
why, when Penelope wishes to speak with him on

---

[1] The visit of Odysseus to the shades carries us to the singular
threat of Hyperion, when he tells Zeus that, if the theft of his
cows be not avenged, he will go down and shine among the
dead (Od. xii. 383). Shelley faithfully represents the spirit of
the old phrase when, in his Hymn of Apollo, he says,
　　'My footsteps pave the clouds with fire: the caves
　　Are filled with my bright presence.'
[2] Od. xviii. 192.
[3] Od. xvii. 31. In the name of her father Autolycos we
have again the same word which gave rise to the story of Lycaon
and to the meaning which Æschylus attached to the name or
Phœbus, the Lykian-born (Λύκειος, Λυκηγενής).
[4] Od. xviii. 321. We see the process by which the force of
the old mythical language was weakened and lost, when the poet
speaks of Melantho as καλλιπάρῃος.
[5] Od. xvii. 300.

his return, she is charged to wait till the evening [1]
—why in his wanderings he should fight not so
much with human enemies as with mighty beings
and monsters of the earth and sea—why his long
voyage and the time of gloomy disguise should be
followed by a triumph so full of blood, ending
with a picture of such serene repose?

In truth, the character of Odysseus was not,
in any greater degree than that of Achilleus, an
original creation of the Homeric poet. In
all its main features it came down ready
to his hand. His wisdom is the wisdom
of Athênê and Prometheus and Medeia, of
Iamos and Asclêpios and Melampus; his
craft is the craft of Hermes, his keen intellect is
the piercing eye of Helios, and from Helios comes
the strange inquisitiveness which must pry into
everything that comes in his path.[2] If he uses
poisoned arrows, it is not because Achaian chieftains were in the habit of using them, but because
the weapons of Heracles were steeped in venom
and the robe of Medeia scorched the body of
Glaukê. If he submits to the love of Kirkê and
Calypso, it is because Achilleus solaced himself
with Diomêdê for the loss of Brisêis, and Heracles
awhile forgot his sorrows in the house of Dêianeira.

How far was the character of Odysseus a creation of the Homeric poet?

---

[1] Od. xvii. 582.

[2] This inquisitiveness is especially seen in the episodes of the
Cyclops and the Seirens.

If he can be a secret stabber, it is not because the heroic ideal could stoop to such baseness, but because Phœbus can smite secretly as well as slay openly, and because it matters not whether the victim be but one man or the fifty who fall by the spear of Bellerophon. If at the end he smites all his enemies, it is not because they have committed an offence which, according to the standard of the age, would deserve such punishment, but because the wrath of Achilleus could only be appeased by the blood of his enemies, as the blazing sun tramples on the dark clouds beneath his feet. We may be well assured that such as these were not the habits of the men who dwelt at Tiryns or in Ithaca—that such as these were not the characteristics of the chieftains who ruled in Mykênæ. But if the character of Odysseus is not strictly Achaian, so, like that of Achilleus, it is not, in strictness of speech, human. Mr. Grote has truly said that the aim of the poet is not ethical or didactic either in the Iliad or the Odyssey,[1] and an examination of the latter poem scatters to the winds all fancies which see in

[1] History of Greece, vol. ii. p. 278. Horace draws but a feeble moral when he says of the Iliad,

'Quidquid delirant reges, plectuntur Achivi.'

Ep. i. 2, 14.

But that this should be the case is perfectly explained by the growth of mythology. The wrath of beings like Achilleus and Odysseus is wide-spreading and indiscriminate.

Odysseus an image of the Christian warrior fighting the good fight of faith, yet yearning for his rest in heaven.[1] The ideal is indeed magnificent, and it has never been more magnificently realised, but it is not the ideal either of Christianity or even of humanity; it is the life of the sun. At the outset of his return from the East, Odysseus has to encounter superhuman foes; and the discomfiture of the Cyclops rouses the wrath of the sea-god Poseidon, as the clouds rise from the waters and curl round the rising sun. Still Zeus is on his side, and Poseidon himself shall not be able to cut short his course,[2] though all his

[1] This higher aim is especially attributed to the poet by the Rev. Isaac Williams, in 'The Christian Scholar,' p. 115, &c.

[2] Od. i. 80. The influence of Polyphêmos on the fortunes of Odysseus curiously perplexes Colonel Mure, who sees in it the chief defect of the Odyssey, as interfering with the 'retributive equity' which he fancies that he finds in the Iliad. 'No reader of taste or judgment,' he thinks, 'can fail to experience in its perusal a certain feeling of impatience, not only that the destinies of a blameless hero and an innocent woman, but that any important trains of events, should hinge on so offensive a mechanism as the blind affection of a mighty deity for so odious a monster as Polyphemus' (Crit. Hist. Gr. Lit. vol. ii. p. 151). Nothing could show more clearly than these words Colonel Mure's inability to enter fairly into the spirit of Greek mythology. It was simply impossible that the poet could make use of any other mechanism. The train of events which he recounts is not the sequence of any human life, but the career of Helios and Daphnê, of Alexandros and Œnônê.

The Cyclops is, according to Homer, the son of Poseidon, the

comrades should fall by the way, as the morning
clouds may be scattered before the noonday. But
while he moves steadily towards his home, that
home is dark and gloomy. There the sun is
hidden, and only from time to time a faint glory
breaks from the sky as Telemachos strives to
maintain the honour of his father's house.[1] So
Penelope remains quiet in her home. Forbidding
forms crowd around her, but her purity remains
unsullied. The web begun is never ended; the
fairy tracery of morning clouds cannot reappear
until the evening. There are others too who
have not forgotten the hero, and Eurycleia seeks
to retain Telemachos when he would go forth to

god of the sea—in other words, the exhalations which form
themselves into the hideous storm-clouds, through which the
sun sometimes glares down like a huge eye in the midst of the
black forehead of the giant. Mr. Kelly, therefore, mistakes the
eye, which really belongs to the sun, for the Cyclops himself,
when he says, 'The Greek mythology shows us a whole people
of suns in the Cyclops, giants with one eye round as a wheel in
their foreheads.' He is right in adding that 'they were akin to
the heavenly giants, and dwelt with the Phæacians, the navi-
gators of the cloud-sea in the broad Hypereia, the upper land,
i. e. heaven, until the legend transplanted them both to the
western horizon' (Indo-European Folk-lore, p. 32).

[1] I must again refer to Mr. Grote's remarks on the merely
secondary character of Telemachos (History of Greece, vol. ii.
p. 238). The name Telemachos comes from the far-darting rays
of the sun, like that of Telephassa. The dawn is always described under names expressive of wide-spreading splendour, as
Euryphaëssa, Euryganeia, and Eurycleia, the nurse of Odysseus.

seek his father.[1]   But he cannot stay.   The
slant rays vanish from the sky, and the house of
Laertes is shadowed with deeper gloom.   Meanwhile Odysseus is hastening on.   For a while he
tarries with Kirkê and Calypso, and makes a
longer sojourn in the house of Alkinoös, even as
Paris abode many months in Sparta. The Phœakian
chieftain would have him stay for ever.   His land
is fair as summer; but the seasons may not tarry,
and Odysseus cannot abide there even with Nausicaâ.   So he hastens home, sometimes showing
his might, as the sun breaks for a moment through
a rift in the clouds; but the darkness is greatest
when he lands on his own shores.   He is surrounded by enemies and spies, and he takes refuge
in craft and falsehood.[2]   The darkness itself must
aid him to win the victory, and Athênê takes all
beauty from his face and all brightness from his
golden hair.[3] These, with all the other ideas which
had come down to him as a fruitful heritage from
the language of his remote forefathers, the Homeric
poet might recombine or develope, but if he brought

[1] Od. ii. 365.
[2] Od. xiii. 255, κ. τ. λ.
[3] Od. xiii. 431.   The language adheres even more closely to
the myth. His locks are actually destroyed—

$$\xi a \nu \theta \grave{a} s \ \grave{\epsilon} \kappa \ \nu \epsilon \phi a \lambda \tilde{\eta} s \ \ddot{\upsilon} \lambda \epsilon \sigma \epsilon \ \tau \rho \acute{\iota} \chi a s.$$

Those which she gave him when she restored his beauty would
be strictly the new rays bursting from behind the clouds.

him to Ithaca under a cloud, he could not but say
that Athênê took away his glory, while yet his dog
Argos, the same hound who crouches at the feet
of Artemis or drives the herds of the sun to their
pastures, knows his old master in all his squalid raiment, and dies for joy at seeing him.[1] When on his
return Telemachos asks whether the bridal couch
of Odysseus is covered with spider's webs, he could
not but say in reply that Penelope still remained
faithful to her only love;[2] and when Telemachos
is once more to see his father, he could not but
make Athênê restore him to more than his ancient
beauty.[3] So the man of many toils and wanderings returns to his home,[4] only to find that his
son is unable to rule his house,[5] as Phaethon and
Patroclos were alike unable to guide the horses of
Helios. Still Penelope is fair as Artemis or
Aphroditê,[6] although Melantho and Melanthios,[7]
the black children of the crafty (Dolios) Night,
strive to dash her life with gloom, and Odysseus
stands a squalid beggar in his own hall.[8] Thence-
forth the poet's path was still more distinctly
marked. He must make the arm of Odysseus
irresistible,[9] he must make Athênê aid him in

[1] Od. xvii. 327.
[2] Od. xvi. 35.
[4] Od. xvi. 175.
[3] Od. i. 2; xvi. 205.
[5] Od. xvi. 256.
[6] Od. xvii. 37.
[7] Od. xvii. 212; xviii. 320.
[8] Od. xvii. 363.
[9] Od. xviii. 95.

storing up weapons for the conflict,[1] as Thetis
brought the armour of Hephaistos to Achilleus;
he must make Penelope tell Odysseus how often
she had woven and undone her web while he tarried so long away.[2]   When Penelope asks tidings
of Odysseus, the poet could not but give an answer
in which the flash of gold and blaze of purple
carry us directly to the arming of Achilleus.[3] As
Eurycleia, the old nurse, tends him at the bath,
he must make her recognise the wound made by
the wild boar[4] who wrought the death of the
fair Adonis, and tell how her foster-child came to
be called Odysseus.[5]   Then, as the day of doom is

[1] Od. xix. 33.

[2] Od. xix. 140.   Penelope is the weaver of the web (πήνη) of
cirri clouds.

In his recent work on the Curiosities of Indo-European
Tradition and Folk-lore, Mr. Kelly, summing up the general
characteristics of Aryan mythology, says, 'Light clouds were
webs spun and woven by celestial women, who also drew water
from the fountains on high and poured it down as rain. The
yellow light gleaming through the clouds was their golden hair.
A fast-scudding cloud was a horse flying from its pursuers. . . .
In all this and much more of the same kind, there was not yet
an atom of that symbolism which has commonly been assumed
as the starting-point of all mythology. The mythic animals, for
example, were, for those who first gave them their names, no
mere images or figments of the mind. They were downright
realities, for they were seen by men who were quick to see, and
who had not yet learned to suspect any collusion between their
eyes and their fancy' (p. 8).

[3] Od. xix. 226.   [4] Od. xix. 393.

[5] Od. xix. 201.   The origin of this name, as of so many others,

ushered in, he must relate how the lightning flashed from the sky,[1] and the rumour went abroad that the chieftain was come again to his home. So Penelope takes down the bow which Iphitos, the mighty, had given to Odysseus,[2] and bids the suitors stretch it; but they cannot, and there is no need that Telemachos should waste his strength now that his father has come home.[3] Then follows the awful tragedy. Zeus must thunder as the beggar seizes the bow.[4] The suitors begin to fall beneath the unerring arrows; but the victory is not to be won without a struggle. Telemachos has left the chamber

is wrongly accounted for; but the explanation is right in so far as it retains the idea of gloomy anger. Odysseus is the angry sun who hides his face behind the clouds, not the man who, like Autolycos, is hated by others for his craft and falsehood. A more curious instance of misinterpretation is the explanation given by Sophocles of the name Œdipus, from the swelling of the ankle caused by tight bandaging (Œd. Tyr. 1033-5). If the poet is right in referring it to οἰδέω at all, the idea conveyed by it is that of the swelling of the sun as it rises from a point of light to a full circle above the horizon. As this swelling is at the base, it might have originated the notion which connected the swelling with the feet of Œdipus. The swelling of the sun may, however, belong us strictly to the time of his setting as of his rising; and it is so understood by M. Bréal. It would thus signify his dilating form as he approaches the horizon, as the other idea would express his growth from a point of light when he left it in the morning.

[1] Od. xx. 105.
[2] Od. xxi. 130.
[3] Od. xxi. 5.
[4] Od. xxi. 413.

door ajar, and the enemy arm themselves with
the weapons which they find there.[1] It is but another version of the battle which Achilleus fought
with Scamandros and Simoeis in the war of elements; and as then the heart of Achilleus almost
failed him, so wavers now the courage of Odysseus.[2]
For a moment the dark clouds seem to be gaining
mastery over the sun. But Athênê comes to his
aid,[3] as before she had come to help Achilleus,
and the arrows of the suitors are in vain aimed
at the hero,[4] although Telemachos is wounded,[5]
though not to the death like Patroclos. Yet
more, Athênê must show her Ægis,[6] dazzling as
the face of the unclouded sun; and when the
victory is won, the corpses of the slain must be
thrust away,[7] like the black vapours driven from
the sky. Only for Melanthios he reserves the
full measure of indignity which Achilleus wreaked
on the body of the dead Hector.[8] Then follows the recognition in which, under another
form, Procris again meets Kephalos and Iolê once
more rejoices the heart of Heracles. For a little
while the brightness rests on Laertes, and the old
man's limbs again grow strong; but the strength
comes from Athênê.[9]

The progress of comparative mythology, with

[1] Od. xxii. 141.   [2] Od. xxii. 147.   [3] Od. xxii. 205.
[4] Od. xxii. 257.   [5] Od. xxii. 277.   [6] Od. xxii. 297.
[7] Od. xxii. 460.   [8] Od. xxii. 475.   [9] Od. xxiv. 367.

that of the science of language, must throw fresh
light on the original construction of the The cha-
great Greek epics; but important and full Odysseus
of interest as the question is, it cannot Achaian.
even be touched on here. Yet one conclusion,
at the least, is forced upon us, and Odysseus is
found to be as much and as little an Achaian
chieftain as Achilleus or Meleagros. The poems
remain, as they were, a mine of wealth for all who
seek to find in them pictures of the manners and
social life of the heroic ages; but all the great
chiefs are removed beyond a criticism which starts
with attributing to them the motives which influence mankind under any circumstances what-
soever.

Thus the Greek, Scandinavian, and Hindoo
epics, the tales told of Hellenic and Teutonic
gods and heroes, alike point to one common The
source from whence all the thousand streams source of
Greek
of mythology have diverged. They carry Norse
us back to ages dimly seen through the mythology.
mists of a hoar antiquity; and yet that age is as
real a portion of the world's history as is our own.
It is beyond the daring of the boldest sceptic to
deny the close kindred between the grammars of
the Greek and the Sanskrit languages; and the
same Titanic assurance would be needed to call
into question the identity, in their essence and in
their chief features, of the Sanskrit and Greek

mythology.   If, then, the Greek said that Apollo
loved Daphnê, and the Aryan of the Five Streams
said that Indra pursued Dahanâ—if the latter
would say

Dyaús me pitá' ganitá,

where the former said

Ζεύς ἐμοῦ πατήρ γενετήρ,[1]—

we can assign their true value to off-hand assertions, mischievous only because they may mislead
the ignorant, that the Aryan race itself, dispersed
or undispersed, is but a creature of the German
imagination.   The name of that race is a matter
of but little moment; yet we have the indisputable fact that certain branches of the one common
stock (whatever it may have been called) drew as
sharp a line between Aryan and non-Aryan tribes,
as ever the Greek drew between Hellên and barba-
rian.   The Persian has his Iran and An-iran; the
Zoroastrian contrasted *vîspem airyô-sayanem*,
the Aryan regions, with those that lay without,
anairyâo dainhâvô;[2] and in all that relates to
this ancient stock, from which we as well as they
are sprung, there is for us, although we may not
heed it, a direct and personal interest.   Nor, if
only we rightly define its limits, is our knowledge
of that race uncertain.   We know not only their

---

[1] Max Müller, Comp. Myth. p. 15.

[2] Max Müller, Lectures on the Science of Language, p. 227
(First Series).

thoughts on the sights and sounds of the visible
world, as declared in their mythical speech and
in the more definite legends of later ages; but we
also know something of their ways and their
doings, from a witness whose testimony we dare
not ignore. We know that they were not a
brutish or degraded race. We know that they
had fixed dwellings, that the relations of father
and mother, of son and daughter, brother and
sister, were as familiar to them as to us. We
know that they were tillers of the earth and
builders of boats, that they had a knowledge of
numbers, and recognised property and law.[1] Nor
does our knowledge end here. The mere analysis
of language will lead us to historical facts. The
common word for a shoe proves that the English
and German tribes had ceased to walk barefooted
before their ways diverged; the difference of their
words for stockings shows that these were a later
acquisition. This is as much an historical fact as
the discovery of gunpowder; and all that need be
said further is that (as in geology) we are dealing with approximate dates, in which it is beyond
our power to determine more than the sequence
of events. We cannot say when the first or last
Sanskrit hymn of the Chandas period was composed; but we can as little deny the fact of their

[1] Max Müller, Lectures on the Science of Language, p. 199
(First Series).

I

composition as we can call into question the fact of a thermal or a glacial period in geological history. Within these limits we may confidently hope to increase our knowledge of that old time. The stream, whose sands have already rewarded our search with so much gold, will most assuredly yield more.

And if the examination of the most complicated epic poetry has disclosed precisely the framework which we find even in the most fragmentary legends [1]—if we have seen that Theseus and Sigurdr, and Phaethon and Phœbus, and Paris and Achilleus, are, though different,

Explanation of the seeming immorality of Aryan mythology.

[1] It is impossible to determine the aid which Comparative Mythology might have received from the lost poems of the epic cycle. There can, however, be little doubt that they would have made still more evident the truth of facts which, even without them, seem to be indisputably established. We might also with their aid have been better able to measure exactly the knowledge which the poets of the Iliad and Odyssey had of legends which they have not mentioned or have treated only incidentally. The epic poem which had for its subject simply the capture of Œchalia by Hercles, the Danais, the Eurôpia, might have added to our knowledge of the materials with which all these poems were built up. The Iliad and Odyssey have assumed in our eyes more than their fair proportions from the mere fact that they alone have survived unhurt the wear and tear of ages. On the whole Grecian epic, see Grote, History of Greece, Part I. ch. xxi.

The so-called Orphic hymns consist almost entirely of invocations to the various beings with which the old mythical language peopled the visible world, followed by a string of all the epithets which were held to be applicable to them. Almost every one of these epithets may be made the germ of a mythical tale. Thus the

yet the same—if we see that their adventures or
their times of inaction are simply the fruit of an
inevitable process going on in all kindred languages—all charges of immorality founded on
the character of these adventures fall more completely to the ground. It is simply impossible to
believe that the great Athenian poets were de-
scended from a people who, some centuries before,
had deliberately sat down to invent the most
loathsome or the most ridiculous fictions about
the gods whom they worshipped and the heroes
whom they revered. To the mind of Æschylus,
there was a depth of almost inexpiable guilt in
the sacrifice of Iphigencia. The imagination of
Sophocles was oppressed by the unconscious incest
of Œdipus and all its frightful consequences,

hymn to Protogonos (who reappears as Protogeneia) hails him
as born from the egg (of night), and having the face of a bull
(Indra), as Phanes, the brilliant, and Antaugès, reflecting the
light of the sun (vi.). Helios (viii.) is Paian, the healer, merging
into the idea of Asclepios; he is also Zeus—a relic of the interchangeable character of the earlier Vedic gods, the moon being
also still male and female (ix.). Heracles (xii.) is the father of
Time, benignant and everlasting, producing and devouring all
things, yet helping all, wearing the dawn and the night round
his head. Adonis (lvi.) dwells partly in Tartarus and partly on
Olympus. The rays of the sun and moon cannot come without
the Charites (lx.) (the Harits, or horses of Indra). Asclepios is
Paian (the healer) as well as Helios, and he has Health as his
spotless bride. The date of these hymns is a matter of little
moment. To whatever age they may belong, they lay bare not
a few of the stages in the mythopœic process.

while Pindar turned aside with almost contemp-
tuous indignation from the stories which told of
gods devouring their own offspring. But we, to
whom the tale of Cronos points to time which
consumes the years to which it has given birth—
we, for whom the early doom of the virgin
Iphigeneia, caused by the wrath of Artemis, is a
mere reflection of the lot which pressed alike on
Dahanâ and Daphnê, on Iolê and Œnônê—we, who
can read in the woful tale of Iocastê the return
of the lord of day, the slayer of the Sphinx and
the Python, to the mother who had borne him in
the morning, must feel that if Greeks or Norsemen who told of such things are to be condemned,
they must be condemned on other grounds, and
not because in Achilleus, or Sigurdr, or Odysseus,
they have given us pictures of obstinate inaction
or brutal revenge. Possibly, to some among those
old poets, the real nature of the tales which they
were telling was not so completely hidden as we
may deem. It is hard to think that the writer of
the Hymn to Hermes knew nothing of the key
which was to unlock all its secrets. The very
form of their language would warrant us in saying
much more. But the words of Kumârila prove
that among the Eastern Aryans the real character
of their mythology had not been forgotten. He
too had to listen to complaints like those which

Pindar brings against the follies or the vices of the gods. His answer is ready.

'It is fabled that Prajâpati, the Lord of Creation, did violence to his daughter. But what does it mean? Prajâpati, the Lord of Creation, is a name of the sun; and he is called so because he protects all creatures [Alexandros]. His daughter Ushas is the dawn. And when it is said that he was in love with her, this only means that, at sunrise, the sun runs after the dawn, the dawn being at the same time called the daughter of the sun, because she rises when he approaches. In the same manner, if it is said that Indra was the seducer of Ahalyâ, this does not imply that the god Indra committed such a crime: but Indra means the sun, and Ahalyâ the night; and, as the night is seduced and ruined by the sun of the morning, therefore is Indra called the paramour of Ahalyâ.'[1]

It is the legend of Œdipus and Iocastê, one of the most awful, and, in some aspects, the most repulsive, in the wide range of Greek mytho- The morally logy.[2] If the real nature of this tale is laid of Hesiod.

[1] Max Müller, History of Sanskrit Literature, p. 530.

[2] Nothing can exceed the coarseness of the legend of Erichthonios as given by Apollodorus, iii. 14, 6. It is, however, nothing more than a strange jumble of images which are found scattered through a hundred legends, and which may be translated into the following phrases:—

bare before us, we may at once assure ourselves
that these stories are not the fruit of depraved
imaginations and brutal lives. There is no longer
any mystery in the strange combination of repulsive
legends with a sensitive morality in the Hesiodic
poem of the Works and Days. We cease to wonder that the same poet who has recounted the tale
of Pandora should tell us that the eye of God is
in every place watching the evil and the good,[1]
that the duty of man is to avoid the smooth road
to evil,[2] and to choose the strait path of good,
which, rough at the first, becomes easy to those
who walk in it.[3]

The Dawn stands before the Sun, and asks him for his
armour.

The face of the Dawn charms the Sun, who seeks to embrace her.

The Dawn flies from the Sun, and a soft shower falls on the
earth, as his piercing rays shoot across the sky after her departing form.

From the soft shower springs the Summer with its fruits.

The Dawn would make the Summer immortal, and intrusts
the Summer to the care of the Dew.

The serpents of night lie coiled round the Summer in the
morning.

The sisters of the Dew are slain by the Dawn.

[1] Works and Days, 252, 253, 265.

[2] Ibid. 286.

[3]
      μακρὸς δὲ καὶ ὄρθιος οἶμος ἐπ' αὐτὴν
καὶ τρηχὺς τὸ πρῶτον· ἐπὴν δ' εἰς ἄκρον ἵκηαι,
ῥηιδίη δὴ ἔπειτα πέλει, χαλεπή περ ἐοῦσα. Ib. 290.

TALES.

MEDUSA.

IN the far western land, where the Hesperides guard the golden apples which Gaia gave to the lady Hêrê, dwelt the maiden Medusa, with her sisters Stheino and Eurualê, in their lonely and dismal home. Between them and the land of living men flowed the gentle stream of ocean,[1] so that only the name of the Gorgon sisters was known to the sons of men, and the heart of Medusa yearned in vain to see some face which might look on her with love and pity. For on her lay the doom of death, but her sisters could neither grow old nor die. For them there was nothing fearful in the stillness of their gloomy home, as they sat with stern unpitying faces, gazing on the silent land beyond the ocean stream. But Medusa wandered to and fro, longing to see something new in a home to which no change ever came; and her heart pined for lack of those things which gladden the souls of mortal men. For where she dwelt there was neither day nor night. She never saw the bright children of

Helios driving his flocks to their pastures in the morning. She never beheld the stars as they look out from the sky, when the sun sinks down into his golden cup[2] in the evening. There no clouds ever passed across the heaven, no breeze ever whispered in the air; but a pale yellow light brooded on the land everlastingly. So there rested on the face of Medusa a sadness such as the children of men may never feel; and the look of hopeless pain was the more terrible because of the greatness of her beauty. She spake not to any of her awful grief, for her sisters knew not of any such thing as gentleness and love, and there was no comfort for her from the fearful Graiæ who were her kinsfolk. Sometimes she sought them out in their dark caves, for it was something to see even the faint glimmer of the light of day which reached the dwelling of the Graiæ; but they spake not to her a word of hope when she told them of her misery, and she wandered back to the land which the light of Helios might never enter. Her brow was knit with pain, but no tear wetted her cheek, for her grief was too great for weeping.

But harder things yet were in store for Medusa; for Athênê, the daughter of Zeus, came from the Libyan land to the dwelling of the Gorgon sisters, and she charged Medusa to go with her to the gardens where the children of Hesperos guard the golden apples of the lady Hêrê. Then Medusa bowed herself down at the feet of Athênê, and besought her to have pity on her changeless sorrow, and she said, ' Child of Zeus, thou dwellest with thy happy kinsfolk, where Helios gladdens all with his light and the Horæ lead the glad dance when Phœbus touches the strings of his golden harp. Here there is neither night nor day, nor cloud or breeze or storm. Let me go forth from this horrible land and look on the face of mortal men; for I too must die, and my heart yearns for the love which my sisters scorn.' Then Athênê looked on her sternly, and said, ' What hast thou to do with love? and what is the love of men for one who is of kin to the beings who may not die? Tarry here till thy doom is accomplished; and then it may be that Zeus will grant thee a place among those who dwell in his glorious home.' But Medusa said, ' Lady, let me go forth now. I cannot tell how many ages may pass before I die, and thou knowest not the yearning which fills the heart of mortal things for tenderness and love.' Then a look of anger came over the fair face of Athênê, and she said, ' Trouble me not. Thy prayer is vain; and the sons of men would shrink from thee, if thou

couldst go among them, for hardly could they
look on the woful sorrow of thy countenance
and live.' But Medusa answered gently, 'Lady,
hope has a wondrous power to kill the deepest
grief, and in the pure light of Helios my face
may be as fair as thine.'

Then the anger of Athênê became fiercer still,
and she said, 'Dost thou dare to vie with me?'
I stand by the side of Zeus, to do his will, and
the splendour of his glory rests upon me; and
what art thou, that thou shouldst speak to me
such words as these? Therefore, hear thy doom.
Henceforth, if mortal man ever look upon thee,
one glance of thy face shall turn him to stone. Thy
beauty shall still remain, but it shall be to thee
the blackness of death. The hair which streams
in golden tresses over thy fair shoulders shall
be changed into hissing snakes, which shall curl
and cluster round thy neck. On thy countenance
shall be seen only fear and dread, that so all
mortal things which look on thee may die.' So
Athênê departed from her, and the blackness of
great horror rested on the face of Medusa, and
the hiss of the snakes was heard as they twined
around her head and their coils were wreathed
about her neck. Yet the will of Athênê was not

wholly accomplished; for the heart of Medusa
was not changed by the doom which gave to her
face its deadly power, and she said, 'Daughter
of Zeus, there is hope yet, for thou hast left me
mortal still, and, one day, I shall die.'

DANAÊ.

FROM the home of Phœbus Apollo at Delphi came words of warning to Acrisios, the king of Argos, when he sent to ask what should befall him in the after-days; and the warning was that he should be slain by the son of his daughter Danaê. So the love of Acrisios was changed towards his child, who was growing up, fair as the flowers of spring, in her father's house; and he shut her up in a dungeon, caring nothing for her wretchedness. But the power of Zeus was greater than the power of Acrisios, and Danaê became the mother of Perseus; and they called her child the son of the Bright Morning,⁴ because Zeus had scattered the darkness of her prison-house. Then Acrisios feared exceedingly, and he spake the word that Danaê and her child should ·die.

The first streak of day was spreading its faint light in the eastern sky when they led Danaê to the sea-shore, and put her in a chest, with a loaf of bread and a flask of water. Her child slept in her arms, and the rocking of the waves, as they bore the chest over the heaving sea, made him slumber yet more sweetly; and the tears of Danaê fell on him as she thought of the days that were past and the death which she must die in the dark waters. And she prayed to Zeus, and said, ' O Zeus, who hast given me my child, canst thou hear me still and save me from this horrible doom?'' Then a deep sleep came over Danaê, and, as she slept with the babe in her arms, the winds carried the chest at the bidding of Poseidôn and cast it forth on the shore of the island of Seriphos.

Now it so chanced that Dictys, the brother of Polydectes, the king of the island, was casting a net into the sea, when he saw something thrown up by the waves on the dry land; and he went hastily and took Danaê with her child out of the chest, and said, ' Fear not, lady; no harm shall happen to thee here, and they who have dealt hardly with thee shall not come nigh to hurt thee in this land.' So he led her to the house of king Polydectes, who welcomed her to his home, and Danaê had rest after all her troubles.

Thus the time went on, and the child Perseus grew up brave and strong, and all who saw him marvelled at his beauty. The light of early morning is not more pure than was the colour on his fair cheeks, and the golden locks streamed brightly over his shoulders, like the rays of the sun when they rest on the hills at midday. And Danaê said, 'My child, in the land where thou wast born, they called thee the son of the Bright Morning. Keep thy faith, and deal justly with all men: so shalt thou deserve the name which they gave thee.' Thus Perseus grew up, hating all things that were wrong and mean; and all who looked on him knew that his hands were clean and his heart pure.

But there were evil days in store for Danaê— for king Polydectes sought to win her love against her will.[6] Long time he besought her to hearken to his prayer; but her heart was far away in the land of Argos, where her child was born, and she said, 'O king, my life is sad and weary; what is there in me that thou shouldest seek my love? There are maidens in thy land fairer far than I; leave me then to take care of my child while we dwell in a strange land.' Then Polydectes said hastily, 'Think not, lady, to escape me thus. If thou wilt not hearken to my words, thy child shall not remain with thee; but I will send him forth far away into the western land, that he may bring me the head of the Gorgon Medusa.'

So Danaê sat weeping when Polydectes had left her, and when Perseus came he asked her why she mourned and wept; and he said, 'Tell me, my mother, if the people of this land have done thee wrong, and I will take a sword in my hand and smite them.' Then Danaê answered, 'Many toils await thee in time to come, but here thou canst do nothing. Only be of good courage, and deal truly, and one day thou shalt be able to save me from my enemies.'

Still, as the months went on, Polydectes sought to gain the love of Danaê, until at last he began to hate her because she would not listen to his prayer. And he spake the word, that Perseus must go forth to slay Medusa, and that Danaê must be shut up in a dungeon until the boy should return from the land of the Graiæ and the Gorgons.

So once more Danaê lay within a prison; and the boy Perseus came to bid her farewell before he set out on his weary journey. Then Danaê folded her arms around him, and looked sadly into his eyes, and said, 'My child, whatever a mortal man can do for his mother, that, I know, thou wilt do for me; but I cannot tell whither thy long toils shall lead thee, save that the land of the Gorgons lies beyond the slow-rolling stream

K

of ocean. Nor can I tell how thou canst do the
bidding of Polydectes, for Medusa alone of the
Gorgon sisters may grow old and die, and the
deadly snakes will slay those who come near, and
one glance of her woful eye can turn all mortal
things to stone. Once, they say, she was fair to
look upon; but the lady Athênê has laid on
her a dark doom, so that all who see the Gorgon's
face must die. It may be, Perseus, that the heart
of Medusa is full rather of grief than hatred, and
that not of her own will the woful glare of her
eye changes all mortal things into stone; and, if
so it be, then the deed which thou art charged to
do shall set her free from a hateful life, and bring
to her some of those good things for which now
she yearns in vain.' Go then, my child, and
prosper. Thou hast a great warfare before thee;
and though I know not how thou canst win the
victory, yet I know that true and fair dealing
gives a wondrous might to the children of men,
and Zeus will strengthen the arm of those who
hate treachery and lies.'

Then Perseus bade his mother take courage,
and vowed a vow that he would not trust in craft
and falsehood; and he said, 'I know not, my
mother, the dangers and the foes which await me,
but be sure that I will not meet them with any

weapons which thou wouldest scorn. Only, as the days and months roll on, think not that evil has befallen me; for there is a hope within me that I shall be able to do the bidding of Polydectes and to bear thee hence to our Argive land.' So Perseus went forth with a good courage to seek out the Gorgon Medusa.

PERSEUS.

THE east wind crested with a silvery foam the waves of the sea of Hellê,[8] when Perseus went into the ship which was to bear him away from Seriphos. The white sail was spread to the breeze, and the ship sped gaily over the heaving waters. Soon the blue hills rose before them, and as the sun sank down in the west, Perseus trod once more the Argive land.

But there was no rest for him now in his ancient home. On and on, through Argos and other lands, he must wander in search of the Gorgon, with nothing but his strong heart and his stout arm to help him. Yet for himself he feared not, and if his eyes filled with tears, it was only because he thought of his mother Danaê; and he said within himself, 'O my mother, I would that thou wert here. I see the towers of the fair city where Acrisios still is king; I see the home which thou longest to behold, and which now I may not enter; but one day I shall bring thee hither in triumph, when I come to win back my birthright.'

Brightly before his mind rose the vision of the
time to come, as he lay down to rest beneath the
blue sky; but when his eyes were closed in sleep,
there stood before him a vision yet more glorious,
for the lady Athênê was come from the home of
Zeus, to aid the young hero as he set forth on his
weary labour. Her face gleamed with a beauty such
as is not given to the daughters of men.   But
Perseus feared not because of her majesty, for the
soft spell of sleep lay on him; but he heard her
words as she said, ' I am come down from Olympus
where dwells thy father Zeus, to help thee in thy
mighty toil.   Thou art brave of heart and strong
of hand, but thou knowest not which way thou
shouldest go, and thou hast no weapons with which
to slay the Gorgon Medusa.   Many things thou
needest, but only against the freezing stare of the
Gorgon's face can I guard thee now.   On her countenance thou canst not look and live ; and even
when she is dead, one glance of that fearful face
will still turn all mortal things to stone.   So,
when thou drawest nigh to slay her, thine eye must
not rest upon her. Take good heed, then, to thyself, for while they are awake the Gorgon sisters
dread no danger, for the snakes which curl around
their heads warn them of every peril.   Only while
they sleep canst thou approach them ; and the face

of Medusa, in life or in death, thou must never
see. Take then this mirror, into which thou canst
look, and when thou beholdest her image there,
then nerve thy heart and take thine aim, and
carry away with thee the head of the mortal maiden.
Linger not in thy flight, for her sisters will pursue
after thee, and they can neither grow old nor die.'

So Athênê departed from him; and early in the
morning he saw by his side the mirror which she
had given to him; and he said, 'Now I know that
my toil is not in vain, and the help of Athênê is
a pledge of yet more aid in time to come.' So he
journeyed on with a good heart over hill and dale,
across rivers and forests, towards the setting of the
sun. Manfully he toiled on, till sleep weighed heavy
on his eyes, and he lay down to rest on a broad stone
in the evening. Once more before him stood a
glorious form. A burnished helmet glistened on
his head, a golden staff was in his hand, and on
his feet were the golden sandals which bore him
through the air with a flight more swift than the
eagle's. And Perseus heard a voice which said,
'I am Hermes, the messenger of Zeus, and I am
come to arm thee against thine enemies. Take
this sword, which slays all mortal things on which
it may fall,[9] and go on thy way with a cheerful
heart. A weary road yet lies before thee, and for

many a long day must thou wander on before
thou canst have other help in thy mighty toil.
Far away, towards the setting of the sun, lies the
Tartessian land, whence thou shalt see the white-
crested mountains where Atlas holds up the pillars
of the heaven.   There must thou cross the dark
waters, and then thou wilt find thyself in the land
of the Graiæ, who are of kin to the Gorgon sisters,
and thou wilt see no more the glory of Helios, who
gladdens the homes of living men.   Only a faint
light from the far-off sun comes dimly to the
desolate land where, hidden in a gloomy cave, lurk
the hapless Graiæ.[10]   These thou must seek out;
and when thou hast found them, fear them not.
Over their worn and wrinkled faces stream tangled
masses of long grey hair; their voice comes hollow
from their toothless gums, and a single eye is
passed from one to the other when they wish to
look forth from their dismal dwelling.   Seek them
out, for these alone can tell thee what more re-
maineth yet for thee to do.'

When Perseus woke in the morning, the sword
of Hermes lay beside him; and he rose up with
great joy, and said, ' The help of Zeus fails me not;
if more is needed, will he not grant it to me?'   So
onward he went to the Tartessian land, and thence
across the dark sea towards the country of the

Graiæ, till he saw the pillars of Atlas rise afar off into the sky. Then, as he drew nigh to the hills which lie beneath them, he came to a dark cave, and as he stooped to look into it, he fancied that he saw the grey hair which streamed over the shoulders of the Graiæ. Long time he rested on the rocks without the cave, till he knew by their heavy breathing that the sisters were asleep. Then he crept in stealthily, and took the eye which lay beside them, and waited till they should wake. At last, as the faint light from the far-off sun [11] who shines on mortal men reached the cave, he saw them groping for the eye which he had taken ; and presently from their toothless jaws came a hollow voice, which said, ' There is some one near us who is sprung from the children of men ; for of old time we have known that one should come and leave us blind until we did his bidding.' Then Perseus came forth boldly and stood before them and said, ' Daughters of Phorkos and of Kêtô, I know that ye are of kin to the Gorgon sisters, and to these ye must now guide me. Think not to escape by craft or guile, for in my hand is the sword of Hermes, and it slays all living things on which it may fall.' And they answered quickly, ' Slay us not, child of man, for we will deal truly by thee, and tell thee of the things which must be done before thou canst reach the dwelling of the Gorgon sisters. Go hence, along the plain which stretches before thee, then over hill and vale, and forest and desert, till thou comest to the slow-rolling ocean stream; there call on the nymphs who dwell beneath the waters, and they shall rise at thy bidding and tell thee of many things which it is not given to us to know.'

Onwards again he went, across the plain, and over hill and vale, till he came to the ocean which flows lazily round the world of living men. No ray of the pure sunshine pierced the murky air, but the pale yellow light, which broods on the land of the Gorgons, showed to him the dark stream, as he stood on the banks and summoned the nymphs to do his bidding. Presently they stood before him, and greeted him by his name; and they said, 'O Perseus, thou art the first of living men whose feet have trodden this desolate shore. Long time have we known that the will of Zeus would bring thee hither to accomplish the doom of the mortal Medusa. We know the things of which thou art in need, and without us thy toil would in very truth be vain. Thou hast to come near to beings who can see all around them, for the snakes which twist about their heads are their eyes; and here is the helmet of Hades, which will enable thee to draw

nigh to them unseen. Thou hast the sword which
never falls in vain; but without this bag which we
give thee, thou canst not bear away the head the
sight of which changes all mortal things to stone.
And when thy work of death is done on the mortal
maiden, thou must fly from her sisters who cannot
die, and who will follow thee more swiftly than
eagles; and here are the sandals which shall waft
thee through the air more quickly than a dream.
Hasten then, child of Danaê, for we are ready to
bear thee in our hands across the ocean stream.'

So they bare Perseus to the Gorgon land, and
he journeyed on in the pale yellow light which
rests upon it everlastingly.

On that night, in the darkness of their lonesome
dwelling, Medusa spake to her sisters of the doom
which should one day be accomplished; and she
said, 'Sisters, ye care little for the grief whose
image on my face turns all mortal things to stone.
Ye who know not old age or death, know not the
awful weight of my agony, and cannot feel the
signs of the change that is coming. But I know
them. The snakes which twine around my head
warn me not in vain; but they warn me against
perils which I care not now to shun. The wrath
of Athênê, who crushed the faint hopes which
lingered in my heart, left me mortal still, and I

am weary with the woe of the ages that are past.
O sisters, ye know not what it is to pity, but something more ye know what it is to love, for even
in this living tomb we have dwelt together in
peace, and peace is of kin to love.   But hearken
to me now.   Mine eyes are heavy with sleep, and
my heart tells me that the doom is coming, for I
am but a mortal maiden ; and I care not if the
slumber which is stealing on me be. the sleep of
those whose life is done.   Sisters, my lot is happier
at the least than yours ; for he who slays me is my
friend.   I am weary of my woe, and it may be that
better things await me when I am dead.'

But, even as Medusa spake, the faces of Stheino
and Eurualê remained unchanged ; and it seemed
as though for them the words of Medusa were
but an empty sound.   Presently the Gorgon sisters were all asleep.   The deadly snakes lay still
and quiet, and only the breath which hissed from
their mouths was heard throughout the cave.

Then Perseus drew nigh, with the helmet of
Hades [11] on his head, and the sandals of the
nymphs on his feet.   In his right hand was the
sword of Hermes, and in his left the mirror of
Athênê.   Long time he gazed on the image of
Medusa's face, which still showed the wreck of
her ancient beauty; and he said within himself,

'Mortal maiden, well may it be that more than mortal woe should give to thy countenance its deadly power. The hour of thy doom is come; but death to thee must be a boon.' Then the sword of Hermes fell, and the great agony of Medusa was ended. So Perseus cast a veil over the dead face, and bare it away from the cave in the bag which the nymphs gave him on the banks of the slow-rolling ocean.

ANDROMEDA.[13]

TERRIBLE was the rage of the Gorgon sisters
when they woke up from their sleep and saw
that the doom of Medusa had been accomplished.
The snakes hissed as they rose in knotted clusters
round their heads, and the Gorgons gnashed their
teeth in fury, not for any love of the mortal
maiden whose woes were ended, but because a
child of weak and toiling men had dared to
approach the daughters of Phorkos and Kêtô.
Swifter than the eagles they sped from their
gloomy cave; but they sought 'in vain to find
Perseus, for the helmet of Hades was on his head,
and the sandals of the nymphs were bearing him
through the air like a dream. Onwards he went,
not knowing whither he was borne, for he saw but
dimly through the pale yellow light which brooded
on the Gorgon land everlastingly; but presently
he heard a groan as from one in mortal pain, and
before him he beheld a giant form, on whose
head rested the pillars of the heaven; and he
heard a voice, which said, 'Hast thou slain the

Gorgon Medusa, child of man, and art thou come
to rid me of my long woe? Look on me, for I am
Atlas, who rose up with the Titans against the
power of Zeus, when Prometheus fought on his
side; and of old time have I known that for me
is no hope of rest till a mortal man should bring
hither the Gorgon head which can turn all living
things to stone. For so was it shown to me from
Zeus, when he made me bow down beneath the
weight of the brazen heaven. Yet, if thou hast
slain Medusa, Zeus hath been more merciful to
me than to Prometheus who was his friend, for
he lies nailed on the rugged crags of Caucasus,
and only thy child in the third generation shall
scare away the vulture which gnaws his heart,
and set the Titan free. But hasten now, Perseus,
and let me look upon the Gorgon's face, for the
agony of my labour is wellnigh greater than I
can bear.' [14] So Perseus hearkened to the words
of Atlas, and he unveiled before him the dead
face of Medusa. Eagerly he gazed for a moment
on the changeless countenance, as though beneath
the blackness of great horror he yet saw the
wreck of her ancient beauty and pitied her for
her hopeless woe. But in an instant the straining
eyes were closed, the heaving breast was still, the
limbs which trembled with the weight of heaven

were stiff and cold; and it seemed to Perseus, as
he rose again into the pale yellow air, that the
grey hairs which streamed from the giant's head
were like the snow which rests on the peaks of a
great mountain, and that in place of the trembling
limbs he saw only the rents and clefts on a rough
hillside.

Onward yet and higher he sped, he knew not
whither, on the golden sandals, till from the
murky glare of the Gorgon land he passed into a
soft and tender light in which all things wore the
colours of a dream.[15] It was not the light of sun
or moon; for in that land was neither day nor
night. No breeze wafted the light clouds of
morning through the sky, or stirred the leaves of
the forest trees where the golden fruits glistened
the whole year round; but from beneath rose the
echoes of sweet music, as he glided gently down
to the earth. Then he took the helmet of Hades
from off his head, and asked the people whom he
met the name of this happy land; and they said,
' We dwell where the icy breath of Boreas cannot
chill the air or wither our fruits; therefore is our
land called the garden of the Hyperboreans.'
There for a while Perseus rested from his toil;
and all day long he saw the dances of happy
maidens fair as Hêbê and Harmonia, and he

shared the rich banquets at which the people of the land feasted with wreaths of laurel twined around their head. There he rested in a deep peace, for no sound of strife or war can ever break it; and they know nothing of malice and hatred, of sickness, or old age.

But presently Perseus remembered his mother Danaê lying in her prison-house at Seriphos, and he left the garden of the Hyperboreans to return to the world of toiling men; but the people of the land knew only that it lay beyond the slow-rolling ocean stream, and Perseus saw not whither he went as he rose on his golden sandals into the soft and dreamy air. Onwards he went, until far beneath he beheld the ocean river, and once more he saw the light of Helios as he drove his fiery chariot through the heaven. Far away stretched the mighty Libyan plain, and further yet beyond the hills which shut it in he saw the waters of the dark sea, and the white line of foam where the breakers were dashed upon the shore. As he came nearer, he saw the huge rocks which rose out of the heaving waters, and on one of them he beheld a maiden whose limbs were fastened to the stone with chains. The folds of her white robe fluttered in the breeze, and her fair face was worn and wasted with the heat by day

and the cold by night. Then Perseus hastened
to her and stood a long time before her, but she
saw him not, for the helmet of Hades was on his
head, and he watched her there till the tears
started to his eyes for pity. Her hands were
clasped upon her breast, and only the moving of
her lips showed the greatness of her misery.
Higher and higher rose the foaming waters, till
at last the maiden said, ' O Zeus, is there none
whom thou canst send to help me?' Then
Perseus took the helmet in his hand, and stood
before her in all his glorious beauty; and the
maiden knew that she had nothing to fear when
he said, ' Lady, I see that thou art in great
sorrow : tell me who it is that has wronged thee,
and I will avenge thee mightily.' And she
answered, ' Stranger, whoever thou art, I will
trust thee, for thy face tells me that thou art
not one of those who deal falsely. My name is
Andromeda, and my father, Kepheus, is king of
the rich Libyan land; but there is strife between
him and the old man Nereus [16] who dwells with
his daughters in the coral caves beneath the sea;
for, as I grew up in my father's house, my mother
made a vain boast of my beauty, and said that
among all the children of Nereus there was none
so fair as I. So Nereus rose from his coral caves,

L

and went to the king Poseidon, and said, "King
of the broad sea, Cassiopeia hath done a grievous
wrong to me and to my children. I pray thee let
not her people escape for her evil words." Then
Poseidon let loose the waters of the sea, and they
rushed in over the Libyan plains till only the
hills which shut it in remained above them, and a
mighty monster came forth and devoured all the
fruits of the land. In grief and terror the
people fell down before my father, Kepheus, and
he sent to the home of Ammon [17] to ask what
he should do for the plague of waters and for the
savage beast who vexed them; and soon the answer
came that he must chain up his daughter on a
rock, till the beast came and took her for his prey.
So they fastened me here to this desolate crag, and
each day the monster comes nearer as the waters
rise; and soon, I think, they will place me within
his reach.' Then Perseus cheered her with kindly
words, and said, 'Maiden, I am Perseus, to whom
Zeus has given the power to do great things. I
hold in my hand the sword of Hermes, which has
slain the Gorgon Medusa, and I am bearing to
Polydectes, who rules in Seriphos, the head which
turns all who look on it into stone. Fear not,
then, Andromeda. I will do battle with the monster,
and, when thy foes are vanquished, I will sue for

the boon of thy love.' A soft blush as of great
gladness came over the pale cheek of Andromeda
as she answered, 'O Perseus, why should I hide
from thee my joy? Thou hast come to me like
the light of morning when it breaks on a woful
night.' But, even as she spake, the rage of the
waves waxed greater, and the waters rose higher
and higher, lashing the rocks in their fury, and
the hollow roar of the monster was heard as he
hastened to seize his prey. Presently by the
maiden's side he saw a glorious form with the
flashing sword in his hand, and he lashed the
waters in fiercer anger. Then Perseus went forth
to meet him, and he held aloft the sword which
Hermes gave to him, and said, 'Sword of Phœbus,
let thy stroke be sure, for thou smitest the enemy
of the helpless.' So the sword fell, and the blood
of the mighty beast reddened the waters of the
green sea.

In gladness of heart Perseus led the maiden to
the halls of Kepheus, and he said, 'O king, I
have slain the monster to whom thou didst give
thy child for a prey: let her go with me now
to other lands, if she gainsay me not.' But
Kepheus answered, 'Tarry with us yet awhile, and
the marriage feast shall be made ready, if indeed
thou must hasten away from the Libyan land.'

So, at the banquet, by the side of Perseus sate the beautiful Andromeda; but there arose a fierce strife, for Phineus had come to the feast, and it angered him that another should have for his wife the maiden whom he had sought to make his bride. Deeper and fiercer grew his rage, as he looked on the face of Perseus, till at last he spake evil words of the stranger who had taken away the prize which should have been his own. But Perseus said calmly, 'Why, then, didst thou not slay the monster thyself and set the maiden free?' When Phineus heard these words, his rage almost choked him, and he charged his people to draw their swords and slay Perseus. Wildly rose the din in the banquet-hall, but Perseus unveiled the Gorgon's face, and Phineus and all his people were frozen into stone.

Then, in the still silence, Perseus bare away Andromeda from her father's home; and when they had wandered through many lands, they came at length to Seriphos. Once more Danaê looked on the face of her son, and said, 'My child, the months have rolled wearily since I bade thee farewell; but sure I am that my prayer has been heard, for thy face is as the face of one who comes back a conqueror from battle.' Then Perseus said, 'Yea, my mother, the help of Zeus has never failed me. When the eastern breeze carried me hence to the Argive land, my heart was full of sorrow, because I saw the city which thou didst yearn to see, and the home which thou couldst not enter; and I vowed a vow to bring thee back in triumph when I came to claim my birthright. That evening, as I slept, the lady Athênê came to me from the home of Zeus, and gave me a mirror so that I might take the Gorgon's head without looking on the face which turns everything into stone; and yet another night, Hermes stood before me, and gave me the sword whose stroke never fails, and the Graiæ told me where I should find the nymphs who gave me the helmet of Hades, and the bag which has borne hither the Gorgon's head, and the golden sandals which carried me like a dream over land and sea. O my mother, I have done wondrous things by the aid of Zeus. By me the doom of Medusa has been accomplished; and I think that the words which thou didst speak were true, for the image of the Gorgon's face, which I saw in Athênê's mirror, was as the countenance of one whose beauty has been marred by a woful agony; and whenever I have looked since on that image, it has seemed to me as though it wore the look of one who rested in death from a mighty pain.

So, as the giant Atlas looked on that grief-stricken
brow, he felt no more the weight of the heaven
as it rested on him; and the grey hair which
streamed from his head seemed to me, when I
left him, like the snow which clothes the moun-
tain-tops in winter. So, when from the happy
gardens of the Hyperboreans I came to the rich
Libyan plain and had killed the monster who
sought to slay Andromeda, the Gorgon's face
turned Phineus and his people into stone, when
they sought to slay me because I had won her
love.'   Then Danaê answered the questions of
Perseus, and told him how Polydectes had vexed
her with his evil words, and how Dictys [16] alone
had shielded her from his brother. And Perseus
bade Danaê be of good cheer, because the recompense of Polydectes was nigh at hand.

There was joy and feasting in Seriphos when
the news was spread abroad that Perseus had
brought back for the king the head of the Gorgon
Medusa; and Polydectes made a great feast, and
the wine sparkled in the goblets as the minstrels
sang of the great deeds of the son of Danaê.
Then Perseus told them of all that Hermes and
Athênê had done for him. He showed them the
helmet of Hades, and the golden sandals, and the
unerring sword, and then he unveiled the face of

Medusa before Polydectes and the men who had
aided him against his mother Danaê. So Perseus
looked upon them, as they sate at the rich banquet, stiff and cold as stone, and he felt that his
mighty work was ended. Then, at his prayer,
came Hermes, the messenger of Zeus, and Perseus
gave him back the helmet of Hades, and the
sword which had slain the Gorgon, and the sandals which had borne him through the air like a
dream. And Hermes gave the helmet again to
Hades, and the sandals to the ocean nymphs; but
Athênê took the Gorgon's head, and it was placed
upon her shield.

Then Perseus spake to Danaê, and said, 'My
mother, it is time for thee to go home. The
Gorgon's face has turned Polydectes and his people
into stone, and Dictys rules in Seriphos.' So
once more the white sails were filled with the
eastern breeze, and Danaê saw once more the
Argive land. From city to city spread the tidings
that Perseus was come, who had slain the Gorgon,
and the youths and maidens sang 'Io Pœan' as
they led the conqueror to the halls of Acrisios.

:

ACRISIOS.

THE shouts of 'Io Pæan' reached the ear of
Acrisios, as he sat in his lonely hall, marvel-
ling at the strange things which must have hap-
pened to waken the sounds of joy and triumph;
for, since the day when Danaê was cast forth
with her babe on the raging waters, the glory of
war had departed from Argos, and it seemed as
though all the chieftains had lost their ancient
strength and courage. But the wonder of Acrisios
was changed to a great fear when they told him
that his child Danaê was coming home, and that
the hero Perseus had rescued her from Polydectes,
the king of Seriphos. The memory of all the
wrong which he had done to his daughter tor-
mented him, and still in his mind dwelt the words
of warning which came from Phœbus Apollo that
he should one day be slain by the hands of her
son; so that, as he looked forth on the sky, it
seemed to him as though he should see the sun
again no more.

In haste and terror Acrisios fled from his home.

He tarried not to hear the voice of Danaê; he
stayed not to look on the face of Perseus, and to
see that the hero who had slain the Gorgon bare
him no malice for the wrongs of the former days.
Quickly he sped over hill and dale, across river
and forest, till he came to the house of Teutamidas, the great chieftain who ruled in Larissa.

The feast was spread in the banquet-hall, and
the Thessalian minstrels sang of the brave deeds
of Perseus, for even thither had his fame reached
already. They told how from the land of toiling
men he had passed to the country of the Graiæ
and the Gorgons, how he had slain the mortal
Medusa and stiffened the giant Atlas into stone;
and then they sang how with the sword of Hermes
he smote the mighty beast which ravaged the
Libyan land, and won Andromeda to be his bride.
Then Teutamidas spake and said, 'My friend, I
envy thee for thy happy lot, for not often in the
world of men may fathers reap such glory from
their children as thou hast won from Perseus.
In the ages to come, men shall love to tell of his
great and good deeds, and from him shall spring
mighty chieftains, who shall be stirred up to a
purer courage when they remember how Perseus
toiled and triumphed before them. And now tell
me, friend, wherefore thou hast come hither?

Thy cheek is pale, and thy hand trembles; and I think not that it can be from the weight of years, for thy old age is yet but green, and thou mayest hope still to see the children of Perseus clustering around thy knees.'

But Acrisios could scarcely answer for shame and fear; for he cared not to tell Teutamidas of the wrongs which he had done to Danaê. So he said hastily that he had fled from a great danger, for the warning of Phœbus was that he should be slain by his daughter's son. And Teutamidas said, ' Has thy daughter yet another son?' And then Acrisios was forced to own that he had fled from the hero Perseus. But the face of Teutamidas flushed with anger as he said, 'O shame, that thou shouldest flee from him who ought to be thy glory and thy pride! Everywhere men speak of the goodness and the truth of Perseus, and I will not believe that he bears thee a grudge for anything that thou hast done to him. Nay, thou doest to him a more grievous wrong in shunning him now than when thou didst cast him forth in his mother's arms upon the angry sea.' So he pleaded with Acrisios for Perseus, until he spoke the word that Danaê and her child might come to the great games which were to be held on the plain before Larissa.[19]

With shouts of 'Io Pæan' the youths and
maidens went out before Perseus as he passed
from the city of Acrisios to go to Larissa, and
everywhere as he journeyed, from town and village the people came forth to greet the bright
hero and the beautiful Andromeda, whom he had
saved from the Libyan dragon.   Onwards they
went, spreading gladness everywhere, till the cold
heart of Acrisios himself was touched with a feeling of strange joy, as he saw the band of youths
and maidens who came before them to the house
of Teutamidas.   So once more his child Danaê
stood before him, beautiful still, although the
sorrows of twenty years had dimmed the brightness of her eye, and the merry laugh of her
youth was gone.   Once more he looked on the face
of Perseus, and he listened to the kindly greet-
ing of the hero whom he had wronged in the
days of his helpless childhood.   But he marvelled yet more at the beauty of Andromeda, and
he thought within himself that throughout the
wide earth were none so fair as Perseus and the
wife whom he had won with the sword of Hermes.

Then, as they looked on the chiefs who strove
together in the games, the shouting of the crowd
told at the end of each that Perseus was the conqueror.   At last they stood forth to see which

should have most strength of arm in hurling the quoit; and, when Perseus aimed at the mark, the quoit swerved aside and smote Acrisios on the head; and the warning of Phœbus Apollo was accomplished.

Great was the sorrow of Teutamidas and his people as the chieftain of Argos lay dead before them; but deeper still and more bitter was the grief of Perseus for the deed which he had unwittingly done; and he said, 'O Zeus, I have striven to keep my hands clean and to deal truly, and a hard recompense hast thou given me.'

So they went back mourning to Argos; but although he strove heartily to rule his people well, the grief of Perseus could not be lessened while he dwelt in the house of Acrisios. So he sent a messenger to his kinsman Megapenthes [20] who ruled at Tiryns, and said, 'Come thou and rule in Argos, and I will come and dwell among thy people.' So Perseus dwelt at Tiryns, and the men of the city rejoiced that he had come to rule over them. Thus the months and years went quickly by, as Perseus strove with all his might to make his people happy and to guard them against their enemies. At his bidding, the Cyclopes came from the far-off Lykian land, and built the mighty walls which gird the city round

about; and they helped him to build yet another
city, which grew in after-times to be even greater
and mightier than Tiryns. So rose the walls of
Mykênæ,[21] and there too the people loved and
honoured Perseus more for his just dealing than
for all the deeds which he had done with the
sword of Hermes. At last the time came when
the hero must rest from his long toil; but as they
looked on his face, bright and beautiful even in
death, the minstrels said, ' We shall hear his voice
no more, but the name of Perseus shall never
die.'

HERMES.[13]

EARLY in the morning, long ago, in a cave of the great Kyllenian hill, lay the new-born Hermes, the son of Zeus and Maia. The cradle-clothes were scarcely stirred by his soft breathing, while he slept as peacefully as the children of mortal mothers. But the sun had not driven his fiery chariot over half the heaven, when the babe arose from his sacred cradle and stepped forth from the dark cavern. Before the threshold a tortoise fed lazily on the grass; and when the child saw it, he laughed merrily. 'Ah! this is luck indeed,' he said; 'whence hast thou come, pretty creature, with thy bright speckled shell? Thou art mine now, and I must take thee into my cave. It is better to be under shelter than out of doors; and though there may be some use in thee while thou livest, it will comfort thee to think that thou wilt sing sweetly when thou art dead.'

So the child Hermes took up his treasure in both arms, and carried it into the cavern. There he took an iron probe, and pierced out the life of the tortoise; and quick as thought, he drilled holes in its shell, and fixed in them reed-canes. Then across the shell he fastened a piece of ox-hide, and with seven sheep-gut cords he finished the making of his lyre. Presently he struck it with the bow, and a wave of sweet music swelled out upon the air. Like the merry songs of youths and maidens, as they sport in village feasts, rose the song of the child Hermes; and his eyes laughed slily as he sang of the loves of Zeus and Maia, and how he himself was born of the mighty race of the gods. Still he sang on, telling of all that he saw around him in the glittering home of the nymph, his mother. But all the while, as he sang, his mind was pondering on other things; and when the song was ended, he went forth from the cave, like a thief in the night, on his wily errand.

The sun was hastening down the slope of heaven with his chariot and horses to the slow-rolling stream of ocean, as Hermes came to the shadowy hills of Pieria, where the cattle of the gods feed in their large pastures. There he took fifty from the herd, and made ready to drive them to the Kyl-lenian hill.[23] But before him lay vast plains of sand; and, therefore, lest the track of the cattle should tell the tale of his thieving, he drove the

beasts round about by crooked paths, until it
seemed as though they had gone to the place from
which he had stolen them.[34]   He had taken good
care that his own footsteps should not betray him,
for with branches of tamarisk and myrtle, well
twisted with their leaves, he hastily made himself
sandals, and sped away from Pieria. One man
alone saw him, a very old man, who was working
in his vineyard on the sunny plain of Onchêstos.
To him Hermes went quickly, and said, ' Old
man, thou wilt have plenty of wine when these
roots come all into bearing trim. Meanwhile,
keep a wise head on thy crumpled shoulders, and
take heed not to remember more than may be
convenient.'

Onwards, over dark hills, and through sounding
dells, and across flowery plains, hastened the child
Hermes, driving his flock before him.   The night
waxed and waned, and the moon had climbed to
her watchtower in the heaven, when, in the flush
of early morning, Hermes reached the banks of
the great Alpheian stream.   There he turned his
herd to feed on the grassy plain, while he gathered
logs of wood, and, rubbing two sticks together,
kindled the first flame that burned upon the earth
where dwell the sons of men.[35]   The smoke went
up to the heaven, and the flame crackled fiercely

beneath it, as Hermes brought forth two of the
herd, and, tumbling them on their back, pierced
out the life of both. Their hides he placed on
the hard rock; their flesh he cut up into twelve
portions; and so Hermes hath the right of order-
ing all sacrifices[26] which the children of men offer
to the undying gods. But he ate not of the flesh
or fat, although hunger sorely pressed him;[27] and
he burnt the bones in the fire, and tossed his
tamarisk sandals into the swift stream of Alpheios.
Then he quenched the fire, and with all his might
trampled down the ashes, until the pale moon
rose up again in the sky. So he sped on his way
to Kyllênê. Neither god nor man saw him as he
went, nor did the dogs bark. Early in the morning he reached his mother's cave, and darted
through the keyhole of the door, softly as a summer breeze. Without a sound, his little feet paced
the stony floor, till he reached his cradle and lay
down, playing like a babe among the clothes with
his left hand, while his right held the tortoise-lyre
hidden underneath them.

But, wily though he was, he could not cheat
his mother. To his cradle she came and said,
'Whither hast thou wandered in the dark night?
Crafty rogue, mischief will be thy ruin. The son
of Leto will soon be here, and bear thee away

M

bound in chains not easily shaken off. Out of my
sight, little wretch, born to worry the blessed gods
and plague the race of men!' 'Mother,' said
Hermes gently, 'why talk thus to me, as though I
were like mortal babes, a poor cowering thing, to
cry for a little scolding? I know thy interest and
mine: why should we stay here in this wretched
cave, with never a gift or a feast to cheer our
hearts? I shall not stay. It is pleasanter to
banquet with the gods than to dwell in a cavern
in draughts of whistling wind. I shall try my
luck against Apollo, for I mean to be his peer;
and if he will not suffer me, and if Zeus my father
takes not up my cause, I will see what I can do
for myself, by going to the shrine of Pytho and
stealing thence the tripods and cauldrons, the iron
vessels and glittering robes. If I may not have
honour in Olympus, I can at least be the prince of
thieves.'

Meanwhile, as they talked together, Eôs rose
up from the deep ocean stream, and her tender
light flushed across the sky, while Apollo hastened to Onchestos and the holy grove of Poseidon.
There the old man was at work in his vineyard,
and to him Phœbus went quickly and said, 'Friend
hedger, I am come from Pieria looking for my
cows. Fifty of th m have been driven away, and

the bull has been left behind with the four dogs
who guarded them as faithfully as men. Tell me,
old man, hast thou seen any one with these cows,
on the road?' But the old man said that it
would be a hard matter to tell of all that he might
chance to see. 'Many travellers journey on this
road, some with evil thoughts, some with good; I
cannot well remember all. This only I know,
that yesterday, from the rising up of the sun to
its setting, I was digging in my vineyard; and I
think, but I am not sure, that I saw a child with
a herd of cattle. A babe he was, and he held a
staff in his hand, and, as he went, he wandered
strangely from the path on either side.'

Then Phœbus stayed not to hear more, for now
he knew of a surety that the new-born son of Zeus
had done him the mischief. Wrapped in a purple
mist, he hastened to beautiful Pylos and came on
the track of cattle. 'O Zeus,' he cried, 'this is
indeed a marvel. I see the footprints of cattle,
but they are marked as though the cattle were
going to the asphodel meadow, not away from it.
Of man or woman, of wolf, bear, or lion, I spy not
a single trace. Only here and there I behold
the footprint of some strange monster, who has
left his mark at random on either side of the road.'
So on he sped to the woody heights of Kyllênê,

and stood on the doorstep of Maia's cave. Straightway the child Hermes nestled under the cradle-
clothes in fear, like a new-born babe asleep. But,
seeing through all his craft, Phœbus looked steadily
through all the cave and opened three secret places
full of the food and drink of the gods, and full
also of gold and silver and raiment; but not a cow
was in any of them. At last he fixed his eyes
sternly on the child and said, 'Wily babe, where
are my cows? If thou wilt not tell me, there
will be strife between us; and then I shall hurl
thee down to the gloomy Tartarus, to the land
of darkness whence neither thy father nor
thy mother can bring thee back, and where
thy kingdom shall be only over the ghosts of
men.' 'Ah!' said Hermes, 'these are dreadful
words indeed; but why dost thou chide me thus,
or come here to look for cows? I have not
seen or heard of them, nor has any one told me
of them. I cannot tell where they are, or get the
reward, if any were promised, for discovering
them. This is no work of mine; what do I care
for but for sleeping and sucking and playing with
my cradle-clothes and being washed in warm
water? My friend, it will be much better that
no one should hear of such a silly quarrel. The
undying gods would laugh at the very thought of

a little babe leaving its cradle to run after cows. I was born but yesterday. My feet are soft, and the ground is hard. But if it be any comfort to thee, I will swear by my father's head (and that is a very great oath) that I have not done this deed, or seen any one else steal your cows, and that I do not know what cows are.'

As he spoke he looked stealthily from one side to the other, while his eyes winked slily, and he made a long soft whistling sound, as if the words of Phœbus had amused him mightily.. 'Well, friend,' said Apollo, with a smile, ' thou wilt break into many a house, I see, and thy followers after thee; and thy fancy for beef will set many a herdsman grieving. But come down from the cradle, or this sleep will be thy last. Only this honour can I promise thee, to be called the prince of thieves for ever.' So without more ado Phœbus caught up the babe in his arms, but Hermes gave so mighty a sneeze that he quickly let him fall, and said to him gravely, ' This is the sign that I shall find my cows: show me, then, the way.' In great fear Hermes started up and pulled the cradle-clothes over both his ears, as he said, ' Cruel god, what dost thou seek to do with me? Why worry me thus about cows? I would there were not a cow in all the earth. I stole them not, nor have I seen any one steal the cows, whatever things cows may be. I know nothing but their name. But come; Zeus must decide the quarrel between us.'

Thus each with his own purpose spake to the other, and their minds grew all the darker, for Phœbus sought only to know where his cows might be, while Hermes strove only to cheat him. So they went quickly and sulkily on, the babe first, and Phœbus following after him, till they came to the heights of Olympus and the home of the mighty Zeus. There he sat on the throne of judgment, and all the undying gods stood around them. Before them in the midst stood Phœbus and the child Hermes, and Zeus said, 'Thou hast brought a fine booty after thy hunt to-day, Phœbus—a child of a day old. A fine matter is this to put before the gods.'

'My father,' said Apollo quickly, 'I have a tale to tell which will show that I am not the only plunderer. After a weary search, I found this babe in the cave of Kyllênê; and a thief he is such as I have never seen whether among gods or men. Yester eve he stole my cattle from the meadow, and drove them straight towards Pylos to the shore of the sounding sea. The tracks left were such that gods and men might well marvel at them. The footprints of the cows on the sand

were as though they were going to my meadows,
not away from them; his own footmarks beggar
all words, as if he had gone neither on his feet nor
on his hands, and as if the oak tops had suddenly
taken to walking. So was it on the sandy soil;
and after this was passed, there remained no
marks at all. But an old man saw him driving
them on the road to Pylos. There he shut up the
cattle at his leisure, and, going to his mother's
cave, lay down in his cradle like a spark in a mass
of cinders, which an eagle could scarcely spy out.
When I taxed him with the theft, he boldly denied
it, and told me that he had not seen the cows or
heard aught of them, and could not get the reward
if one were offered for restoring them.'

So the words of Phœbus were ended, and the
child Hermes made obeisance to Zeus, the lord of
all the gods, and said, 'Father Zeus, I shall tell
thee the truth, for I am a very truthful being, and
I know not how to tell a lie. This morning, when
the sun was but newly risen, Phœbus came to my
mother's cave, looking for cows. He brought no
witnesses; he urged me by force to confess; he
threatened to hurl me into the abyss of Tartarus.[28]
Yet he has all the strength of early manhood,
while I, as he knows, was born but yesterday, and
am not in the least like a cattle-reiver. Believe

me (by thy love for me, thy child). that I have not brought these cows home, or passed beyond my mother's threshold. This is strict truth, Nay, by Helios and the other gods, I swear that I love thee and have respect for Phœbus. Thou knowest that I am guiltless, and, if thou wilt, I will also swear it. But, spite of all his strength, I will avenge myself some day on Phœbus for his unkindness; and then help thou the weaker.'

So spake Hermes, winking his eyes and holding the clothes to his shoulders; and Zeus laughed aloud at the wiliness of the babe, and bade Phœbus and the child be friends. Then he bowed his head and charged Hermes to show the spot where he had hidden the cattle, and the child obeyed, for none may despise that sign and live. To Pylos they hastened and to the broad stream of Alpheios, and from the fold Hermes drove forth the cattle. But as he stood apart, Apollo beheld the hides flung on the rock, and he asked Hermes, ' How wast thou able, cunning rogue, to flay two cows, thou a child but one day old? I fear thy might in time to come, and I cannot let thee live.' Again he seized the child, and bound him fast with willow bands, but the child tore them from his body like flax, so that Phœbus marvelled greatly. In

vain Hermes sought a place wherein to hide himself, and great fear came upon him till he thought
of his tortoise-lyre. With his bow he touched
the strings, and the wave of song swelled out
upon the air more full and sweet than ever. He
sang of the undying gods and the dark earth,
how it was made at the first, and how to each of
the gods his own appointed portion was given,
till the heart of Apollo was filled with a mighty
longing, and he spake to Hermes, and said,
'Cattle-reiver, wily rogue, thy song is worth fifty
head of cattle. We will settle our strife by-and-
by. Meanwhile, tell me, was this wondrous gift
of song born with thee, or hast thou it as a gift
from any god or mortal man? Never on Olympus,
from those who cannot die, have I heard such
strains as these. They who hear thee may have
what they will, be it mirth, or love, or sleep.
Great is thy power, and great shall be thy renown,
and by my cornel staff I swear that I will not
stand in the way of thy honour or deceive thee in
anywise.'

Then said Hermes, 'I grudge thee not my
skill, son of Letó, for I seek but thy friendship.
Yet thy gifts from Zeus are great. Thou knowest
his mind, thou canst declare his will, and reveal
what is stored up in time to come for undying

gods or mortal men. This knowledge I fain would
have. But my power of song shall this day be
thine. Take my lyre, the soother of the wearied,
the sweet companion in hours of sorrow or of
feasting. To those who come skilled in its language, it can discourse sweetly of all things, and
drive away all thoughts that annoy and cares that
vex the soul. To those who touch it, not knowing
how to draw forth its speech, it will babble strange
nonsense, and rave with uncertain moanings. But
thy knowledge is born with thee, and so my lyre
is thine. Wherefore now let us feed the herds
together, and with our care they shall thrive and
multiply. There is no more cause for anger.'

So saying, the babe held out the lyre, and
Phœbus Apollo took it. In his turn he gave to
the child Hermes a glittering scourge, with charge
over his flocks and herds. Then, touching the
chords of the lyre, he filled the air with sweet
music, and they both took their way to Olympus,
and Zeus was glad at heart to see that the wrath
of Apollo had passed away. But Phœbus dreaded
yet the wiles of Hermes, and said, 'I fear me
much, child of Maia, that in time to come thou
mayest steal both my harp and my bow, and take
away my honour among men. Come now, and
swear to me by the dark water of Styx that thou

wilt never do me wrong.' Then Hermes bowed
his head, and sware never to steal anything from
Apollo, and never to lay hands on his holy shrine;
and Phœbus sware that of all the undying gods
there should be none so dear to him as Hermes.
'And of this love,' he said, 'I will give thee a
pledge. My golden rod shall guard thee, and
teach thee all that Zeus may say to me for the
well or ill doing of gods or men. But the higher
knowledge for which thou didst pray may not be
thine; for that is hidden in the mind of Zeus,
and I have sworn a great oath that none shall
learn it from me. But the man who comes to me
with true signs, I will never deceive; and he who
puts trust in false omens and then comes to in-
quire at my shrine,[29] shall be answered according to
his folly, but his offering shall go into my treasure-
house. Yet further, son of Maia, in the clefts of
Parnassus far away dwell the winged Thriæ,[30] who
taught me long ago the secret things of times to
come. Go thou then to the three sisters, and
thus shalt thou test them. If they have eaten of
the honeycomb before they speak, they will answer thee truly; but if they lack the sweet food
of the gods, they will seek to lead astray those
who come to them. These I give thee for thy
counsellors; only follow them warily; and have

thou dominion over all flocks and herds, and over all living things that feed on the wide earth; and be thou the guide to lead the souls of mortal men to the dark kingdom of Hades.'

So was the love of Apollo for Hermes made sure; and Hermes hath his place amongst all the deathless gods and dying men. Nevertheless, the sons of men have from him no great gain, for all night long he vexes them with his treacherous wiles.[31]

IAMOS.

ON the banks of Alpheios, Evadnê watched
over her new-born babe, till she fled away
because she feared the wrath of Æpytos, who
ruled in Phæsana. The tears streamed down her
cheeks as she prayed to Phœbus Apollo who
dwells at Delphi, and said, 'Lord of the bright
day, look on thy child, and guard him when he
lies forsaken, for I may no longer tarry near him.'
So Evadnê fled away ; and Phœbus sent two serpents, who fed the babe with honey as he lay
amid the flowers which clustered round him.
And ever more and more, through all the land
went forth the saying of Phœbus, that the child
of Evadnê should grow up mighty in wisdom and
in the power of telling the things that should
happen in the time to come. Then Æpytos asked
of all who dwelt in his house to tell him where
he might find the son of Evadnê. But they knew
not where the child lay, for the serpents had
hidden him far away in a thicket, where the wild
flowers sheltered him from wind and heat. Long

time they searched amid the tall reeds which clothe the banks of Alpheios, until at last they found the babe lying on a bed of violets. So Æpytos took the child and called his name Iamos, and he grew up brave and wise of heart, pondering well the signs of coming grief and joy, and the tokens of hidden things which he saw in the heaven above him or on the wide earth beneath. He spake but little to the youths and maidens who dwelt in the house of Æpytos, but he wandered on the bare hills or by the stream side, musing on many things. And so it came to pass that one night, when the stars glimmered softly in the sky, Iamos plunged beneath the waters of Alpheios, and prayed to Phœbus who dwells at Delphi, and to Poseidon, the lord of the broad sea; and he besought them to open his eyes, that he might reveal to the sons of men the things which of themselves they could not see. Then they led him away to the high rocks which look down on the plain of Pisa, and they said, 'Look yonder, child of Evadné, where the white stream of Alpheios winds its way gently to the sea. Here, in the days which are to come, Heracles, the son of the mighty Zeus, shall gather together the sons of Hellen, and give them in the solemn games the mightiest of all bonds;[33] hither shall

they come to know the will of Zeus, and here
shall it be thy work and the work of thy children
to read to them the signs which of themselves
they cannot understand.' Then Phœbus Apollo
touched his ears, and straightway the voices of
the birds spake to him clearly of the things which
were to come, and he heard their words as a man
listens to the speech of his friend. So Iamos
prospered exceedingly, for the men of all the
Argive land sought aid from his wisdom, and laid
rich gifts at his feet. And he taught his children
after him to speak the truth and to deal truly, so
that none envied their great wealth, and all men
spake well of the wise children of Iamos.

SKYLLA.

FROM the turret of her father's house, Skylla, the daughter of Nisos, watched the ships of king Minos,[88] as they drew near from the island of Crete. Their white sails, and the spears of the Cretan warriors, sparkled in the sunshine, as the crested waves rose and fell, carrying the long billows to the shore. As she watched the goodly sight, Skylla thought sadly of the days that were gone, when her father had sojourned as a guest in the halls of king Minos, and she had looked on his face as on the face of a friend. But now there was strife between the chieftains of Crete and Megara, for Androgeôs, the son of Minos, had been slain by evil men as he journeyed from Megara to Athens, and Minos was come hither with his warriors to demand the price of his blood. But when the herald came with the message of Minos, the face of Nisos the king flushed with anger, as he said, 'Go thy way to him that sent thee, and tell him that he who is guarded by the undying gods cares not for the wrath of men

whose spears shall be snapped like bulrushes.'
Then said the herald, 'I cannot read thy riddle,
chieftain of Megara; but the blood of the gods
runs in the veins of Minos, and it cannot be that
the son of Europa shall fall under the hands of
thee or of thy people.'

The sun went down in a flood of golden glory
behind the purple heights of Geraneia; and as
the mists of evening fell upon the land, the warriors of Minos made ready for the onset on the
morrow. But when the light of Eôs flushed the
eastern sky, and the men of Crete went forth to
the battle, their strength and their brave deeds
availed them nothing, for the arms of the mightiest
became weak as the hands of a little child, because
the secret spell, in which lay the strength of the
undying gods, guarded the city of Nisos. And so
it came to pass that, as day by day they fought in
vain against the walls of Megara, the spirit of the
men of Crete waxed feeble, and many said that
they came not thither to fight against the deathless gods.

But each day as Minos led his men against the
city, the daughter of Nisos had looked forth from
her turret, and she saw his face, beautiful as in
the days when she had sojourned in his house at
Gnossos, and flushed with the pride and eagerness

N

of war. Then the heart of Skylla was filled with a
strange love, and she spake musingly within herself,
'To what end is this strife of armed men? Love
is beyond all treasures, and brighter for me than
the love of others would be one kindly look from
the bright son of Europa. I know the spell which
keeps the city of the Megarians; and where is the
evil of the deed, if I take the purple lock of hair
which the gods have given to my father as a
pledge that, so long as it remains untouched, no
harm shall befall his people? If I give it to
Minos, the struggle is ended, and it may be that I
shall win his love.'

So, when the darkness of night fell again upon
the earth, and all the sons of men were buried in
a deep sleep, Skylla entered stealthily into her
father's chamber, and shore off the purple lock in
which lay his strength and the strength of his
people. Then, as the tints of early morning stole
across the dark heavens, the watchman of the
Cretans beheld the form of a woman as she drew
nigh to them and bade them lead her to the tent
of king Minos. When she was brought before
him, with downcast face she bowed herself to the
earth and said, 'I have sojourned in thy halls in
the days that are gone, when there was peace
between thee and the house of my father Nisos.

O Minos, peace is better than war, and of all treasures the most precious is love. Look on me then
gently, as in the former days, for at a great price
do I seek thy kindness. In this purple lock is
the strength of my father and of his people.'
Then a strange smile passed over the face of
Minos, as he said, 'The gifts of fair maidens must
not be lightly cast aside; the requital shall be
made when the turmoil of strife is ended.'

With a mighty shout the Cretan warriors went
forth to the onset as the fiery horses of Helios
rose up with his chariot into the kindled heaven.
Straightway the walls of Megara fell, and the men
of Crete burst into the house of Nisos. So the city
was taken, and Minos made ready to go against
the men of Athens, for on them also he sought
to take vengeance for the death of his son Andro-
geos. But even as he hastened to his ship, Skylla
stood before him on the sea-shore. 'Thy victory
is from me,' she said; 'where is the requital of
my gift?' Then Minos answered, 'She who cares
not for the father that has cherished her has her
own reward; and the gift which thou didst bring
me is beyond human recompense.' The light
southern breeze swelled the outspread sail, and
the ship of Minos danced gaily over the rippling
waters. For a moment the daughter of Nisos

stood musing on the shore. Then she stretched forth her arms, as, with a low cry of bitter anguish, she said, ' O Love, thy sting is cruel; and my life dies poisoned by the smile of Aphroditê!' So the waters closed over the daughter of Nisos, as she plunged into the blue depths; but the strife which vexes the sons of men follows her still, when the eagle swoops down from the cloud for his prey in the salt sea.[34]

DIONYSOS.

IN the dark land beneath the earth, where
wander the ghosts of men, lay Semelê, the
daughter of Cadmus, while her child Dionysos
grew up full of strength and beauty on the flowery
plain of Orchomenos. But the wrath of the lady
Hêrê still burned alike against the mother and the
child. No pity felt she for the hapless maiden
whom the fiery lightning of Zeus had slain; and
so in the prison-house of Hades Semelê mourned
for the love which she had lost, waiting till her
child should lead her forth to the banquet of the
gods. But for him the wiles of Hêrê boded long
toil and grievous peril. On the land and on the
sea strange things befell him, but from all dangers
his own strong arm and the love of Zeus, his
father, rescued him. Thus throughout the land
men spake of his beauty and his strength, and
said that he was worthy to be the child of the
maiden who had dared to look on the majesty
of Zeus. At length the days of his youth were
ended, and a great yearning filled his heart to

wander through the earth and behold the cities
and the ways of men. So from Orchomenos
Dionysos journeyed to the sea-shore, and he stood
on a jutting rock to gaze on the tumbling waters.
The glad music of the waves fell upon his ear
and filled his soul with a wild joy. His dark locks
streamed gloriously over his shoulders, and his
purple robe rustled in the soft summer breeze.
Before him on the blue waters the ships danced
merrily in the sparkling sunlight, as they hastened from shore to shore on the errands of war
or peace. Presently a ship drew near to the
beach. Her white sail was lowered hastily to
the deck, and five of her crew leaped out and
plunged through the sea-foam to the shore, near
the rock on which stood Dionysos. 'Come with
us,' they said, with rough voices, as they seized
him in their brawny arms. 'It is not every day
that Tyrrhenian mariners fall in with youths like
thee.' With rude jests they dragged him to the
ship, and there made ready to bind him. 'A
brave youth and fair he is,' they said; 'we shall
not lack bidders when we put forth our goods for
sale.' So round his limbs they fastened stout
withy bands, but they fell from off him as withered
leaves fall from trees in autumn; and a careless
smile played on his face as he sat down and looked

calmly on the robbers who stood before him.
Then on a sudden the voice of the helmsman
was heard as he shouted, 'Fools, what do ye?
The wrath of Zeus is hurrying you to your doom.
This youth is not of mortal race; and who can
tell which of the undying gods has put on this
beautiful form? Send him straightway from the
ship in peace, if ye fear not a deadly storm as
we cross the open sea.' Loud laughed the crew,
as their chief answered jeeringly, 'Look out for
the breeze, wise helmsman, and draw up the sail
to the wind. That is more thy task than to busy
thyself with our doings. Fear not for the boy.
The withy bands were but weak; it is no great
marvel that he shook them off. He shall go with
us, and before we reach Egypt or Cyprus, or the
land of the Hyperboreans, doubtless he will tell
us his name and the name of his father and
his mother. Fear not; we have found a godsend.'

So the sail was drawn up to the mast, and it
swelled proudly before the breeze as the ship
dashed through the crested waves. And still the
sun shone brightly down on the water, and the
soft white clouds floated lazily in the heaven, as the
mighty Dionysos began to show signs and wonders
before the robbers who had seized him. Over the
deck ran a stream of purple wine, and a fragrance

as of a heavenly banquet filled the air. Over mast and sailyard clambered the clustering vine, and dark masses of grapes hung glistening from the branches. The ivy twined in tangled masses round the tackling, and bright garlands shone, like jewelled crowns, on every oar-pin. Then a great terror fell on all, as they cried to the old helmsman, 'Quick, turn the ship to the shore; there is no hope for us here.' But there followed a mightier wonder still. A loud roar broke upon the air, and a tawny lion stood before them, with a grim and grisly bear by his side.[85] Cowering like pitiful slaves, the Tyrrhenians crowded to the stern, and crouched round the good helmsman. Then the lion sprang and seized the chief, and the men leaped in their agony over the ship's side. But the power of Dionysos followed them still; and a change came over their bodies as they heard a voice which said, 'In the form of dolphins shall ye wander through the sea for many generations. No rest shall ye have by night or by day, while ye fly from the ravenous sharks that shall chase you through the seas.'

But before the old helmsman again stood Dionysos, the young and fair, in all the glory of undying beauty. Again his dark locks flowed gently over his shoulders, and the purple robe rustled softly in the breeze. 'Fear not,' he said, 'good friend and true, because thou hast aided one who is sprung from the deathless race of the gods. I am Dionysos, the child of Zeus, the lord of the wine-cup and the revel. Thou hast stood by me in the hour of peril; wherefore my power shall shield thee from the violence of evil men, and soothe thee in a green old age, till thine eyes close in the sleep of death and thou goest forth to dwell among brave heroes and good men in the asphodel meadows of Elysium.'

Then, at the bidding of Dionysos, the north wind came and wafted the ship to the land of Egypt, where Proteus was king. And so began the long wanderings of the son of Semelê, through the regions of the Ethiopians and the Indians, towards the rising of the sun. Whithersoever he went, the women of the land gathered round him with wild cries and songs, and he showed them of his secret things, punishing grievously all who set at nought the new laws which he ordained. So, at his word, Lycurgus, the Edonian chieftain, was slain by his people, and none dared any more to speak against Dionysos, until he came back [34] to the city where Semelê, his mother, had been smitten by the lightnings of Zeus.

ASCLEPIOS.

ON the shores of the lake Bœbæis, the golden-haired Apollo saw and loved Corônis, the beautiful daughter of Phlegyas.[37] Many a time they wandered beneath the branching elms while the dewdrops glistened like jewels on the leaves, or sat beneath the ivy bowers as the light of evening faded from the sky and the blue veil of mist fell upon the sleeping hills. But at length the day came when Apollo must journey to the western land, and as he held Corônis in his arms, his voice fell softly and sadly on her ear. 'I go,' he said, 'to a land that is very far off, but surely I will return. More precious to me than aught else on the wide earth is thy love, Corônis. Let not its flower fade, but keep it fresh and pure as now, till I come to thee again. The dancing Horæ trip quickly by, Corônis, and when they bring the day on which I may clasp thee in mine arms once more, it may be that I shall find thee watching proudly over the child of our love.'

He was gone; and for Corônis it seemed as

though the sun had ceased to shine in the heaven.
For many a day she cared not to wander by the
winding shore in the light of early morning, or to
rest in the myrtle bowers as the flush of evening
faded from the sky. Her thoughts went back to
the days that were past, when Apollo the golden-
haired made her glad with the music of his voice.
But at length a stranger came to the Bœbœan
land, and dwelt in the house of Phlegyas, and the
spell of his glorious beauty fell upon Corônis, and
dimmed the love which she had borne for Apollo
who was far away. Again for her the sun shone
brightly in the heaven, and the birds filled the
air with a joyous music; but the tale went swiftly
through the land, and Apollo heard the evil
tidings as he journeyed back with his sister Artemis to the house of Phlegyas. A look of sorrow
that may not be told passed over his fair face;
but Artemis stretched forth her hand towards the
flashing sun and sware that the maiden should
rue her fickleness. Soon, on the shore of the lake
Bœbœis, Corônis lay smitten by the spear which
may never miss its mark, and her child Asclepios
lay a helpless babe by her side. Then the voice
of Apollo was heard saying, ' Slay not the child
with the mother;[38] he is born to do great things;
but bear him to the wise centaur Cheiron, and bid

him train the boy in all his wisdom and teach
him to do brave deeds, that men may praise his
name in the generations that shall be hereafter.'

So in the deep glens of Pelion the child Asclepios grew up to manhood, under the teaching of
Cheiron the wise and good. In all the land there
was none that might vie with him in strength of
body; but the people marvelled yet more at his
wisdom, which passed the wisdom of the sons of
men, for he had learnt the power of every herb
and leaf to stay the pangs of sickness and bring
back health to the wasted form. Day by day the
fame of his doings was spread abroad more widely
through the land, so that all who were sick hastened
to Asclepios and besought his help. But soon
there went forth a rumour that the strength of
death had been conquered by him, and that
Athênê, the mighty daughter of Zeus, had taught
Asclepios how to bring back the dead from the
dark kingdom of Hades. Then, as the number of
those whom he brought from the gloomy Stygian
land increased more and more, Hades went in hot
anger to Olympus, and spake bitter words against
the son of Corônis, so that the heart of Zeus was
stirred with a great fear lest the children of men
should be delivered from death and defy the
power of the gods. So Zeus bowed his head, and

the lightnings flashed from heaven, and Asclepios
was smitten down by the scathing thunderbolt.

Then a mighty and terrible grief stirred the
soul of the golden-haired Apollo. The sun shone
dimly from the heaven; the birds were silent in
the darkened groves; the trees bowed down their
heads in sorrow; and the hearts of all the sons of
men fainted within them, because the healer of
their pains and sickness lived no more upon the
earth. But the wrath of Apollo was mightier
than his grief, and he smote the giant Cyclopes
who shaped the fiery lightnings far down in the
depths of the burning mountain.[39] Then the
anger of Zeus was kindled against his own child,
the golden-haired Apollo, and he spake the word
that he should be banished from the home of the
gods to the dark Stygian land. But the lady
Leto fell at his knees and besought him for her
child, and the doom was given that a whole year
long he should serve as a bondman in the house
of Admetos, who ruled in Pheræ.

THERE was high feasting in the halls of Pheres, because Admetos, his son, had brought home Alkêstis, the fairest of all the daughters of Pelias,[40] to be his bride. The minstrels sang of the glories of the house of Pheræ, and of the brave deeds of Admetos—how, by the aid of the golden-haired Apollo, he had yoked the lion and the boar, and made them drag his chariot to Iolcos, for Pelias had said that only to one who came thus would he give his daughter Alkêstis to be his wife. So the sound of mirth and revelry echoed through the hall, and the red wine was poured forth in honour of Zeus and all the gods, each by his name; but the name of Artemis only was forgotten, and her wrath burned sore against the house of Admetos.

But one, mightier yet than Artemis, was nigh at hand to aid him, for Apollo, the son of Leto, served as a bondman in the home of Pheres, because he had slain the Cyclopes who forged the thunderbolts of Zeus. No mortal blood flowed in his veins; but, though he could neither grow old

nor die, nor could any of the sons of men do him
hurt, yet all loved him for his gentle dealing, for
all things had prospered in the land from the day
when he came to the house of Admetos. And so
it came to pass that, when the sacrifice of the
marriage feast was ended, he spake to Admetos
and said, 'The anger of Artemis my sister is
kindled against thee, and it may be that she will
smite thee with her spear which can never miss
its mark. But thou hast been to me a kind task-
master; and though I am here as thy bondservant,
yet have I power still with my father Zeus, and I
have obtained for thee this boon, that, if thou art
smitten by the spear of Artemis, thou shalt not
die, if thou canst find one who in thy stead will go
down to the dark kingdom of Hades.'

Many a time the sun rose up into the heaven
and sank down to sleep beneath the western
waters; and still the hours went by full of deep
joy to Admetos and his wife Alkêstis, for their
hearts were knit together in a pure love, and no
cloud of strife spread its dark shadow over their
souls. Once only Admetos spake to her of the
words of Apollo, and Alkêstis answered, with a
smile, 'Where is the pain of death, my husband,
for those who love truly? Without thee I care not
to live; wherefore, to die for thee will be a boon.'

Once again there was high feasting in the house of Admetos, for Heracles, the mighty son of Alcménê, had come thither as he journeyed through many lands, doing the will of the false Eurystheus. But, even as the minstrels sang the praises of the chieftains of Pheræ, the flush of life faded from the face of Admetos, and he felt that the hour of which Apollo had warned him was come. But soon the blood came back tingling through his veins, when he thought of the sacrifice which alone could save him from the sleep of death. Yet what will not a man do for his life? and how shall he withstand when the voice of love pleads on his side? So once again the fair Alkêstis looked lovingly upon him as she said, 'There is no darkness for me in the land of Hades, if only I die for thee;' and even as she spake, the spell passed from Admetos, and the strength of the daughter of Pelias ebbed slowly away.

The sound of mirth and feasting was hushed. The harps of the minstrels hung silent on the wall, and men spake in whispering voices, for the awful Mœræ were at hand to bear Alkêstis to the shadowy kingdom. On the couch lay her fair form, pale as the white lily which floats on the blue water, and beautiful as Eôs when her light dies out of the sky in the evening.⁴¹ Yet a little while, and the strife was ended, and Admetos mourned in bitterness and shame for the love which he had lost.

Then the soul of the brave Heracles was stirred within him, and he sware that the Mœræ should not win the victory. So he departed in haste, and far away in the unseen land he did battle with the powers of death, and rescued Alkêstis from Hades, the stern and rugged king.

So once more she stood before Admetos, more radiant in her beauty than in the former days, and once more in the halls of Pheræ echoed the sound of high rejoicing, and the minstrels sang of the mighty deed of the good and brave Heracles, as he went on his way from the home of Admetos to do in other lands the bidding of the mean Eurystheus.

DEUCALION.

FROM his throne on the high Olympus, Zeus looked down on the children of men, and saw that everywhere they followed only their lusts and cared nothing for right or for law. And ever, as their hearts waxed grosser in their wickedness, they devised for themselves new rites to appease the anger of the gods, till the whole earth was filled with blood. Far away in the hidden glens of the Arcadian hills the sons of Lycaon feasted and spake proud words against the majesty of Zeus, and Zeus himself came down from his throne to see their way and their doings.

The sun was sinking down in the sky when an old man drew nigh to the gate of Lycosura. His grey locks streamed in the breeze, and his beard fell in tangled masses over his tattered mantle. With staff in hand he plodded wearily on his way, listening to the sound of revelry which struck upon his ear. At last he came to the Agora, and the sons of Lycaon crowded round him. 'So the wise seer is come,' they said; 'what

tale hast thou to tell us, old man? Canst thou
sing of the days when the earth came forth from
Chaos? Thou art old enough to have been there
to see.' Then with rude jeering they seized him
and placed him on the ground near to the place
where they were feasting. 'We have done a
great sacrifice to Zeus this day; and thy coming
is timely, for thou shalt share the banquet.' So
they placed before him a dish, and the food that
was in it was the flesh of man, for with the blood
of men they thought to turn aside the anger of
the gods.[12] But the old man thrust aside the
dish, and, as he rose up, the weariness of age
passed away from his face, and the sons of
Lycaon[13] were scorched by the glory of his
countenance; for Zeus stood before them and
scathed them all with his lightnings, and their
ashes cumbered the ground.

Then Zeus returned to his home on Olympus,
and he gave the word that a flood of waters
should be let loose upon the earth, that the sons
of men might die for their great wickedness. So
the west wind rose in his might, and the dark
rain-clouds veiled the whole heaven, for the winds
of the north which drive away the mists and
vapours were shut up in their prison-house. On
hill and valley burst the merciless rain, and the

rivers, loosened from their courses, rushed over the wide plains and up the mountain side. From his home on the highlands of Phthia, Deucalion looked forth on the angry sky, and, when he saw the waters swelling in the valleys beneath, he called Pyrrha, his wife, the daughter of Epimetheus, and said to her, 'The time is come of which my father, the wise Prometheus, forewarned me. Make ready, therefore, the ark which I have built, and place in it all that we may need for food while the flood of waters is out upon the earth. Far away on the crags of Caucasus the iron nails rend the flesh of Prometheus, and the vulture gnaws his heart, but the words which he spake are being fulfilled, that for the wickedness of men the flood of waters would come upon the earth; for Zeus himself is but the servant of one that is mightier than he, and must do his bidding.'

Then Pyrrha hastened to make all things ready, and they waited until the waters rose up to the highlands of Phthia and floated away the ark of Deucalion. The fishes swam amidst the old elmgroves, and twined amongst the gnarled boughs of the oaks, while on the face of the waters were tossed the bodies of men; and Deucalion looked on the dead faces of stalwart warriors, of maidens,

and of babes, as they rose and fell upon the heaving
waves. Eight days the ark was borne on the flood,
while the waters covered the hills, and all the
children of men died save a few who found a place
of shelter on the summits of the mountains. On
the ninth day the ark rested on the heights of
Parnassus, and Deucalion, with his wife Pyrrha,
stepped forth upon the desolate earth. Hour by
hour the waters fled down the valleys, and dead
fishes and sea-monsters lay caught in the tangled
branches of the forest. But, far as the eye could
reach, there was no sign of living thing, save of
the vultures who wheeled in circles through the
heaven to swoop upon their prey; and Deucalion
looked on Pyrrha; and their hearts were filled with
a grief which cannot be told. 'We know not,'
he said, 'whether there live any one of all the
sons of men, or in what hour the sleep of death
may fall upon us. But the mighty being who
sent the flood has saved us from its waters: to
him let us build an altar and bring our thank-offer-
ing.' So the altar was built, and Zeus had respect
to the prayer of Deucalion, and presently Hermes
the messenger stood before him. 'Ask what thou
wilt,' he said, 'and it shall be granted thee, for
in thee alone of all the sons of men hath Zeus
found a clean hand and a pure heart.' Then

Deucalion bowed himself before Hermes and said,
'The whole earth lies desolate; I pray thee, let
men be seen upon it once more.' 'Even so shall
it come to pass,' said Hermes, 'if ye will cover
your faces with your mantles and cast the bones
of your mother behind you as ye go upon your
way.'

So Hermes departed to the home of Zeus, and
Deucalion pondered his words, till the wisdom of
his father Prometheus showed him that his mother
was the earth, and that they were to cast the stones
behind them as they went down from Parnassus.
Then they did each as they were bidden, and the
stones which Deucalion threw were turned into
men, but those which were thrown by Pyrrha
became women; and the people which knew
neither father nor mother went forth to their toil
throughout the wide earth.   The sun shone
brightly in the heaven and dried up the slime
beneath them; yet was their toil but a weary
labour, and so hath it been until this day—a
struggle hard as the stones from which they have
been taken.[44]

But, as the years passed on, there were children
born to Pyrrha and Deucalion,[45] and the old race
of men still lived on the heights of Phthia. From

Hellen, their son, sprang the mighty tribes of the
Hellenes, and from Protogeneia, their daughter,
was born Aëthlios, the man of toil and suffering,
the father of Endymion the fair who sleeps on
the hill of Latmos.[46]

THESEUS.

MANY a long year ago a little child was playing on the white sands of the bay of Trœzen.
His golden locks streamed in the breeze as he ran
amongst the rippling waves which flung themselves
lazily on the beach. Sometimes he clapped his
hands in glee as the water washed over his feet,
and he stopped again to look with wondering
eyes at the strange things which were basking on
the sunny shore, or gazed on the mighty waters
which stretched away bright as a sapphire stone
into the far distance. But presently some sadder
thought troubled the child, for the look of gladness passed away from his face, and he went
slowly to his mother, who sat among the weed-
grown rocks, watching her child at play.

'Mother,' said the boy, 'I am very happy here,
but may I not know to-day why I never see my
father as other children do? I am not now so
very young, and I think that you feel sometimes
lonely, for your face looks sad and sorrowful as if
you were grieving for some one who is gone away.'

Fondly and proudly the mother looked on her boy, and smoothed the golden locks on his forehead, as she said, 'My child, there is much to make us happy, and it may be that many days of gladness are in store for us both. But there is labour and toil for all, and many a hard task awaits thee, my son. Only have a brave heart, and turn away from all things mean and foul, and strength will be given thee to conquer the strongest enemy. Sit down then here by my side, and I will tell thee a tale which may make thee sad, but which must not make thee unhappy, for none can do good to others who waste their lives in weeping. Many summers have come and gone since the day when a stranger drew nigh to the house of my father Pittheus. The pale light of evening was fading from the sky; but we could see, by his countenance and the strength of his stalwart form, that he was come of a noble race and could do brave deeds. When Pittheus went forth from the threshold to meet him, the stranger grasped his hand and said, " I come to claim the rights of our ancient friendship; for our enemies have grown too mighty for us, and Pandion my father rules no more in Athens. Here then let me tarry till I can find a way to punish the men who have driven away their king and made his

children wanderers on the earth." So Ægeus
sojourned in my father's house, and soon he won
my love, and I became his wife. Swiftly and
happily the days went by, and one thing only
troubled me, and this was the thought that one
day he must leave me, to fight with his enemies
and place his father again upon his throne. But
even this thought was forgotten for a while, when
Ægeus looked on thee for the first time, and,
stretching forth his hands towards heaven, said,
"O Zeus, that dwellest in the dark cloud, look
down on my child, and give him strength that he
may be a better man than his father; and if thou
orderest that his life shall be one of toil, still let
him have the joy which is the lot of all who do
their work with a cheerful heart and keep their
hands from all defiling things." Then the days
passed by more quickly and happily than ever; but
at last there came messengers from Athens, to tell
him that the enemies of Pandion were at strife
among themselves, and that the time was come
that Ægeus should fight for his father's house.
Not many days after this we sat here, watching
thee at play among the weeds and flowers that
climb among the rocks, when thy father put his
arms gently round me and said, "Æthra, best gift
of all that the gods have ever given to me, I leave

thee to go to my own land; and I know not what things may befall me there, or whether I may return hither to take thee to dwell with me at Athens. But forget not the days that are gone, and faint not for lack of hope that we may meet again in the days that are coming. Be a brave mother to our child, that so he too may grow up brave and pure; and when he is old enough to know what he must do, tell him that he is born of a noble race, and that he must one day fight stoutly to win the heritage of his fathers." And now, my son, thou seest yonder rock, over which the wild briars have clambered. No hands have moved it since the day when thy father lifted it up and placed beneath it his sword and his sandals. Then he put back the stone as it was before, and said to me, " When thou thinkest fit, tell our child that he must wait until he is able to lift this stone. Then must he put my sandals on his feet, and gird my sword on his side, and journey to the city of his forefathers." From that day, my child, I have never seen thy father's face, and the time is often weary, although the memory of the old days is sweet, and my child is by my side to cheer me with his love. So now thou knowest something of the task that lies before thee. Think of thy father's words, and make thyself ready for the toil and danger that may fall to thy lot in time to come.'[47]

The boy looked wistfully into his mother's face, and a strange feeling of love and hope and strength filled his heart, as he saw the tears start to her eyes when the tale was ended. His arms were clasped around her neck; but he said only, 'Mother, I will wait patiently till I am strong enough to lift the stone; but before that time comes, perhaps my father may come back from Athens.'

So for many a year more the days went by, and the boy Theseus grew up brave, truthful, and strong. None who looked upon him grudged him his beauty, for his gentleness left no room for envy; and his mother listened with a proud and glad heart to the words with which the people of the land told of his kindly deeds. At length the days of his youth were ended, but Ægeus came not back; and Theseus went to Æthra, and said, 'The time is come, my mother; I must see this day whether I am strong enough to lift this stone.' And Æthra answered gently, 'Be it as thou wilt, and as the undying gods will it, my son.' Then he went up to the rock, and nerved himself for a mighty effort, and the stone yielded slowly to his strength, and the sword and sandals lay before him.[48] Presently he stood before Æthra, and to

her it seemed that the face of Theseus was as the
face of one of the bright heroes who dwell in the
halls of Zeus. A flush of glorious beauty lit up
his countenance, as she girt the sword to his side
and said, 'The gods prosper thee, my son; and
they will prosper thee, if thou livest in time to
come as thou hast lived in the days that are gone.'

So Theseus bade his mother farewell, there on
the white sea-shore, where long ago he had asked
her first to tell him of his name and kindred.
Sadly, yet with a good hope, he set out on his
journey. The blue sea lay before him, and the
white sails of ships glistened as they danced on
the heaving waters. But Theseus had vowed a vow
that he would do battle with the evil-doers who
filled the land with blood, and for terror of whom
the travellers walked in byways. So at Epidauros
he fought with the cruel Periphêtes, and smote him
with his own club; and at the Megarian isthmus
he seized the robber Sinis, and tare him to pieces
between the trunks of pines, even as he had been
wont to do with the wayfarers who fell into his
hands. Then in the thickets of Crommyon he
slew the huge sow that ravaged the fair cornfields,
and on the borderland he fought a sore fight with
Skiron, who plundered all who came in his path,
and, making them wash his feet, hurled them, as

they stooped, down the cliffs which hung over the
surging sea. Even so did Theseus to him, and,
journeying on to the banks of Kephisos, stretched
the robber Procrustes on the bed on which he had
twisted and tortured the limbs of his victims till
they died.

Thus, amid the joyous shoutings of the people
whom he had set free, Theseus entered into the
city of his fathers; and the rumour of him was
brought to Ægeus the king. Then the memory
of the days that were gone came back to Ægeus,
and his heart smote him as he thought within
himself that this must be the child of Æthra,
whom he had left mourning on the shore of
Trœzen. But soon there was a strife in the city,
for among the mightiest of the people were many
who mocked at Theseus and said, ' Who is this
stranger that men should exalt him thus, as
though he came of the race of heroes? Let
him show that he is the child of Ægeus, if he
would win the heritage which he claims.' So
was Theseus brought before the king, and a blush
of shame passed over the old man's face when he
saw the sword and sandals which he had left
beneath the great stone near the Trœzenian shore.
Few words only he spake of welcome, and none
of love or kindness for his child or for the wife

who still yearned for the love of the former days. Then, at his father's bidding, Theseus made ready to go forth once again on his path of toil, and he chafed not against the hard lot which had fallen to his portion. Only he said, 'The love of a father would sweeten my labour; but my mother's love is with me still, and the battle is for right and for law.'

So in after-times the minstrels sang of the glorious deeds of Theseus the brave and fair. They told how at the bidding of his father he went forth from the gates of Athens and smote the bull which ravaged the broad plains of Marathon, and how in the secret mazes of the labyrinth he smote the Minotauros. They sang of his exploits in the day when the Amazons did battle with the men of Athens—how he went with Meleagros and his chieftains to the chase of the boar in Calydon—how with the heroes in the ship Argo he brought back the golden fleece from Colchis. They told how at the last he went down with Peirithoös his comrade into the gloomy kingdom of Hades and seized on the daughter of Dêmêtêr, to bring her to the land of living men. They sang of the fierce wrath of Hades when his lightnings burst forth and smote Peirithoös—of the dark prison-house where Theseus lay while many a rolling year went round, until at the last the mighty Heracles passed the borders of the shadowy land and set the captive free.

And so it was that, when the heroes had passed to the home of Zeus and the banquet of the gods, the glory of Theseus was as the glory of the brave son of Alcmênê who toiled for the false Eurystheus; and ever, in the days of feasting, the minstrels linked together the names of Heracles and of Theseus.[19]

LAÏOS.

ON the throne of Cadmos, in the great city of Thebes, sat Laïos, the son of Labdacos. He had passed through many and sore troubles since his father died, for Amphion and Zethos, the sons of Antiopê, had driven him from his kingdom, and for a long time Laïos dwelt in a strange land. But now he trusted to live in peace with his wife Iocastê, the daughter of Menœkeus, and to die happily in a good old age. Still, although all things seemed to go well with him, he could not forget the words which Phœbus Apollo spake when he sent to Delphi to ask what should befall him in the after days ; and so it came to pass that, while others rejoiced to hear the merry laughter of children in their homes, Laïos trembled when he heard the tidings that a son had been born to him. For the warning was that he should be slain by his own child.[60]

Many days he spent in sadness and gloom, and he spake no word of love or tenderness to Iocastê, nor did he look on the child as he lay helpless in

P

his cradle. At last he bade his servants to take the child and leave him on the rugged heights of Kithairôn. So Iocastê sat in silence although her heart was breaking with grief, for she knew that it was vain to plead for the life of her babe; and presently the servants set forth from the house of Laïos to go to the mountain where his flocks were feeding. There, in a hollow cleft, they placed the child, and, as they went away, they said, ' If the nymphs see him not as they wander along the rough hillside, Laïos will have no need to fear the warnings of Apollo.'

So once more there was seeming peace in the king's house at Thebes; and the grief of Iocastê was soothed as the months passed by, for she said, ' It is better that my child should sleep the sleep of death than that he should live to slay his father.'

But the danger had not passed away, for the babe was in the house of Polybos, who ruled at Corinth. Once had the sun gone down beneath the sea, and once had the light of Eôs tinged the eastern sky, when a shepherd who tended his flocks on the cool hillside saw the babe wrapped in his white shroud. Then his heart was touched with pity, and he said, ' I will take him to my master's house; for if his parents will it not that

the child should live, it will profit nothing to
take him back to Thebes, and he cannot do harm
to any one in the Corinthian land.'

So Meropê, the wife of Polybos, received the
babe with great gladness, for she had no child;
and she called his name Œdipus, because his feet
were swollen with the linen bands which were
bound about them when they took him away
from the house of Laïos. Many times the year
went round, and Œdipus grew up with fair and
ruddy countenance, and all men loved him. No
cloud dimmed the brightness of his childhood and
his youth, for Polybos and Meropê looked on him
with a happy pride, and thought how the love of
Œdipus should cheer them in the days of weakness and old age. So the fame of the young man
was spread abroad, for he was foremost in every
sport and game, and none returned from the chase
more laden with booty. But one day it came to
pass that there was a feast in the house of Polybos,
and one of the guests, whom Œdipus had beaten
in the foot-race, spake out in his anger and said
that he was not in very truth the child of Meropê.

The feast went on with mirth and song; but
there was a dark cloud on the face of Œdipus,
for the words of the stranger had sunk deep in.
his heart, and he sate still and silent till the

banquet was ended. When the morning was
come, he went to Meropê and said, 'Tell me the
truth, my mother; am I not indeed thy son?'
Then she cast her arms around him and said,
'Who hath beguiled thee thus, Œdipus? Can
any know better than I that thou art my child
indeed? and never was a son more dear to his
parents than thou art to us.' But, although he
asked no more questions, yet after a while the
doubt came back, and he said within himself,
'None can be more tender and loving than
Meropê, but she did not tell me plainly that I
really am her son.' So in the darkness of the night
he went sadly from the home where he had lived
without care or trouble till the misery of this
doubt came upon him.   Once more he passed
along the heathy sides of Kithairôn, not knowing
that there he had been cast forth to die; and he
journeyed on to the shrine of Phœbus Apollo at
Delphi.   There, as he stood before the holy place,
a voice came to him which said, 'Thy doom is
that thou shalt slay thy father.'

Then Œdipus was bowed down with the weight
of his fear and sorrow; and he resolved within
himself that he would never go back to Corinth,
that so he might not become the slayer of Polybos.
So he went away from Delphi, heavy and dis-

pleased, and he journeyed on in moody silence, with his heart full of bitter thoughts. He cared not whither the road might lead him, and it chanced that as he came near to the meeting of the roads which go to Daulis and to Thebes, he heard suddenly the voice of one who bade him turn aside from the path while his chariot passed by. Then Œdipus started like one awaking from a dream, and looking up he saw an old man sitting in the chariot. An angry flush was on his face, as he charged his servant to thrust aside the stranger who dared to stand in his path. So the servant lifted up his whip to strike Œdipus; and Œdipus said, 'Who are ye that ye should smite me? and why should I yield to thee, old man, because thou ridest in a fine chariot and seekest to turn others aside from the road which is open for all men?' But when the driver of the chariot sought again to strike him, Œdipus smote him with the full strength of his arm, so that he sank down from his seat. Then the face of the old man grew pale with fury, and he leaned forth to strike down Œdipus with the dagger which was in his hand. But he smote him not, for Œdipus turned aside the blow, and he struck the old man on his temples, and left him lying dead by the side of the chariot.

So he journeyed onwards; but as he drew near to the great city of Cadmos he saw mothers sitting with their children by the wayside, and the air was filled with their wailing. Their faces were pale as though from a deadly plague, and their limbs quivered as if from mortal fear; and Œdipus said, 'Children of Cadmos, what evil has befallen you, that ye have fled from your homes and are sunk down thus on the hard earth?' Then they told him how on a high cliff near the city of Thebes a horrible monster, with a maiden's face and a lion's body, sate looking on the plain below, and how the breath of the Sphinx poisoned the pure air of the heaven and filled their dwellings with a noisome pestilence. And they said, 'Help us, stranger, if thou canst, for if help come not soon, the city and people of Cadmos will be destroyed; for like a black cloud in the sky the Sphinx rests on the cliff, and none can drive her away unless he answer first the riddle with which she baffles the wisest of the land. Every day she utters her dark speech, and devours all who seek to answer it and fail.' Then said Œdipus, 'What may the riddle be?' and they answered, 'This much only does the Sphinx say, "On the earth is a two-footed living thing which has four feet and three and only one voice. Alone of all

creatures it changes in its form, and moves most
slowly when it uses all its feet." Now, therefore,
stranger, if thou canst answer the riddle, thou
wilt win a mighty prize; for Laïos, our king, has
been slain, we know not by whom, and the elders
have spoken the word that he who slays the
Sphinx shall have Iocastê for his wife and sit on
the throne of Cadmos.'

Then, with a cheerful heart, Œdipus went
onwards, until he drew near to the cliff on which
the Sphinx was sitting. With a steady gaze he
looked on her stern unpitying face, and said to her,
' What is thy riddle?' and all who heard trembled
as she spake to Œdipus. Then he thought within
himself for a while, and at last he looked up and
said, ' Listen, O Sphinx: the creature of whom
thou hast asked me is man. In the days of his
helpless childhood he crawls on his four feet; in
his old age a staff is his third foot, and his move-
ment is slowest when he crawls on four feet.'

The paleness of death came over the face of the
Sphinx, and every limb quivered with fear, until,
as Œdipus drew nearer, she flung herself with a
wild roar from the cliff. Presently the men of
Thebes trampled on her ghastly carcase; and they
led Œdipus [51] in triumph to the elders of the city,
shouting ' Io Pæan ' for the mighty deed which he

had done. Then was the feast spread in the great
banquet-hall, and the minstrels sang his praise,
and besought strength and wealth for him and
for the people. So Iocastê became the wife of
Œdipus,[12] and all men said, 'Since the days of
Cadmos, the son of Telephassa, no king hath
ruled us so wisely and justly;' and the name of
the gloomy Laïos was forgotten.

ŒDIPUS.

FOR many years Œdipus reigned gloriously in
Thebes, and the fame of his wisdom was
spread abroad in the countries round about. He
looked on his sons and daughters as they grew
up in health and strength, filling his house with
gladness and merriment; and it seemed to him as
though trouble and sorrow could scarcely vex him
more. But the terrible Erinnys, who takes vengeance for blood, had not forgotten the day when
Laïos fell smitten by the wayside; and, at the
bidding of Zeus, Phœbus Apollo sent a plague
upon the Theban land. The people died like
sheep in the city and the field, and the pestilence
was more grievous than in the days when the
Sphinx uttered her dark riddle from the cliff. At
last the elders of the city came to Œdipus and
said, 'O king, thou didst save the city and the
people long ago, when we were sore pressed by a
horrible monster; save us now, if thou canst, by
thy great wisdom.' But Œdipus said, 'Friends,
the plague which is slaying us now comes from no

monster, but from Zeus who dwells on Olympus ;
and my wisdom therefore cannot avail to take it
away.   But I have sent Creon my brother to the
shrine of Phœbus Apollo at Delphi to ask him
wherefore these evils have come upon us.'

But the coming of Creon brought strife only
and anguish to the city, and the fearful Erinnys
who wanders through the air waved her dark
wings over the house of Œdipus; for Phœbus had
told him that there was no hope for the land until
they cast forth the man whose hands were polluted
with blood.   Then said Œdipus, ' This were. an
easy task if we only knew on whom lies the
bloodguiltiness,[13] but I know neither the man nor
the deed for which this doom is laid upon him.'
And Creon answered, ' O king, it is for Laïos, who
was slain as he was journeying into the Phokian
land.'

Then everywhere through the city and in the
field went the messengers of Œdipus, charging
all to bring forth the murderer, and threatening
grievous pains to any who should hide or shelter
him.   But none stood forth to own his guilt or
to charge it on another ; and in his sore strait
Œdipus sent for the blind seer Teiresias, who
knew the speech of birds and the hidden things
of earth and heaven.   But when he was led before

the king, Œdipus saw that the heart of the wise prophet was troubled, and he said gently, 'Teiresias, thou understandest things that are hidden from other men; tell me now, I beseech thee, on whose hands is the stain from the blood of Laïos. Let me but know this, and the pestilence will straightway cease from the land.' But Teiresias answered hastily, 'Ask me not, O king, ask me not. Let me go again to my home, and let us bear each his own burden.' So Teiresias kept silence, and many times Œdipus prayed him to speak, until his wrath was roused, and he spake unseemly words to the prophet, and said, 'If thou answerest not my question, it must be because thine own hands are polluted with the blood of Laïos.' Then from the countenance of the prophet flashed unutterable scorn, as he said slowly, so that none might hear but Œdipus, 'O king, thou hast sealed thine own doom. On thine hand lies his blood, not on mine; and thou rememberest the words which Phœbus spake to thee at Delphi, when thou hadst gone thither from the house of Polybos.' But, in his rage and madness, Œdipus took no heed of prudence and wisdom, and he cried with a loud voice, and said, 'Hearken, O people, to the words of Teiresias; hath he not spoken well when he said that Laïos was smitten by my hand?' Then there rose wild cries and shoutings, and bitter words were spoken against the seer, who had dared to revile the king; but as he turned to go, Teiresias said only, 'It is easy to cry aloud, it is harder to judge and to find out the truth; search ye it out well before ye say that I have spoken falsely.'

So once more a terrible doubt filled the mind of Œdipus. In the day his thoughts vexed him, and evil dreams stood before him in the dark hours of night; and daily the plague pressed more heavily on the people, until at length he asked Iocastê of the time when Laïos had been slain, and what tidings were brought of the deed. And she said, 'One only lives to tell the tale, and he said that, at a place where three ways met, robbers fell on the king and slew him; and the deed was done not long before thy coming to Thebes.' Then a strange fear came over Œdipus, as he remembered the old man whom he had smitten in his chariot, and he told her of all the things which befell him as he journeyed to Thebes from Delphi. 'But in thy words is hope,' he said, 'for if Laïos fell by a band of thieves, then am I guiltless of his blood. Yet hasten now, and bring hither the man who saw the deed, for I will not close my eyes in sleep until this secret is made known.'

But while one went for the man, there came a
messenger from Corinth with tidings that Polybos
the king was dead ; and Œdipus lifted up his hands
and said, 'I thank thee, O Zeus; for the words of
Phœbus Apollo, that I should slay my father,
can never be accomplished.' But the messenger
answered hastily, 'Thy thanks are wasted, O king,
for the blood of Polybos runs not in thy veins. I
found thee on the rugged heights of Kithairôn,
and saved thee from the doom which was prepared
for thee. So from the house of Polybos there is
for thee neither hope nor fear.' Then the heart of
Œdipus beat wildly with a horrible dread, and he
said, 'O thou that dwellest at Delphi, have thy
words in very deed been accomplished, and I knew
it not ?' Presently the hope, which the words of
Iocastê had waked up in him, was taken away; for
the old man who had seen the deed said now that
one only had slain the king, and the tokens remained sure that the hands of Œdipus were polluted with his father's blood.

Then was there woe unspeakable in the city of
Cadmos, and the hearts of all the people were
bowed down with grief for all the miseries which
had burst like a flood on the house of Labdacos,
and a great cry went up to heaven. For the lady
Iocastê lay dead, and Œdipus had done a fearful

deed when he saw her stretched cold and lifeless before him. With his own hands he tore out his eyes and hurled them away; for he said, 'It is not fit that the eyes which have seen such things should ever look upon the sun again.'

From that day forth the terrible Erinnys who hovers in the air, and the awful Atê[54] who visits the sins of the fathers upon the children, abode by day and by night in the house of Œdipus. His sons strove together in their vain and silly pride, and each sought to be king in his father's place, till at last they cast Œdipus forth, and he wandered in wretchedness and misery from the land of the Cadmeians. His grievous sorrow had quenched his love for his people, and he said, in bitterness of spirit, that his body should not be buried in the Theban land. So his child Antigonê led him onwards, and sought to cheer him in his fierce agony. But the dark cloud rested ever on his countenance, until, one day, he said to Antigonê, 'My child, I think that the end of my long suffering is nigh at hand; for there came to me last night a vision of a dream which said, "Man of many troubles, thou shalt lie down to rest in the grove of the Eumenides, and for the land in which thy body shall lie there shall be wealth in peace and victory in war."' So he went

on with a good heart, journeying towards rocky
Athens, and as he passed through a wood where
the waters of a little stream murmured pleasantly
in the still summer air, he sat down on a seat
carved in the living rock, while Antigonê stood by
his side. But presently a rough voice bade him
rise and depart. 'Stranger, dost thou not dread
the wrath of the mighty beings whose very name
we fear to utter? In this grove of the Eumenides
no mortal man may rest or tarry.' But Œdipus
said gently, 'Yet move me not, I pray thee, for I
am not as other men, and the visions of Zeus have
told me that this shall be the place of my rest.
Go then to Theseus who rules at Athens, and
bid him come to one who has suffered much and
who will do great things for him and for his
people.' So Theseus came at the bidding of
Œdipus; and there were signs in the heaven above
and on the earth beneath, that the end was nigh
at hand, for the ground shook beneath their feet,
and the thunder was heard in the cloudless sky.
Then Œdipus bade Antigonê farewell, and said,
'Weep not, my child; I am going to my home,
and I rejoice to lay down the burden of my woe.'
And to Theseus he said, 'Follow me, O friend, for
the blind shall guide thee this day. The dreams
which Zeus sends have shown me the place where

I must sleep after the fever of my life is ended;
and so long as thou revealest not my resting-place
to men, thou and thy people shall prosper and
wax mighty in peace and in war.' But even while
he yet spake, there came a voice which said,
' Œdipus, why tarriest thou?' and the sound of
the thunder echoed again through the cloudless
sky. Then he spake the parting words to Theseus,
and besought him to guard his child Antigonê;
and he said, ' Here must thou stay until thou
seest that the things are accomplished of which
the vision hath forewarned me. Follow me not
further.' So Œdipus departed alone, and Theseus
knew presently that Zeus had fulfilled his word.[55]

From that day forth, the city of Athênê grew
mighty in the earth, and no enemy prevailed
against it. For to no one did Theseus show the
place where Œdipus rested in the hidden dells
of Colonos, save to the man who should rule at
Athens after him. Thus only the king knew
where lay the secret spell which made the city of
Erechtheus mightier than the city of Cadmos; and
the men of Thebes sought in vain to find the
grave of Œdipus where the Kephisos flows by the
sacred grove of the Eumenides.

POLYNEIKES.

THERE was strife between Eteocles and Polyneikes, when they had driven forth their
father from the city of Cadmos; for Œdipus had
laid on them a heavy curse for their cruel deed,
and the awful Erinnys heard it, and she sware
with an oath that there should be no peace for the
men of Thebes until the whole house of Laïos
should be utterly destroyed. At first the brothers
agreed that each should be king in his turn, and
that the power should pass daily from the one to
the other; but soon there grew up jealousy between them and hatred, and bitter words were
spoken, until at last Eteocles rose up against his
brother and thrust him out of the city.

So Polyneikes went away in rage and sorrow,
and took the road which goes to Argos; and as he
came near to it, he met a stranger by the wayside,
and they talked together, until there arose a
quarrel between them. But while they were fighting, Adrastos the king passed by, and he saw that

Q

on the shield of Polyneikes was a boar, and a lion
on the shield of the other stranger, whose name
was Tydeus; and he said within himself, 'Long
ago Phœbus forewarned me that my daughters
must be married to a lion and a boar; surely these
must be they of whom he spake.' And he went
up to them and parted them in their battle, and
said, 'Come with me, friends. I am Adrastos, and
I rule in this city of Argos. There are better things
in store for you than vain strife and hard blows.'
So, when Argeia became the wife of Polyneikes,
and Dêipylê was given to Tydeus, who came from
the rugged mountains of Ætolia, Adrastos sware
to avenge the wrongs of both the strangers and to
place them again on the thrones of their fathers.

Then throughout the land of Argos the messengers went to and fro to summon the chieftains to
the war; but when they met in council at Argos,
Amphiaraos rose up and said, 'Friends, ye are
going to your death, for to me are shown many
things which are hidden from your eyes; and I
see the eagles gathered which shall tear the flesh
from your bones, if ye go against the city and
people of Cadmos.' But none hearkened to his
warnings, and they dragged Amphiaraos to the
war against his will.

So round the walls of Thebes camped the army
of the great Argive chieftains; and within the city
was fear and trembling, until Teiresias the wise
seer spake and said, 'Thebans, the victory shall
be yours, and your enemies shall perish utterly, if
ye offer a great sacrifice to Ares.' Then Menœkeus, the son of Creon, answered, 'What can a
man give better than his life?' and he went forth
and slew himself without the city.[54] Then the
Argives battered more fiercely against the gates,
and put ladders to climb the walls; but the thunderbolt fell from heaven, and smote many of them,
and the Thebans hurled mighty stones from the
wall, and crushed the foremost of their warriors.
Still the battle raged fiercely, until Eteocles went
forth and said, 'Men of Argos, ye are fighting in
a vain quarrel; for ye have no cause to hate the
men of Thebes. Bring forth Polyneikes my
brother, that we may fight together, and so shall
the strife be ended, and ye shall go back to your
homes in peace.'

Then the awful Erinnys, as she hovered unseen
in the air, waved her dark wings over the brothers
when they came forth to meet each other. On
their faces was the blackness of hatred strong as
death; but no word was spoken as they drew

each his sword, and the mortal strife began.
Then the Erinnys gave to their arms an unearthly
strength, and presently the bodies of the two
brothers were stretched dead upon the plain.
But the men of Argos and of Thebes said that
there was no victory where none lived to claim it,
and again they fought, until Tydeus the Ætolian
fell with a deadly wound, and a mighty crowd of
enemies pressed hard to slay Amphiaraos. Then
he rose up in his chariot, and, lifting up his hands
to the broad heaven, he said, ' O Zeus, the hour is
come; and the things of which thou didst show
me the tokens have been accomplished. Yet save
me from the sword of men, if the doom is that I
must die.' So his prayer was heard, and the earth
clave asunder, and the chariot of Amphiaraos was
seen no more; and the place where it sank down
became holy ground, for the flocks and herds
would not touch the grass which grew soft and
green upon it,[67] and the birds lighted not near the
pillars of his temple.

Then a mighty terror fell on the men of Argos,
when they knew that Amphiaraos had been taken
from the land of living men; and the chieftains
fled away each to his own home. With the swiftness of the wind as it sweeps over the waters,

Adrastos rode on his horse Areiôn, over hill and vale and along the sea-shore; and as they saw his blood-stained raiment streaming on the breeze, the people of the land knew that Zeus had accomplished the doom of the chiefs who went to place Polyneikes on the throne of his father Œdipus.

WHEN the army of the Argives was scattered and the two sons of Œdipus had slain each other, Creon became king in Thebes, and he sent messengers through the city, who said, ' Hearken, ye people, to the words of the king. Eteocles has fallen in a righteous quarrel, and a great sacrifice shall be done to the gods who dwell beneath the earth, that they may welcome him when he comes before them: but the body of Polyneikes shall be cast forth to the beasts of the field and the fowls of the air; and the man who dares to lay it in the ground, or so much as to sprinkle earth upon it, shall be stoned to death before the people of the city.'

So the body of Polyneikes was cast forth on a mound of earth, and guards were placed there to see that none should bury it or sprinkle earth upon it. But Antigonê spake to Ismênê, her sister, and besought her help that the fitting things might be done for the body of their brother; but Ismênê said, ' What good can come

from despising the words of those who rule in
the city? Hath anything prospered in the house
of Laios since the plague came to search out the
pollution of blood? and how shall it profit to
bring another woe on the woes that are past?'
And Antigonê answered, 'Be it even as thou wilt,
my sister; thou knowest, it may be, what it is
best for thee to do. I speak not for any love
which Polyneikes showed to us or to our father;
but there are other laws besides the laws of gentleness and pity; and justice, which lives for ever,
cries out that the offerings must be given for
those who wander on the banks of the Stygian
stream.'

So the maiden went forth, and when the shades
of night covered the earth, she scraped away the
sand until the body of Polyneikes sank down
into the shallow grave. But the men who were
placed to guard the body woke up from their
sleep, and seized the maiden, and carried her in
the morning before the king. And Creon said,
'Thou hast sealed thine own doom, Antigonê, for
the word which I have spoken may not be re-
called, and this day thou shalt die.' But the
maiden answered, 'Do with me as thou wilt;
I have obeyed a law which is higher and stronger
than thy word.' So they carried the maiden to a

hollow rock, and there they placed her with a loaf of bread and a flask of water.

But dark signs were seen again in the heavens, and the seer Teiresias came before Creon, and said,[59] 'Take good heed, O king, what thou doest. The wrath of the awful Erinnys is coming again upon the city, and few hours shall pass before thou shalt atone with the life of one whom thou dost love for the death of the maiden Antigonê. I have heard the strange voices of birds, which told me of fresh woes for this hapless land; and I have listened to the sounds which tell of strife and war. The fire burns not on the altar of sacrifice, and the flesh of the victim wastes away in the smouldering cinders; for the gods who dwell beneath the earth are wroth with thee, and thou hast done to them a grievous wrong while thy thought was how thou mightest do hurt to Polyneikes.' Then Creon said, 'The evil may be yet undone. The traitor's body shall be buried, and we will bring forth Antigonê from the cave where they have left her to die.'

Hastily and in much fear they went to save the maiden; but when they entered the cave, the body of Antigonê lay before them stiff and cold in death, and by her side sat Hæmon, the son of

the king; but when Creon bade him rise and go
home, he said, ' It is too late; the joy of my life
is gone; what have I to live for now?'   Then he
plunged a dagger into his heart, and in the home
of Hades and Persephonê he won again the love
which Creon had denied to him in the land of
living men.

So the years went on, but the days of Creon
passed in gloom and sorrow, for the light which
had risen for a little while on the house of Laïos
was quenched at the death of Hœmon; and there
came rumours of war from Argos, for the sons of
the chieftains who had fought for Polyneikes were
grown up to manhood, and they had vowed a vow
to avenge the blood of their fathers.   Once more
Creon sent for the blind prophet; but Teiresias
would not come, for he said, ' There is no hope,
and the undying gods fight against the children
of Cadmos.'   So the hearts of the Thebans were
bowed down with fear, and Creon fled away in
terror when the army of the Argives drew nigh
to the walls of the city.   Thus was the house of
Laïos rooted utterly out of the land, and the vengeance of the awful Erinnys was accomplished.

ERIPHYLÉ.

W HEN the first war of the seven chiefs against Thebes was ended, the men of Argos, with the help of the men of Athens, took from the Thebans the dead bodies of their comrades and burnt them with fire, and then went back to their own land. But the words of Amphiaraos were yet to be accomplished, which he spake to Alcmæon his son when he departed for the war.

Now the wisdom of the far-seeing gods had rested on Amphiaraos, for he was sprung from the seer Melampus, who knew the speech of birds. And thus it was that, when Adrastos besought his aid against the men of Thebes, Amphiaraos forewarned him of the evils which should come upon them. 'The Até of Zeus presses sore upon Polyneikes,' he said, 'for the curse of a father has a mighty power. Wherefore I go not to the war.' Then was there great fear, and the chieftains took counsel hurriedly in the hall of Adrastos, for of all the warriors of the land none had so great fame as the wise seer Amphiaraos. His spear had wounded the great boar of Calydon, which was slain by the beautiful Atalantê, and his wisdom had guided the chiefs who sailed in the ship Argo to fetch away the golden fleece. But Amphiaraos dwelt with his wife Eriphylê, and in an evil hour he had sworn to Adrastos her brother that, if ever there rose up strife between them, he would follow the bidding of Eriphylê. So the chieftain of Argos went to his sister, and said, ' Our task is vain, if Amphiaraos goes not forth with us to the war. Wherefore I have brought thee a rich gift, that thou mayest persuade him to go.. Lo! here is the necklace which Hephaistos wrought and Cadmos gave to his wife Harmonia when he had come to Thebes from the far-off Eastern land.' The lustre of gold and gems dazzled the eyes of Eriphylê, and her heart was corrupted by the bribe, so that she said, ' Fear not, my brother. It shall be even as thou wilt.' So her word was spoken, and Amphiaraos bade farewell to his home and to his children; but to Alcmæon his eldest-born he said, ' The treachery of thy mother sends me forth to an evil war; if I come not back, avenge me of her.'

Then Alcmæon remembered his father's words when the remnant of the host of the Argives returned faint of heart from the seven-gated walls

of Thebes, and when they told him how Zeus had
opened the earth and taken to himself his child
Amphiaraos. So Eriphylê died, and the awful
Erinnys, who hovers in the air, came down to take
vengeance for the deed. Unheard by others, the
waving of her dark wings and the hiss of her
poisoned breath fell loud and harsh on the ear of
Alcmæon, and gave him neither peace by day nor
sleep by night. In madness of spirit he wandered
through the land, driven by her merciless scourge,
till he came to the shrine of Phœbus Apollo at
Delphi. There the priestess bade him offer the
necklace which Adrastos gave to Eriphylê, and told
him that, if he would have rest from the scourge
of Erinnys, he must find a spot which the sun had
not yet seen when he avenged his father. In
sorrow of heart Alcmæon wandered from Delphi,
over mountain and through valley, seeking in vain
for the place of which the priestess had spoken,
until he came to the shores of the mighty Ache-
lôos, where it flows slowly out into the sea.
There the slime, borne down by the waters, rises
higher and higher as the years roll round, and
makes new land, gaping and desolate, where the
lank and coarse grass sweeps in a wild tangle over
the ground. Here, as he sank down in utter
weariness, Alcmæon heard a voice which said,

' This is the place of thy rest, for here the blood
which thou hast shed cannot taint the air; and
here, when ten years have passed away, thy hands
shall again be pure, and thou shalt return and
lead thy kinsfolk to avenge the blood of their
fathers against the men of Thebes.' [60]

Even so it came to pass; and when the Epigoni [61]
made ready for the war, Alcmæon went forth from
his hiding-place, and led them from Argos against
the city of Cadmos. But the undying gods cared
no more to shield Creon, and all things came to
pass according to the words of the seer Teiresias,
and the chiefs of Argos burst through the seven
gates and smote the men of Thebes, and made
Thersander, the son of Polyneikes, king in the
stead of Creon, the son of Menœkeus.

NINE years the Achaians had fought against Ilion to avenge the wrongs and the woes of Helen, and still the war went on, and only the words of Calchas, which he spake long ago in Aulis,[62] cheered them with the hope that the day of vengeance was near at hand. For strife had arisen between the king Agamemnon and the mighty son of Peleus, and it seemed to the men of Argos that all their toil must be for naught. In fierce anger, Achilleus vowed a vow that he would go forth no more to the battle, and he sat in sullen silence within his tent, or wandered gloomily along the sea-shore. With fresh courage the hosts of the Trojans poured out from their walls when they knew that Achilleus fought no more on the side of the Achaians, and the chieftains sought in vain for his help when the battle went against them. Then the face of the war was changed; for the men of Ilion came forth from their city, and shut up the Achaians within their camp, and fought fiercely to take

the ships. Many a chief and warrior was smitten
down, and still Achilleus sat within his tent,
nursing his great wrath, and reviling all who
came before him with gifts and prayers.

But dearer than all others to the child of the
sea-nymph Thetis was Patroclos, the son of Me-
nœtios, and the heart of Achilleus was touched
with pity when he saw the tears stream down his
face ; and he said, ' Dear friend, tell me thy grief,
and hide nothing from me. Hast thou evil
tidings from our home at Phthia, or weepest
thou for the troubles which vex us here?' Then
Patroclos spake out boldly, and said, 'Be not
angry at my words, Achilleus. The strength of
the Argives is wasted away, and the mightiest of
their chieftains lie wounded or dead around their
ships. They call thee the child of Peleus and of
Thetis; but men will say that thou art sprung
from the rugged rocks and the barren sea, if thou
seest thy people undone and liftest not an arm to
help them.' Then Achilleus answered, ' O friend,
the vow is on me, and I cannot go; but put thou
on my armour, and go forth to the battle. Only
take heed to my words, and go not in my chariot
against the city of Ilion. Drive our enemies
from the ships, and let them fight in the plain,
and then do thou come back to my tent.'

Then the hearts of the Achaians were cheered,
for next to Achilleus there was not in all the host
a warrior more brave and mighty than Patroclos.
At his word, the Myrmidons started up from their
long rest, and hastily snatched their arms to follow him to the battle.   Presently Patroclos came
forth.   The glistening helmet of Achilleus was
on his head, and his armour was girt around
his body.   Only he bare not his mighty spear, for
no mortal man might wield that spear in battle
but Achilleus.   Before the tent stood the chariot,
and harnessed to it were the horses Xanthos and
Balios, who grow not old nor die.[63]

So Patroclos departed for the fight, and Achilleus went into his tent, and as he poured out the
dark wine from a golden goblet, he prayed to
Zeus, and said, ' O thou that dwellest far away in
Dodona,[64] where the Selloi do thy bidding and
proclaim thy will, give strength and victory to
Patroclos my friend.   Let him drive the men of
Ilion from the ships and come back safe to me
after the battle.'   But Zeus heard the prayer in
part only, for the doom was that Achilleus should
see Patroclos alive no more.

Then the hosts of the Trojans trembled as
Patroclos drew nigh on the chariot of Achilleus,
and none dared to go forth against him. Onwards

sped the undying horses, and wherever they went the ground was red with the blood of the Trojans who were smitten down by his spear. Then Sarpedon,[65] the great chief of the Lykians, spake to Glaucos, and said, ' O friend, I must go forth and do battle with Patroclos. The people fall beneath his sword, and it is not fit that the chieftains should be backward in the strife.' But the doom of Sarpedon was sealed, and presently his body lay lifeless on the ground, while the men of Argos and of Ilion fought for his glittering arms.

Then the doom came on Patroclos also, for Phœbus Apollo fought against him in the battle, and in the dust was rolled the helmet which no enemy had touched when it rested on the head of Achilleus. Before him flashed the spear of Hector, as he said, 'The hour of thy death is come, Patroclos, and the aid of Achilleus cannot reach thee now.' But Patroclos said only, 'It is thy time for boasting now; wait yet a little while, and the sword of Achilleus shall drink thy life-blood.'

So Patroclos died, and there was a fierce fight over his body, and many fell on both sides, until there was a great heap of dead around it. But away from the fight, the horses Xanthos and Balios wept for their charioteer, and they would

R

not stir with the chariot, but stood fixed firm as
pillars on the ground, till Zeus looked down in
pity on them and said, 'Was it for this that I
gave you to Peleus, the chieftain of Phthia—
horses who cannot grow old or die, to a mortal
man, the most wretched thing that crawls upon
the earth? But fear not; no enemy shall lay
hands on the chariot of Achilleus, or on the immortal horses which bear it. Your limbs shall
be filled with new strength, and ye shall fly like
birds across the battle-field till ye come to the
tent of your master.' Then the horses wept no
more, but swift as eagles they bare Automedon
through the fight,[60] while Hector and his people
strove fiercely to seize them. At last the battle
was over, and, while the Achaians bore the body
of Patroclos to the ships, Antilochos, the son of
Nestor, went to the tent of Achilleus, and said,
'Thy friend is slain, and Hector has his armour.'

Then the dark cloud of woe fell on the soul
of Achilleus. In a fierce grief he threw earth
with both hands into the air, and rent his clothes,
and lay down weeping in the dust. Far away in
her coral caves beneath the sea Thetis heard the
deep groans of her child, and, like a white mist,
she rose from the waters and went to comfort
him; and she said, 'Why weepest thou, my son?

When Agamemnon did thee wrong, thou didst
pray that the Achaians might sorely need thy aid
in the battle, and thy wish has been accomplished.
So may it be again.' But Achilleus answered,
'Of what profit is it to me, my mother, that my
prayer has been heard, since Patroclos my friend
is slain, and Hector has my armour? One thing
only remains to me now. I will slay Hector, and
avenge the slaughter of Patroclos.' Then the
tears ran down the cheeks of Thetis as she said,
'Then is thine own doom accomplished, for when
thou slayest Hector, thou hast not many days to
live.' 'So then let it be,' said Achilleus; 'the
mighty Heracles tasted of death: therefore let me
die also, so only Hector dies before me.'[67]

Then Thetis sought no more to turn him from his
purpose, but she went to the house of Hephaistos
to get armour for her child in place of that which
Hector had taken from Patroclos. And Achilleus
vowed a vow that twelve sons of the Trojans
should be slain at the grave of Patroclos, and that
Hector should die before the funeral rites were
done. Then Agamemnon sent him gifts, and
spake kindly words,[68] so that the strife between
them was ended, and Achilleus might now go
forth to fight for the Achaians. So, in the armour
which Hephaistos had wrought at the prayer of

Thetis, he mounted his chariot, and bade his
horses bring him back safe from the battle-field.
Then the horse Xanthos bowed his head, and the
long tresses of his mane flowed down to the earth
as he made answer, 'We will in very truth save
thee, O mighty Achilleus, but thy doom is near
at hand, and the fault rests not with us now, or
when we left Patroclos dead on the battle-field,
for Phœbus Apollo slew him and gave the glory
and the arms to Hector.' And Achilleus said,
'Why speak to me of evil omens? I know that
I shall see my father and my mother again no
more; but if I must die in a strange land, I will
first take my fill of vengeance.'[69]

Then the war-cry of Achilleus was heard again,
and a mighty life was poured into the hearts of
the Achaians, as they seized their arms at the
sound. Thick as withering leaves in autumn fell
the Trojans beneath his unerring spear. Chief
after chief was smitten down, until their hosts
fled in terror within the walls of Ilion. Only
Hector awaited his coming; but the shadow of
death was stealing over him, for Phœbus Apollo
had forsaken the great champion of Troy because
Zeus so willed it. So in the strife the strength of
Hector failed, and he sank down on the earth.
The foot of Achilleus rested on his breast, and
the spear's point was on his neck, while Hector

said, 'Slay me if thou wilt, but give back my body to my people. Let not the beasts of the field devour it, and rich gifts shall be thine from my father and my mother for this kindly deed.' But the eyes of Achilleus flashed with a deadly hatred as he answered, 'Were Priam to give me thy weight in gold, it should not save thy carcase from the birds and dogs.' And Hector said, 'I thought not to persuade thee, for thy heart is made of iron ; but see that thou pay not the penalty for thy deed, on the day when Paris and Phœbus Apollo shall slay thee at the Skaian gates of Ilion.' Then the life-blood of Hector reddened the ground as Achilleus said, 'Die, wretch! My fate I will meet in the hour when it may please the undying gods to send it.'

But not yet was the vengeance of Achilleus accomplished. At his feet lay Hector dead, but the rage in his heart was fierce as ever; and he tied the body to his chariot and dragged it furiously, till none who looked on it could say, 'This was the brave and noble Hector.' But things more fearful still came afterwards, for the funeral rites were done for Patroclos, and twelve sons of the Trojans were slain in the mighty sacrifice. Still the body of Hector lay on the ground, and the men of Ilion sought in vain to redeem it from Achilleus. But Phœbus Apollo came down to guard it, and he spread over it his golden shield to keep away all unseemly things.[70] And at the last king Priam mounted his chariot, for he said, 'Surely he will not scorn the prayer of a father when he begs the body of his son.' Then Zeus sent Hermes to guide the old man to the tent of Achilleus, so that none others of the Danai might see him. Then he stood before the man who had slain his son, and he kissed his hands and said, ' Hear my prayer, Achilleus. Thy father is an old man like me, but he hopes one day to see thee come back with great glory from Ilion. My sons are dead, and none had braver sons in Troy than I; and Hector, the flower and pride of all, has been smitten by thy spear. Fear the gods, Achilleus, and pity me for the remembrance of thy father, for none has ever dared like me to kiss the hand of the man who has slain his son.' So Priam wept for his dear child Hector, and the tears flowed down the cheeks of Achilleus as he thought of· his father Peleus and his friend Patroclos, and the cry of their mourning went up together.[71]

So the body of Hector was borne back to Ilion, and a great sacrifice was done to the gods beneath the earth, that Hector might be welcomed in the kingdom of Hades and Persephoné. But the

time drew nigh that the doom of Achilleus
must be accomplished, and the spear of Phœbus
Apollo [72] pierced his heart as they fought near
the Skaian gates of Ilion. In the dust lay the
body of Achilleus, while the Achaians fought the
whole day long around it, till a mighty storm
burst forth from the heaven.[73] Then they carried
it away to the ships, and placed it on a couch, and
washed it in pure water. And once more from her
coral caves beneath the sea rose the silver-footed

hetis, and the cry of the nymphs who followed
her filled the air, so that the Achaians who
heard it trembled and would have fled to the
ships; but Nestor, the wise chief of the Pylians,
said, ' Flee not, ye Argives, from those who come
to mourn for the dead Achilleus.' So Thetjs
stood weeping by the body of her child, and
the nymphs wrapped it in shining robes. Many
days and nights they wept and watched around it,
until at last they raised a great pile of wood on
the sea-shore, and the flame went up to heaven.
Then they gathered up the ashes, and placed them,
with the ashes of Patroclos, in a golden urn which
Hephaistos wrought and gave to Dionysos; and
over it they raised a great cairn on the shore
of the sea of Hellê, that men might see it afar
off as they sailed on the broad waters.[74]

IXION.

FAIR as the blushing clouds which float in early
morning across the blue heaven, the beautiful
Dia gladdened the hearts of all who dwelt in the
house of her father Hesioneus. There was no
guile in her soft clear eye, for the light of Eôs
was not more pure than the light of the maiden's
countenance. There was no craft in her smile,
for on her rested the love and the wisdom of
Athênê. Many a chieftain sought to win her for
his bride, but her heart beat with love only for
Ixion the beautiful and mighty, who came to the
halls of Hesioneus with horses which cannot grow
old or die.[75]   The golden hair flashed a glory
from his head dazzling as the rays which stream
from Helios when he drives his chariot up the
heights of heaven; and his flowing robe glistened
as he moved, like the vesture which the sun-god
gave to the wise maiden Medeia who dwelt in
Colchis.

Long time Ixion abode in the house of Hesio-

neus, for Hesioneus was loth to part with his child.
But at the last Ixion sware to give for her a
ransom precious as the golden fruits which Helios
wins from the teeming earth. So the word was
spoken, and Dia the fair became the wife of the
son of Amythaon, and the undying horses bare
her away in his gleaming chariot. Many a day
and month and year the fiery steeds of Helios
sped on their burning path, and sank down hot
and wearied in the western sea; but no gifts came
from Ixion,[76] and Hesioneus waited in vain for the
wealth which had tempted him to barter away his
child. Messenger after messenger went and came,
and always the tidings were that Ixion had better
things to do than waste his wealth on the mean
and greedy. ' Tell him,' he said, ' that every day
I journey across the wide earth, gladdening the
hearts of the children of men, and that his child
has now a more glorious home than that of the
mighty gods who dwell on the high Olympus.
What would he have more?' Then day by day
Hesioneus held converse with himself, and his
people heard the words which came sadly from
his lips. ' What would I more?' he said; 'I would
have the love of my child. I let her depart,
when not the wealth of Phœbus himself could
recompense me for her loss. I bartered her for

gifts, and Ixion withholds the wealth which he
sware to give. Yet were all the riches of his
treasure-house lying now before me, one loving
glance from the eyes of Dia would be more than
worth them all.'

But when his messengers went yet again to plead
with Ixion, and their words were all spoken in
vain, Hesioneus resolved to deal craftily, and he
sent his servants by night and stole the undying
horses which bare his gleaming chariot. Then
the heart of Ixion was humbled within him, for
he said, ' My people look for me daily throughout
the wide earth. If they see not my face, their
souls will faint with fear; they will not care to
sow their fields, and the golden harvests of Démêtêr will wave no more in the summer breeze.'
So there came messengers from Ixion, who said,
' If thou wouldest have the wealth which thou
seekest, come to the house of Ixion, and the gifts
shall be thine, and thine eyes shall once more
look upon thy child.' In haste Hesioneus went
forth from his home, as the dark and lonely cloud
steals across the broad heaven. All night long he
sped upon his way, and, as the light of Eôs flushed
the eastern sky, he saw afar off the form of a fair
woman who beckoned to him with her long white
arms. Then the heart of the old man revived,

and he said, 'It is Dia, my child. It is enough if
I can but hear her voice and clasp her in mine
arms and die.' But his limbs trembled for joy,
and he waited until presently his daughter came
and stood beside him. On her face there rested
a softer beauty than in the former days, and the
sound of her voice was more tender and loving,
as she said, 'My father, Zeus has made clear to
me many dark things, for he has given me power
to search out the secret treasures of the earth, and
to learn from the wise beings who lurk in its
hidden places the things that shall be hereafter.
And now I see that thy life is wellnigh done, if
thou seekest to look upon the treasures of Ixion,
for no man may gaze upon them and live. Go
back then to thy home, if thou wouldest not die.
I would that I might come with thee, but so it
may not be. Each day I must welcome Ixion
when his fiery horses come back from their long
journey, and every morning I must harness them
to his gleaming chariot before he speeds upon his
way. Yet thou hast seen my face, and thou
knowest that I love thee now even as in the days
of my childhood.' But the old greed filled again
the heart of Hesioneus, and he said, 'The faith of
Ixion is pledged. If he withhold still the treasures which he sware to give, he shall never more

see the deathless horses. I will go myself into his treasure-house, and see whether in very truth he has the wealth of which he makes such proud boasting.' Then Dia clasped her arms once again around her father, and she kissed his face, and said sadly, 'Farewell, then, my father; I go to my home, for even the eyes of Dia may not gaze on the secret treasures of Ixion.' So Dia left him, and when the old man turned to look on her departing form, it faded from his sight as the clouds melt away before the sun at noonday. Yet once again he toiled on his way, until before his glorious home he saw Ixion, radiant as Phœbus Apollo in his beauty; but there was anger in his kindling eye, for he was wroth for the theft of his undying horses. Then the voice of Ixion smote the ear of Hesioneus, harsh as the flapping of the wings of Erinnys when she wanders through the air. 'So thou wilt see my secret treasures. Beware that thy sight is strong.' But Hesioneus spake in haste and said, 'Thy faith is pledged, not only to let me see them, but to bestow them on me as my own, for therefore didst thou win Dia my child to be thy wife.' Then Ixion opened the door of his treasure-house, and thrust in Hesioneus, and the everlasting fire devoured him.

But far above, in the pure heaven, Zeus beheld

the deed of Ixion, and the tidings were sent abroad to all the gods of Olympus, and to all the sons of men, that Ixion had slain Hesioneus by craft and guile. A horror of great blackness fell on the heaven above and the earth beneath for the sin of which Zeus alone can purge away the guilt. Once more Dia made ready her husband's chariot, and once more he sped on his fiery journey; but all men turned away their faces, and the trees bowed their scorched and withered heads to the ground. The flowers drooped sick on their stalks and died, the corn was kindled like dried stubble on the earth, and Ixion said within himself, 'My sin is great; men will not look upon my face as in the old time, and the gods of Olympus will not cleanse my hands from the guilt of my treacherous deed.' So he went straightway and fell down humbled before the throne of Zeus, and said, 'O thou that dwellest in the pure air far above the dark cloud, my hands are foul with blood, and thou alone canst cleanse them: therefore purge mine iniquity, lest all living things die throughout the wide earth.' Then the undying gods were summoned to the judgment-seat of Zeus. By the side of the son of Cronos stood Hermes, ever bright and fair, the messenger who flies on his golden sandals more swiftly than a

dream; but fairer and more glorious than all who
stood near his throne was the lady Hêrê, the queen
of the blue heaven. On her brow rested the majesty
of Zeus, and the glory of a boundless love which
sheds gladness on the teeming earth and the broad
sea. And even as he stood before the judgment-
seat, the eyes of Ixion rested with a strange
yearning on her undying beauty, and he scarce
heard the words which cleansed him from bloodguiltiness.

So Ixion tarried in the house of Zeus, far above
in the pure æther, where only the light clouds
weave a fairy network at the rising and the setting
of the sun. Day by day his glance rested more
warm and loving on the countenance of the lady
Hêrê, and Zeus saw that her heart too was kindled
by a strange love, and a fierce wrath was stirred
within him.

Presently he called Hermes the messenger and
said, ' Bring up from among the children of Nephelê one who shall wear the semblance of the
lady Hêrê, and place her in the path of Ixion
when he wanders forth on the morrow.' So
Hermes sped away on his errand, and on that day
Ixion spake secretly with Hêrê, and tempted her
to fly from the house of Zeus. ' Come with me,'
he said; ' the winds of heaven cannot vie in speed

with my deathless horses; and the palace of Zeus
is but as the house of the dead by the side of my
glorious home.' Then the heart of Ixion bounded
with a mighty delight as he heard the words of
Hêrê. 'To-morrow I will meet thee in the land of
the children of Nephêle.' So on the morrow, when
the light clouds had spread their fairy network over
the heaven, Ixion stole away from the house of Zeus
to meet the lady Hêrê. As he went, the fairy
web faded from the sky, and it seemed to him that
the lady Hêrê stood before him in all her beauty.
'Hêrê, great queen of the unstained heaven,' he
said, 'come with me, for I am worthy of thy love,
and I quail not for all the awful majesty of Zeus.'
But even as he stretched forth his arms, the bright
form vanished away. The crashing thunder rolled
through the sky, and he heard the voice of Zeus
saying, 'I cleansed thee from thy guilt; I sheltered thee in my home ; and thou hast dealt with
me treacherously as thou didst before with Hesioneus. Thou hast sought the love of Hêrê, but the
maiden which stood before thee was but a child of
Nephelê, whom Hermes brought hither to cheat
thee with the semblance of the wife of Zeus.
Wherefore hear thy doom. No more shall thy
deathless horses speed with thy glistening chariot
over the earth, but high in the heaven a blazing

wheel shall bear thee through the rolling years;
and the doom shall be on thee for ever and ever.'

So was Ixion bound on the fiery wheel, and the
sons of men see the flashing spokes [77] day by day
as it whirls in the high heaven.

TANTALOS.

BENEATH the mighty rocks of Sipylos stood
the palace of Tantalos the Phrygian king,
gleaming with the blaze of gold and jewels. Its
burnished roofs glistened from afar like the rays
which dance on ruffled waters. Its marble columns
flashed with hues rich as the hues of purple clouds
which gather round the sun as he sinks down in
the sky. And far and wide was known the name
of the mighty chieftain, who was wiser than all
the sons of mortal men; for his wife Euryanassa,[78]
they said, came of the race of the undying gods,
and to Tantalos Zeus had given the power of
Helios, that he might know his secret counsels
and see into the hidden things of the earth and
air and sea. Many a time, so the people said, he
held converse with Zeus himself in his home on
the high Olympus; and day by day his wealth
increased, his flocks and herds multiplied exceedingly, and in his fields the golden corn waved like
a sunlit sea.

But, as the years rolled round, there were dark

s

sayings spread abroad, that the wisdom of Tantalos was turned to craft, and that his wealth and
power were used for evil ends. Men said that he
had sinned like Prometheus, the Titan, and had
stolen from the banquet-hall of Zeus the food and
drink of the gods, and given them to mortal men.
And tales yet more strange were told, how that
Pandareôs brought to him the hound which Rhea
placed in the cave of Dictê to guard the child
Zeus, and how, when Hermes bade him yield up
the dog, Tantalos laughed him to scorn, and said,
‘ Dost thou ask me for the hound which guarded
Zeus in the days of his childhood? It were as
well to ask me for the unseen breeze which sighs
through the groves of Sipylos.’

Then, last of all, men spake in whispers of a sin
yet more fearful which Tantalos had sinned, and
the tale was told that Zeus and all the gods came
down from Olympus to feast in his banquet-hall,
and how, when the red wine sparkled in the golden
goblets, Tantalos placed savoury meat before Zeus,
and bade him eat of a costly food, and, when the
feast was ended, told him that in the dish had lain
the limbs of the child Pelops, whose sunny smile
had gladdened the hearts of mortal men. Then
came the day of vengeance, for Zeus bade Hermes
bring back Pelops again from the kingdom of

Hades to the land of living men, and on Tantalos
was passed a doom which should torment him for
ever and ever. In the shadowy region where
wander the ghosts of men, Tantalos, they said, lay
prisoned in a beautiful garden, gazing on bright
flowers and glistening fruits and laughing waters;
but for all that his tongue was parched, and his
limbs were faint with hunger. No drop of water
might cool his lips, no luscious fruit might soothe
his agony. If he bowed his head to drink, the
water fled away; if he stretched forth his hand to
pluck the golden apples, the branches vanished
like mists before the face of the rising sun; and
in place of ripe fruits glistening among green
leaves a mighty rock beetled above his head, as
though it must fall and grind him to powder.
Wherefore men say, when the cup of pleasure is
dashed from the lips of those who would drink of
it, that on them has fallen the doom of the Phrygian Tantalos.[79]

THE BATTLE OF THE FROGS AND THE MICE.[80]

A THIRSTY mouse, who had just escaped from a weasel, was drinking from a pool of water, when a croaking frog saw him, and said, 'Stranger, whence hast thou come to our shore, and who is thy father? Tell me the truth, and deceive me not, for if thou deservest it, I will lead thee to my house and give thee rich and beautiful gifts. My name is Puffcheek, and I rule over the frogs who dwell in this lake, and I see that thou too art an excellent prince and a brave warrior. So make haste, and tell me to what race thou dost belong.'

Then the mouse answered him, and said, 'Friend, why dost thou ask me of my race? It is known to all the gods, and to men, and all the birds of heaven. My name is Crumbfilcher, and I am the son of the great-hearted Bread-gnawer, and my mother is Lickmill, the daughter of king Hamnibbler. I was born in a hovel, and fed on figs and nuts and on all manner of good things. But how can we be friends? We are not at all

like each other. You, frogs, live in the water;
we feed on whatever is eaten by man. No dainty
escapes my eye, whether it be bread, or cake, or
ham, or new-made cheese, or rich dishes prepared
for feasts. As to war, I have never dreaded its
din, but, going straight into it, have taken my
place among the foremost warriors.[81] Nor do I
fear men, although they have large bodies; for
at night I can bite a finger or nibble a heel without waking the sleeper from his pleasant slumber.
But there are two things which I dread greatly—
a mouse-trap and a hawk; but worse than these
are the weasels, for they can catch us in our holes.
What then am I to do? for I cannot eat the cab-
bages, radishes, and pumpkins, which furnish food
to the race of frogs.'

Then Puffcheek answered with a smile, 'My
friend, thou art dainty enough, but we have fine
things to show on the dry land and in the marsh, for
the son of Cronos has given us the power to dwell
on land or in the water as it may please us. If thou
wouldest see these things, it is soon done. Get
on my back and hold on well, so that thou mayest
reach my house with a cheerful heart.' So he
turned his back to the mouse, who sprang lightly
on it and put his arms round his soft neck. Much
pleased he was at first to swim on the back of

Puffcheek, while the haven was near; but when
he got out into midwater he began to weep and
curse his useless sorrow. He tore his hair, and
drew his feet tightly round the frog's stomach.
His heart beat wildly, and he wished himself well
on shore, as he uttered a pitiful cry and spread
out his tail on the water, moving it about like an
oar. Then in the bitterness of his grief he said,
'Surely it was not thus that the bull carried the
beautiful Europa on his back over the sea to
Crete; surely——' But before he could say more,
a snake, of which frogs and mice alike are afraid,
lifted up his head straight above the water. Down
dived Puffcheek, when he saw the snake, never
thinking that he had left the mouse to die. The
frog was safe at the bottom of the marsh, but the
mouse fell on his back and screamed terribly.
Many times he sank and many times he came up
again, kicking hard, but there was no hope. The
hair on his skin was soaked with wet and weighed
him down, and with his last breath he cried,
'Puffcheek, thou shalt not escape for thy treachery.
On the land I could have beaten thee in boxing,
wrestling, or running, but thou hast beguiled me
into the water, where I can do nothing. The eye
of justice sees thee, and thou shalt pay a fearful
penalty to the great army of the mice.'

So the Crumbfilcher died, but Lickplatter saw him as he sat on the soft bank, and, uttering a sharp cry, went to tell the mice. Then was there great wrath among them, and messengers were sent to bid all come in the morning to the house of Breadgnawer, the father of the luckless Crumbfilcher, whose body could not even be buried, because it was floating in the middle of the pond. So they came at dawn, and then Breadgnawer, rising in grief and rage, said, 'Friends, I may be the only one whom the frogs have sorely injured, but we all live but a poor life, and I am in sad plight, for I have lost three sons. The first was slain by a hateful weasel who caught him outside his hole. The next one cruel men brought to his death by a newfangled device of wood, which they call a trap; and now my darling Puffcheek has been choked in the waters. Come and let us arm ourselves for the war and go forth to do battle.'

So they put on each his armour; and for greaves around their legs they used the beans on which they fed at night, and their breastplates they made cunningly out of the skin of a dead weasel. For spears they carried skewers, and the shell of a nut for a helmet. So they stood in battle array, and the frogs, when they heard of it, rose from the water and summoned a council in a corner of the pond. As they wondered what might be the cause of these things, there came a messenger from the mice, who declared war against them and said, 'Ye frogs, the mice bid you arm yourselves and come forth to the battle, for they have seen Crumbfilcher, whom your king Puff-cheek drowned, floating dead on the water.' Then the valiant frogs feared exceedingly, and blamed the deed of Puffcheek; but the king said, 'Friends, I did not kill the mouse or see him die ; of course he was drowned while he amused himself in the pond by imitating the swimming of a frog, and the wretches now bring a charge against me who am wholly guiltless. But come, let us take counsel how we may destroy these mice ; and this, I think, is the best plan. Let us arm ourselves and take our stand where the bank is steepest, and when they come charging against us, let us seize their helmets and drag them down into the pond. Thus we shall drown them all and set up a trophy for our victory.' So they put on each his armour. They covered their legs with mallow leaves, and carried radish leaves for shields, and rushes for spears, and snail-shells for helmets. So they stood in array on the high bank, brandishing their spears and shouting for the battle.

But Zeus summoned the gods to the starry

heaven, and, pointing to the hosts of the frogs
and mice, mighty as the armies of the Kentaurs
or the giants, he asked who would aid each side
as it might be hard pressed in the strife; and he
said to Athênê, 'Daughter, thou wilt go surely to
the aid of the mice, for they are always running
about thy shrine, and delight in the fat and the
morsels which they pick from the sacrifices.'

But Athênê said to the son of Cronos, 'O father,
I go not to help the mice, for they have done me
grievous mischief, spoiling the garlands and the
lamps for the sake of the oil. Nay, I have greater
cause for anger, for they have eaten out the robe
which I wove from fine thread, and made holes
in it; and the man who mended it charges a
high price, and, worse still, I borrowed the stuff
of which I wove it, and now I cannot pay it back.
Yet neither will I aid the frogs, for they are not
in their right senses. A little while ago, I came
back tired from war, and wanting sleep, but they
never let me close my eyes with their clatter, and
I lay sleepless with a headache till the cock crew
in the morning. But, O ye gods, let us aid neither
side, lest we be wounded with their swords or
spears, for they are sharp and strong even against
gods; but let us take our sport by watching the
strife in safety out of heaven.' [82]

Then the gods did as Athênê bade them, and went all into one place; and the gnats, with their great trumpets, gave the signal for the battle, and Zeus thundered out of the sky because of the woes that were coming. Mighty were the deeds which were done on both sides, and the earth and the pond were reddened with the blood of the slain. So, as the fight went on, Crumbstealer slew Garlicenter before he came to land; and Mudwalker, seeing it, threw at him a clod of earth, and, hitting him on the forehead, almost blinded him. Then, in his fury, Crumbstealer seized a great stone, and crushed the leg of the frog, so that he fell on his back in the dust. Then Breadgnawer wounded Puffcheek in the foot, and made him limp into the water.

But among the mice was a young hero, with whom none could be matched for boldness and strength, and whose name was Bitstealer. On the bank of the pond he stood alone, and vowed a vow to destroy the whole race of the frogs. And the vow would have been accomplished, for his might was great indeed, had not the son of Cronos pitied the frogs in their misery, and charged Pallas Athênê and Arês to drive Bitstealer from the battle. But Arês made answer and said, 'O Zeus, neither Athênê nor Arês alone can save the

frogs from death. Let us all go and help them; [83]
and do thou, son of Cronos, wield thy mighty
weapon with which thou didst slay the Titans, and
Capaneus, and Enkelados, and the wild race of
the giants, for thus only can the bravest of them
be slain.' So spake Arês; and Zeus hurled his
scathing thunderbolts, and the lightnings flashed
from the sky, and Olympus shook with the earth-
quake. The frogs and mice heard and trembled,
but the mice ceased not yet from the battle, and
strove only the more to slay their enemies, until
Zeus, in his pity, sent a new army to aid the frogs.

Suddenly they came on the mice, with mailed
backs and crooked claws, with limping gait, with
mouths like shears, and skins like potsherds.
Their backs were hard and horny, their arms were
long and lean, and their eyes were in their
breasts. They had eight feet and two heads,
and no hands. Men call them crabs. With
their mouths they bit the tails and feet and
hands of the mice, and broke their spears, and
great terror came on all the mice, so that they
turned and fled. Thus was the battle ended, and
the sun went down. [84]

NOTES TO TALES.

Note 1, page 121.

THE ocean of Greek mythology, with its unbroken calm, has nothing to do with Thalassa, the rough and angry sea. Tales of the Gods and Heroes, note 61, p. 314.

Note 2, page 122.

A phrase from a beautiful fragment of Archilochus, quoted in Tales from Greek Mythology, p. 107. In it we have a picture of the serene and cloudless sunset which, after the slaughter of the suitors, brings to an end the long toils of Odysseus. Introduction, p. 00.

Note 3, page 124.

The Homeric poets mention but one Gorgon, and in their descriptions she retains no trace of beauty. It matters little whether the legends which speak of the change in her form are older than Homer or later. Both are equally true to the mythical phraseology from which all such tales were derived (Introd. p. 32.) The story which says that from her head sprang the winged horse Pegasos (another form of the Harits, χάριτς, or horses of Indra) is remarkable chiefly because it makes her also the mother of Chrysaor, which occurs elsewhere simply as an epithet of Apollo (with the golden sword). Hesiod, Works and Days, 700.

NOTES TO TALES.

Note⁴, page 120.

Χρυσόπατρος, the child of the golden shower—a fitting name for the son of Danaê, Dahanâ, the Dawn.   Introd. p. 53.

Note⁵, page 127.

The Lament of Danaê, by Simonides of Keos, exists only as a fragment. Mr. Isaac Williams has given a translation of it in his Christian Scholar, p. 181.

Note⁶, page 128.

The name Polydectes is only another form of Polydegmon; and it is under both these names that Hades steals away Persephonê (Hymn to Dêmêtêr, 0, 17). We have not far to go for the meaning. It is but the love of the night for the evening. In Homer, Eôs ends as well as begins the day (Od. v. 390); and Danaê here represents the beautiful hues of twilight, which the darkness vainly strives to make its own. It is true that Hades wins the love of Persephonê; but Persephonê is the summer, whom the winter, another image of darkness, steals from the mourning earth, her mother. Thus the vain attempt of Polydectes to win the love of Danaê is a mere counterpart to that of Apollo when he seeks to embrace Daphnê.

Note⁷, page 130.

Mr. Kingsley, in his Heroes, introduces a strong moral element into the tale, when he says that she lost her beauty for sinning 'a sin at which the sun hid his face.' But Medusa cannot in any sense be either morning, day, or evening; and hence the sun could not be said to see her deeds.

Note⁸, page 132.

Not the narrow strait to which we confine the name, but the broad Hellespontos, from which the storm-tossed mariner might see the distant cairn on the grave of Achilleus (Od. xxiv. 82). See, further, Tales from Greek Mythology, note 11, p. 112.

Note, *page* 134.

Introduction, p. 41.

Note 10, *page* 135.

The idea of age would be directly suggested whenever the evening was regarded as the lingering survivor mourning for the departed glories of the day.

Note 11, *page* 136.

Introd. p. 32.

Note 12, *page* 139.

This 'invisible cap' is worn by Athênê in Iliad, v. 845, and is represented on the shield of Heracles (Asp. Heracl. 222).

Note 13, *page* 141.

It is scarcely necessary to refer to Mr. Kingsley's fine poem, in which he has made the episode of the Dragon as attractive as it can be made in hexameters which are really anapæstic.

Note 14, *page* 142.

The idea of a weighty and solid heaven would seem to be a much later conception than that of Ouranos, Varuna, who, spread over all things, looks down on the earth which he loves. The idea of the brazen firmament found no disfavour with Greek astronomers.

Note 15, *page* 143.

Introd. p. 33.

Note 16, *page* 145.

Tales from Greek Mythology, note 2, p. 105.

Note 17, *page* 146.

The celebrated oracle of Zeus Ammon, in the Libyan

desert. The name was then referred to the sands by which
the temple was surrounded, although it was only a Greek
form of the Egyptian Amoun (Herod. ii. 42).

Note ¹⁸, page 150.

Dictys is made a fisherman, in the same way that Lycaon
is turned into a wolf—to account for the name. The name
points more probably to the root of δίκνυμι, and so is connected with the idea of light as revealing the secrets of
darkness. Hence the brother of Polydectes would be a
fitting friend for Danaê.

Note ¹⁹, page 154.

Achilleus, also, presides at games after his victory over
Hector—the reason in both cases being the same. Introd.
p. 08.

Note ²⁰, page 150.

The man of sorrow comes naturally to Argos, when the
bright hero, the sun of the land, has departed from it.

Note ²¹, page 157.

These are simply local legends, to account for certain
cities and their buildings. Still the myths adhere to the
old idea, for the builders come from Lykia, the land of
light, which gives to Phœbus the name Lykêgenês, and
they are the Cyclopes, who sometimes forge the thunderbolts of Zeus beneath the burning mountain, and sometimes,
as in the Odyssey, appear as (the mists and black clouds)
the monstrous offspring of the sea-god Poseidon. Here, as
elsewhere, we cannot infer from the silence of Homer that
the latter is the older myth. Probably both may have
come down together. Introd. p. 104.

Note ²², page 158.

Shelley's Translation of this hymn is a marvel of power
and beauty. It is also on the whole a remarkably faithful

version; and the vein of sly humour running through the
poem is admirably preserved.

The analysis of this hymn (Introd. p. 40) seems to furnish a sufficient explanation of the comic air with which
certain portions of the narrative are invested. The remembrance of the old myth, although not fully retained, was by
no means wholly effaced; and under these conditions it was
impossible that the result should be any other than what it
is. The burlesque into which the adventures of Heracles
easily pass, arose from no intention of disparaging the
hero's greatness; and Mr. Grote would appear to be mistaken when he says (Hist. of Greece, vol. i. p. 82) that the
hymnographer concludes the song to Hermes 'with frankness
unusual in speaking of a god.' Nor can we determine,
from the mere existence of this comic element, the particular use for which these hymns were composed. Colonel
Mure (Crit. Hist. Gr. Lit. vol. ii. p. 316) has little hesitation
in concluding, 'from the discreditable and even ludicrous
light in which the character and conduct of the deities
are often exhibited in their text,' that many 'even of the
earlier more genial among them' were composed, not for
recitation in any religious solemnities, but 'for familiar
occasions of festive conviviality, where the adventures of
the popular objects of worship were made, like all other
subjects, to contribute their share to the common fund of
mirthful entertainment.' That they may have been so used,
it is impossible to deny; but an equally strong argument
against such exclusive use might be drawn from those
graver passages, even in the Hymn to Hermes, which are
scarcely surpassed for beauty and dignity even in the Lay
of Démêtêr. Colonel Mure has summed up all the reasons
against assigning the authorship of these hymns to the poets
of the Iliad or the Odyssey; and these reasons are conclusive. Yet, if the composition of the greater epics belongs
to an age much earlier than that to which it is generally

T

assigned, these hymns may well have been written at a time which, in the belief of Herodotus or Thucydides, was the age of Homer. These hymns, as Colonel Mure has well remarked, are epical lays, complete in themselves; and among their number he reckons the lay of Demodocos, recited in the Odyssey, as being 'in all essential respects an epic hymn to Vulcan.' His remark seems to militate slightly against his own theory of the complete unity of the Odyssey.

Note ¹², page 159.

Dr. Mommsen (Hist. of Rome, vol. i. p. 18) believes that 'the enigmatical Hellenic story of the stealing of the cattle of Helios' by Hermes 'is beyond doubt connected with the Roman legend about Cacua.' It is also connected with that of Heracles and Echidna in the Scythian tale; but the solution of the enigma is, in all, the same.

Note ¹⁴, page 160.

Mr. Grote, in his short analysis of this hymn, says of this incident that Hermes 'stole the cattle of Apollo in Pieria, dragging them backwards to his cave in Arcadia' (Hist. of Greece, vol. i. p. 80). This is no necessary inference from the passage in the hymn (75, 76), although Livy (i. 7) has accepted this clumsy addition in the story of Cacus. The poet means apparently that he so varied the track of the cattle that no one could know whence they had come or whither they were going; and so Shelley has understood it.

'Backward and forward drove he them astray,
So that the tracks which seemed before were aft.' (xiii.)

This would accurately describe the action of wind, while the other device would not.

Note ¹⁵, page 160.

The Hymn to Hermes (111) ascribes to him the gift of

fire, thus asserting more and less than Shelley in his translation—

' Mercury first found out for human weal
Tinder-box, matches, fire-irons, flint and steel.'   (xviii.)

The list should be brought down to the mere item of tinder-
wood.   Mr. Kelly would refer this legend to the Sanskrit
chark, in which the fire is churned.   See his Curiosities of
Indo-European Folk-lore.

Note²⁶, page 101.

Hymn, 130.   This line is unfortunately diluted by
Shelley—

' His mind became aware
Of all the joys which in religion are.'   (xxi.)

Note²⁷, page 101.

Introd. p. 48.

Note²⁸, page 107.

Hymn, 372-3.   This seems by far the keenest piece of
satire to be found in the poem.   The passage, in fact, lays
down the great principles of English law, that a criminal
charge must be proved by witnesses, and that prisoners are
not to be threatened or coerced into confession.   It is a
passage which might come from the poet of a people who
met in Agora in the age of the Iliad, but could never have
come from the Asiatic.   It would be well for French
justice if it might less frequently be said of the judge—

μηνύειν ἐπέλευεν ἀναγκαίης ὕπο πολλῆς.

Note²⁹, page 171.

The contrast in the tone of this passage (Hymn, 549)
with the concluding lines of the Hymn to Apollo is manifest.   See, further, Tales of the Gods and Heroes, note 13,
p. 203.

Note [30], *page* 171.

The Thriæ are beings of the same type with the Graiæ and the Gorgons.

Note [31], *page* 172.

Colonel Mure, who with Mr. Grote thinks that the oxen were dragged by their tails, holds that 'it is the supernatural element of the subject which alone gives point and seasoning to an otherwise palpable extravaganco' (Crit. Hist. Gr. Lit. vol. ii. p. 330). His explanation apparently fails altogether to account for the character of the hymn. It may be true that 'Hermes, in his capacity of god, is gifted from the first moment of his existence with divine power and energy,' but so also is Apollo; and if, 'as a member of the Hellenic pantheon, he is subjected to the natural drawbacks of humanity, and, by consequence, at his birth to those of infancy,' so also, again, is Apollo. Nor does this help to explain why Hermes should go off to play, sing, and thieve, when but a few hours old. Colonel Mure believes that the 'spirit of the jest' lies in 'the obligation to perform, through the agency of his imbecile human personality, the mighty deeds' by which he seeks 'at once to assert his rank among his fellow-gods;' but he forgot that the real point to be explained is, why Hermes should have to do this any more than Apollo or Dionysos. It is characteristic of Colonel Mure's criticism to pronounce the making of the lyre 'an elegant expedient,' hit on by the poet, for 'accommodating the dispute (between Hermes and Apollo) on terms honourable to each party' (p. 349).

Note [32], *page* 174.

Mr. Grote (Hist. of Greece, vol. ii. p. 320, &c.) has brought out very vividly the influence of the great festivals at Olympia and elsewhere in imparting to the various Hellenic tribes something like a national character.

Note **33**, *page* 170.

In Minos Professor Max Müller recognises the Sanskrit Manu, a mortal Zeus (Comp. Myth. p. 61).

Note **34**, *page* 180.

Skylla, according to one version, was changed into a fish, Nisos into an eagle. This is one of the many involuntary transformations which occur in Greek mythology. See, further, note 43.

Note **35**, *page* 184.

The power of transformation at will, exercised by Phœbus Apollo (Gods and Heroes, p. 115) as well as Dionysos, is embodied especially in Proteus, who, in the familiar legends of the North, appears as ' Farmer Weatheraky.'

Note **36**, *page* 185.

Gods and Heroes, p. 171.

Note **37**, *page* 186.

The king of the flaming fire. His daughter Corónis (who is the same as Danaê or Procris) is here, like the Sanskrit Ahalyâ, represented as the daughter of the sun, because, in the words of Kumârila, she goes before him at his rising.

Note **38**, *page* 187.

The story of Corónis is in all essential points the same as that of the Arcadian Callisto (Paus. viii. 3; Apollod. iii. 8, 2). As in other legends, the real origin of the tale is seen at once in the almost transparent account of Apollodorus.

Note **39**, *page* 180.

For the Cyclopes of Homer, see p. 104. The influence of the Iamidæ is described by Pindar as strictly a moral one :—

τιμῶντες ἀρετάς,
ἰς φανερὰν ὁδὸν ἔρχονται.   Ol. vi. 122.

Note ⁴⁰, page 100.

Gods and Heroes, p. 105.

Note ⁴¹, page 103.

ἀλλ' ὅτε δὴ τρίτον ἦμαρ ἰϋπλόκαμος τέλεσ' ἠώς.   Od. v. 390.

Note ⁴², page 105.

On the extent to which human sacrifices prevailed in
Greece within any historic or semi-historical period, see
Grote, Hist. of Greece, vol. ii. p. 170, &c.   The origin of the
practice may be traced either to a perverted notion of
human duty, or to such etymological mistakes (whether
wilful or not) as led to the institution of the Suttee sacrifice
in India.   Max Müller, Comp. Myth. p. 22.

Note ⁴³, page 105.

Apollodorus (iii. 8, 1) merely says that Lycaon was with
his sons killed by the thunderbolt.   Pausanias (viii, 2, 1), on
high religious and moral grounds, is firmly convinced that
he was transformed into a wolf.   The story, however, is
simply a device to explain the origin and meaning of a
name; but the Greek explanations of mythical names are
much more frequently wrong than right.   If the original force
of each word had been thoroughly remembered, the great
fabric of their mythology could never have been built up.
But the growth of precisely such tales as those into which
they were expanded was inevitable, as soon as the meaning
of the old names was either half understood or altogether
forgotten.   Under the former class stand Melantho and
Melanthios, the children of Dolios and enemies of Odysseus.
But the explanation became utterly wrong when the name
of Iolê was referred to poison, and the epithet of Lykeios,
applied to Apollo, was connected, like that of Lycaon, with
wolves.   Midway between these two classes stand such
names as Odysseus and Œdipus, in which a faint link, still

perceptible in the spirit of the tale, carries us to the old mythical phrase. See Introduction, note 5, p. 108.

But such transformations, few as they are, seem in no way to be relics, as Mr. Gladstone contends, of original nature-worship among the Greeks (Homer and the Homeric Age, vol. ii. p. 412). Most of them are to be explained by refer-ring to the language of tho oldest Vedic hymns. The bull of Europa is the bull Indra, who is afterwards degraded into the Minotauros and other monsters. On these and on the frequently recurring dragons and serpents, enough has already been said. But there appears to be no attempt in the Homeric poetry to analyse accurately the characteristics of beasts, and to frame tales in illustration of them. The Battle of the Frogs and Mice (xxii.) is a sharp satire, valuable as showing the estimate of a later age for what is called the supernatural mechanism of Homer; and the fables of Æsop cannot be held to prove the existence of such stories during the age in which the Homeric poems were composed. Simonides of Amorgos, in his satirical portraiture of women, shows much the same power of dis-crimination with Æsop; but he simply uses the main features in brute character to point his sarcasm, without any attempt to depict brute life. The theory which traces all such indications in Greek poetry to an old nature-worship thus becomes utterly untenable. Such a suppo-sition might possibly account for the sacredness of the sun's oxen in Thrinakia, but it cannot account for Hermes steal-ing them when he is but an hour old. Hence some little uncertainty is also thrown over Mr. Dasent's hypothesis of a primæval belief that 'men under certain conditions could take the shape of animals' (Norse Tales, cxix.) There is no doubt that such a belief prevailed long before the time of Herodotus; but if, as it would seem, there is no trace of it in Homer, it is at the least possible that tho idea, with all its consequences of wehrwolves and loupgarous, may

be traced to the same sort of mistake which connected the
name of the Lykian sun-god with the destruction of wolves,
and so gave rise to the fable of Lycaon. To this origin
may perhaps be assigned the involuntary transformations to
which so many of the personages in the Norse tales are
subjected. But there still remains the genuine Beast epic
of the North, which accurately describes the relations of
brute animals with one another, and, in Mr. Dasent's words,
' is full of the liveliest traits of nature.' These tales Mr.
Dasent traces, not to nature-worship, but to ' that deep love
of nature and close observation of the habits of animals
which is only possible in an early and simple stage of
society,' and he refers to similar stories in the Hindu
Pantcha Tantra and the Hitopadesa. Hence we have to
seek for the common origin of both; but the mere fact of
their composition seems to be conclusive against the idea of
nature-worship, which, of all forms of thought, would most
completely blind the eyes and dull the minds of men to the
real characters whether of men or beasts. Had Norsemen
really worshipped bulls, bears, and wolves, they would never
have written of them with an affectionate familiarity.

Note 44, page 108.

Professor Max Müller, in the passage (Comp. Myth. p. 8)
where he shows the absurdity of supposing that Greeks sat
down deliberately to concoct ridiculous legends, says that
this myth of Deucalion and Pyrrha ' owes its origin to a
mere pun on λάος and λᾶας.' (See also Grote, History of
Greece, vol. i. p. 134; Pind. Ol. ix. 71.) But Delitzch, in his
commentary on Genesis, asserts that, ' according to the
legend of the Macusi-Indians in South America, the only
man who survived the flood repeopled the earth by changing
stones into men. According to that of the Tamanaks of
Orinoko, it was a pair of human beings who cast behind
them the fruit of a certain palm, and out of the kernels

sprang men and women.' The chief suspicion about American native traditions arises from the possible intermeddling of Christian missionaries, who may have thought it to their interest to make out a correspondence of such legends with those of the old world, and especially with the records of the Hebrew Scriptures. Hence Burton, in the volume which relates his visit to the Great Salt Lake City, does not hesitate to ascribe the alleged original belief of the North American Indians in a great Spirit, unseen but omnipotent, to the Jesuit missionaries, who first instilled the belief into them, and then asserted that the Indians had the belief before their arrival. But if the idea of such interference is rejected (and it is, very possibly, worth little), then the harmony of many of their legends with those of the old world increases the marvel, if not the mystery, which attaches to the diffusion of Aryan mythology. The legend on the subject of women, which Mr. Hind, in his Labrador Explorations, says that he heard from wandering native tribes, presents the closest correspondence with that of Pandora in Hesiod. If, then, these Labrador Indians did not learn it from Jesuit missionaries (and it seems highly improbable that they should so have learnt it, nor can we conceive the motive which could have led the Jesuits to impart this legend rather than others), then we must carry back these tales still further to a common source from which the mythology of the Aryan and the North American Indian may both have taken their rise. The agreement of many negro stories with European traditions still further complicates the problem. Dasent, Popular Tales from the Norse, p. xxxi. &c.

Note [45], page 108.

Nothing, it would seem, can be gained by attempts to prove that the legend of Deucalion is derived directly from the account of the Noachian deluge as given in the Pentateuch. It is impossible to deny that essentially the

two stories are the same: but so also are the Babylonian and
other legends on the same subject; and if we resort to the
supposition of conscious borrowing in this case, we must
take up the same hypothesis in every other—a labour before
which the stoutest would quail. Further, we should have
to determine first which is the oldest tale of the flood, to
be found in what is called profane history; and this is a
task for which at present we appear scarcely to have
sufficient materials. It is of no slight moment that the
Egyptians, with whom the Hebrews were in earliest and
closest intercourse, had no traditions of a flood (Edinburgh
Review, July 1802, p. 100), while the Babylonian and
Hellenic tales bear a strong resemblance in many points to
the narrative in Genesis. But we have no warrant for
assuming any intercourse between Jews and Greeks in or
before the Hesiodic age; and the legend of Deucalion was
known to the author of the Catalogue of Women, a poem
which, if not written by Hesiod, belongs certainly to his
age, or to the age immediately succeeding.

> Ἤτοι γὰρ Λοκρὸς Λελίγων ἡγήσατο λαῶν,
> Τούς ῥά ποτε Κρονίδης Ζεὺς, ἄφθιτα μήδεα εἰδώς,
> Λεκτοὺς ἐκ γαίης λάας πόρε Δευκαλίωνι.

Mr. Grote refers to conflicting accounts of the genealogy of
Deucalion, as given by the Scholiast on Homer, on the
authority both of Hesiod and Acusilaos (History of Greece,
Part I. ch. v.) It is seemingly doubtful whether the story
of Ogyges is earlier or later than that of Deucalion. It has
certainly assumed more strictly the form of a local legend;
but Mr. Grote supposes it to refer to Deucalion's deluge
(Ibid. ch. xi. vol. i. p. 200). As evidence of an historical
flood, these tales have as much and as little value as the
lay of Achilleus for determining the reality of the Trojan
war. In Deucalion's flood those who can reach the top of
the hills escape: the flood of Xisuthrus, in the Babylonian

mythology, spares all the pious (Niebuhr's Lectures on Ancient History, vol. i. p. 18). In the Hindu version, the flood is universal; but Manu, the man, enters the ark with the seven sages, who remain with him till it is landed on the peak called Naubandhana, from the binding of the ship (Story of Nala and Damhyanti, Milman's translation).

The names occurring in the legend of Deucalion are significant. His own name suggests a comparison with that of Polydeukes, the glittering son of Leda. His father is Prometheus, in whom we recognise (not, according to Mr. Kingsley, in his pleasant tale of the Waterbabies, p. 286, the false system of deductive philosophers, but) the same idea of piercing forethought, which comes out again in Athênê, Asclepios, and Iamos, the children or the kinsfolk of the sun-god Phœbus Apollo. His wife is Pyrrha, the red, a name which to the Greek mythographers expressed the colour of the earth, but which may rather belong to the class of names of which Phoinix, Iolê, Iolaos, Iocastê, are examples. Pyrrha, again, is the daughter of Epimetheus, the passive receiver of impressions, and so passing into the receptive character of Dêmêtêr and Persephonê. Deucalion is, moreover, the father of Minos, who is connected with a large family of solar legends, running into the mythology of Argos, Megara, Thebes, and Athens.

Note ⁴⁶, *page* 199.

Tales from Greek Mythology, pp. 8, 107.

Note ⁴⁷, *page* 204.

According to the version of Apollodorus (iii. 10, 7), Æthra was brought by force from Athens to Trœzen. The tale is a curious complication of myths. Having related the story which made Helen the daughter of Zeus and Nemesis, he goes on to tell how Theseus stole Helen and brought her to Athens, and how Castor and Polydeukes,

while Theseus was absent in Hades, took Athens and
brought away thence not only Helen but Æthra. It is
easy to see that they could only have been taken while
Theseus was in the kingdom of the dead.

Note 48, page 204.
Introduction, p. 14; p. 43, note 1.

Note 49, page 208.

'It was not without reason that Theseus was said to
have given rise to the proverb, *Another Hercules*; for not
only is there a strong resemblance between them in many
particular features, but it also seems clear that Theseus was
to Attica what Hercules was to the rest of Greece, and
that his career likewise represents the events of a period
which cannot have been exactly measured by any human
life, and probably includes many centuries' (Thirlwall, Hist.
of Greece, ʳol. i. p. 139). It would have been still more
true to say that his life, like that of Theseus, Bellerophon,
Achilleus, Meleagros, and Odysseus, is but the sun's life of
a day or the yearly life of the seasons.

Note 50, page 209.
Introduction, p. 9.

Note 51, page 215.

The victory of Œdipus over the Sphinx is but the slaying
of the serpent Fafnir or the Pythian dragon, by one who
to the strength and beauty of Sigurdr or Phœbus adds the
wisdom of Prometheus and Medeia. There can be no
doubt that the riddle of the feet is a late insertion. It is
one of the enigmas in which a rude people take delight;
and a different riddle might be introduced in all the versions of the tale. It mattered not what the dark saying
might be, as long as it was a dark saying, like the in-
articulate growl of the thunder.

Note [32], *page* 210.

As long as this incident retained any part of the meaning still seen in the myth which tells us how Iolê at the last came back to Heracles, here the tale of Œdipus doubtless ended. When translated into the ordinary relations of life, the unwitting marriage of a son with his mother might well give rise to such a tragedy as that which Sophocles has immortalised.

Note [33], *page* 218.

Gods and Heroes, note 73, p. 310.

Note [34], *page* 222.

Gods and Heroes, note 46, p. 307.

Note [35], *page* 224.

So ends the tale of the long toil and sorrows of Œdipus. The last scene exhibits a manifest return to the spirit of the solar myth. His beauty is utterly marred, and his disguise is as complete as that of Odysseus when he first trod the soil of Ithaca after his return from Troy. Still there is about him a more than human power. He must not die the common death of all men, for no disease or corruption can touch the body of the brilliant sun; and so the poet says, with instinctive truthfulness, that his departure forms no matter for weeping—

οὐ στενακτὸς οὐδὲ σὺν νόσοις
ἀλγεινὸς ἐξεπέμπετ', ἀλλ' εἴ τις βροτῶν
θαυμαστός.　　　　　　Soph. Œd. Col. 1007.

And not less truly does he associate the very sorrows of Œdipus with the long struggle of the sun against the clouds who are arrayed against him. It is a lifelong toil, and his trials come—

αἱ μὲν ἀπ' ἀελίου δυσμᾶν,
αἱ δ' ἀνατέλλοντος,
αἱ δ' ἀνὰ μέσσαν ἀκτῖν',
αἱ δὲ νυχιᾶν ἀπὸ ῥιπᾶν.　　Œd. Tyr. 1243.

Note 56, *page* 227.

A counterpart to this act is found in the Roman tales of
the self-devotion of Curtius and the Decii.

Note 57, *page* 228.

Paus. ix. 8, 2. The same tokens were alleged as proof
of the burial-place of many a mediæval saint. See also
Grote, History of Greece, vol. i. p. 374.

Note 58, *page* 231.

The reason which Antigoné gives as determining her
conduct is eminently characteristic. If her husband die,
she may marry again; if she lose one child, she may have
another; but when her parents are dead she cannot hope
for more brothers. Herodotus represents the wife of Inta-
phernes as choosing to save her brother and abandon her
husband and children to death (iii. 119). Now, that the
tone of thought in both these stories is precisely the same,
all must admit; but Mr. Grote apparently takes this coinci-
dence as conclusively proving that Sophocles was the companion of Herodotus. He refuses to determine 'which of
the two obtained the thought from the other,' but thinks
that 'the comparison of Herodot. iii. 119 with Soph. Antig.
905, proves a community of thought . . . hardly explicable
in any other way' (History of Greece, vol. viii. p. 440). But
this only starts a fresh difficulty, for it implies that either
Herodotus or Sophocles originated this thought, which, as
Mr. Grote asserts, 'is certainly not a little far-fetched,'
and, as we might safely add, is to all appearance decidedly
non-Hellenic. It is possible that Herodotus may have
brought the Persian legend into closer harmony with
Western forms of expression; but we lose ourselves in an
inextricable labyrinth when we say that it was borrowed
directly by the one from the other. The bear and the

hyæna have no tails. The Norseman and the negro not only say that they lost them long ago, but they account for the fact in the same way—'that both owe their loss to the superior cunning of another animal' (Dasent, Tales from the Norse, Introd. li.) The cases are almost parallel. In each case we have fragments of primæval thought which have floated at random down the stream of time.

Note [59], page 232.
Soph. Antig. 1000.

Note [60], page 237.

The rising of land from alluvial deposit at the mouth of the Acheloös was a fact of sufficient importance to demand and receive its own local legend. Thucydides was somewhat prone to believe in epónymi—that is, he had no objection to say that Italy was named after Italos, king of the Sikels; but when he has to speak of mythical heroes, he generally lays the burden of responsibility on popular tradition: λέγεται δὲ καὶ Ἀλκμαίωνι, κ. τ. λ. (ii. 102), or else reduces the tale to his own standard of credibility. See Grote, Hist. of Greece, i. 547.

Note [61], page 237.

The sons of the seven chieftains who had attacked Thebes in the former war. Apollod. iii. 72 ; Grote, Hist. of Greece, vol. i. p. 378.

Note [62], page 238.

The sign of the snake and the sparrows. Il. 300–331.

Note [63], page 240.

These are, in fact, the immortal Harits, who draw the car of Indra up the heaven. Introd. p. 72, note 1.

Note [64], page 240.

This Dodóna is not the later and more widely known

Dodóna of Epeiros. Gladstone, Homer and the Homeric Age, vol. i. p. 104; Iliad, xvi. 233.

Note 63, page 241.
Gods and Heroes, p. 224.

Note 66, page 242.
Il. xvii. 438–460.

Note 67, page 243.
Il. xviii. 117.

Note 68, page 243.
Il. xix. 137.

Note 69, page 244.
Il. xix. 409–423.

Note 70, page 246.
Il. xxiii. 185, xxiv. 20.

Note 71, page 246.
Il. xxiv. 512.

Note 72, page 247.
Il. xxii. 360. This passage furnishes conclusive evidence that the poets of the Iliad were well acquainted with many mythical tales which it formed no part of their object to recount.

Note 73, page 247.
Od. xxiv. 42. Ζεὺς λαίλαπι παύσιν.

Note 74, page 247.
Od. xxiv. 84. For a comparison of the groundwork of the Iliad (or rather of the Achilléis) with that of the Odyssey, see Introd. p. 87, &c.

Note 75, page 248.
These are, again, the horses which Zeus gave to Peleus, the Harits (χάριτες) of Vedic mythology.

Note [76], *page* 249.

This withholding of the gifts is the drought which follows when the summer sun journeys through an unclouded sky. The incident occurs again in the story of Hesionê, where Laomedon plays the part of Ixion.

Note [77], *page* 256.

Pind. Pyth. ii. 74.

Note [78], *page* 257.

This is one more among the many names which describe the wide-spreading light of the dawn—Europa, Eurydikê, Eurymedê, Euryphaëssa, &c.

Note [79], *page* 259.

To be tantalised is therefore only a phrase expressive of the disappointment of Orpheus when he turns to embrace Eurydikê, whom he recovers only to lose again. In the restoration of Pelops to life, we see simply the power of the Colchian Medeia, which she can exercise at her will; and thus is dispelled the moral horror which roused the special indignation of Pindar against this tale.

Note [80], *page* 260.

The question of the date of this poem has been examined by Colonel Mure (Crit. Hist. Gr. Lit. vol. ii. p. 300). He regards the poem itself as 'conceived in a very happy spirit of mixed Homeric and Aristophanic satire against the absurdities of the popular religion.' Yet it is, after all, simply the inevitable extension of a principle which is seen at work in the Iliad and the Odyssey. In those poems, it is true, some of the gods and heroes are saved from the indignity of sarcasm; and the reasons why they should be so preserved are plain. But the transition to the temper of actual satire becomes natural, when we look to the singular passage in which Héré, Poseidon, and Athéné are represented as absurdly foiled by a mere giant in their attempt to bind the father of gods and men (Il. i. 400). It may well be doubted whether even the lay of Demodocos would furnish a more powerful stimulus to the sarcasm of a later age than this passage which Mr. Gladstone has unaccountably ignored in his description of the attributes and character of the spotless Athéné.

Professor Max Müller quotes (Hist. of Sanskrit Literature, p. 494) a hymn in the 7th Mandala, which, under form of a panegyric of the frogs, 'is clearly a satire on the priests.' 'It is curious to observe,' he adds, 'that the same animal should have been chosen by the Vedic satirist to represent the priests, which by the earliest satirist of Greece was selected as the representative of the Homeric heroes.'

Note ⁸¹, page 201.

It seems almost profane to point out the sarcasm which attacks the words of Hector in what is perhaps the most beautiful passage of the Iliad—

μάθον ἔμμεναι ἐσθλός
αἰεὶ καὶ πρώτοισι μετὰ Τρώεσσι μάχεσθαι.

Note ⁸², page 205.

A privilege which, before the final struggle between Achilleus and his enemies, Zeus reserves to himself, that he may gladden his heart with the sight of the battle (Il xix. 23).

Note ⁸³, page 207.

A reference to the mission of all the gods, by Zeus, to take part in the final conflict of the Iliad.

Note ⁸⁴, page 207.

The names of the frog and mouse warriors are scarcely more transparent than those of many heroes and minor characters in the Iliad and Odyssey. Euryeleia and Melantho tell their tale as clearly as Psicharpax and Troxartes; but those names of the later poem are, in Colonel Mure's words, 'the more interesting to the modern reader from the light they throw on many petty details of social life in the age from which the poem has been transmitted' (Crit. Hist. Gr. Lit. vol. ii. p. 359).

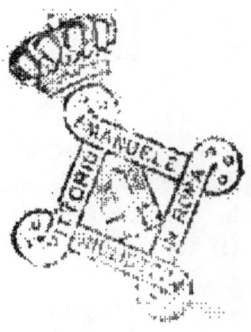

LONDON
PRINTED BY SPOTTISWOODE AND CO.
NEW-STREET SQUARE

GENERAL LIST OF WORKS

PUBLISHED BY

MESSRS. LONGMANS, GREEN, AND CO.

PATERNOSTER ROW, LONDON.

Historical Works.

LORD MACAULAY'S WORKS. Complete and Uniform Library Edition. Edited by his Sister, Lady TREVELYAN. 8 vols. 8vo. with Portrait, price £5 5s. cloth, or £8 8s. bound in tree-calf by Rivière.

The **HISTORY of ENGLAND** from the Fall of Wolsey to the Death of Elizabeth. By JAMES ANTHONY FROUDE, M.A. late Fellow of Exeter College, Oxford.

 VOLS. I. to IV. the Reign of Henry VIII. Third Edition, 54s.

 VOLS. V. and VI. the Reigns of Edward VI. and Mary. Second Edition, 28s.

 VOLS. VII. and VIII. the Reign of Elizabeth, VOLS. I. and II. Fourth Edition, 28s.

 VOLS. IX. and X. the Reign of Elizabeth, VOLS. III. and IV.
             [In October.

The **HISTORY of ENGLAND** from the Accession of James II. By Lord MACAULAY.

 LIBRARY EDITION, 5 vols. 8vo. £4.

 CABINET EDITION, 8 vols. post 8vo. 48s.

 PEOPLE'S EDITION, 4 vols. crown 8vo. 16s.

REVOLUTIONS in ENGLISH HISTORY. By ROBERT VAUGHAN, D.D. 3 vols. 8vo. 45s.

 VOL. I. Revolutions of Race, Second Edition, revised, 15s.

 VOL. II. Revolutions in Religion, 15s.

 VOL. III. Revolutions in Government, 15s.

An **ESSAY** on the **HISTORY** of the **ENGLISH GOVERNMENT** and Constitution, from the Reign of Henry VII. to the Present Time. By JOHN EARL RUSSELL. Fourth Edition, revised. Crown 8vo. 6s.

The **HISTORY of ENGLAND** during the Reign of George the Third. By the Right Hon. W. N. MASSEY. Cabinet Edition. 4 vols. post 8vo. 24s.

The **CONSTITUTIONAL HISTORY** of **ENGLAND**, since the Accession of George III. 1760—1860. By THOMAS ERSKINE MAY, C.B. Second Edition. 2 vols. 8vo. 33s.

A

CONSTITUTIONAL HISTORY of the **BRITISH EMPIRE** from the Accession of Charles 1. to the Restoration. By G. BRODIE, Esq. Historiographer-Royal of Scotland. Second Edition. 3 vols. 8vo. 36s.

HISTORICAL STUDIES. I. On Some of the Precursors of the French Revolution; II. Studies from the History of the Seventeenth Century; III. Leisure Hours of a Tourist. By HERMAN MERIVALE, M.A. 8vo. price 12s. 6d.

LECTURES on the **HISTORY** of **ENGLAND.** By WILLIAM LONGMAN. VOL. I. from the earliest times to the Death of King Edward II. with 6 Maps, a coloured Plate, and 53 Woodcuts. 8vo. 15s.

HISTORY of **CIVILISATION.** By HENRY THOMAS BUCKLE. 2 vols. 8vo. £1 17s.
VOL. I. *England and France*, Fourth Edition, 21s.
VOL. II. *Spain and Scotland*, Second Edition, 16s.

DEMOCRACY in **AMERICA.** By ALEXIS DE TOCQUEVILLE. Translated by HENRY REEVE, with an Introductory Notice by the Translator. 2 vols. 8vo. 21s.

The **SPANISH CONQUEST** in **AMERICA,** and its Relation to the History of Slavery and to the Government of Colonies. By ARTHUR HELPS. 4 vols. 8vo. £3. VOLS. I. and II. 28s. VOLS. III. and IV. 16s. each.

HISTORY of the **REFORMATION** in **EUROPE** in the Time of Calvin. By J. H. MERLE D'AUBIGNÉ, D.D. VOLS. I. and II. 8vo. 28s. and VOL. III. 12s. VOL. IV. 16s.

LIBRARY HISTORY of **FRANCE,** in 5 vols. 8vo. By EYRE EVANS CROWE. VOL. I. 14s. VOL. II. 15s. VOL. III. 18s. VOL. IV. in October.

LECTURES on the **HISTORY** of **FRANCE.** By the late Sir JAMES STEPHEN, LL.D. 2 vols. 8vo. 24s.

The **HISTORY** of **GREECE.** By C. THIRLWALL, D.D. Lord Bishop of St. David's. 8 vols. 8vo. £3; or in 8 vols. fcp. 28s.

The **TALE** of the **GREAT PERSIAN WAR,** from the Histories of Herodotus. By GEORGE W. COX, M.A. late Scholar of Trin. Coll. Oxon. Fcp. 7s. 6d.

GREEK HISTORY from Themistocles to Alexander, in a Series of Lives from Plutarch. Revised and arranged by A. H. CLOUGH. Fcp. with 44 Woodcuts, 6s.

CRITICAL HISTORY of the **LANGUAGE** and **LITERATURE** of Ancient Greece. By WILLIAM MURE, of Caldwell. 5 vols. 8vo. £3 9s.

HISTORY of the **LITERATURE** of **ANCIENT GREECE.** By Professor K. O. MÜLLER. Translated by the Right Hon. Sir GEORGE CORNEWALL LEWIS, Bart. and by J. W. DONALDSON, D.D. 3 vols. 8vo. 36s.

HISTORY of the **CITY** of **ROME** from its Foundation to the Sixteenth Century of the Christian Era. By THOMAS H. DYER, LL.D. 8vo. with 2 Maps, 15s.

HISTORY of the **ROMANS** under the **EMPIRE.** By CHARLES MERIVALE, B.D. Chaplain to the Speaker. Cabinet Edition, with Maps complete in 8 vols. post 8vo. 48s.

The **FALL** of the **ROMAN REPUBLIC**: a Short History of the Last Century of the Commonwealth. By CHARLES MERIVALE, B.D. Chaplain to the Speaker. Fourth Edition. 12mo. 7s. 6d.

The **CONVERSION** of the **ROMAN EMPIRE**: the Boyle Lectures for the year 1864, delivered at the Chapel Royal, Whitehall. By CHARLES MERIVALE, B.D. Chaplain to the Speaker. Second Edition, 8vo. 8s. 6d.

The **CONVERSION** of the **NORTHERN NATIONS**; the Boyle Lectures for 1865. By the same Author. 8vo. 8s. 6d.

CRITICAL and **HISTORICAL ESSAYS** contributed to the *Edinburgh Review*. By the Right Hon. LORD MACAULAY.

    LIBRARY EDITION, 3 vols. 8vo. 36s.

    TRAVELLER'S EDITION, in 1 vol. 21s.

    CABINET EDITION, 3 vols. fcp. 21s.

    PEOPLE'S EDITION, 2 vols. crown 8vo. 8s.

HISTORICAL and **PHILOSOPHICAL ESSAYS**. By NASSAU W. SENIOR. 2 vols. post 8vo. 16s.

HISTORY of the **RISE** and **INFLUENCE** of the **SPIRIT** of RATIONALISM in EUROPE. By W. E. H. LECKY, M.A. Second Edition, revised. 2 vols. 8vo. 25s.

The **HISTORY** of **PHILOSOPHY**, from Thales to the Present Day. By GEORGE HENRY LEWES. Third Edition, partly rewritten and greatly enlarged. In 2 vols. VOL. I. *Ancient Philosophy*; VOL. II. *Modern Philosophy*. [*Nearly ready*.

HISTORY of the **INDUCTIVE SCIENCES**. By WILLIAM WHEWELL, D.D. F.R.S. late Master of Trin. Coll. Cantab. Third Edition. 3 vols. crown 8vo. 24s.

HISTORY of **SCIENTIFIC IDEAS**; being the First Part of the Philosophy of the Inductive Sciences. By the same Author. 2 vols. cr. 8vo. 14s.

EGYPT'S PLACE in **UNIVERSAL HISTORY**; an Historical Investigation. By C. C. J. BUNSEN, D.D. Translated by C. H. COTTRELL, M.A. With many Illustrations. 4 vols. 8vo. £3 8s. VOL. V. is nearly ready.

MAUNDER'S HISTORICAL TREASURY; comprising a General Introductory Outline of Universal History, and a series of Separate Histories. Fcp. 10s.

HISTORICAL and **CHRONOLOGICAL ENCYCLOPÆDIA**, presenting in a brief and convenient form Chronological Notices of all the Great Events of Universal History. By B. B. WOODWARD, F.S.A. Librarian to the Queen. [*In the press*.

HISTORY of the **CHRISTIAN CHURCH**, from the Ascension of Christ to the Conversion of Constantine. By E. BURTON, D.D. late Prof. of Divinity in the Univ. of Oxford. Eighth Edition. Fcp. 3s. 6d.

SKETCH of the **HISTORY** of the **CHURCH** of **ENGLAND** to the Revolution of 1688. By the Right Rev. T. V. SHORT, D.D. Lord Bishop of St. Asaph. Seventh Edition. Crown 8vo. 10s. 6d.

HISTORY of the **EARLY CHURCH**, from the First Preaching of the Gospel to the Council of Nicæa, A.D. 325. By the Author of 'Amy Herbert.' Fcp. 4s. 6d.

The **ENGLISH REFORMATION**. By F. C. MASSINGBERD, M.A. Chancellor of Lincoln and Rector of South Ormsby. Fourth Edition, revised. Fcp. 8vo. 7s. 6d.

HISTORY of WESLEYAN METHODISM. By GEORGE SMITH, F.A.S. Fourth Edition, with numerous Portraits. 3 vols. cr. 8vo. 7s. each.

LECTURES on the **HISTORY of MODERN MUSIC**, delivered at the Royal Institution. By JOHN HULLAH. FIRST COURSE, with Chronological Tables, post 8vo. 6s. 6d. SECOND COURSE, on the Transition Period, with 40 Specimens, 8vo. 16s.

Biography and Memoirs.

EXTRACTS of the **JOURNALS** and **CORRESPONDENCE** of **MISS BERRY**, from the Year 1783 to 1852. Edited by Lady THERESA LEWIS. Second Edition, with 3 Portraits. 3 vols. 8vo. 42s.

The **DIARY** of the Right Hon. **WILLIAM WINDHAM, M.P.** From 1783 to 1809. Edited by Mrs. HENRY BARING. 8vo. 18s.

LIFE of the DUKE of WELLINGTON. By the Rev. G. R. GLEIG, M.A. Popular Edition, carefully revised; with copious Additions. Crown 8vo. with Portrait, 5s.

Brialmont and Gleig's Life of the Duke of Wellington. (The Parent Work.) 4 vols. 8vo. with Illustrations, £2 14s.

Life of the Duke of Wellington, Intermediate Edition, partly from the French of M. BRIALMONT, partly from Original Documents. By the Rev. G. R. GLEIG, M.A. 8vo. with Portrait, 15s.

HISTORY of MY RELIGIOUS OPINIONS. By J. H. NEWMAN, D.D. Being the Substance of Apologia pro Vita Suâ. Post 8vo. 6s.

FATHER MATHEW: a Biography. By JOHN FRANCIS MAGUIRE, M.P. Popular Edition, with Portrait. Crown 8vo. 3s. 6d.

Rome; its Rulers and its Institutions. By the same Author. New Edition in preparation.

LIFE of AMELIA WILHELMINA SIEVEKING, from the German. Edited, with the Author's sanction, by CATHERINE WINKWORTH. Post 8vo. with Portrait, 12s.

MOZART'S LETTERS (1769–1791), translated from the Collection of Dr. LUDWIG NOHL by Lady WALLACE. 2 vols. post 8vo. with Portrait and Facsimile, 18s.

BEETHOVEN'S LETTERS (1790–1826), from the Two Collections of Drs. NOHL and discovered Letters to the Archduke Rudolph, Cardinal-Archbishop of Olmütz, VON KÖCHEL. Translated by Lady WALLACE. 2 vols. post 8vo. with Portrait.

FELIX MENDELSSOHN'S LETTERS from *Italy and Switzerland*, and *Letters from 1833 to 1847*, translated by Lady WALLACE. New Edition, with Portrait. 2 vols. crown 8vo. 5s. each.

RECOLLECTIONS of the late WILLIAM WILBERFORCE, M.P. for the County of York during nearly 30 Years. By J. S. HARFORD, F.R.S. Second Edition. Post 8vo. 7s.

MEMOIRS of SIR HENRY HAVELOCK, K.C.B. By JOHN CLARK MARSHMAN. Second Edition. 8vo. with Portrait, 12s. 6d.

THOMAS MOORE'S MEMOIRS, JOURNAL, and CORRESPONDENCE. Edited and abridged from the First Edition by Earl RUSSELL. Square crown 8vo. with 8 Portraits, 12s. 6d.

MEMOIR of the Rev. SYDNEY SMITH. By his Daughter, Lady HOLLAND. With a Selection from his Letters, edited by Mrs. AUSTIN. 2 vols. 8vo. 28s.

VICISSITUDES of FAMILIES. By Sir BERNARD BURKE, Ulster King of Arms. FIRST, SECOND, and THIRD SERIES. 3 vols. crown 8vo. 12s. 6d. each.

ESSAYS in ECCLESIASTICAL BIOGRAPHY. By the Right Hon. Sir J. STEPHEN, LL.D. Fourth Edition. 8vo. 14s.

BIOGRAPHIES of DISTINGUISHED SCIENTIFIC MEN. By FRANÇOIS ARAGO. Translated by Admiral W. H. SMYTH, F.R.S. the Rev. D. POWELL, M.A. and R. GRANT, M.A. 8vo. 18s.

MAUNDER'S BIOGRAPHICAL TREASURY: Memoirs, Sketches, and Brief Notices of above 12,000 Eminent Persons of All Ages and Nations. Edited by W. L. R. CATES. Fcp. 10s. 6d.

LETTERS and LIFE of FRANCIS BACON, including all his Occasional Works. Collected and edited, with a Commentary, by J. SPEDDING, Trin. Coll. Cantab. VOLS. I. and II. 8vo. 24s.

Criticism, Philosophy, Polity, &c.

The INSTITUTES of JUSTINIAN; with English Introduction, Translation, and Notes. By T. C. SANDARS, M.A. Barrister, late Fellow of Oriel Coll. Oxon. Third Edition. 8vo. 15s.

The ETHICS of ARISTOTLE. Illustrated with Essays and Notes. By Sir A. GRANT, Bart. M.A. LL.D. Director of Public Instruction in the Bombay Presidency. Second Edition, revised and completed. 2 vols. 8vo. 28s.

ELEMENTS of LOGIC. By R. WHATELY, D.D. late Archbishop of Dublin. Ninth Edition. 8vo. 10s. 6d. crown 8vo. 4s. 6d.

Elements of Rhetoric. By the same Author. Seventh Edition. 8vo. 10s. 6d. crown 8vo. 4s. 6d.

English Synonymes. Edited by Archbishop WHATELY. 5th Edition. Fcp. 3s.

BACON'S ESSAYS with ANNOTATIONS. By R. WHATELY, D.D. late Archbishop of Dublin. Sixth Edition. 8vo. 10s. 6d.

LORD BACON'S WORKS, collected and edited by R. L. Ellis, M.A. J. Spedding, M.A. and D. D. Heath. Vols. I. to V. *Philosophical Works*, 5 vols. 8vo. £4 6s. Vols. VI. and VII. *Literary and Professional Works*, 2 vols. £1 16s.

On **REPRESENTATIVE GOVERNMENT**. By John Stuart Mill, M.P. for Westminster. Third Edition, 8vo. 9s. crown 8vo. 2s.

On **Liberty.** By the same Author. Third Edition. Post 8vo. 7s. 6d. crown 8vo. 1s. 4d.

Principles of Political Economy. By the same. Sixth Edition. 2 vols. 8vo. 30s. or in 1 vol. crown 8vo. 5s.

A System of Logic, Ratiocinative and Inductive. By the same. Sixth Edition. Two vols. 8vo. 25s.

Utilitarianism. By the same. Second Edition. 8vo. 5s.

Dissertations and Discussions. By the same Author. 2 vols. 8vo. price 24s.

Examination of Sir W. Hamilton's Philosophy, and of the Principal Philosophical Questions discussed in his Writings. By the same Author. Second Edition. 8vo. 14s.

MISCELLANEOUS REMAINS from the Common-place Book of Richard Whately, D.D. late Archbishop of Dublin. Edited by Miss E. J. Whately. Crown 8vo. 7s. 6d.

ESSAYS on the **ADMINISTRATIONS of GREAT BRITAIN** from 1783 to 1830. By the Right Hon. Sir G. C. Lewis, Bart. Edited by the Right Hon. Sir E. Head, Bart. 8vo. with Portrait, 15s.

By the same Author.

Inquiry into the Credibility of the Early Roman History, 2 vols. price 30s.

On the **Methods of Observation and Reasoning in Politics,** 2 vols. price 28s.

Irish Disturbances and Irish Church Question, 12s.

Remarks on the Use and Abuse of some Political Terms, 9s.

The Fables of Babrius, Greek Text with Latin Notes, Part I. 5s. 6d. Part II. 3s. 6d.

An OUTLINE of the NECESSARY LAWS of THOUGHT: a Treatise on Pure and Applied Logic. By the Most Rev. W. Thomson, D.D. Archbishop of York. Crown 8vo. 5s. 6d.

The ELEMENTS of LOGIC. By Thomas Shedden, M.A. of St. Peter's Coll. Cantab. 12mo. 4s. 6d.

ANALYSIS of Mr. MILL'S SYSTEM of LOGIC. By W. Stebbing, M.A. Fellow of Worcester College, Oxford. Second Edition. 12mo. 3s. 6d.

The ELECTION of REPRESENTATIVES, Parliamentary and Municipal: a Treatise. By Thomas Hare, Barrister-at-Law. Third Edition, with Additions. Crown 8vo. 6s.

SPEECHES of the RIGHT HON. LORD MACAULAY, corrected by Himself. Library Edition, 8vo. 12s. People's Edition, crown 8vo. 3s. 6d.

LORD MACAULAY'S SPEECHES on PARLIAMENTARY REFORM in 1831 and 1832. 16mo. 1s.

A DICTIONARY of the ENGLISH LANGUAGE. By R. G. LATHAM, M.A. M.D. F.R.S. Founded on the Dictionary of Dr. S. JOHNSON, as edited by the Rev. H. J. TODD, with numerous Emendations and Additions. Publishing in 36 Parts, price 3s. 6d. each, to form 2 vols. 4to.

THESAURUS of ENGLISH WORDS and PHRASES, classified and arranged so as to facilitate the Expression of Ideas, and assist in Literary Composition. By P. M. ROGET, M.D. 16th Edition. Crown 8vo. 10s. 6d.

LECTURES on the SCIENCE of LANGUAGE, delivered at the Royal Institution. By MAX MÜLLER, M.A. Taylorian Professor in the University of Oxford. FIRST SERIES, Fourth Edition, 12s. SECOND SERIES, 18s.

CHAPTERS on LANGUAGE. By FREDERIC W. FARRAR, M.A. late Fellow of Trin. Coll. Cambridge, Author of 'The Origin of Language,' &c. Crown 8vo. 8s. 6d.

The DEBATER; a Series of Complete Debates, Outlines of Debates, and Questions for Discussion. By F. ROWTON. Fcp. 6s.

A COURSE of ENGLISH READING, adapted to every taste and capacity; or, How and What to Read. By the Rev. J. PYCROFT, B.A. Fourth Edition. Fcp. 5s.

MANUAL of ENGLISH LITERATURE, Historical and Critical: with a Chapter on English Metres. By THOMAS ARNOLD, M.A. Post 8vo. New Edition, revised. [In November.

SOUTHEY'S DOCTOR, complete in One Volume. Edited by the Rev. J. W. WARTER, B.D. Square crown 8vo. 12s. 6d.

HISTORICAL and CRITICAL COMMENTARY on the OLD TESTA-MENT; with a New Translation. By M. M. KALISCH, Ph.D. VOL. I. *Genesis,* 8vo. 18s. or adapted for the General Reader, 12s. VOL. II. *Exodus,* 15s. or adapted for the General Reader, 12s.

A Hebrew Grammar, with Exercises. By the same. PART I. *Outlines with Exercises,* 8vo. 12s. 6d. KEY, 5s. PART II. *Exceptional Forms and Constructions,* 12s. 6d.

A LATIN-ENGLISH DICTIONARY. By J. T. WHITE, M.A. of Corpus Christi College, and J. E. RIDDLE, M.A. of St. Edmund Hall, Oxford. Imperial 8vo. pp. 2,128, price 42s. cloth.

A New Latin-English Dictionary, abridged from the larger work of *White* and *Riddle* (as above), by J. T. WHITE, M.A. Joint-Author. Medium 8vo. pp. 1,048, price 18s. cloth.

The Junior Scholar's Latin-English Dictionary, abridged from the larger works of *White* and *Riddle* (as above), by J. T. White, M.A. surviving Joint-Author. Square 12mo. pp. 662, price 7s. 6d. cloth.

8   NEW WORKS published by LONGMANS and CO.

An **ENGLISH-GREEK LEXICON**, containing all the Greek Words used by Writers of good authority. By C. D. YONGE, B.A. Fifth Edition. 4to. 21s.

Mr. **YONGE'S NEW LEXICON**, English and Greek, abridged from his larger work (as above). Revised Edition. Square 12mo. 8s. 6d.

A **GREEK-ENGLISH LEXICON**. Compiled by H. G. LIDDELL, D.D. Dean of Christ Church, and R. SCOTT, D.D. Master of Balliol. Fifth Edition. Crown 4to. 31s. 6d.

A **Lexicon, Greek and English**, abridged from LIDDELL and SCOTT's *Greek-English Lexicon*. Eleventh Edition. Square 12mo. 7s. 6d.

A **SANSKRIT-ENGLISH DICTIONARY**, the Sanskrit words printed both in the original Devanagari and in Roman letters; with References to the Best Editions of Sanskrit Authors, and with Etymologies and Comparisons of Cognate Words chiefly in Greek, Latin. Gothic, and Anglo-Saxon. Compiled by T. BENFEY, Prof. in the Univ. of Göttingen. 8vo. 52s. 6d.

A **PRACTICAL DICTIONARY** of the **FRENCH** and **ENGLISH LANGUAGES**. By L. CONTANSEAU. Eleventh Edition. Post 8vo. 10s. 6d.

Contanseau's Pocket Dictionary, French and English, abridged from the above by the Author. New and Cheaper Edition, 18mo. 3s. 6d.

NEW PRACTICAL DICTIONARY of the **GERMAN LANGUAGE**; German-English and English-German. By the Rev. W. L. BLACKLEY, M.A. and Dr. CARL MARTIN FRIEDLANDER. Post 8vo. 14s.

Miscellaneous Works and Popular Metaphysics.

RECREATIONS of a COUNTRY PARSON. By A. K. H. B. FIRST SERIES, with 41 Woodcut Illustrations from Designs by R. T. Pritchett. Crown 8vo. 12s. 6d.

Recreations of a Country Parson. SECOND SERIES. Cr. 8vo. 3s. 6d.

The Common-place Philosopher in Town and Country. By the same Author. Crown 8vo. 3s. 6d.

Leisure Hours in Town; Essays Consolatory, Æsthetical, Moral, Social, and Domestic. By the same Author. Crown 8vo. 3s. 6d.

The Autumn Holidays of a Country Parson; Essays contributed to *Fraser's Magazine* and to *Good Words*. By the same. Crown 8vo. 3s. 6d.

The Graver Thoughts of a Country Parson. SECOND SERIES. By the same Author. Crown 8vo. 3s. 6d.

Critical Essays of a Country Parson. Selected from Essays contributed to *Fraser's Magazine*. By the same Author. Post 8vo. 9s.

Sunday Afternoons at the Parish Church of a University City. By the same Author.   [*In October.*

A **CAMPAIGNER AT HOME.** By SHIRLEY, Author of 'Thalatta' and 'Nugæ Criticæ.' Post 8vo. with Vignette, 7s. 6d.

STUDIES in PARLIAMENT. A Series of Sketches of Leading Politicians. By R. H. Hutton. [Reprinted from the 'Pall Mall Gazette.'] Crown 8vo. 4s. 6d.

LORD MACAULAY'S MISCELLANEOUS WRITINGS.
Library Edition. 2 vols. 8vo. Portrait, 21s.
People's Edition. 1 vol. crown 8vo. 4s. 6d.

The REV. SYDNEY SMITH'S MISCELLANEOUS WORKS; including his Contributions to the *Edinburgh Review.*
Library Edition, 3 vols. 8vo. 36s.
Traveller's Edition, In 1 vol. 21s.
Cabinet Edition, 3 vols. fcp. 21s.
People's Edition, 2 vols. crown 8vo. 8s.

Elementary Sketches of Moral Philosophy, delivered at the Royal Institution. By the same Author. Fcp. 7s.

The Wit and Wisdom of the Rev. Sydney Smith: a Selection of the most memorable Passages in his Writings and Conversation. 16mo. 5s.

EPIGRAMS, Ancient and Modern; Humorous, Witty, Satirical, Moral, and Panegyrical. Edited by Rev. John Booth, B.A. Cambridge. Second Edition, revised and enlarged. Fcp. 7s. 6d.

From MATTER to SPIRIT: the Result of Ten Years' Experience in Spirit Manifestations. By Sophia E. De Morgan. With a Preface by Professor De Morgan. Post 8vo. 8s. 6d.

ESSAYS selected from CONTRIBUTIONS to the *Edinburgh Review.* By Henry Rogers. Second Edition. 3 vols. fcp. 21s.

The Eclipse of Faith; or, a Visit to a Religious Sceptic. By the same Author. Eleventh Edition. Fcp. 5s.

Defence of the Eclipse of Faith, by its Author; a rejoinder to Dr. Newman's *Reply.* Third Edition. Fcp. 3s. 6d.

Selections from the Correspondence of R. E. H. Greyson. By the same Author. Third Edition. Crown 8vo. 7s. 6d.

Fulleriana, or the Wisdom and Wit of Thomas Fuller, with Essay on his Life and Genius. By the same Author. 16mo. 2s. 6d.

An ESSAY on HUMAN NATURE; showing the Necessity of a Divine Revelation for the Perfect Development of Man's Capacities. By Henry S. Boase, M.D. F.R.S. and G.S. 8vo. 12s.

The PHILOSOPHY of NATURE; a Systematic Treatise on the Causes and Laws of Natural Phænomena. By the same Author. 8vo. 12s.

An INTRODUCTION to MENTAL PHILOSOPHY, on the Inductive Method. By J. D. Morell, M.A. LL.D. 8vo. 12s.

Elements of Psychology, containing the Analysis of the Intellectual Powers. By the same Author. Post 8vo. 7s. 6d.

B

The **SECRET** of **HEGEL**: being the Hegelian System in Origin, Principle, Form, and Matter. By JAMES HUTCHISON STIRLING. 2 vols. 8vo. 28s.

SIGHT and **TOUCH**: an Attempt to Disprove the Received (or Berkeleian) Theory of Vision. By THOMAS K. ABBOTT, M.A. Fellow and Tutor of Trin. Coll. Dublin. 8vo. with 21 Woodcuts, 5s. 6d.

The **SENSES** and the **INTELLECT**. By ALEXANDER BAIN, M.A. Professor of Logic in the University of Aberdeen. Second Edition. 8vo. price 15s.

The **Emotions** and the **Will**, by the same Author; completing a Systematic Exposition of the Human Mind. 8vo. 15s.

On the **Study** of **Character**, including an Estimate of Phrenology. By the same Author. 8vo. 9s.

TIME and **SPACE**: a Metaphysical Essay. By SHADWORTH H. HODGSON. 8vo. pp. 588, price 16s.

The **WAY** to **REST**: Results from a Life-search after Religious Truth. By R. VAUGHAN, D.D. Crown 8vo. 7s. 6d.

HOURS WITH THE MYSTICS: a Contribution to the History of Religious Opinion. By ROBERT ALFRED VAUGHAN, B.A. Second Edition. 2 vols. crown 8vo, 12s.

The **PHILOSOPHY** of **NECESSITY**; or Natural Law as applicable to Mental, Moral, and Social Science. By CHARLES BRAY. Second Edition. 8vo. 9s.

The **Education** of the **Feelings** and **Affections**. By the same Author. Third Edition. 8vo. 3s. 6d.

On **Force**, its **Mental** and **Moral Correlates**. By the same Author. 8vo. 5s.

CHRISTIANITY and **COMMON SENSE**. By Sir WILLOUGHBY JONES, Bart. M.A. Trin. Coll. Cantab. 8vo. 6s.

Astronomy, Meteorology, Popular Geography, &c.

OUTLINES of **ASTRONOMY**. By Sir J. F. W. HERSCHEL, Bart. M.A. Eighth Edition, revised; with Plates and Woodcuts. 8vo. 18s.

ARAGO'S POPULAR ASTRONOMY. Translated by Admiral W. H. SMYTH, F.R.S. and R. GRANT, M.A. With 25 Plates and 358 Woodcuts. 2 vols. 8vo. £2 5s.

SATURN and its **SYSTEM**. By RICHARD A. PROCTOR, B.A. late Scholar of St. John's Coll. Camb. and King's Coll. London. 8vo. with 14 Plates, 14s.

The **Handbook** of the **Stars**. By the same Author. 3 Maps. Square fcp. 5s.

CELESTIAL OBJECTS for **COMMON TELESCOPES**. By the Rev. T. W. WEBB, M.A. F.R.A.S. With Map of the Moon, and Woodcuts. 16mo. 7s.

PHYSICAL GEOGRAPHY for **SCHOOLS** and **GENERAL READERS**. By M. F. MAURY, LL.D. Fcp. with 2 Charts, 2s. 6d.

M'CULLOCH'S DICTIONARY, Geographical, Statistical, and Historical, of the various Countries, Places, and Principal Natural Objects in the World. Revised Edit. printed in a larger type, with Maps, and with the Statistical Information throughout brought up to the latest returns by P. MARTIN. 4 vols. 8vo. 21s. each. Vols. I. and II. now ready.

A GENERAL DICTIONARY of GEOGRAPHY, Descriptive, Physical, Statistical, and Historical; forming a complete Gazetteer of the World. By A. KEITH JOHNSTON, F.R.S.E. 8vo. 31s. 6d.

A MANUAL of GEOGRAPHY, Physical, Industrial, and Political. By W. HUGHES, F.R.G.S. Professor of Geography in King's College, and in Queen's College, London. With 6 Maps. Fcp. 7s. 6d.

The Geography of British History; a Geographical Description of the British Islands at Successive Periods. By the same. With 6 Maps. Fcp. 8s. 6d.

Abridged Text-Book of British Geography. By the same. Fcp. 1s. 6d.

MAUNDER'S TREASURY of GEOGRAPHY, Physical, Historical, Descriptive, and Political. Edited by W. HUGHES, F.R.G.S. With 7 Maps and 16 Plates. Fcp. 10s. 6d.

Natural History and Popular Science.

The **ELEMENTS of PHYSICS** or **NATURAL PHILOSOPHY.** By NEIL ARNOTT, M.D. F.R.S. Physician Extraordinary to the Queen. Sixth Edition, rewritten and completed. 2 Parts, 8vo. 21s.

HEAT CONSIDERED as a MODE of MOTION. By Professor JOHN TYNDALL, LL.D. F.R.S. Second Edition. Crown 8vo. with Woodcuts, 12s. 6d.

VOLCANOS, the Character of their Phenomena, their Share in the Structure and Composition of the Surface of the Globe, &c. By G. POULETT SCROPE, M.P. F.R.S. Second Edition. 8vo. with Illustrations, 15s.

A TREATISE on ELECTRICITY, in Theory and Practice. By A. DE LA RIVE, Prof. in the Academy of Geneva. Translated by C. V. WALKER, F.R.S. 3 vols. 8vo. with Woodcuts, £3 13s.

The **CORRELATION of PHYSICAL FORCES.** By W. R. GROVE, Q.C. V.P.R.S. Fourth Edition. 8vo. 7s. 6d.

MANUAL of GEOLOGY. By S. HAUGHTON, M.D. F.R.S. Fellow of Trin. Coll. and Prof. of Geol. in the Univ. of Dublin. Revised Edition, with 66 Woodcuts. Fcp. 6s.

A GUIDE to GEOLOGY. By J. PHILLIPS, M.A. Professor of Geology in the University of Oxford. Fifth Edition, with Plates. Fcp. 4s.

A GLOSSARY of MINERALOGY. By H. W. BRISTOW, F.G.S. of the Geological Survey of Great Britain. With 486 Figures. Crown 8vo. 12s.

PHILLIPS'S ELEMENTARY INTRODUCTION to MINERALOGY, with extensive Alterations and Additions, by H. J. BROOKE, F.R.S. and W. H. MILLER, F.G.S. Post 8vo. with Woodcuts, 18s.

VAN DER HOEVEN'S HANDBOOK of ZOOLOGY. Translated from the Second Dutch Edition by the Rev. W. CLARK, M.D. F.R.S. 2 vols. 8vo. with 24 Plates of Figures, 60s.

The COMPARATIVE ANATOMY and PHYSIOLOGY of the VERTE-brate Animals. By RICHARD OWEN, F.R.S. D.C.L. 3 vols. 8vo. with upwards of 1,200 Woodcuts. VOLS. I. and II. price 21s. each, now ready.

HOMES WITHOUT HANDS: a Description of the Habitations of Animals, classed according to their Principle of Construction. By Rev. J. G. WOOD, M.A. F.L.S. With about 140 Vignettes on Wood (20 full size of page). Second Edition. 8vo. 21s.

MANUAL of CORALS and SEA JELLIES. By J. R. GREENE, B.A. Edited by the Rev. J. A. GALBRAITH, M.A. and the Rev. S. HAUGHTON, M.D. Fcp. with 39 Woodcuts, 5s.

Manual of Sponges and Animalculæ; with a General Introduction on the Principles of Zoology. By the same Author and Editors. Fcp. with 16 Woodcuts, 2s.

Manual of the Metalloids. By J. APJOHN, M.D. F.R.S. and the same Editors. Revised Edition. Fcp. with 38 Woodcuts, 7s. 6d.

The HARMONIES of NATURE and UNITY of CREATION. By Dr. GEORGE HARTWIG. 8vo. with numerous Illustrations, 18s.

The Sea and its Living Wonders. By the same Author. Second (English) Edition. 8vo. with many Illustrations. 18s.

The Tropical World. By the same Author. With 8 Chromoxylographs and 172 Woodcuts. 8vo. 21s.

SKETCHES of the NATURAL HISTORY of CEYLON. By Sir J. EMERSON TENNENT, K.C.S. LL.D. With 82 Wood Engravings. Post 8vo. price 12s. 6d.

Ceylon. By the same Author. Fifth Edition; with Maps, &c. and 90 Wood Engravings. 2 vols. 8vo. £2 10s.

The Wild Elephant, its Structure and Habits, with the Method of Taking and Training it in Ceylon. By the same Author. With Illustrations. In 1 vol.   [Nearly ready.

A FAMILIAR HISTORY of BIRDS. By E. STANLEY, D.D. F.R.S. late Lord Bishop of Norwich. Seventh Edition, with Woodcuts. Fcp. 3s. 6d.

MARVELS and MYSTERIES of INSTINCT; or, Curiosities of Animal Life. By G. GARRATT. Third Edition. Fcp. 7s.

HOME WALKS and HOLIDAY RAMBLES. By the Rev. C. A. JOHNS, B.A. F.L.S. Fcp. 8vo. with 10 Illustrations, 6s.

KIRBY and SPENCE'S INTRODUCTION to ENTOMOLOGY, or Elements of the Natural History of Insects. Seventh Edition. Crown 8vo. price 5s.

MAUNDER'S TREASURY of NATURAL HISTORY, or Popular Dictionary of Zoology. Revised and corrected by T. S. COBBOLD. M.D. Fcp. with 900 Woodcuts, 10s.

The TREASURY of BOTANY, or Popular Dictionary of the Vegetable Kingdom; with which is incorporated a Glossary of Botanical Terms. Edited by J. LINDLEY, F.R.S. and T. MOORE, F.L.S. assisted by eminent Contributors. Pp. 1,274, with 274 Woodcuts and 20 Steel Plates. 2 Parts, fcp. 20s.

The **ELEMENTS** of **BOTANY** for **FAMILIES** and **SCHOOLS**. Tenth Edition, revised by THOMAS MOORE, F.L.S. Fcp. with 154 Woodcuts, 2s. 6d.

The **ROSE AMATEUR'S GUIDE**. By THOMAS RIVERS. New Edition. Fcp. 4s.

The **BRITISH FLORA**; comprising the Phænogamous or Flowering Plants and the Ferns. By Sir W. J. HOOKER, K.H. and G. A. WALKER-ARNOTT, LL.D. 12mo. with 12 Plates, 14s. or coloured, 21s.

BRYOLOGIA BRITANNICA; containing the Mosses of Great Britain and Ireland, arranged and described. By W. WILSON. 8vo. with 61 Plates 42s. or coloured, £4 4s.

The **INDOOR GARDENER**. By Miss MALING. Fcp. with Frontispiece, printed in Colours, 5s.

LOUDON'S ENCYCLOPÆDIA of PLANTS; comprising the Specific Character, Description, Culture, History, &c. of all the Plants found in Great Britain. With upwards of 12,000 Woodcuts. 8vo. £3 13s. 6d.

Loudon's Encyclopædia of Trees and Shrubs; containing the Hardy Trees and Shrubs of Great Britain scientifically and popularly described. With 2,000 Woodcuts. 8vo. 50s.

MAUNDER'S SCIENTIFIC and LITERARY TREASURY; a Popular Encyclopædia of Science, Literature, and Art. Fcp. New Edition. [Nearly ready.

A DICTIONARY of SCIENCE, LITERATURE, and ART. Fourth Edition, re-edited by W. T. BRANDE (the Author), and GEORGE W. COX. M.A. assisted by gentlemen of eminent Scientific and Literary Acquirements. 3 vols. medium 8vo. price 63s. cloth.

ESSAYS on **SCIENTIFIC** and other **SUBJECTS**, contributed to Reviews. By Sir H. HOLLAND, Bart. M.D. Second Edition. 8vo. 14s.

ESSAYS from the **EDINBURGH** and **QUARTERLY REVIEWS**; with Addresses and other Pieces. By Sir J. F. W. HERSCHEL, Bart. M.A. 8vo. 18s.

– –

Chemistry, Medicine, Surgery, and the Allied Sciences.

A DICTIONARY of CHEMISTRY and the Allied Branches of other Sciences: founded on that of the late Dr. Ure. By HENRY WATTS, F.C.S. assisted by eminent Contributors. 5 vols. medium 8vo. in course of publication in Parts. VOL. L. 31s. 6d. VOL. II. 26s. VOL. III. 31s. 6d. VOL. IV. 24s. are now ready.

HANDBOOK of CHEMICAL ANALYSIS. Adapted to the Unitary System of Notation. By F. T. CONINGTON, M.A. F.C.S. Post 8vo. 7s. 6d.— TABLES of QUALITATIVE ANALYSIS adapted to the same, 2s. 6d.

A HANDBOOK of VOLUMETRICAL ANALYSIS. By ROBERT H. SCOTT, M.A. T.C.D. Post 8vo. 4s. 6d.

ELEMENTS of CHEMISTRY, Theoretical and Practical. By WILLIAM A. MILLER, M.D. LL.D. F.R.S. F.G.S. Professor of Chemistry, King's College, London. 3 vols. 8vo. £2 13s. PART I. CHEMICAL PHYSICS. Third Edition. 12s. PART II. INORGANIC CHEMISTRY, 21s. PART III. ORGANIC CHEMISTRY, Second Edition, 20s.

A MANUAL of CHEMISTRY, Descriptive and Theoretical. By WILLIAM ODLING, M.B. F.R.S. PART I. 8vo. 9s.

A Course of Practical Chemistry, for the use of Medical Students. By the same Author. Second Edition, with 70 new Woodcuts. Crown 8vo. price 7s. 6d.

Lectures on Animal Chemistry, delivered at the Royal College of Physicians in 1865. By the same Author. Crown 8vo. 4s. 6d.

The DIAGNOSIS and TREATMENT of the DISEASES of WOMEN; including the Diagnosis of Pregnancy. By GRAILY HEWITT, M.D. 8vo. 16s.

LECTURES on the DISEASES of INFANCY and CHILDHOOD. By CHARLES WEST, M.D. &c. Fifth Edition, revised and enlarged. 8vo. 16s.

EXPOSITION of the SIGNS and SYMPTOMS of PREGNANCY: with other Papers on subjects connected with Midwifery. By W. F. MONTGOMERY, M.A. M.D. M.R.I.A. 8vo. with Illustrations, 25s.

A SYSTEM of SURGERY, Theoretical and Practical. In Treatises by Various Authors. Edited by T. HOLMES, M.A. Cantab. Assistant-Surgeon to St. George's Hospital. 4 vols. 8vo. £4 13s.

Vol. I.   **General Pathology.** 21s.

Vol. II.   **Local Injuries:** Gunshot Wounds, Injuries of the Head, Back, Face, Neck, Chest, Abdomen, Pelvis, of the Upper and Lower Extremities, and Diseases of the Eye. 21s.

Vol. III.   **Operative Surgery   Diseases of the Organs of Circulation,** Locomotion, &c. 21s.

Vol. IV.   **Diseases of the Organs of Digestion, of the Genito-Urinary System,** and of the Breast, Thyroid Gland, and Skin; with APPENDIX and GENERAL INDEX. 30s.

LECTURES on the PRINCIPLES and PRACTICE of PHYSIC. By THOMAS WATSON, M.D. Physician-Extraordinary to the Queen. Fourth Edition. 2 vols. 8vo. 34s.

LECTURES on SURGICAL PATHOLOGY. By J. PAGET, F.R.S. Surgeon-Extraordinary to the Queen. Edited by W. TURNER, M.B. 8vo. with 117 Woodcuts, 21s.

A TREATISE on the CONTINUED FEVERS of GREAT BRITAIN. By C. MURCHISON, M.D. Senior Physician to the London Fever Hospital. 8vo. with coloured Plates, 18s.

ANATOMY, DESCRIPTIVE and SURGICAL. By HENRY GRAY, F.R.S. With 410 Wood Engravings from Dissections. Third Edition, by T. HOLMES, M.A. Cantab. Royal 8vo. 28s.

The CYCLOPÆDIA of ANATOMY and PHYSIOLOGY. Edited by the late R. B. TODD, M.D. F.R.S. Assisted by nearly all the most eminent cultivators of Physiological Science of the present age. 5 vols. 8vo. with 2,853 Woodcuts, £6 6s.

PHYSIOLOGICAL ANATOMY and PHYSIOLOGY of MAN. By the late R. B. Todd, M.D. F.R.S. and W. Bowman, F.R.S. of King's College. With numerous Illustrations. Vol. II. 8vo. 25s.

A DICTIONARY of PRACTICAL MEDICINE. By J. Copland, M.D. F.R.S. Abridged from the larger work by the Author, assisted by J. C. Copland, M.R.C.S. and throughout brought down to the present State of Medical Science. Pp. 1,560 in 8vo. price 36s.

Dr. Copland's Dictionary of Practical Medicine (the larger work). 3 vols. 8vo. £5 11s.

The WORKS of SIR B. C. BRODIE, Bart. collected and arranged by Charles Hawkins, F.R.C.S.E. 3 vols. 8vo. with Medallion and Facsimile, 48s.

Autobiography of Sir B. C. Brodie, Bart. Printed from the Author's materials left in MS. Second Edition. Fcp. 4s. 6d.

The TOXICOLOGIST'S GUIDE: a New Manual on Poisons, giving the Best Methods to be pursued for the Detection of Poisons (post-mortem or otherwise). By John Horsley, F.C.S. Analytical Chemist. Post 8vo. 3s. 6d.

A MANUAL of MATERIA MEDICA and THERAPEUTICS, abridged from Dr. Pereira's *Elements* by F. J. Farre, M.D. assisted by R. Bentley, M.R.C.S. and by R. Warington, F.R.S. 8vo. with 90 Woodcuts, 21s.

Dr. Pereira's Elements of Materia Medica and Therapeutics. Third Edition. By A. S. Taylor, M.D. and G. O. Rees, M.D. 3 vols. 8vo. with Woodcuts, £3 15s.

THOMSON'S CONSPECTUS of the BRITISH PHARMACOPŒIA. Twenty-fourth Edition, corrected and made conformable throughout to the New Pharmacopœia of the General Council of Medical Education. By E. Lloyd Birkett, M.D. 18mo. 5s. 6d.

MANUAL of the DOMESTIC PRACTICE of MEDICINE. By W. B. Kesteven, F.R.C.S.E. Second Edition, revised, with Additions. Fcp. 5s.

The RESTORATION of HEALTH; or, the Application of the Laws of Hygiene to the Recovery of Health: a Manual for the Invalid, and a Guide in the Sick Room. By W. Strange, M.D. Fcp. 6s.

SEA-AIR and SEA-BATHING for CHILDREN and INVALIDS. By the same Author. Fcp. boards, 3s.

MANUAL for the CLASSIFICATION, TRAINING, and EDUCATION of the Feeble-Minded, Imbecile, and Idiotic. By P. Martin Duncan, M.B. and William Millard. Crown 8vo. 5s.

The Fine Arts, and Illustrated Editions.

The NEW TESTAMENT, illustrated with Wood Engravings after the Early Masters, chiefly of the Italian School. Crown 4to. 63s. cloth, gilt top; or £5 5s. elegantly bound in morocco.

LYRA GERMANICA; Hymns for the Sundays and Chief Festivals of the Christian Year. Translated by CATHERINE WINKWORTH; 125 Illustrations on Wood drawn by J. LEIGHTON, F.S.A. Fcp. 4to. 21s.

The **LIFE of MAN SYMBOLISED** by the **MONTHS** of the **YEAR** in their Seasons and Phases; with Passages selected from Ancient and Modern Authors. By RICHARD PIGOT. Accompanied by a Series of 25 full-page Illustrations and numerous Marginal Devices, Decorative Initial Letters, and Tailpieces, engraved on Wood from Original Designs by JOHN LEIGHTON, F.S.A. 4to. 42s.

CATS' and FARLIE'S MORAL EMBLEMS; with Aphorisms, Adages, and Proverbs of all Nations: comprising 121 Illustrations on Wood by J. LEIGHTON, F.S.A. with an appropriate Text by R. PIGOT. Imperial 8vo. 31s. 6d.

SHAKSPEARE'S SENTIMENTS and **SIMILES**, printed in Black and Gold, and illuminated in the Missal Style by HENRY NOEL HUMPHREYS. In massive covers, containing the Medallion and Cypher of Shakspeare. Square post 8vo. 21s.

The **HISTORY of OUR LORD**, as exemplified in Works of Art. Being the fourth and concluding series of 'Sacred and Legendary Art.' By Mrs. JAMESON and Lady EASTLAKE. Second Edition, with 13 Etchings and 281 Woodcuts. 2 vols. square crown 8vo. 42s.

In the same Series, by Mrs. JAMESON.

Legends of the Saints and Martyrs. Fourth Edition, with 19 Etchings and 187 Woodcuts. 2 vols. 31s. 6d.

Legends of the Monastic Orders. Third Edition, with 11 Etchings and 88 Woodcuts. 1 vol. 21s.

Legends of the Madonna. Third Edition, with 27 Etchings and 165 Woodcuts. 1 vol. 21s.

Arts, Manufactures, &c.

DRAWING from **NATURE**; a Series of Progressive Instructions in Sketching, from Elementary Studies to Finished Views, with Examples from Switzerland and the Pyrenees. By GEORGE BARNARD, Professor of Drawing at Rugby School. With 18 Lithographic Plates, and 108 Wood Engravings. Imp. 8vo. 25s.

ENCYCLOPÆDIA of ARCHITECTURE, Historical, Theoretical, and Practical. By JOSEPH GWILT. With more than 1,000 Woodcuts. 8vo. 42s.

TUSCAN SCULPTORS, their Lives, Works, and Times. With 45 Etchings and 28 Woodcuts from Original Drawings and Photographs. By CHARLES C. PERKINS. 2 vols. imperial 8vo. 63s.

The **GRAMMAR of HERALDRY**: containing a Description of all the Principal Charges used in Armory, the Signification of Heraldic Terms, and the Rules to be observed in Blazoning and Marshalling. By JOHN E. CUSSANS. Fcp. with 106 Woodcuts, 4s. 6d.

The **ENGINEER'S HANDBOOK**; explaining the Principles which should guide the young Engineer in the Construction of Machinery. By C. S. LOWNDES. Post 8vo. 5s.

The **ELEMENTS** of **MECHANISM**. By T. M. GOODEVE, M.A. Professor of Mechanics at the R. M. Acad, Woolwich. Second Edition, with 217 Woodcuts. Post 8vo. 6s. 6d.

URE'S DICTIONARY of ARTS, MANUFACTURES, and **MINES.** Re-written and enlarged by ROBERT HUNT, F.R.S. assisted by numerous gentlemen eminent in Science and the Arts. With 2,000 Woodcuts. 3 vols. 8vo. £4.

ENCYCLOPÆDIA of CIVIL ENGINEERING, Historical, Theoretical, and Practical. By E. CRESY, C.E. With above 3,000 Woodcuts. 8vo. 42s.

TREATISE on **MILLS** and **MILLWORK.** By W. FAIRBAIRN, C.E. Second Edition, with 18 Plates and 322 Woodcuts. 2 vols. 8vo. 32s.

Useful Information for Engineers. By the same Author. FIRST and SECOND SERIES, with many Plates and Woodcuts. 2 vols. crown 8vo. 10s. 6d. each.

The Application of Cast and Wrought Iron to Building Purposes. By the same Author. Third Edition, with 6 Plates and 118 Woodcuts. 8vo. 16s.

IRON SHIP BUILDING, its History and Progress, as comprised in a Series of Experimental Researches on the Laws of Strain; the Strengths, Forms, and other conditions of the Material; and an Inquiry into the Present and Prospective State of the Navy, including the Experimental Results on the Resisting Powers of Armour Plates and Shot at High Velocities. By the same Author. With 4 Plates and 130 Woodcuts. 8vo. 18s.

The **PRACTICAL MECHANIC'S JOURNAL:** an Illustrated Record of Mechanical and Engineering Science, and Epitome of Patent Inventions. 4to. price 1s. monthly.

The **PRACTICAL DRAUGHTSMAN'S BOOK of INDUSTRIAL DE-SIGN.** By W. JOHNSON, Assoc. Inst. C.E. With many hundred Illustrations, 4to. 28s. 6d.

The **PATENTEE'S MANUAL**. a Treatise on the Law and Practice of Letters Patent for the use of Patentees and Inventors. By J. and J. H. JOHNSON. Post 8vo. 7s. 6d.

The **ARTISAN CLUB'S TREATISE** on the **STEAM ENGINE,** in its various Applications to Mines, Mills, Steam Navigation, Railways and Agriculture. By J. BOURNE, C.E. Seventh Edition; with 37 Plates and 546 Woodcuts. 4to. 42s.

Catechism of the Steam Engine, in its various Applications to Mines, Mills, Steam Navigation, Railways, and Agriculture. By the same Author. With 199 Woodcuts. Fcp. 9s. The INTRODUCTION of 'Recent Improvements' may be had separately, with 110 Woodcuts, price 3s. 6d.

Handbook of the Steam Engine. By the same Author, forming a KEY to the Catechism of the Steam Engine, with 67 Woodcuts. Fcp. 9s.

A **TREATISE** on the **SCREW PROPELLER, SCREW VESSELS,** and Screw Engines, as adapted for purposes of Peace and War; illustrated by many Plates and Woodcuts. By the same Author. New and enlarged Edition, in course of publication in 24 Parts. Royal 4to. 2s. 6d. each.

The **THEORY of WAR** Illustrated by numerous Examples from History. By Lieut.-Col. P. L. MACDOUGALL. Third Edition, with 10 Plans, Post 8vo. 10s. 6d.

c

The ART of PERFUMERY; the History and Theory of Odours, and the Methods of Extracting the Aromas of Plants. By Dr. Piesse, F.C.S. Third Edition, with 53 Woodcuts. Crown 8vo. 10s. 6d.

Chemical, Natural, and Physical Magic, for Juveniles during the Holidays. By the same Author. Third Edition, enlarged, with 38 Woodcuts. Fcp. 6s.

TALPA; or the Chronicles of a Clay Farm. By C. W. Hoskyns, Esq. Sixth Edition, with 24 Woodcuts by G. Cruikshank. 16mo. 5s. 6d.

LOUDON'S ENCYCLOPÆDIA of AGRICULTURE: comprising the Laying-out, Improvement, and Management of Landed Property, and the Cultivation and Economy of the Productions of Agriculture. With 1,100 Woodcuts. 8vo. 31s. 6d.

Loudon's Encylopædia of Gardening: comprising the Theory and Practice of Horticulture, Floriculture, Arboriculture, and Landscape Gardening. With 1,000 Woodcuts. 8vo. 31s. 6d.

Loudon's Encyclopædia of Cottage, Farm, and Villa Architecture and Furniture. With more than 2,000 Woodcuts. 8vo. 42s.

HISTORY of WINDSOR GREAT PARK and WINDSOR FOREST. By William Menzies, Resident Deputy Surveyor. With 2 Maps and 20 Photographs. Imp. folio, £3 8s.

BAYLDON'S ART of VALUING RENTS and TILLAGES, and Claims of Tenants upon Quitting Farms, both at Michaelmas and Lady-Day. Eighth Edition, revised by J. C. Morton. 8vo. 10s. 6d.

Religious and Moral Works.

An EXPOSITION of the 39 ARTICLES, Historical and Doctrinal. By E. Harold Browne, D.D. Lord Bishop of Ely. Seventh Edit. 8vo. 16s.

The Pentateuch and the Elohistic Psalms, in Reply to Bishop Colenso. By the same. Second Edition. 8vo. 2s.

Examination Questions on Bishop Browne's Exposition of the Articles. By the Rev. J. Gorle, M.A. Fcp. 3s. 6d.

FIVE LECTURES on the CHARACTER of ST. PAUL; being the Hulsean Lectures for 1862. By the Rev. J. S. Howson, D.D. Second Edition. 8vo. 9s.

The LIFE and EPISTLES of ST. PAUL. By W. J. Conybeare, M.A. late Fellow of Trin. Coll.Cantab. and J. S. Howson, D.D. late Principal of Liverpool College.

LIBRARY EDITION, with all the Original Illustrations, Maps, Landscapes on Steel, Woodcuts, &c. 2 vols. 4to. 48s.

INTERMEDIATE EDITION, with a Selection of Maps, Plates, and Woodcuts. 2 vols. square crown 8vo. 31s. 6d.

PEOPLE'S EDITION, revised and condensed, with 46 Illustrations and Maps. 2 vols. crown 8vo. 12s.

The VOYAGE and SHIPWRECK of ST. PAUL; with Dissertations on the Life and Writings of St. Luke and the Ships and Navigation of the Ancients. By James Smith, of Jordanhill, F.R.S. Third Edition, with Frontispiece, 4 Charts, and 11 Woodcuts. Crown 8vo. 1s. 6d.

FASTI SACRI, or a Key to the Chronology of the New Testament; comprising an Historical Harmony of the Four Gospels, and Chronological Tables generally from B.C. 70 to A.D. 70; with a Preliminary Dissertation on the Chronology of the New Testament, and other Aids to the elucidation of the subject. By THOMAS LEWIN, M.A. F.S.A. Imperial 8vo. 42s.

A CRITICAL and GRAMMATICAL COMMENTARY on ST. PAUL'S Epistles. By C.J. ELLICOTT, D.D. Lord Bishop of Gloucester and Bristol. 8vo.

Galatians, Third Edition, 8s. 6d.

Ephesians, Third Edition, 8s. 6d.

Pastoral Epistles, Third Edition, 10s. 6d.

Philippians, Colossians, and Philemon, Third Edition, 10s. 6d.

Thessalonians, Second Edition, 7s. 6d.

Historical Lectures on the Life of our Lord Jesus Christ: being the Hulsean Lectures for 1859. By the same Author. Fourth Edition. 8vo. price 10s. 6d.

The Destiny of the Creature; and other Sermons preached before the University of Cambridge. By the same. Fourth Edition. Post 8vo. 5s.

The Broad and the Narrow Way; Two Sermons preached before the University of Cambridge. By the same. Crown 8vo. 2s.

Rev. T. H. HORNE'S INTRODUCTION to the CRITICAL STUDY and Knowledge of the Holy Scriptures. Eleventh Edition, corrected and extended under careful Editorial revision. With 4 Maps and 22 Woodcuts and Facsimiles. 4 vols. 8vo. £3 13s. 6d.

Rev. T. H. Horne's Compendious Introduction to the Study of the Bible, being an Analysis of the larger work by the same Author. Re-edited by the Rev. JOHN AYRE, M.A. With Maps. &c. Post 8vo. 9s.

The TREASURY of BIBLE KNOWLEDGE; being a Dictionary of the Books, Persons, Places, Events, and other matters of which mention is made in Holy Scripture: intended to establish its Authority and illustrate its Contents. By Rev. J. AYRE, M.A. With Maps, 16 Plates, and numerous Woodcuts. Fcp. 10s. 6d.

The GREEK TESTAMENT; with Notes, Grammatical and Exegetical. By the Rev. W. WEBSTER, M.A. and the Rev. W. F. WILKINSON, M.A. 2 vols. 8vo. £2 4s.

> VOL. I. the Gospels and Acts, 20s.
>
> VOL. II. the Epistles and Apocalypse, 24s.

EVERY-DAY SCRIPTURE DIFFICULTIES explained and illustrated. By J. E. PRESCOTT, M.A. VOL. I. *Matthew* and *Mark*; VOL. II. *Luke* and *John.* 2 vols. 8vo. 9s. each.

The PENTATEUCH and BOOK of JOSHUA CRITICALLY EXAMINED. By the Right Rev. J. W. COLENSO, D.D. Lord Bishop of Natal. People's Edition, in 1 vol. crown 8vo. 6s. or in 5 Parts, 1s. each.

The PENTATEUCH and BOOK of JOSHUA CRITICALLY EXAMINED. By Prof. A. KUENEN, of Leyden. Translated from the Dutch, and edited with Notes, by J. W. COLENSO, D.D. Bishop of Natal. 8vo. 8s. 6d.

The CHURCH and the WORLD: Essays on Questions of the Day. By Various Writers. Edited by the Rev. ORBY SHIPLEY, M.A. 8vo. 15s.

The FORMATION of CHRISTENDOM. Part I. By T. W. Allies, 8vo. 12s.

CHRISTENDOM'S DIVISIONS: a Philosophical Sketch of the Divisions of the Christian Family in East and West. By Edmund S. Ffoulkes, formerly Fellow and Tutor of Jesus Coll. Oxford. Post 8vo. 7s. 6d.

Christendom's Divisions, Part II. Greeks and Latins, being a History of their Dissensions and Overtures for Peace down to the Reformation. By the same Author. [Nearly ready.]

The LIFE of CHRIST: an Eclectic Gospel, from the Old and New Testaments, arranged on a New Principle, with Analytical Tables, &c. By Charles De La Pryme, M.A. Trin. Coll. Camb. Revised Edition, 8vo. 5s.

The HIDDEN WISDOM of CHRIST and the KEY of KNOWLEDGE; or, History of the Apocrypha. By Ernest De Bunsen. 2 vols. 8vo. 28s.

ESSAYS on RELIGION and LITERATURE. Edited by the Most Rev. Archbishop Manning. 8vo. 10s. 6d.

The TEMPORAL MISSION of the HOLY GHOST; or, Reason and Revelation. By the Most Rev. Archbishop Manning. Second Edition. Crown 8vo. 6s. 6d.

ESSAYS and REVIEWS. By the Rev. W. Temple, D.D. the Rev. R. Williams, B.D. the Rev. B. Powell, M.A. the Rev. H. B. Wilson, B.D. C. W. Goodwin, M.A. the Rev. M. Pattison, B.D. and the Rev. B. Jowett, M.A. Twelfth Edition. Fcp. 8vo. 5s.

MOSHEIM'S ECCLESIASTICAL HISTORY. Murdock and Soames's Translation and Notes, re-edited by the Rev. W. Stubbs, M.A. 3 vols. 8vo. 45s.

BISHOP JEREMY TAYLOR'S ENTIRE WORKS: With Life by Bishop Heber. Revised and corrected by the Rev. C. P. Eden, 10 vols. price £5 5s.

PASSING THOUGHTS on RELIGION. By the Author of 'Amy Herbert.' New Edition. Fcp. 8vo. 5s.

Thoughts for the Holy Week, for Young Persons. By the same Author. Third Edition. Fcp. 8vo. 2s.

Night Lessons from Scripture. By the same Author. Second Edition. 32mo. 3s.

Self-Examination before Confirmation. By the same Author. 32mo. price 1s. 6d.

Readings for a Month Preparatory to Confirmation, from Writers of the Early and English Church. By the same. Fcp. 4s.

Readings for Every Day in Lent, compiled from the Writings of Bishop Jeremy Taylor. By the same. Fcp. 5s.

Preparation for the Holy Communion; the Devotions chiefly from the works of Jeremy Taylor. By the same. 32mo. 3s.

MORNING CLOUDS. Second Edition. Fcp. 5s.

PRINCIPLES of EDUCATION Drawn from Nature and Revelation and applied to Female Education in the Upper Classes. By the same. 2 vols. fcp. 12s. 6d.

The **WIFE'S MANUAL**; or, Prayers, Thoughts, and Songs on Several Occasions of a Matron's Life. By the Rev. W. CALVERT, M.A. Crown 8vo. price 10s. 6d.

SPIRITUAL SONGS for the **SUNDAYS** and **HOLIDAYS** throughout the Year. By J. S. B. MONSELL, LL.D. Vicar of Egham. Fourth Edition. Fcp. 4s. 6d.

The **Beatitudes**: Abasement before God ; Sorrow for Sin ; Meekness of Spirit ; Desire for Holiness ; Gentleness ; Purity of Heart ; the Peacemakers ; Sufferings for Christ. By the same. Third Edition, fcp. 3s. 6d.

LYRA DOMESTICA; Christian Songs for Domestic Edification. Translated from the *Psaltery and Harp* of C. J. P. SPITTA, and from other sources, by RICHARD MASSIE. FIRST and SECOND SERIES, fcp. 4s. 6d. each.

LYRA SACRA; Hymns, Ancient and Modern, Odes and Fragments of Sacred Poetry. Edited by the Rev. B. W. SAVILE, M.A. Third Edition, enlarged and improved. Fcp. 5s.

LYRA GERMANICA, translated from the German by Miss C. WINKWORTH. FIRST SERIES, Hymns for the Sundays and Chief Festivals ; SECOND SERIES, the Christian Life. Fcp. 5s. each SERIES.

Hymns from Lyra Germanica, 18mo. 1s.

LYRA EUCHARISTICA; Hymns and Verses on the Holy Communion, Ancient and Modern: with other Poems. Edited by the Rev. ORBY SHIPLEY, M.A. Second Edition. Fcp. 7s. 6d.

Lyra Messianica; Hymns and Verses on the Life of Christ, Ancient and Modern ; with other Poems. By the same Editor. Second Edition, altered and enlarged. Fcp. 7s. 6d.

Lyra Mystica; Hymns and Verses on Sacred Subjects, Ancient and Modern. By the same Editor. Fcp. 7s. 6d.

The **CHORALE BOOK** for **ENGLAND**; a complete Hymn-Book in accordance with the Services and Festivals of the Church of England: the Hymns translated by Miss C. WINKWORTH ; the tunes arranged by Prof. W. S. BENNETT and OTTO GOLDSCHMIDT. Fcp. 4to. 12s. 6d.

Congregational Edition. Fcp. 2s.

The **CATHOLIC DOCTRINE** of the **ATONEMENT**: an Historical Inquiry into its Development in the Church ; with an Introduction on the Principle of Theological Developments. By H. N. OXENHAM, M.A. formerly Scholar of Balliol College, Oxford. 8vo. 8s. 6d.

FROM SUNDAY TO SUNDAY: an attempt to consider familiarly the Weekday Life and Labours of a Country Clergyman. By R. GEE, M.A. Vicar of Abbott's Langley and Rural Dean. Fcp. 5s.

Our Sermons; An Attempt to consider familiarly, but reverently, the Preacher's Work in the present day. By the same Author. [*In October.*

FIRST SUNDAYS at **CHURCH**; or, Familiar Conversations on the Morning and Evening Services of the Church of England. By J. E. RIDDLE, M.A. Fcp. 2s. 6d.

The **JUDGMENT** of **CONSCIENCE**, and other Sermons. By RICHARD WHATELY, D.D. late Archbishop of Dublin. Crown 8vo. 4s. 6d.

PALEY'S MORAL PHILOSOPHY, with Annotations. By RICHARD WHATELY, D.D. late Archbishop of Dublin. 8vo. 7s.

Travels, Voyages, &c.

OUTLINE SKETCHES of the **HIGH ALPS** of **DAUPHINÉ**. By T.
G. BONNEY, M.A. F.G.S. M.A.C. Fellow of St. John's Coll. Camb. With 13
Plates and a Coloured Map. Post 4to. 16s.

ICE-CAVES of **FRANCE** and **SWITZERLAND**; a Narrative of Sub-
terranean Exploration. By the Rev. G. F. BROWNE, M.A. Fellow and
Assistant-Tutor of St. Catherine's Coll. Cambridge, M.A.C. With 11 Illustrations on Wood. Square crown 8vo. 12s. 6d.

VILLAGE LIFE in **SWITZERLAND**. By SOPHIA D. DELMARD.
Post 8vo. 9s. 6d.

HOW WE SPENT the SUMMER; or, a Voyage en Zigzag in Switzerland and Tyrol with some Members of the ALPINE CLUB. From the Sketch-
Book of one of the Party. Third Edition, re-drawn. In oblong 4to. with
about 300 Illustrations, 15s.

BEATEN TRACKS; or, Pen and Pencil Sketches in Italy. By the
Authoress of 'A Voyage en Zigzag.' With 42 Plates, containing about 200
Sketches from Drawings made on the Spot. 8vo. 16s.

MAP of the **CHAIN** of **MONT BLANC**, from an actual Survey in
1863—1864. By A. ADAMS-REILLY, F.R.G.S. M.A.C. Published under the
Authority of the Alpine Club. In Chromolithography on extra stout
drawing-paper 28in. × 17in. price 10s. or mounted on canvas in a folding
case, 12s. 6d.

TRANSYLVANIA, its **PRODUCTS** and its **PEOPLE**. By CHARLES
BONER. With 5 Maps and 43 Illustrations on Wood and in Chromolithography. 8vo. 21s.

EXPLORATIONS in **SOUTH WEST AFRICA**, from Walvisch Bay to
Lake Ngami and the Victoria Falls. By THOMAS BAINES, F.R.G.S. 8vo.
with Map and Illustrations, 21s.

VANCOUVER ISLAND and **BRITISH COLUMBIA**; their History,
Resources, and Prospects. By MATTHEW MACFIE, F.R.G.S. With Maps
and Illustrations. 8vo. 18s.

HISTORY of **DISCOVERY** in our **AUSTRALASIAN COLONIES**,
Australia, Tasmania, and New Zealand, from the Earliest Date to the
Present Day. By WILLIAM HOWITT. With 3 Maps of the Recent Explora-
tions from Official Sources. 2 vols. 8vo. 20s.

The **CAPITAL** of the **TYCOON**; a Narrative of a Three Years' Resi-
dence in Japan. By Sir RUTHERFORD ALCOCK, K.C.B. 2 vols. 8vo. with
numerous Illustrations, 42s.

LAST WINTER in **ROME**. By C. R. WELD. With Portrait and
Engravings on Wood. Post 8vo. 14s.

Florence, the **New** Capital of Italy. By the same Author. Post
8vo.   [In October.

AUTUMN RAMBLES in **NORTH AFRICA**. By JOHN ORMSBY,
of the Middle Temple. With 16 Illustrations. Post 8vo. 8s. 6d.

The **DOLOMITE MOUNTAINS**. Excursions through Tyrol, Carinthia,
Carniola, and Friuli in 1861, 1862, and 1863. By J. GILBERT and G. C.
CHURCHILL, F.R.G.S. With numerous Illustrations. Square crown
8vo. 21s.

A SUMMER TOUR in the GRISONS and ITALIAN VALLEYS of the Bernina. By Mrs. HENRY FRESHFIELD. With 2 Coloured Maps and 4 Views. Post 8vo. 10s. 6d.

Alpine Byeways; or, Light Leaves gathered in 1859 and 1860. By the same Authoress. Post 8vo. with Illustrations, 10s. 6d.

A LADY'S TOUR ROUND MONTE ROSA; including Visits to the Italian Valleys. With Map and Illustrations. Post 8vo. 14s.

GUIDE to the PYRENEES, for the use of Mountaineers. By CHARLES PACKE. With Maps, &c. and Appendix. Fcp. 6s.

The ALPINE GUIDE. By JOHN BALL, M.R.I.A. late President of the Alpine Club. Post 8vo. with Maps and other Illustrations.

Guide to the Eastern Alps, *nearly ready.*

Guide to the Western Alps, including Mont Blanc, Monte Rosa, Zermatt, &c. 7s. 6d.

Guide to the Oberland and all Switzerland, excepting the Neighbourhood of Monte Rosa and the Great St. Bernard; with Lombardy and the adjoining portion of Tyrol. 7s. 6d.

A GUIDE to SPAIN. By H. O'SHEA. Post 8vo. with Travelling Map, 15s.

CHRISTOPHER COLUMBUS; his Life, Voyages, and Discoveries. Revised Edition, with 4 Woodcuts. 18mo. 2s. 6d.

CAPTAIN JAMES COOK; his Life, Voyages, and Discoveries. Revised Edition, with numerous Woodcuts. 18mo. 2s. 6d.

HUMBOLDT'S TRAVELS and DISCOVERIES in SOUTH AMERICA. Third Edition, with numerous Woodcuts. 18mo. 2s. 6d.

MUNGO PARK'S LIFE and TRAVELS in AFRICA, with an Account of his Death and the Substance of Later Discoveries. Sixth Edition, with Woodcuts. 18mo. 2s. 6d.

NARRATIVES of SHIPWRECKS of the ROYAL NAVY between 1793 and 1857, compiled from Official Documents in the Admiralty by W. O. S. GILLY; with a Preface by W. S. GILLY, D.D. Third Edition, fcp. 5s.

A WEEK at the LAND'S END. By J. T. BLIGHT; assisted by E. H. RODD, R. Q. COUCH, and J. RALFS. With Map and 96 Woodcuts. Fcp. price 6s. 6d.

VISITS to REMARKABLE PLACES: Old Halls, Battle-Fields, and Scenes Illustrative of Striking Passages in English History and Poetry. By WILLIAM HOWITT. 2 vols. square crown 8vo. with Wood Engravings, price 25s.

The RURAL LIFE of ENGLAND. By the same Author. With Woodcuts by Bewick and Williams. Medium 8vo. 12s. 6d.

Works of Fiction.

ATHERSTONE PRIORY. By L. N. COMYN. 2 vols. post 8vo. 21s.

Ellice: a Tale. By the same Author. Post 8vo. 9s. 6d.

STORIES and **TALES** by the Author of ' Amy Herbert,' uniform Edition, each Tale or Story complete in a single Volume.

AMY HERBERT, 2s. 6d.	IVORS, 3s. 6d.
GERTRUDE, 2s. 6d.	KATHARINE ASHTON, 3s. 6d.
EARL'S DAUGHTER, 2s. 6d.	MARGARET PERCIVAL, 5s.
EXPERIENCE OF LIFE, 2s. 6d.	LANETON PARSONAGE, 4s. 6d.
CLEVE HALL, 3s. 6d.	URSULA, 4s. 6d.

A Glimpse of the World. By the Author of 'Amy Herbert.' Fcp. 7s. 6d.

THE SIX SISTERS of the **VALLEYS**: an Historical Romance. By W. BRAMLEY-MOORE. M.A. Incumbent of Gerrard's Cross, Bucks. Third Edition, with 14 Illustrations. Crown 8vo. 5s.

The **GLADIATORS**: A Tale of Rome and Judæa. By G. J. WHYTE MELVILLE. Crown 8vo. 5s.

Digby Grand, an Autobiography. By the same Author. 1 vol. 5s.

Kate Coventry, an Autobiography. By the same. 1 vol. 5s.

General Bounce, or the Lady and the Locusts. By the same. 1 vol. 5s.

Holmby House, a Tale of Old Northamptonshire. 1 vol. 5s.

Good for Nothing, or All Down Hill. By the same. 1 vol. 6s.

The Queen's Maries, a Romance of Holyrood. 1 vol. 6s.

The Interpreter, a Tale of the War. By the same. 1 vol. 5s.

TALES from **GREEK MYTHOLOGY**. By GEORGE W. COX, M.A. late Scholar of Trin. Coll. Oxon. Second Edition. Square 16mo. 3s. 6d.

Tales of the Gods and Heroes. By the same Author. Second Edition. Fcp. 5s.

Tales of Thebes and Argos. By the same Author. Fcp. 4s. 6d.

BECKER'S GALLUS; or, Roman Scenes of the Time of Augustus: with Notes and Excursuses illustrative of the Manners and Customs of the Ancient Romans. New Edition. Post 8vo. 7s. 6d.

BECKER'S CHARICLES; a Tale illustrative of Private Life among the Ancient Greeks: with Notes and Excursuses. New Edition. Post 8vo. 7s. 6d.

ICELANDIC LEGENDS. Collected by JON ARNASON. Selected and Translated from the Icelandic by G. E. J. POWELL and E. MAGNUSSON. SECOND SERIES, with Notes and an Introductory Essay on the Origin and Genius of the Icelandic Folk-Lore, and 3 Illustrations on Wood. Cr. 8vo. 21s.

The **WARDEN**: a Novel. By ANTHONY TROLLOPE. Crown 8vo. 2s. 6d.

Barchester Towers : a Sequel to ' The Warden.' By the same Author. Crown 8vo. 3s. 6d.

Poetry and The *Drama*.

GOETHE'S SECOND FAUST. Translated by JOHN ANSTER, LL.D. M.R.I.A. Regius Professor of Civil Law in the University of Dublin. Post 8vo. 15s.

TASSO'S JERUSALEM DELIVERED. Translated into English Verse by Sir J. KINGSTON JAMES, Kt. M.A. 2 vols. fcp. with Facsimile, 14s.

POETICAL WORKS of JOHN EDMUND READE; with final Revision and Additions. 3 vols. fcp. 18s. or each vol. separately, 6s.

MOORE'S POETICAL WORKS, Cheapest Editions complete in 1 vol. including the Autobiographical Prefaces and Author's last Notes, which are still copyright. Crown 8vo. ruby type, with Portrait, 6s. or People's Edition, in larger type, 12s. 6d.

Moore's Poetical Works, as above, Library Edition, medium 8vo. with Portrait and Vignette, 14s. or in 10 vols. fcp. 3s. 6d. each.

MOORE'S IRISH MELODIES, 32mo. Portrait, 1s. 16mo. Vignette, 2s. 6d.

Maclise's Edition of Moore's Irish Melodies, with 161 Steel Plates from Original Drawings. Super-royal 8vo. 31s. 6d.

Maclise's Edition of Moore's Irish Melodies with all the Original Designs (as above) reduced by a New Process. Imp. 16mo. 10s. 6d.

MOORE'S LALLA ROOKH. 32mo. Plate, 1s. 16mo. Vignette, 2s. 6d.

Tenniel's Edition of Moore's Lalla Rookh, with 68 Wood Engravings from original Drawings and other Illustrations. Fcp. 4to. 21s.

SOUTHEY'S POETICAL WORKS, with the Author's last Corrections and copyright Additions. Library Edition. in 1 vol. medium 8vo. with Portrait and Vignette, 14s. or in 10 vols. fcp. 3s. 6d. each.

LAYS of ANCIENT ROME; with Ivry and the Armada. By the Right Hon. LORD MACAULAY. 16mo. 4s. 6d.

Lord Macaulay's Lays of Ancient Rome. With 90 Illustrations on Wood, Original and from the Antique, from Drawings by G. SCHARF. Fcp. 4to. 21s.

Lord Macaulay's Lays of Ancient Rome, with all the Original Designs (as above) reduced by a New Process. Imp. 16mo. price 10s. 6d. cloth, gilt edges; or 21s. bound in morocco by Rivière.

POEMS. By JEAN INGELOW. Eleventh Edition. Fcp. 8vo. 5s.

Poems by Jean Ingelow. A New Edition, with nearly 100 Illustrations by Eminent Artists, engraved on Wood by the Brothers DALZIEL. Fcp. 4to. 21s.

POETICAL WORKS of LETITIA ELIZABETH LANDON (L.E.L.) 2 vols. 16mo. 10s.

PLAYTIME with the POETS: a Selection of the best English Poetry for the use of Children. By a LADY. Revised Edition. Crown 8vo. 5s.

BOWDLER'S FAMILY SHAKSPEARE, cheaper Genuine Edition, complete in 1 vol. large type, with 36 Woodcut Illustrations, price 14s. or with the same ILLUSTRATIONS, in 6 pocket vols. 3s. 6d. each.

ARUNDINES CAMI, sive Musarum Cantabrigiensium Lusus canori. Collegit atque edidit H. DRURY, M.A. Editio Sexta, curavit H. J. HODGSON, M.A. Crown 8vo. 7s. 6d.

The ILIAD of HOMER TRANSLATED into BLANK VERSE. By ICHABOD CHARLES WRIGHT, M.A. late Fellow of Magd. Coll. Oxon. 2 vols. crown 8vo. 21s.

The ILIAD of HOMER in ENGLISH HEXAMETER VERSE. By J. HENRY DART, M.A. of Exeter College, Oxford: Author of 'The Exile of St. Helena, Newdigate, 1838.' Square crown 8vo. 21s.

D

DANTE'S DIVINE COMEDY, translated in English Terza Rima by
JOHN DAYMAN, M.A. [With the Italian Text, after *Brunetti*, interpaged.]
8vo. 21s.

Rural Sports, &c.

ENCYCLOPÆDIA of RURAL SPORTS; a complete Account, Historical, Practical, and Descriptive, of Hunting, Shooting, Fishing, Racing,
&c. By D. P. BLAINE. With above 600 Woodcuts (20 from Designs by
JOHN LEECH). 8vo. 42s.

NOTES on RIFLE SHOOTING. By Captain HEATON, Adjutant of
the Third Manchester Rifle Volunteer Corps. Revised Edition. Fcp. 2s. 6d.

COL. HAWKER'S INSTRUCTIONS to YOUNG SPORTSMEN in all
that relates to Guns and Shooting. Revised by the Author's Son. Square
crown 8vo. with Illustrations, 18s.

The RIFLE, its THEORY and PRACTICE. By ARTHUR WALKER
(79th Highlanders), Staff. Hythe and Fleetwood Schools of Musketry.
Second Edition. Crown 8vo. with 125 Woodcuts, 5s.

The DEAD SHOT, or Sportsman's Complete Guide; a Treatise on
the Use of the Gun, Dog-breaking, Pigeon-shooting, &c. By MARKSMAN.
Revised Edition. Fcp. 8vo. with Plates, 5s.

HINTS on SHOOTING, FISHING, &c. both on Sea and Land and in
the Fresh and Saltwater Lochs of Scotland; being the Experiences of
C. IDLE. Second Edition, revised. Fcp. 4s.

The FLY-FISHER'S ENTOMOLOGY. By ALFRED RONALDS. With
coloured Representations of the Natural and Artificial Insect. Sixth
Edition; with 20 coloured Plates. 8vo. 14s.

HANDBOOK of ANGLING : Teaching Fly-fishing, Trolling, Bottom-
fishing, Salmon-fishing; with the Natural History of River Fish, and the
best modes of Catching them. By EPHEMERA. Fcp. Woodcuts, 5s.

The CRICKET FIELD; or, the History and the Science of the Game
of Cricket. By JAMES PYCROFT, B.A. Fourth Edition. Fcp. 5s.

The Cricket Tutor; a Treatise exclusively Practical. By the same.
18mo. 1s.

Cricketana. By the same Author. With 7 Portraits. Fcp. 5s.

The HORSE-TRAINER'S and SPORTSMAN'S GUIDE: with Considerations on the Duties of Grooms, on Purchasing Blood Stock, and on Veterinary Examination. By DIGBY COLLINS. Post 8vo. 6s.

The HORSE'S FOOT, and HOW to KEEP IT SOUND. By W.
MILES, Esq. Ninth Edition, with Illustrations. Imperial 8vo. 12s. 6d.

A Plain Treatise on Horse-Shoeing. By the same Author. Post
8vo. with Illustrations, 2s. 6d.

Stables and Stable-Fittings. By the same. Imp. 8vo. with 13 Plates, 15s.

Remarks on Horses' Teeth, addressed to Purchasers. By the same.
Post 8vo. 1s. 6d.

On DRILL and MANŒUVRES of CAVALRY, combined with Horse
Artillery. By Major-Gen. MICHAEL W. SMITH, C.B. Commanding the
Poonah Division of the Bombay Army. 8vo. 12s. 6d.

BLAINE'S VETERINARY ART; a Treatise on the Anatomy, Physiology, and Curative Treatment of the Diseases of the Horse, Neat Cattle and Sheep. Seventh Edition, revised and enlarged by C. STEEL, M.R.C.V.S.L. 8vo. with Plates and Woodcuts, 18s.

The **HORSE**: with a Treatise on Draught. By WILLIAM YOUATT. New Edition, revised and enlarged. 8vo. with numerous Woodcuts, 10s. 6d.

The **Dog**. By the same Author. 8vo. with numerous Woodcuts, 6s.

The **DOG in HEALTH and DISEASE**. By STONEHENGE. With 70 Wood Engravings. Square crown 8vo. 15s.

The **Greyhound**. By the same Author. Revised Edition, with 24 Portraits of Greyhounds. Square crown 8vo. 21s.

The **OX**; his Diseases and their Treatment: with an Essay on Parturition in the Cow. By J. R. Donson, M.R.C.V.S. Crown 8vo. with Illustrations, price 7s. 6d.

Commerce, Navigation, and Mercantile Affairs.

PRACTICAL GUIDE for BRITISH SHIPMASTERS to UNITED States Ports. By PIERREPONT EDWARDS, Her Britannic Majesty's Vice-Consul at New York. Post 8vo. 8s. 6d.

A **NAUTICAL DICTIONARY**, defining the Technical Language relative to the Building and Equipment of Sailing Vessels and Steamers, &c. By ARTHUR YOUNG. Second Edition; with Plates and 150 Woodcuts. 8vo. 18s.

A **DICTIONARY**, Practical, Theoretical, and Historical, of Commerce and Commercial Navigation. By J. R. M'CULLOCH, Esq. 8vo. with Maps and Plans, 50s.

A **MANUAL for NAVAL CADETS**. By J. M'NEIL BOYD, late Captain R.N. Third Edition; with 240 Woodcuts and 11 coloured Plates. Post 8vo. 12s. 6d.

The **LAW of NATIONS** Considered as Independent Political Communities. By TRAVERS TWISS, D.C.L. Regius Professor of Civil Law in the University of Oxford. 2 vols. 8vo. 30s. or separately, PART I. Peace, 12s. PART II. War, 18s.

Works of Utility and General Information.

MODERN COOKERY for PRIVATE FAMILIES, reduced to a System of Easy Practice in a Series of carefully-tested Receipts. By ELIZA ACTON. Newly revised and enlarged; with 8 Plates, Figures, and 150 Woodcuts. Fcp. 7s. 6d.

The **HANDBOOK of DINING**; or, Corpulency and Leanness scientifically considered. By BRILLAT-SAVARIN, Author of 'Physiologie du Goût.' Translated by L. F. SIMPSON. Revised Edition, with Additions. Fcp. 3s. 6d.

On **FOOD and its DIGESTION**; an Introduction to Dietetics. By W. BRINTON, M.D. Physician to St. Thomas's Hospital, &c. With 48 Woodcuts. Post 8vo. 12s.

WINE, the VINE, and the CELLAR. By Thomas G. Shaw. Second Edition, revised and enlarged, with Frontispiece and 31 Illustrations on Wood. 8vo. 16s.

HOW TO BREW GOOD BEER. a complete Guide to the Art of Brewing Ale, Bitter Ale, Table Ale, Brown Stout, Porter, and Table Beer. By John Pitt. Revised Edition. Fcp. 4s. 6d.

A PRACTICAL TREATISE on BREWING; with Formulæ for Public Brewers, and Instructions for Private Families. By W. Black. 8vo. 10s. 6d.

SHORT WHIST. By Major A. Sixteenth Edition, revised, with an Essay on the Theory of the Modern Scientific Game by Prof. P. Fcp. 3s. 6d.

WHIST, WHAT TO LEAD. By Cam. Third Edition. 32mo. 1s.

HINTS on ETIQUETTE and the USAGES of SOCIETY; with a Glance at Bad Habits. Revised, with Additions, by a Lady of Rank. Fcp. price 2s. 6d.

TWO HUNDRED CHESS PROBLEMS, composed by F. Healey, including the Problems to which the Prizes were awarded by the Committees of the Era, the Manchester, the Birmingham, and the Bristol Chess Problem Tournaments; accompanied by the Solutions. Crown 8vo. with 200 Diagrams, 5s.

The CABINET LAWYER; a Popular Digest of the Laws of England, Civil and Criminal. Twenty-second Edition, extended by the Author; including the Acts of the Session 1860. Fcp.   [Ready.

The PHILOSOPHY of HEALTH; or, an Exposition of the Physiological and Sanitary Conditions conducive to Human Longevity and Happiness. By Southwood Smith, M.D. Eleventh Edition, revised and enlarged: with 113 Woodcuts, 8vo. 15s.

HINTS to MOTHERS on the MANAGEMENT of their HEALTH during the Period of Pregnancy and in the Lying-in Room. By T. Bull, M.D. Fcp. 5s.

The Maternal Management of Children in Health and Disease. By the same Author. Fcp. 5s.

The LAW RELATING to BENEFIT BUILDING SOCIETIES; with Practical Observations on the Act and all the Cases decided thereon; also a Form of Rules and Forms of Mortgages. By W. Tidd Pratt, Barrister. Second Edition. Fcp. 3s. 6d.

NOTES on HOSPITALS. By Florence Nightingale. Third Edition, enlarged; with 13 Plans. Post 4to. 18s.

C. M. WILLICH'S POPULAR TABLES for ascertaining the Value of Lifehold, Leasehold, and Church Property, Renewal Fines, &c.; the Public Funds; Annual Average Price and Interest on Consols from 1731 to 1861; Chemical, Geographical, Astronomical, Trigonometrical Tables, &c. Post 8vo. 10s.

THOMSON'S TABLES of INTEREST, at Three, Four, Four and a Half, and Five per Cent. from One Pound to Ten Thousand and from 1 to 365 Days. 12mo. 3s. 6d.

MAUNDER'S TREASURY of KNOWLEDGE and LIBRARY of Reference: comprising an English Dictionary and Grammar, Universal Gazetteer, Classical Dictionary, Chronology, Law Dictionary, a Synopsis of the Peerage, useful Tables, &c. Revised Edition. Fcp. 10s. 6d.

INDEX.

www.ingramcontent.com/pod-product-compliance
Lightning Source LLC
Chambersburg PA
CBHW020933030726
47496CB00005B/1164